AF521201

BREACH

Amrita Verma Chowdhury is the author of *Faking It*, an art crime thriller about fake modern and contemporary Indian art.

She holds engineering degrees from IIT Kanpur and UC Berkeley, where she was a Jane Lewis Fellow, and an MBA from Carnegie Mellon (Tepper Business School). Her work as an engineer in Silicon Valley led to seven US patents for semi-conductor fabrication – something to show for those bad-haired days. She has done Strategy Consulting and Board Effectiveness work in the US and Australia and has spent long nights fitting five-syllable words inside two-by-two squares. She has worked in the rarefied bastions of Ivy League education bringing together ideas and people. She currently works in publishing.

She lives in Mumbai with her husband Sumit, their two children Shoumik and Aishani, and an assortment of pets including a cocker spaniel, a guinea pig and two turtles. She loves travelling, baking cupcakes with her daughter and hearing from her readers.

You can find her at www.amritachowdhury.com or connect with her on Facebook (Author Amrita Chowdhury) or Twitter (@vc_amrita).

You can learn more about the book and the world of cyber crime and safety on www.BREACH.co.in.

Advance Praise for *Breach*

'A gripping, transcontinental drama steeped in well-researched global pharma geopolitics. A must read cyber-crime thriller that is hard to put down.'

– Rohit Deshpande, Professor, Harvard Business School

'*Breach* is a superlative rendering of the state of cyber crime, not what might be but what is. Amrita Chowdhury delivers a multi-layered and nuanced work, with a broad array of characters and an authentic feel of big pharma and IT.'

– Vijay Ramachandran, Editor-in-Chief, IDG Media India, publisher of *Computer World*, *PC World* and *CIO* magazines

'*Breach* offers an expeditious, fascinating and compelling narrative that is unafraid to explore the dark and murky world of cyber crime. Amrita writes with such veracity: the characters so well-nuanced in a setting that is deeply authentic. Riveting!'

– Vishal Dhupar, Former MD, India and SAARC, Symantec

'A fascinating thriller, which blends together elements of real-world data theft, counter surveillance, crisis management and incident reconstruction to uncover the modus operandi and motives of the criminals. Cybercrime is on the rise in India, and this book is a timely reminder to stay safe in an increasingly digital world.'

– D Sivanandan, Former Police Commissioner of Mumbai and Former Director General of Police, Maharashtra

'An intelligent, page-turning cyber thriller written in a lucid style, *Breach* eerily reflects real world online threats. It's an eye-opener for anyone who surfs the web without understanding its risks.'

– Vijay Mukhi, Cyber Crime Expert

'A globe-trotting, detail-driven, tech-powered thriller for today's India.'

– Rachel Lopez, *Hindustan Times*

Praise for *Faking It*

'A socialite thriller with diamond-dripping and Birkin-bearing ladies.'

– *India Today*

'A cross between chick-lit and crime thriller.'

– *DNA India*

'A perfectly enjoyable read that focuses completely around Indian art.'

– *Bangalore Mirror*

'A fast-paced thriller in the dizzying backdrop of Indian art; the engrossing crime tale is deceptively woven around a frantic chase for trophy art.'

– *The Arts Trust*

'Set mostly in urban India, the fast-paced entertainer is a reverse-migration story. It gives an insider's view of the art world and takes you through the world of elusive artistes, gallery owners, art auctions and explores art writing and criticism in true settings.'

– *The Hindu*

'All about art and crime in high-end society. The drab world of brushes and strokes springs to life, mainly because of the energy levels of the now-confused-now-determined protagonist Tara.'

– *Deccan Herald*

'Written in a fluid yet literary language, it is about the scintillating, almost-glass world of the Mumbai elite and the glitterati. At a more macro level, it is a commentary on fast-changing India and about the multiple realities in our lives.'

– *New Indian Express*

'The racy tale tracks down a fake Amrita Sher-Gil painting, with exciting traps laid out for the leading character, a diamond-dripping lady of leisure.'

– *Indian Express*

BREACH

Amrita Chowdhury

hachette
INDIA

First published in 2014 by Hachette India
(Registered name: Hachette Book Publishing India Pvt. Ltd)
An Hachette UK company
www.hachetteindia.com

SRD

ISBN 978-93-5009-855-4

Hachette Book Publishing India Pvt. Ltd
4th & 5th Floors, Corporate Centre
Plot No. 94, Sector 44, Gurgaon 122003, India

Typeset in Sabon 10/12
by Ram Das Lal, NCR Delhi

Printed and bound in India by
Manipal Technologies Limited, Manipal

FSC
www.fsc.org
MIX
Paper from
responsible sources
FSC™ C104740

For my mother, Dr. Purnima Prasad (d. 2013)
You were a graceful warrior.

Your strength, generosity, and ability to multi-task
and listen with stillness shall inspire me forever.

For Papa, Sumit, Chetan, Shalu
My rocks in our journey together!

FRIDAY, 10.00 A.M.

Rockville, Maryland

'Andy.' Dr Small pushed his rimless glasses up the bridge of his broad nose and stood in greeting.

He had left a voicemail for Andrew Rudd, the Head of Research at Acel Biosciences, on the internal phone system just fifteen minutes back, reporting unusual data. Andy had walked over immediately. 'What's happened?' he said impatiently.

'It's an unusual trend, Andy.' Dr Small appeared hesitant. Andy scared him.

Dr Small sat down in front of his large-screen monitor, explaining the statistical analysis results. He had various windows open, charting metastatic cell growth, immune response, and physiological symptoms over time across different animals.

'We've been getting the best results with 15 per cent virulence. You've seen this before.' The chart tracked six-month reduction in melanoma growth of in vivo testing.

'But see this dip here.' He zoomed on to the end of the chart and pointed towards the slight dip towards the end.

Andy sat on a revolving leather chair, silent and forbidding, entirely focused on the screen.

'See, what happens when I remove the data from India,' Dr Small continued, flipping open another chart. A near flat line! Repeatable results, as expected.

Andy sat still, watching Dr Small flip between the two charts.

'Is it a data error?'

'I have asked the data centre guys to look at the backup. They will respond tonight I suppose. Their morning time.'

The data centre had been shifted to India two years ago, much to Andy's chagrin. A decision taken above him, at the board level, where the clinical virtue of balance sheet benefits outweighed the concerns of control.

Andy drummed his fingers on the table, tension writ large on his stiff frame. Dr Small observed the forbidding look on Andy's face. Andy was famous for his blowups.

'Have you shown this to Peter?'

'He called in sick.'

'Peter?' Andy looked quizzical. Dr Peter Lee, the lead scientist working on Colare, was never sick. Ever. In all his fifteen years of working at Acel. He was one of those who lived and breathed for work, turning up in the lab even on weekends.

'Have you spoken to the research team in India?'

'No...' Dr Small stammered. 'I wanted to speak with you first.'

'It could also be an error in the India Lab,' Andy barked.

That was his other pet peeve. The new offshore research centre in India, conceived by the smooth-talking Udai Vir Dhingra and blessed by Acel's CEO. Despite all the misgivings he had openly shared.

Now this! Andy seethed in anger. This had *implications*.

Colare was at the end of the pre-clinical phase. After much experimentation, it had come together.

Three years.

A hundred million dollars invested.

A wonder drug to cure late-stage metastic pancreatic cancer.

The US patent application had been filed. They had just started clinical testing on live patients. The animal testing phase was supposed to be a mere extended formality to show additional data for the global patent filing. The drug would offer hope to patients around the world. Acel, which had created several wonder cures in the past thirty years, had been dreaming of a new breakthrough: Colare.

It was slated to possibly garner billions in revenue for Acel, and stabilize its fortunes for the next decade.

Now was not the time for data to go awry.

SATURDAY, 4.55 A.M.

Gaithersburg, Maryland

He woke up with a jerk.

Bitterness swelled like dry ash in his mouth. Tossing the blanket away, he swallowed. His heart pounded in sharp incisive thuds like it was going to pummel out of his body. His mind felt cluttered like a rabid kaleidoscope of fragmented images. He reached out to the bedside table for a bottle of water and guzzled it down. Instead of calming down, he felt anger rising within him again like liquid warmth. It was an anger that had been latent for years, simmering from a lifetime of discontent. Now, fanned by the last one, it had flamed into an inferno.

His smartphone was blinking red. His heart lurched in anticipation. There were work messages and updates. Nothing new! He scrolled down through the app icons and pressed on Scrabble. He had three ongoing games – two with random players and one with *Tau Neutrino*.

It wasn't about word play. It was his communication lifeline.

Two years ago, he used to prefer free email alias accounts, rotating through them to connect with different people. Pure precaution, in case anyone was monitoring those accounts. Now, untraceability was paramount. Not every contact could be on the dark net. With emails under the scanner of cyber security hounds and phone text messages that could be wire tapped, newer communication channels had to be used; even those with weaker security. Like the free text messaging service inside a gaming app! *Tau Neutrino* had created a new word – *when* – innocuous enough, but a portent for the message in the text bar below.

P.S. The sun is setting. It's getting late.

He quickly opened the Pinterest link and searched for

photographs of sunsets. He scrolled down the page, till he found what he thought he was supposed to look for. He clicked on the image. A surreally beautiful sky, marigold bleeding into plum that melded into deepest cyan, with an intricate shadow of a pagoda at its centre. Below the photograph was a caption:

It's getting late.

He clicked on the image. It had originally been pinned by someone called Melissa Y, whose digital photo was a fluffy, green-eyed Siamese kitten.

He downloaded the image. On first glance, it was a harmless photo, serene and moody, clicked perhaps to accompany a travel blog. That was the beauty of it. The layers of hints and clues, like a cyber treasure hunt. You had to know what you were looking for, and where.

He saved the sunset using an imaging software, clicked edit to open the colour saturation bar and set the colour Y from the CMYK palette to zero. At least, that's what he hoped the Y in Melissa's name implied. Bingo!

The image morphed. The colours swirled and etched in the middle in weak dots were the words:

Plan B.

Plan B. Something he was not privy to. Something he intuitively knew would not be good for him, whatever it was. Advance payment had already exchanged hands. A hefty sum had arrived to him as a bundle of bitcoins. He had instantly encashed it at his local exchange and converted it into silver. Some money had also flown down the channel, for work done on the ground. Small change in comparison, yes. He vaguely knew the details, happier to focus on managing the task at hand than understanding the intricately tortuous ways in which unaccounted money flowed on its intercountry course. The remaining payment had been kept aside, possibly in a spurious offshore escrow account or as gemstones. Ready to be paid to him against promised delivery.

Plan B. It would surely be set in motion. Those that dealt in hot money never exhibited any patience for long-term gains.He swung his legs down from the bed, stood up, and padded out to the study room.

Through the blinds in the tall window, a dull greyness crept in. Without switching on any lights, he walked steadily towards the long wooden table and switched on his laptop.

He logged on to an email account he had created two weeks ago. He noted with some satisfaction the single message in his inbox, one of those welcome confirmations; he never sent messages. Not from these accounts anyway. The Drafts box was highlighted in bold. There was just one message in Drafts. Communication that had never been sent across any network, defying detection. It was the message he himself had created last night. A single-line message – *Send me an update.*

The other party had password access to the account; login details shared initially through another spurious account that had been deleted immediately after. He always deleted the trail of messages after each interaction.

There was no response from the other end.

His fingers raced across the keyboard, firing up another laptop. He connected through his second broadband connection to SSH, an open server in Nebraska, the first one his scanning bots found. If anyone out there was monitoring machine IPs and accounts, they would see no pattern. He scrolled amid his favourite icons and clicked on a small square of leaping yellow-brown flames. *brownphyre.com.* He signed in, his name online – *Mystic Mir*. There were a string of posts. *Viral*, *Plastic Nuke*, and *Malingomer* exchanging tips on a new worm that could hole its way through an open source code mobile platform. He waited a few minutes, looking at the names as messages popped up.

No sign of *Manic18*. If he was there, he was anonymous. Observing, not participating. Where was the guy when urgency called? Or did he have multiple aliases? *Manic18* was a mystery. Unknown, as he was meant to be. A shadow player in online murk, like a Wayang Kulit puppet, identifiable only in outline, through a snippet he had let loose during one of their chat sessions exchanging notes about coding a new jailbreak app. *Manic18* lived in Mumbai. Found by absolute chance and recruited with strategic intent.

Mystic Mir looked out through the window. Streaks of aubergine leavened the heavy predawn sky. He let out a small sigh. His back felt tense, his muscles lethargic. The bed in the other room beckoned him. If only he cound find peace. But the clock on the screen suggested it was time to stay awake. There was work to be done, *Manic18* to be contacted. Offline if he did not appear in cyberspace.

TWO WEEKS EARLIER

THURSDAY, 4.00 P.M.

Andheri, Mumbai

'Ooh, don't you look handsome, boss,' Delna trilled, and tilted her head. 'But peaky. You have dark shadows under your eyes.'

Vir glanced at his photograph in *Business Now* magazine. Sharp red tie, blue gabardine suit. Face angled to the camera. Just another executive in a general interest story. The staple of monthly mags.

'Indeed,' Vir said, smiling affably. Delna was a generously proportioned woman of indeterminate age, with such a kind smile that Vir had hired her on the spot six months ago, and never regretted it.

The photo had been taken at the end of a long tiring day, he recalled. A day that had started with a sunrise run along the Carter Road promenade, was later crammed with meetings, a speech at a conference, and then the photo shoot in a posh, teak-panelled midtown hotel. It was a feature story on the new Country Head of a global pharma and biotech firm. Complete with a peach-coloured sidebar on the rise of diabetes and cancer patients in India, and the drugs in Acel's arsenal that targeted these diseases.

The real scoop is yet to come, Vir knew. Restlessness returned. What would give him peace? Applauds for the success of Colare? Or, was it something else?

Five years ago, propped by his Ivy League pedigree, he had his trajectory all mapped out: multi-millionaire by thirty, retired by forty. But market forces had colluded to slow down the march, with events beyond control yet forbidding in their stance. He had been successful, just not as much and as fast as he had wanted. This move to India, this sidestep from the single-mindedness of dealmaking to managing the messiness of operations, to disrupt life as he had defined it, had seemed a way to get the brio back. But, was it?

'You work too hard. You need to slow down. Go out more. Enjoy life, no?'

Vir shrugged. He had been weary of late, and the idea of fun had lost its enchantment.

'You should get married,' Delna said.

Vir quirked an eyebrow. It appeared to be Delna's pet project. *Operation Matchmake Vir.* 'Jump into the *band-baaja-baraat* mode just when Colare is about to be unveiled?'

'Should life stop for a product launch? Have they even decided the launch date?'

'Soon. Our lawyers are working on it.'

'What about Tracey's trip? Has she finalized her dates?' Delna fished for information, glancing at the framed photograph on Vir's desk. A white girl. Pretty, if you liked them tall and skinny. She had fielded many a question and deflected several invitations from women trying to get to know Vir.

Tracey. His fiancée. A sinking feeling returned to him. He nodded. 'She is coming in two weeks.'

'You're taking some holiday, na?'

'Just a few days. Solan, to meet my parents and then a trip to Goa.'

Vir glanced at his chronograph. Time to rework the numbers on the new licensing deal he was trying to put together, before his last meeting of the day.

'There's so much to wrap up.'

Delna took the hint. 'Anything else you need, boss?'

He stood up, flexed his neck and shoulders. 'Some coffee before you go, Delna.'

Delna sensed he was tense again. About what, she could not understand. He was thirty-three, and the youngest Country Head in Acel's global empire. It seemed quite a coup to Delna. Feted by market and media, his mugshot gracing many a newspaper and magazine, his degrees in bioengineering and business from Ivy League universities.

What was the worry and the hurry?

He just needs a woman, she told herself.

'It will all settle down soon, don't worry,' she said, walking away.

THURSDAY, 4.00 P.M.

Annasalai, Chennai

Annaswamy Cherian wiped his brow and his bald pate. The world seemed to impinge upon him. The import of his words on India's patent law would reverberate for decades – on people, on companies, on governments.

Outside his office at the Intellectual Property Appellate Board, life went on as usual. Colourfully dressed women went about their daily shopping. Hundreds of enthusiasts in dark shades stood outside a villa, waiting to catch a glimpse of their hero – the reigning superstar of Tamil cinema. At a nearby hospital, doctors and patients went on, as usual, in that game of triumph and failure against disease.

'It would be the wrong precedent, Anna,' Vaidyanathan, the sharp-suited intellectual property lawyer, said, breaking Anna's thoughts.

Annaswamy nodded. That was *his* fear too.

'Think of the headlines. New York. London. Geneva. Not just in New Delhi.'

'But what about ethics, Vaidy, what about that?'

'There is only the Law, Anna. Dispassionate. Firm. Sound.'

'But...'

'Think of Brand India, too, for a moment. Of how this will affect our entire stance towards growth, towards finding our spot on the global stage.'

Annaswamy thought, instead, of the report sitting in the pile of papers on his desk. An independent study that had been commissioned by the ministry. It laid out the need for access to affordable medical care. Detailing statistics of the rise in critical diseases in India. It was a case being eyed by governments around the world. Armies of scientists, statisticians and lawyers had been appointed by both sides. Creating reams and reams of background material, stating their stances, defending their approaches.

One faction within the Indian government maintained the stance of affordability and curtailing the spread of diseases. Another, more globally minded faction, argued the case for global citizenship, of subscribing to the international patent norms, of the need to be trusted by global partners.

'The crux is the idea, Anna. The invention. The path to get there. The investment to make it happen,' Vaidy pressed on. His clients stood for global openness.

'But the idea is usually from some academic, right? Some researcher at a university or a government-funded medical facility, in a cramped laboratory doing primary research, only too happy to sell out to a pharma major for a pittance?' Annaswamy shrugged.

'Perhaps,' Vaidy replied curtly. 'But that does not bring down the millions spent thereafter, to bring the drug to market. That's what matters, Anna.'

'Does it?' Annaswamy questioned.

He was beginning to feel hot in his white bush shirt and pants, wishing he could have spent the day in his study, jotting down in points and sub-points his own thoughts. Getting ready for the deliberation next month.

Annaswamy had started his career as a junior lawyer in the dusty offices of Veluthayan & Associates, rising through the legal ranks, pouring his heart and soul into difficult cases that required endless nights of reading and reflecting. Decades of uprightness stood between that humble start and now. Doing right was important above everything else.

'I can see the merit of the idea and the investment, but the path?'

The *path* was what allowed Indian firms to reconstruct and manufacture certain global drugs.

India's patent law had been first enacted in 1856, aiming to protect the rights of the English inventors, while bolstering the economic flow of goods. In the shadow of the independence movement, the imperative for the new government had been to ensure food and medicines were available to the masses at affordable prices. In 1957, a one-man committee set up by Justice Rajagopala Ayyangar argued that the political and economic reality of the country demanded a different interpretation of patent law. He cited that no country other than the US allowed unrestricted protection of medicines at that time. The German system of process patents seemed more suited for India. His opinions led to the much debated Indian Patent Act of 1970 granting five-year protection on process and not on the products, thus allowing local manufacturers to make cheaper medicines available to hundreds of millions of patients.

As the cost of drug development escalated across the world, with hundreds of millions spent to create one blockbuster drug, the pressure to protect it for significant periods escalated. Global firms could make minor changes in drug composition, allowing them to extend their patent protection period through evergreening.

Since the process patent was what mattered in India, local firms could identify alternative processes for making the same medicine, or perhaps change one ingredient, or mix the ingredients of multiple bestselling drugs, run quick trials and bring the drug to market. At a fraction of the cost. At a fraction of the price. Then export these medicines to other cash-strapped markets. Was the effectiveness of the cure altered? Perhaps. But in a billion-strong country, getting some medicines, some hope was important.

That was what was at stake. *That* was what was about to change. By the deliberations of the committee, with Annaswamy as its Chairman.

'The path matters, Anna sir. The path is the legal loophole at the moment. That is what is allowing these firms to infringe global patent laws. To be predatory.'

'Predatory?' Annaswamy's dark forehead furrowed.

'Predatory,' Vaidy said firmly. 'Undercutting, underpricing, reverse engineering. That is predatory, Anna.'

Not according to the report that sat on his desk. Which

suggested that restricting access by increasing prices was predatory. Which said that changing one ingredient and filing another application to increase the life of patent protection was predatory. Especially in a country with five hundred million below the poverty line. That change in price meant life and death for many of them.

Annaswamy stared into the distance, beyond the small window, outside which the hot afternoon sun glittered.

'Think about the long-term repercussions, Anna,' Vaidy argued for economics. 'Firms spend billions on research, and only a few ideas ever make it to market. Those billions are justified because firms can earn reasonable profits for a period of time from a few blockbuster drugs. If the protections are not there, firms will stop investing in research and eventually people will suffer when newer cures are no longer available.'

'Reasonable is the operative word, no?' said Annaswamy. 'What is reasonable in the West may not hold true for the Indian hinterland. Look at what happened with the AIDS medicines in Africa.'

For all the political activism of artists and rock concerts in aid of the disease-ridden across sub-Saharan Africa, millions had died due to lack of affordable antiretroviral medicines. Until an intrepid Indian manufacturer had stepped in with a concoction, possible under the permissive process patent regime, to supply medicines at one-twentieth the cost.

'What happened was piracy, Anna. The patent holder should determine reasonable price, not a healthcare Robin Hood.'

Annaswamy returned to the moment and looked back inside the room, at the aggravated lawyer sitting across his table, impatient to prove his point.

With all the weariness of age, Annaswamy sighed. 'Go now, Vaidy. Let me think.'

THURSDAY, 4.00 P.M.

Bandra, Mumbai

Raghu stood on the dilapidated balcony, looking down. A bus shifted its lane, throwing traffic in disarray. Scooters and rickshaws honked. Cars screeched to a halt. Pedestrians cursed. It never failed to amuse him, the continuous drama on this street, everyone always rushing to or from Bandra station. Like life depended on motion and the commotion.

His phone rang. 'Maganbhai? What is it?' He whispered.

'Get me the new Anya video.' Maganbhai said abruptly. 'It has been advertised to be released in two weeks, but I have clients who want it now.'

'I am in class, Maganbhai. In a few days, maybe.' Raghu looked behind him. He was in his coaching class, on a break between the sessions. Suv had gone to the toilet. Girls and boys stood about, gripping their books, munching snacks, talking of theorems or films. Their break would end in ten minutes.

'Come after class, Raghu. You are right here.'

'What's the urgency, Maganbhai?'

Maganbhai ran a small stall off Linking Road, selling all manner of counterfeit and pirated products, thumping the noses of the anti-piracy squad in full daylight, not even bothering to hide his duplicate items behind posters of bosomy starlets or stacks of used books and porn rags. The sapient but illiterate Maganbhai was quite a tout. Always on the lookout for new youngsters who could extract digital video data from poorly protected sites for little money.

'Tough *hain*, Raghu,' Maganbhai gurgled on the phone, his voice filtering and distorting through the mouthful of tobacco he was chomping. 'See if you can crack it. Double pay *hain*.'

Double? Raghu knew Amma would kill him if she knew. But he wasn't harming national security, was he?

Raghu tapped into his smartphone. *Anya. Images.*

His was not a sleek top-of-the-line model like Suv's. But it had been purchased from the money earned from Maganbhai. Raghu had met Maganbhai last year, when he had bought an MP3 phone of dubious origin from the stall. Somehow the two had got chatting. Maganbhai had enquired about Raghu's internet skills. One thing had led to another, and Raghu had surreptitiously procured some poor quality versions of internet games and porn for Maganbhai. He had neatly copied them onto a CD, which Maganbhai copied many times over and sold to select customers. He had created bittorrents, for which Maganbhai created his own pay-per-view model for clients who could not afford a computer, but aspired to use one. And, Raghu had earned several hundreds in pocket money in the process! Now those same customers were clamouring for Anya, and Maganbhai, eager to oblige, had called Raghu.

So, *double* meant he could combine his earnings from his Systems Security part-time job to buy that bass guitar he wanted.

Photographs of a seductive girl filled the screen.

He shot a furtive glance around him. How hard could it be? Surely there was a bittorrent file of the song somewhere. If not, how long could it possibly take to find a backdoor entry to the music company's intranet. Ping. Find open port. Tunnel in. Download.

THURSDAY, 5.00 P.M.

Andheri, Mumbai

'Vir's core team had assembled in his office. There was a bustle of greetings and shuffle of chairs. It was their weekly huddle, to pore over charts and updates.

Prashant Mehra, tall and balding, with a rounded belly from days on the road, headed sales. Arnab Mazumder, mid-height, mid-weight, unassuming and erudite, looked after finance.

'How's the new out-licensing contract going?' Prashant asked.

'Slow,' Arnab said.

The deal had been signed in intent. Their second one in India. But some tax issues had cropped up, and he had been trying hard to get the US legal team and the local manufacturer to agree upon some details.

Vir nodded. Keen as he was to close the deal, he knew it was better to stay out of the whys and wherefores. 'Let's see the numbers.'

Prashant slid a sheet towards him. The top-line sales data for the week. Gathered from data submitted by a national team of some 200-odd people, and sliced and diced by a team of analysts.

'Sales are flat.'

'We are holding our own. Not to be scoffed at in today's market.'

'The new out-licensing deal would be good, though.'

'Yup, Vir's *shaadi-dot-com* service for Acel,' Arnab quipped. It had to be a careful orchestration. Like many frogs kissed before finding the one prince.

Vir let out a laugh.

Acel's highly regarded curative drugs had limited reach,

preferred by the larger hospitals and prescribed to well-heeled patients. Prices were a major deterrent to mass-scale adoption.

India's medical needs defied imagination. Old, ageing, harried, haggard, decrepit, hopeless – every category of patient abounded. Yet sales belied mythical forecasts. Few consumers could afford to pay for expensive imported medicines. The mass market category was very price conscious. Patients could only afford inexpensive medicines. Just the usual woes of every global executive in the region.

Contract licence agreements, for older drugs and those getting off their patent cycles soon, were a way to reach more people. Acel would never dream of out-licensing either of its two blockbuster drugs for cancer treatments. Even selling a few of those at a lakh of rupees per cycle was much better than selling higher numbers at lower prices. But its older formulations, still effective, had potential.

Vir oversaw the team that marketed and sold, convinced doctors and patients, ran local clinical trials and offered promotions, created ads and hosted events to drive up sales from current products. But above all, he played the roving matchmaker, identifying suitable partners, ensuring a melding of hearts and minds, vision and philosophy, to expand the India portfolio. His particular strengths – persuasion and negotiation.

Trouble was everything dragged out in India. Like stars aligning in slow motion.

'It's a worry, all this talk of compulsory licensing,' Vishal said.

'I know,' Vir exhaled. With so many of Acel's portfolio of drugs focusing on life-threatening diseases, the threat of being mandated to supply them at throwaway prices was a real risk.

'There will be a hue and cry around the world.'

'Back to sales figures. The trouble is,' Arnab said, 'we were projecting to do better. We need to ramp up numbers somehow.'

'No immediate potential from new hospital majors at this stage,' Vishal added. 'We've been in long talks with some new hospitals down south; that will take some time. Maybe on the back of Colare we can energize some new deals.'

Vir nodded in agreement.

Colare. It was an experiment of a kind. A clean room had been specially built above their Mumbai office, away from the hustle and bustle of selling biochemical concoctions. Acel's pre-clinical research, closely guarded by its team of pharmacologists, medical oncologists, biochemistry doctorates and bio-informatics geniuses housed in a leafy campus in Rockville, had been tag-teamed with this new facility. Pressures of long product development cycles and delays in approval and release of new discoveries weighed on Acel. Vir had convinced the Chairman, Adam Janlowski, to open this centre in India, the time difference aimed at speeding up the entire lab to market process.

For the first time in the history of Acel, it was doing multi-country research for this new dream drug for treating late-stage and metastatic pancreatic cancers. It was a deadly disease that shimmied in on silken toes, undetected until too late, claiming millions around the world.

Different researchers around the world were working on finding a cure. One precocious sixteen-year-old had even designed a basic screening test, which more distinguished scientists were now working to perfect and standardize. A screening test marked the pathways lit up by the one protein in a complex array of proteins that always went in hyper mode when this type of cancer was present in a patient, triggering the multiplying switch of the cancerous cells inside and outside the pancreas.

Colare was a complex virus bonded onto a molecule, targeted to reduce the splitting of cells gone berserk with auto-division, and stopping the formation of new blood vessels around this writhing mass of cells, thus preventing their spread. Complemented by a forgotten biomarker, dusted out for new usage, it provided a combination cure. Like a lock and key. Detection and prevention.

This was not the kind of last-minute clinical trials that had become fashionable of late, targeting poor emerging markets and garnering much flak from local activists. This was real, hands-on, post-molecular-stage testing on animals to increase the speed and volume of data gathering and fast track the global patent approval process. Initial results were dramatic. Medical journals were already excited.

With the market in such flux – media riffing about the generic medicine business and its future, lobbyists from all continents chasing ministerial bigwigs and global white knights swooping in to buy local manufacturers – this story of innovation, of twinned research, was bound to capture the imagination of all once it hit the newswire.

It could change the course of a disease. Provide relief to those who had lost hope, expand their life expectancy by several years. It could change the course of a company. Add billions to Acel's coffers. There were hushed whispers that Pharma bigwigs were circling Acel, eager to acquire its stable of two blockbuster drugs and two upcoming cures, to lift their diminishing fortunes. It could change the course of careers of the team working on it.

His career. A hot flash of dark bitterness ran through Vir.

A knock sounded on the door. Dr Amin Ali, who looked after Colare R&D in India, walked in.

'Sorry guys, I'm late.'

'Yeah, because you had the longest commute!' Arnab said. The rest of them were on the same floor, while Ali's lab was on the floor above.

'Yeah, yeah,' Ali said. 'The US is getting ready for the global patent filing. There's lots of momentum in our work.'

'What's the latest?' Vir asked.

Ali beamed, a wide smile, adding a sparkle to his bulbous-nosed face. 'All well, Vir, all well. I am super excited. Colare is going to make news.'

THURSDAY, 6.00 P.M.

Bandra, Mumbai

The skyline of suburban Mumbai spread in a vertical display of twinkling lights, jaggedly piercing the dark heart of the night and reflecting into the wavering strip of inky sea spread before it.

Sandman, as he liked his friends to call him, sat on his haunches and positioned the cut-top plastic canister in his hands to collect the narrow trickle of water flowing from the municipal tap. His task completed, he shoved an old cork to stopper the flow. Drops continued to drip from the broken faucet. Carefully, he hoisted the canister and walked home. Soon the water would be needed to cook dinner.

Once inside, he put the canister next to a makeshift table – a plank balanced on two columns of bricks, and checked the time on his phone. *Just six*. An hour before his mother returned from work.

He kneeled on the floor and from inside an old cardboard box, underneath the wooden bed, took out a blue bubble-wrapped packet. He unwrapped it to take out his netbook. He no longer had to use UC browser on a basic phone to access the internet.

He switched on the laptop, searched for an open insecure hotspot and logged in, rotating by habit from Facebook to email to *whyweprotest.com*. He scrolled down the screen. *A secret protest in Brisbane against unsafe mining practices in the Kalgoorie range; an open call for action against genetically modified seeds in Malaysia; an all-night seance against Scientology in Haight Ashbury in San Francisco*. He scrolled down some more, and his eyes chanced upon a heading: *Stop Clinical Trials Battle in Mumbai*. The post followed by the cyber war cry. *Lets Lulz*.

Fragmented images flitted across *Sandman*'s mind, a

sensory video of memories. A man, grown old before his time, twisting and arcing as spasms of radial pain spread through him. His father. Lain on a steel cot in a government hospital in Parel, breathing on a prayer, his last hope lost, the last possible medicine unavailable, after he was refused to be signed for a clinical trial. Patients like him were just data for the clinical trial firms. He felt his pulse race. Wiping a thin string of perspiration off his upper lip, he leaned forward involuntarily, reading the post.

I've often wondered how much patients understand the risks of a randomized clinical trial. It is a legal and a moral issue.

The blogger went on to describe the incidents of five deaths of young girls in a cancer trial being run by an NGO under the guise of an aid project. It spoke of how the government had allowed certain medicines to be sold in the country without holding local clinical trials, and ended with a quote from a US firm rubbishing the slow and stringent regulatory framework around clinical trials in India.

There were posts below the main article expressing outrage on the trials that had been conducted on the poor, the infirm and the demented, without due disclosures and paperwork.

A hot rush of rage coursed through him, molten and intense.

Knowledge was power. Power was responsibility. He had to do something. He started typing.

THURSDAY 2.00 P.M.

Rockville, Maryland

The door to the conference room opened, and the sallow-faced Dr Peter Lee peered inside.

The room was in disarray, the table moved to one side like a stage prop, with an assortment of equipment and books artfully arranged on it and a row of chairs placed in front. A camera with heavy duty lens stood on a tripod. Andy Rudd stood in the middle of the hubbub with people Peter vaguely recalled as being in Acel's legal and marketing teams.

'Join us, Peter.' Andrew Rudd waved his arms. 'Meet Thomas Varmore from *Health* magazine.'

'Thomas is writing a special feature on Colare,' said a sharp-suited marketer. 'Time we unveiled its wonders to the world.'

This was the first Peter had heard of any marketing plans for Colare. All he had heard till date was the need for utmost secrecy.

The door opened again, and Dr Terence Small from the analytics team walked in.

'Great to meet the Colare team.' Thomas shook hands with Peter and Terence. 'I have been reading the advance reports. Amazing is all I can say.'

Peter stood uncertainly, not knowing what was expected of him next. He had been called from the lab just five minutes back. *Come down if you are free.* The tableau here indicated hours of advance planning.

A woman with a makeup case moved towards Andy.

'Sit, gentlemen, will you?' the marketing guy said. 'A few solo shots of Andy first.'

Peter and Terry sank into chairs set up against the wall, observing the activity of the makeup artist trussing up Andy, lightly powdering his nose.

'Our readers like the human interest angle,' Thomas Varmore said. 'We will explain the technology, of course. For the lay reader. But your background as the person heading this is great.'

'We need to blend science and commerce today,' the marketing guy added.

Peter shifted in his chair.

Andy was tall and broad, in his trademark look of a loud shirt worn underneath a sober suit. More like a British banker than an American researcher. In a firm of intellectual dreamers, for whom routine meant profiling RNA sequences to detect protein level variations in diseased tissue or using polymerase reaction to amplify or multiply a DNA strand, Andy was a strict realist. An operational genius who understood the interplay of biology, disease, informatics and technology, yet relied on factual statistics and repeatable results to steer research towards success. In an industry where hundreds of millions could be spent upon a dream over several long years, Andy knew, almost intuitively, when to pull the plug and when to persevere. In his ten years as Head of Research, he had led Acel through four successful drug launches, which had earned the firms hundreds of millions in global revenue. Of course, Colare would be the biggest product of his career so far.

The photographer took over, making Andy sit first in one pose then in another, shouting instructions to his assistant to hold up the light reflectors at different angles.

'It's amazing, the feat, Andy.' Thomas Varmore kept a steady conversation going on the pitfalls of research and the path of exploration taken by Acel.

'It's been teamwork,' Andy said.

'And you led that team.'

Andy was manic obsessive, his team thought. Unable to make it to medical school, he now lorded over highly qualified docs, tearing down their best mapped ideas with the poke of commerce.

'We managed the breakthrough,' the marketing guy said, flashing his perfect teeth. 'Isn't that right?' He smiled at Peter and Terry.

Terry nodded.

Peter looked impassively at the thicket of bare-branched trees visible through the window. He had left midway through designing the logic of a database to tabulate clinical trial data, and he couldn't wait to get back to his desk. He had worked alone for years, trying to graft that impossible bond of an arenavirus on a human embryo stem cell. An idea he had thought of after a rare conversation with Acel's Chairman Adam Janlowski. He had dogged every detail of the project. Now that Colare was near full definition, he wanted to work on every detail himself. Not sit around in a silly photo shoot.

'Join us now, guys,' Thomas Varmore called out.

Peter looked questioningly at his white lab coat.

'Don't lose the lab coat,' Thomas Varmore said. 'Gives you the scientist look.'

Peter felt like scowling. Scientist look indeed. But he obeyed, his face impassive as ever.

'We need one shot of the team,' said Thomas Varmore, as he made Peter and Terry sit next to Andy, and observed the picture they made.

'It looks bare. You guys join in too.'

Terry rolled his eyes and winked at Peter. Peter looked away in response. He wondered since when legal and marketing had become the key Colare team. He was the one who had made Colare possible. But he stepped in as instructed, making room for the others. The hot flashlight shone on them.

'Just a few more shots,' the photographer called out. 'Change the tilt of your head, Andy.'

Standing next to Peter, Andy shifted a bit.

'Be still, sir,' the photographer looked at Peter, then back into his camera viewfinder.

FRIDAY, 6.00 P.M.

Bandra, Mumbai

'Oh Anki, you wicked girl you.' Madhu's hazel eyes darkened to match the brown of her Maheshwari silk dupatta.

'Wait, there's more.' Ankita scrunched her slim face to mimic their physics teacher and continued to imitate his thick Mallu accent.

Madhu giggled.

'Girls, you are driving me crazy,' Ankita's mother, Mrs Sharma, entered the room, uncoiling her bun. '*Chatar-patar! Khil-khil!* I could not be heard when I was your age!'

Anki winked at Madhu. 'Just going, Ma. Is my room done yet?'

Mrs Sharma looked hassled. 'Incompetent fools. No sense.'

She had spent the last hour screaming at the furniture shop guys about a new desk for the girls' room. It had arrived half-finished. To add to her ire, the workers had spread out an oily knapsack and started to cut a hole for the wires with a tiny saw.

'Ma, you have smoke coming out of your ears,' Ankita teased.

'Enough cheekiness, miss.' Mrs Sharma's eyes glinted. 'I need to start preparing dinner. The Khatris are coming.'

She looked at her watch. 'Where is this Lalti? Just when there is more work, she takes off. No sense of duty.'

'True, madam,' the kitchen maid muttered, sweeping furry balls of dust, grease and hair onto a plastic tray. She was deeply suspicious that the cleaning bai secreted away fistfuls of rice under her pallav as she went home. More than that, she resented having to do the cleaning work, which was Lalti's duty.

'We'll watch TV, Ma. Tell me when my room is done.' Ankita sank into the sofa, already switched off from the domestic drama.

Mrs Sharma went inside to supervise the workers.

The doorbell rang, a loud ting-tong sound over the buzz of the drilling machine in the bedroom and the snappy tunes of TV ads in the living room.

'Anki,' Mrs Sharma shouted. 'Check who's there!'

Ankita sloped off to open the door.

A boy about her age stood there, in a much washed striped tee shirt Anki thought her dad used to wear last year. His hair fell messily on his forehead. His eyes were watery and slightly blank.

'Madam there?' There was a gap between his front teeth.

'Who are you?' Ankita asked imperiously, annoyed at what she felt was a leering look in his eyes.

'Lalti's son.'

'Who is it?' Mrs Sharma came out.

The boy stood stiffly at the door. There was a pinched look on his lopsided face. 'Mother is sick, I need some money for medicine.'

'Again?' Mrs Sharma frowned. 'Tell your mother she is always making these excuses.'

Sullenness crept into the boy's eyes.

'These maids,' Mrs Sharma scorned, 'they hold you at ransom!' Her mind ran ahead. Just when you think a maid is working well, something would happen. Usually sick leave for herself or one of her umpteen relatives. Leaving the household in a lurch!

'What's your name?' Mrs Sharma wrinkled her eyes. She usually paid Lalti some extra money for this boy's education, salving her conscience.

'Sandesh,' the boy mumbled, staring beyond her.

'Look down, boy. Show respect when you speak to elders.'

Grumbling, Mrs Sharma went to rummage inside her purse and dug out a few hundred-rupee notes. She looked towards the sofa. Anki was not there.

'Madhu, give this to the boy.'

Madhu walked to the door to give the cash to the boy. He stood there with a vacuous stare, not noticing her, an odd belligerence on his face.

'Here,' said Madhu, a kind note in her voice. She used to volunteer with her mother to teach the kids of the tribal workers, and had seen that expression of pride mixed with need. She extended her hand, holding on to the very edge of the crisp notes. 'Sandesh?'

The boy looked at her, startled. Colour suffused his dark face. His eyes dropped down. He clamped the notes in his fingers, crumpled them and did a quick about turn.

FRIDAY, 7.40 P.M.

Chembur, Mumbai

'Come back. *Enakku puriyala!*' Mrs Revathy Damodaran shouted, her voice as rigid as her pose. 'When will you study, Raghu? Didn't I tell you to give up this stupid job? Why do you need pocket money at this age?'

'It's good for my IT course, Amma.' Raghu tried resignedly.

'Entrance exams are no joke, Raghu. These two years will determine your future,' she reasoned.

'Night duty is not hectic, Amma.'

It was true. It was quiet enough to study in the computer lab, where he worked the night shift. Not that he studied. Who would, given high speed broadband, unlimited access, and no one to peep over the shoulder? Not that he surfed either. That was just uncool. Not for Raghu Damodaran.

'Focus! You don't want to become overconfident now.'

As if. 'I know what I am doing, Ma'.

'This is crazy. Why can't you listen to any logic?'

Mrs Damodaran was a professor at the Tata Institute of Social Sciences and got hyper only over two things – her field projects with rural child welfare organizations and the future well-being of her brilliant son.

Raghu picked up his bag jerkily and walked out, slamming the door without a backward glance.

Mrs Damodaran's voice echoed in the cement-floored room, the dim light masking the tired fabric of the thin sofa cushions and the chipped edges of the white sunmica table.

Raghu got on his bicycle and pedalled off furiously. Blood swelled inside him, throbbing his arteries. *I am seventeen!* he fumed. *And she treats me like I'm still a clueless child!* He sped, pedalling faster, leaning into the handlebar, feeling his thigh muscles burn, and then let go, till just the creaky whirr of the wheels disrupted the silence and exhilaration flowed in his veins, the wind ruffling his hair. A bird fluttered somewhere. The avenue of feathery-leaved tamarinds and dense peepuls, interspersed with tall toddy palms, formed a canopy over the road. The leaves sieved the sodium glow of street lamps, dappling the deep shadows. The campus road twined away from the residential blocks towards the larger academic buildings.

He let his cycle come to a slow halt, hopped off and leaned it against a tree. His shift at the computer centre began in ten minutes. His mind wandered to his mother, her skeletal arms like bent sticks planted upon her thin frame, dressed in one of her usual block-printed Dastakar saris. He could not recall its colour. So blended were the beiges and browns and dove greys she wore, that colour lost all vibrancy. Like the rest of her life. *Their lives!* Leached of colour.

That's what she wished for him too! *Colourlessness.* No fun, no games. No coffees with friends, no pocket money. Just study, study, study.

Amma's expectations were palpable, like some raw unyielding need, wanting to propel him towards a destiny that he never questioned, simply submitted to. Of carrying forward the scientific legacy of his father, of taking it to the next level, of becoming someone successful.

He could not recall life with his father. Just a few pictures that had survived – of Raghu as a baby clambering on dad's shoulders while he played the veena, dad flying a kite while chubby little Raghu looked up at him enamoured, dad steadying a young Raghu on his first small bicycle. The pictures made Raghu feel nostalgic for what could have been. There was also a wedding picture – dad in a thin zari bordered white sarong, another zari-edged cloth wrapped around his shoulders, a bejewelled Amma resplendent in a deep magenta and emerald Kanjivaram, both drowned in fat garlands of marigold and rose and hibiscus, little tinsel strands spreading out from them.

Dr Damodaran had been a physicist who had returned from Imperial College to work at the Tata Institute of Fundamental Research and had posthumously won the prestigious Bhatnagar

Award for scientific research. A non-smoking, non-drinking vegetarian, his only passion other than his work in asymmetric string theories had been his love of the stringed instrument veena. He had died of a cerebral haemorrhage at the relatively young age of forty. Raghu had been five then.

Raghu had inherited his father's mathematical genius. He topped exams effortlessly. Mrs Damodaran had high hopes for him and strict views on what he should do. His job as Sys Sec, the systems security person, had never met her approval. He sat quietly for a few minutes, drawing interlinked patterns of eight on the dirt. Loud guffaws announced a group of young students walking past, breaking his reverie. Once they walked past, he got up, brushed his trousers and rode off to the computer centre.

'You're late,' Sanker, the afternoon Sys Sec, a scrawny doctoral student in sociology, looked up from his swivel chair.

'Mom.' Raghu rolled his eyes. Sanker knew of his ongoing scuffles with his mother over his evening job.

'All yours, then.' Sanker sloped off with his bulging backpack.

Raghu sat down. Momentarily annoyed to sit in another's body warmth, he surveyed the room. Rows of computers were kept on grey sunboard tables. The room was empty. After all, it was a Friday night. Most students were possibly in places more exciting than a computer lab, hanging out in coffee shops, perhaps cheering some sports team on television, or drinking litres of Old Monk and Coke.

His fingers raced across the keyboard now, tapping away, in and out of sites to find Anya. Her old songs were everywhere. On YouTube. On BitTorrent downloads. But not the new song. He went to the website of Desi Rhythm, the post-production company working on Anya's music video. It advertised a flashing image. *Coming Soon* – the new video of Anya. The girl herself blinkered on the screen, zooming in and out, delectable in black lace, her back facing the camera, just her face turned to the front. The full song had to be in there somewhere. In their servers.

Fired with determination, Raghu pinged the site and

scanned the ports. The security team had done their job well. All entries were blocked, except Port 22. Which meant some intrusion detection software was running underneath. Could he brute-force it to get through? He ran a vulnerability scan. *Yes.* It needed buffer overload to break in. Simple.

Raghu sneaked another look around the room. All was quiet. He went back to the screen and telnetted to a site in Iran. From there, he searched for and found a free online hacking tool for buffer overload.

He went back to the Desi Rhythm website, and tried running the tool in the search bar on the page. He waited. Nothing happened for a minute. Just a little cursor flashed and rotated. Then it stopped. He refreshed the screen and repeated the actions. Nothing. He stretched his arms, thinking. What next?

Anya continued to stare back at him from another window on the screen. Raghu stared back at her, taking in the flushed face, the inviting eyes. Damn.

Well, if Anya stymied him, there were other things he could do. With a smile, he started typing again.

FRIDAY, 9.00 P.M.

Pali Hill, Mumbai

Vir dabbed Chanel Allure Homme Sport Eau, and tucked his checked Abercrombie shirt inside his jeans. He was freshly showered and rejuvenated, post a game of squash in Otters.

His phone rang.

'Hi Trace. Hugs to you, baby. Wish you were here already. I really want to hold you close,' Vir said, meaning it.

He missed talking to her. Six months of international calls and instant messages and chats at odd hours could not fill the void of real conversations. The first few weeks had been emotional, laden with the misery and longing of the newly separated, then desultoriness had crept in.

'Well,' she offered tetchily. 'You should have thought of it before going off ten thousand miles away.'

Why was she pereniallly grumpy? 'What's the matter, Trace?'

'The usual.' She talked about the latest work gossip, the cold that refused to thaw. 'To top it, the boiler stopped working last night. Can you even imagine how freezing it was? I had to come home at midday so the guy could fix it.'

'I miss DC weather,' he cut in, recalling the chilly pre-spring days, waiting for those first snowbells to sprout and the first cherry blossoms to flourish.

'Hah. All good for you to say it while soaking up the sunshine.'

'Come to sunshine, Trace.'

'I am ready for my trip, Vir. But where are we headed?' Vir felt denseness returning upon him. He exhaled, the tiny sound carrying through the phone.

'Its annoying, how you react,' she said.

'Trace. Darling.'

'I don't want to talk about it any more. So, what are you doing now?'

'Heading out for a friend's birthday party now.'

'A party again?' She flared up. 'My God! Is that why you moved, Vir, to play the scene?'

'That's unfair, Trace.'

'Unfair? What's unfair is that I am here alone, working hard, staying in, minding the house. While you waltz from party to party!' She snapped and killed the connection.

Vir tried calling her back. She did not pick up.

He had been a player once. Before he had met her. A scuba-diving, mountain-scaling, adrenaline junkie, OD-ing on acquisition deals between his globetrotting jaunts.

He had met Tracey at a medical fundraising dinner. She was one of the resident research fellows in paediatric oncology, having recently completed her specialization from Columbia Med School. His company had been one of the sponsors. She looked striking – tall, blonde and pretty. But her seriousness had struck him. They had started dating soon after, spending more and more time together. It had taken him nearly two years to propose. Commitment meant vulnerability, he had learnt early in life. Why set yourself up for rejection, when the present was all that could be controlled. Strange how a few months of living together had domesticated him.

Yet their conversations were stilted now, the arguments sharper. Was there truth in Tracey's questions? Did they have a future any more? They had set a date for an autumn wedding. But that had been then. When he had been in DC. Together still. Not living parallel lives halfway across the world.

He tried calling Tracey's number several times, checked to see if he could chat or Facetime her. She had switched off completely.

The irony of it.

A sliver of disappointment stabbed him, its blue-tinged tip raking up a much forgotten image, a pretty sylph bidding a younger him a clipped goodbye in the serene greens of Kamla Nehru Ridge, ending their relationship, unwilling to face time and distance for love, for him.

Was it happening all over again?

FRIDAY, 9.00 P.M.

Bandra, Mumbai

'This is perfect. Thank you, Mausi.' Madhu hugged Mrs Sharma.

Their room had been cleaned and organized. Two desks on two sides; a new Mac on Anki's table, and an old desktop on Madhu's.

The girls sat companionably. Ankita surfing the internet, checking out social media posts and taking a picture on her mobile to upload and share, Madhu writing a long email to her parents. Madhu described the new room arrangement in detail. The pink braided dhurrie, the rose-printed bedsheets, the two computers, the new desk. *Something nice to write about. Without fibbing. Or pretending she liked her new college and new classmates.*

Madhu Mishra, a girl who preferred calculus to couture, had recently come to Mumbai to attend junior college and coaching classes and live with her cousin's family. The girls were together constantly, chatting late into the night and going to college and tuition together.

A hazy image of home fluttered into Madhu's mind – a large whitewashed bungalow with high-ceiling rooms and a verdant garden with mango and *jamun* trees and climbing *raat-ki-rani* and *madhumalati*. Korba, a small industrial mining township in Chhattisgarh, where her father was the Head of Engineering in the coal plant. The only way to reach Korba was by a train that sped across the heartland of the country, loading and unloading passengers at one small mining town after another, on its cross-country trek along the Mumbai–Howrah line, and getting off at the grimy station of Champa, the nearest railhead to Korba. Madhu remembered chasing her twin brothers about the garden, drinking Thums Up, picnicking behind the mulberry bush, plucking guavas to make jelly, watching open-air movie screenings in the colony club, and most of all, cycling. That feeling of freedom, her dupatta billowing in the cool night air, the wind in her face, as she raced in the campus.

She missed home.

Wistfully, she went back to her email.

The maid walked in, carrying a tray with glasses of Fanta and plates of hot fried *hara bhara* kebabs.

There was a new message in her inbox. From desi-card-dot-com. She clicked on it. A cuddly little fluffy leopard cub appeared on the screen, its plump brown nose and large liquid brown eyes staring off the screen, the enticing button for a site for e-cards.

'Awww, this is so cute!' Madhu said. 'Anki, look at this.'

Anki put down her comic book and stood behind Madhu.

'You be careful of what you click on, princess.'

'Hah.'

The bear picture flashed and changed into a cute shaggy dog.

'Aww,' the girls cried in unison.

Madhu clicked on the link, and registered on the site by keying in her email ID and password.

Piggybacking on the link, a remote administration malware automatically installed itself on her computer and instead of waiting for an external command, it reached out to the host directly, giving it permission to open a tunnel to Madhu's computer. It took a few seconds, perhaps, for this background process to click in.

The site opened to a beautifully laid out selection of card images and searchable database tagged by categories of friends, romance, father, mother, and so on.

The computer, meanwhile, became accessible. Like an open book, for someone to enter its recesses, access all stored information, retrieve any files and see the on-screen activity in real time.

While the girls trawled through the images, the intruder digitally shoulder-surfed, watching them like a remote voyeur as they chose cards, typed in messages, and keyed in email ids of friends.

FRIDAY 10.00 P.M.

Bandra, Mumbai

Vir stepped out of his blue BMW and entered the dimly lit inside of Pali Village Café, which had been closed for the night for a private party. The music was loud and all-encompassing. Bips was in the back of the faux-rustic space leaning into a sizzling young thing in a peach bandage dress.

That's a player, he thought ruefully, as he made his way to the back to envelop his newfound friend Bipin Prasad in a bear hug and congratulate him on hitting the big three-o, then moved to find himself a glass of Laphroaig.

Taking a sip, he surveyed the scene. Men standing around clinking glasses, ruing the slide of the rupee while sipping expensive Single Malts and Grey Goose martinis.

Vir did drop in late at night at the parties thrown by his Mumbai friends when he could. There was always something on, even on week nights. Most of which he spent trying to avoid the lavish matchmaking attempts of their wives, girlfriends and mothers. Thirty-three and unmarried! Successful, to boot. Curiosity simmered in every meeting.

'Hey, we met at Bips' before.' A hip-looking guy in denims, plaid shirt and goatee offered a handshake and introduced himself. 'How's biotech doing in India?'

Vir breathed out, letting go of his personal worries. He dived into an animated discussion with the wannabe investor on the buccaneering field that biotech had become globally, with feisty funders chasing a bunch of molecule concocters and firms ascending by sizing up and swooping down on potential start-ups with great ideas on molecular biochemistry.

'It's the next phase,' Vir concluded. 'The future. The space where bigger pharma companies want to play.'

'Hey there,' a girl in a black dress, wavy hair and nose

ring interrupted them and introduced herself. She had recently returned from Oxford to work for a non-profit in slum child education.

'Takes a lot of courage to do what you do,' Arun said.

'How do you contribute?' she asked Vir, her diamond nose-ring glinting in the low light.

'We don't have the wherewithal to run projects ourselves,' Vir said. 'But we support some non-profits that work in rural healthcare.'

'That's the way it should be. Business should create goods and services. Let the experts in operating agencies do field development work.'

'You speak like an economist.' Vir grinned.

'But I am.' The girl explained why she wanted to work at the ground level, and not in some apex money management agency.

Discussion turned on the practices of corporate giving and personal donations.

'Excuse me,' Vir said after some time, and walked towards the bar to get himself another drink.

A tall girl in a long burgundy dress stood at the bar, her hair bunched on one side to reveal a tattooed ampersand on her slender neck. Vir squinted at the tattoo as he squeezed up to the counter to order a refill. He shouted out his order, but his voice did not carry over the din of the crowd. He waved his hand to catch the busy waiter's attention and accidentally bumped the girl's shoulder.

'Excuse me!' She turned, her hair tumbling in glossy curls down one side. 'Vir!'

'Diti?'

'Oh my god, are you for real?' She cupped her mouth with her palm awkwardly.

Vir felt his breath stop. A floodgate of memories opened, that *kabuli keekar* tree in Kamla Nehru Ridge overlooking a mossy pond, underneath which they used to sit wrapped up in each other.

Where they had last met. Where she had bid goodbye.

FRIDAY, 2.00 P.M.

Rockville, Maryland

The standing Friday meeting was usually a drab affair, a weekly round-up, where researchers shared project status and discussed challenges to be solved against elongated timelines. Nothing in drug discovery moved fast.

'Welcome all.' Andy Rudd asked people to sit down.

Today's meeting had been taken over by the marketing team. Neat folders labelled *Colare: Prep* had been placed at every seat. A stack of glossy brochures with large photos of happy people and small charts explaining the new drug had been kept in the middle. A pile of merchandise – colourful foos balls, double helical keychains, assorted coasters and mugs and mint boxes – all suitably adorned with the Acel logo and the name Colare had been placed on trolley carts along one wall.

Peter Lee flipped through the folder. He had seen this hype. When another drug he had worked on had been taken to market.

Colare, the latest wonder product in Acel's stable of biotech solutions, was about to be launched.

Pure magic, Adam Janlowski, Acel Chairman, had called it in an internal announcement meeting.

Colare was a complex product. *Colombian porcine pericarditis virus,* a species of arenavirus, had been attenuated to delete certain genes, thus stripping the virus to reduce its virulence. For the first time ever, the virus had then been grafted with human embryonic stem cells and cultured fibroblast cells. The cultured cells had been implanted with a microdose of a special protein tagged with a radioactive marker. The result was a special oncolytic virus that could selectively target cancerous cells. The tagged protein allowed microdose radiation therapy to be used in conjunction with the virus for targeted blasting of the irregular cells.

Lara Andrews, Acel Chief Legal Counsel, stood out in a shocking blue power suit. 'Before we begin, I cannot stress enough on the need for confidentiality.'

Her keen eyes bored into everyone around the table.

'Then why the early marketing drama?' Peter said, horrified immediately that he had spoken aloud. He could feel the room staring at him.

'Leave the business road map to us, Peter,' Andy was curt, barely looking up from the dossier he was reading.

Peter looked down, mortified. Had Andy just snubbed him? Data was decipherable. People were not. Peter sneaked a look around the silent room. What were they thinking?

Lara smiled kindly. 'As you know, the FDA has already approved our clinical trial.'

She was going to ignore the interchange, wasn't she? Peter clenched his fist. He very well knew of the approval and that doctors had already signed on. As Chief Scientist, he oversaw the clinical trial process.

'This is just advance prep for the roadshow. We are going to carefully monitor and curate any external communication. As you know, we are going to file the global patent in a few weeks.'

She peered at everyone again, intimidating her audience.

'The last of the in vivo tests are wrapping up in our labs in Rockville and Mumbai.'

Darkness shot through Peter, as always, on mention of the Mumbai lab. True, he oversaw their work. But did Acel really need to split Colare in two? Not that his protest had mattered. He absently scratched on the marketing folder with his pen, till the nib bore a hole into the glossy paper.

'Now the video.' Lara gestured to the marketing team to take charge.

The projector came to life with a video and catchy background music. Double helical strands of DNA rotated on the screen, then morphed into Acel's logo.

Andy appeared. 'Three years of hard work have gone into Colare: two years in primary research, followed by a year of in vivo testing.'

Andy's face was replaced by computer animation with a clipped voiceover. Inside the host body, the rogue tumour cells spread by self-replicating, swarming around the good cells. The oncolytic virus, like a guided missile, went through the capillaries and tissues of the host body, attaching itself on rogue dendritic cells. But instead of just relying on cell lysis to kill the cancerous cells, Colare did a double whammy. It also allowed the normal cells to multiply.

The marketing guys sat smug, pleased at this high quality video that would be shown to clinicians and the media.

Peter thought of the early years.

It had been a tough balancing act. And a risk. As the lone scientist on it in the early days, he knew the human embryonic stem cell had high telomerase activity. So, potentially, it could enhance even the rogue cell multiplication. But careful manipulation of telomerase levels and expression of binding proteins led to transcription and higher connective cellular growth. Normal cells multiplied, crowding out malignant ones.

He leaned back in his chair, satisfied that his solitary dream was close to reality.

The drug offered hope to patients with advanced metastases, where the disease had spread beyond the effective use of normal chemotherapy and radiation therapy treatments.

Andy came on screen again. 'Results have been revolutionary.'

Peter felt boredom kick in. He had lived and breathed these details. While Andy droned on screen, he recalled his mentor Dr Ron Johnson.

As Chief Scientist on another product, Ron had been the face of those infomercials. Quite the East Coast patrician, making stately appearances in magazines and channels, feted by masses and the media as a messiah. That had been then. Andy had been new, and Ron too much of an evangelist to stand behind. Peter had learned everything about managing drug discovery from Ron. But could charisma be imbibed?

Plus Andrew Rudd ran a tight ship, keeping close track of research results and taking on the complete mantle of interacting with the business teams and the market. No one could be the face of the product but him.

The video dissolved into Acel's logo.

The projector was switched off. An executive detailed the marketing plan. The technical articles co-authored by Andy and Peter, the peer reviews in medical journals, had been the careful start. The full-blown campaign would launch soon. Not just apprising doctors, but courting the public and the investors. Going to mass media. Hobnobbing with Washington. And Andy at the nub of all projections as Acel's Head of Research.

Peter shifted in his seat restlessly. This was *his* baby they were talking about. Without his diligence, Colare would've never been possible. Except he stood on the side, watching the jamboree like some bystander. Why did they make him waste time sitting in useless meetings like this, when he had piles of data analysis waiting on his desk?

SATURDAY, 9.00 P.M.

Juhu, Mumbai

'You never reached out.' Vir almost winced as he heard the words come out of his mouth. Did he sound whiny? Needy? Diti simply quirked her eyebrows. 'You never did, either.' Her dark eyes flashed in the glimmer of the candlelight. 'So we're even.'

The sound of the waves swishing in filled the momentary silence, over the lively strains of the remixed piano music. They sat in the outdoor pavilion at a beachside restaurant, reclined against plush silky cushions on a Balinese bed which served as a seating area. A breeze blew in. Floating wisps of curtains hung from the bedposts. A large moon hung low in the sky, its yellow lustre shimmering upon the rippled slate of the sea. It was romantic beyond belief, and Vir wondered what Diti would be reading into it all. What did she think of him now?

'And, you have moved to Mumbai?' Diti folded one leg over the other.

'Yes, but how come I've never bumped into you till now?'

'Because I haven't been here.'

'No? Then?'

'First tell me all about you. Enjoying India?'

Vir shrugged. 'It has its moments.'

'Jaded, are we?'

'Pragmatic,' he replied. A thrill furled inside him, somewhere. 'Lets get back to you now.'

'Well,' she sighed. 'Where do I begin?'

'From the start, I guess. Since you don't show up on Google, you need to spill the details.'

'And you are all over!' Diti grinned, teasing, her full lips a flush of pink. 'My God, I feel I know every little twist and turn of the life and times of Udai Vir Dhingra.'

'So you checked.'

'Journalism 101,' she shot back, amused. 'Don't get your hopes high.'

'Me? Never.'

He felt about as gauche as his twenty-five-year-old self, who had been awestruck by her even back then. They had met accidentally, at some fundraising meeting in Hauz Khas. He had been in Delhi, back from his studies in the US, aiming to start a healthcare business and she had been a first-year student at St Stephen's. Bright, beautiful and full of vim and vigour about changing the world. Spouting Socrates and Shakespeare to him. It had been incandescent attraction on his part, and much imperious ribbing on hers. But he had chased her, till she'd agreed to go out with him. Two years of an intensity like never before. Or after. Till she had shattered his world. Devastated his confidence by breaking up with him. Refusing to wait for him while he went away for his business degree. Just like that! Because she was too young to be tied down.

'Go on then. About you,' Vir urged, at once defensive about her teasing and glad that she had looked him up. 'Journalism, did you say?'

She forked a tiny garlic butter drizzled morsel, and paused.

'Minx,' he bent forward to touch her nose, almost from some past habit. 'You're teasing.'

'I'm not.' She leaned back into her cushion, an odd smile on her face. She relayed her journey. From Delhi to Oxford for a degree in International Human Rights Law. Several years at the UN Human Rights Council, doing stints across Africa and Asia.

'Wow,' he marvelled, thinking of the wisp of a girl she had looked like to the gritty woman she had become.

'You may see a lot more of me in a month though,' she said. 'I will be anchoring my own talk show from Mumbai starting next month. One last report on Namibia to complete, and then I'll be spending some time with my parents in Mysore.'

'Won't you get bored being an anchor?'

'I'll figure it out.' She sipped her champagne. Vir had given in to impulse and ordered a bottle of Bollinger, a far cry from the sweet Nescafés and occasional Old Monks they had shared before.

'Eight years.' He folded his arms, his broad frame stretching his shirt taut, a boyish smile softening his usual harshness.

'Stop sounding like some middle-aged filmi type.'

'Middle-aged? Me?' He laughed, eyes aglitter, giving her his best flirtatious grin. 'At thirty-three?'

'Yes. You. So how come, I don't see the mention of a Mrs Dhingra and mini munchkins in these interviews you give so freely?'

The question he knew would come. 'Because there isn't a Mrs Dhingra.' Something inside him wished she hadn't asked. Or that he did not have to answer. 'Yet.'

'Yet?'

'I'm engaged.'

'Knew it.' She wiggled her finger. 'Come now, spill the beans.'

Vir told her about Tracey, about how he had met her, about what she did. She asked him to show a photograph and he scrolled through the pictures on his iPhone.

What he did not share was his bafflement, years ago, when Diti had left him. The years and years it took for him to emotionally connect with anyone again. The hollowness he had felt through all his seeming successes. The hollowness that was back again, as he sat here having this surreal conversation with a girl who had broken his heart once, talking about the woman he was about to marry.

'So, that's the dream, hmm? The white picket fence, three kids and a dog?'

'What?' Vir goggled.

'You know. The American ideal. What you had dreamed of back then. Money. Success. Life.'

Was it? Questions clouded his mind, robbing him of the pleasure of the present. Was that really where he had dreamt of being? Was this it?

'I have to ask,' Diti said, leaning into the table, face resting on one hand, suddenly too close for his comfort. 'What with all the hoopla around patent law and stuff. Don't you ever think that instead of protecting profits you should do something for your countrymen?'

'Woah. That's dramatic.'

'No. Just set aside your Yankee hat for a sec. You were born here. Surely you feel some solidarity for the plight of the poor patients who cannot afford the fancy medications you produce?'

'Its business, Diti, with huge investments.'

'Hmm.' She leaned back, eyes afire. 'Perhaps there is room for a new model – for patient capitalism and fair profit?'

Vir shrugged.

With disquiet, he deflected the conversation.

Questions rolled in his mind, even as they spoke of Darfur and Windhoek and other troubled hotspots she had been to. Of youthful idealism when he had started and sold his small healthcare products company, and the path he was currently on, slower than imagined.

'That's why I am back.' Diti sipped her Bolly, bringing Vir back to the present. 'To try and make a difference. I cannot talk of developmental economics and not work in my own country.'

Vir felt overwhelmed by her passion, her idealism.

Did he yearn for anything deeper? Questions crowded his mind again, swelling into a quagmire.

'Will I see you again?' Vir asked later, after they had finished the rest of their dinner over meaningless natter that had washed over him, mostly about Diti drawing him out about his work and travels and Tracey.

The earlier magic had dissolved.

They stood up to leave.

She took his hand in a formal shake and stood still, considering.

'Maybe.'

With that, she turned and took off into the warm night.

MONDAY, 6.00 P.M.

Rockville, Maryland

Mystic Mir reached out a thin hand to pick up a medical journal and absent-mindedly flipped through the pages.

The cut yellow roses and large framed photographs of spring blossoms did little to alleviate the antiseptic gloom of the room. Dr Sandler, though still in her thirties, was one of the best-known medical oncologists at the Shady Grove Adventist Hospital, rated with a double thumbs-up by the *Washingtonian*. But even the precision of her diagnosis and the diligence of her palliative care did not take away one penultimate reality. That even her best efforts failed to save many of the patients in her care in their fight against cancer.

The door to the inner chamber opened. A family emerged, with a spindly teenaged boy. Despite himself, sadness tugged at *Mystic Mir's* heart. A wasted life, before it even began. Dr Sandler came out, looking near angelic with curly chestnut hair and a warm candid face, and took the last patient in.

Without even a glance at me, he noted.

That was him. An outsider, whom women passed by without a glance. All his life. He had tried reaching out in his youth, eager for a fresh-faced smile, for a soft embrace, for sweet words of affection, commonplace wishes that never came his way. He had always been slight and unsure, painfully aware of being different. Of being invisible. Women ignored his very presence, and never approached him even for his meticulously kept study notes. They never even *knew* he kept meticulous notes, all colour-coded in reds, blues and greens. Even his mother had abandoned him, first in ill health and then in death. It had just been his father and him, and the long shadows and empty silences that inhabited their house. He had thrown himself into study instead, scoring high grades, and later chained himself to his work and office, in an emotional bond that surpassed all others.

Mystic Mir drummed his fingers upon a *Scientifc American.* He caught his fuzzy-angled reflection in the glass door: a slight figure with inscrutable features, sitting alone. A neat black moustache pasted against his upper lip. He rubbed his palms against his pants.

The door opened again.

'How may I help you?' Dr Sandler asked. There was nothing listed in her appointments calendar. Puzzlement laced her voice; he hardly looked like a patient. More like a travelling salesman. His limp dark hair making him look sallower, the thick glasses adding weight to an otherwise thin face.

'I'm from Acel.' He went by many names. One at work. A few different ones online, *Mystic Mir* being one of them. He told her yet another name now, briefly flashing an ID card and holding out a thick brochure.

A medical rep, thought Dr Sandler. 'I'm in a rush, sir, please call my assistant to take an appointment for next week.'

'Sorry, I did take a last-minute appointment, I'm sure your assistant must have forgotten to put it on your calendar.' He offered an apologetic shrug. 'It won't take long – it's an update on Colare. A new data collection app. It's important. Time bound.'

Dr Sandler looked at her watch and sighed. She had recently signed up to become a Principal Investigator with Acel and had started clinical trials for a new anti-cancer drug, which had received great pre-trial hype.

'Ten minutes, tops, okay?'

She led him inside her spare chamber. Just her certificates from Tufts and Massachusetts General hung on the wall behind her.

He switched on his laptop. 'We've been testing a new tool. It's a beta algorithm. Patient data records get created into image files. This update runs an auto-regression over time on the underlying data to create time deviant response.'

Dr Sandler nodded. Not that she cared much for autoregressions, but her training course in how to run clinical trials had emphasized the importance of correct data capture and analysis against well-calibrated control groups.

'We sent you an email link for the plug-in tool.'

'I can't recall seeing an email.'

'I can show you how it works.'

'Let's see it quick.' She had a dinner reservation and did not want to be late.

His laptop flickered and blanked out.

'Oh no.' He jabbed at the buttons.

'Why don't you take another appointment?'

'The plug-in goes live tomorrow. If you don't set up the tool before that, you will have to manually enter all old data.'

'Then?'

'We have a demo version online…' His voice wavered.

'Let's see it on my computer then,' Dr Sandler said decisively.

Finally, he had access to her computer. He opened a site with the Acel logo on the sidebar and clicked on a link.

'Just a few minutes now.'

TUESDAY, 1.00 P.M.

Churchgate, Mumbai

Madhu entered the college canteen, back stiff, gait taut and her orange dupatta trailing the floor.

A guffaw followed, as one of the boys behind her made a mooing sound and the others giggled.

'Pick up your dupatta, Mads,' Anki said, with gritted teeth.

Madhu picked up her dupatta with a jerk and flung it back on her shoulder. Tears of frustration brimmed in her eyes. It seemed a regular episode, this ribbing, every time she answered in class or solved a complex problem.

'Why can't they leave me alone?' she hissed.

'Because you appear to get teased,' Anki snapped.

Always one of the in-gang through school, this not fitting in was new to Ankita. She loved her cousin, was pleased to spend all her waking time with her, but sometimes Madhu annoyed the hell out of her. Especially, this babe-in-the-woods routine.

'Why don't you just slam into them a few times? They will stop.' God knew, she had tried standing up for Madhu a few times. It had only backfired. The gang had started looping her into their taunts, so she had stepped back. It hadn't done any good, anyway.

'Come,' Anki said, grabbing a table in an already full corner.

The canteen was packed. Anki waved to call a waiter, and ordered masala Maggi and nimbu pani for both.

The gang was now sitting at a table on the other side of the room. They were chuckling.

'Ignore them,' Anki told Madhu sternly.

Madhu wiped a tear with a slim hand.

Anki shook her wispily cut hair. She looked at Madhu, in her slim-fitting long-sleeved kurta and churidar. Beauiful as ever, in her long braid, but a bit too traditional. She scanned the room. There were others in churidars too, but there was something in the way they carried themselves. Perhaps the hair cuts were trendier, the nailpolish vampish, the nose-rings and bangles modern.

'It's Raghu and Suv, isn't it?' Madhu said bitterly.

Anki shot her a surprised glance. She had known Raghu and Suv since junior school. They had been her best buddies throughout. They still hung out with her despite their teasing Madhu. They even acted nice. Well, mostly.

'They started it,' Madhu said vehemently.

Raghu Damodaran. Saurav Paul. Her classmates in junior college and the coaching centre. Their mission in life seemed to be to torment her. They had started sniggering each time she raised her hand in class. Others had followed suit. Some of it she had expected. To be from a never-heard-of small mining town, deep in the heart of Chhattisgarh, where coal pulsed into power, was to invite hazing. There were jokes circulating on the class email lists and WhatsApp groups.

'Dude, Raghu was the state topper. Till you came in. With your national rankings and all!'

'So that justifies misbehaviour?'

Anki shrugged. 'Calm down, Mads. They don't bother you as much now, na?'

Madhu looked thoughtful for a second. Had they calmed down? But what they had started had been taken to the next degree by others.

Steaming plates of Maggi arrived.

'I really miss home,' Madhu said wistfully. 'I belonged there. Everyone is nasty here.'

'Forget them. Dig in now,' Anki advised.

The girls ate their Maggi in silence.

'Girls, may we join you?' Suv said.

Madhu glowered.

'Only if you promise not to bother her,' Anki said.

'Me?' Suv feigned surprise.

He sat down, with Raghu next to him.

The boys spread out their gadgets – laptops and mobile phones and ordered bhurji-toast.

'Excuse me,' Madhu snapped, feeling irritated.

It was an impossible situation. She hated the two, and Anki thought of them as friends. She got up. Chocolate. That's what she needed. Something to lift her mood. She walked towards the counter that stocked chocolates. She bought two bars and stood at the counter flipping the newspaper, breaking bits of chocolate and popping them into her mouth, reluctant to go back to her table yet.

'Oh, she left her phone,' Suv said.

'She'll be back.' Madhu said, eyeing them sternly. 'She's touchy, guys. Don't bug her so much.' They looked at each other.

'Now when do I do that?' Suv said.

'Oh, her phone's flashing,' Raghu said. 'Battery's run out, it seems.'

'Let me see,' said Suv. 'I have the same jack. Let me charge it for a few minutes.'

'Your good Samaritan act?' Anki winked.

'Absolutely!' Suv gave her a cheesy smile, plugging Madhu's phone to his laptop. The phone screen flashed green then darkened, only a little red blinking light indicated the running of some background process.

TUESDAY, 4.00 P.M.

Bandra, Mumbai

Sandman stood in the narrow lane, in the spot of shade beneath a frangipani tree, ensconced between a Skoda and a Cielo parked on the street, biding his time. He knew the routine. He checked his watch. A few more minutes.

He had dithered over his clothes earlier in the afternoon, glad that he had been home alone. His mother had gone to the doctor, puzzled by her persistent cough, throat pain and sluggish energy, wanting medicines that might do the trick.

He had taken out his shirts and had worried which one looked the best, the newest. Finally he had chosen a check shirt in green, blue and black, with a nifty logo emblazoned on the pocket with his six-pocket cargo pants. His sneakers one size too large, but original Nike that his mother had procured from some house she worked in. Stored in a plastic bag for special occasions. Like today. Seeing that little blue swoosh on white gave his heart a lurch every time he tied the laces.

Sandman bent a bit to check his reflection in the side mirror of the Cielo. His smartest best, he felt. He flicked his hair, scanning the street.

'Here, boy, why are you standing here?' A security guard from one of the buildings on the road walked up to him, twirling a little baton.

'Why? The road belongs to the government,' *Sandman* said, feeling a bit annoyed. 'What is it with you?'

'As long as you don't touch my Saheb's Cielo,' the guard said, pointing behind him.

Sandman scowled. 'I'm not even touching your Saheb's precious car,' he said, taking a step into the road.

The security guard moved away, and *Sandman* went back to his lonely vigil.

A blur of colour caught his attention at the end of the lane. He had eyes only for one, as two girls walked up the lane. Her orange dupatta trailing, looking vibrant even in the shade of the tall buildings. His heart hammered. He had dreamt of her again last night. He stood straighter now, his tongue glued to his palate. His thoughts racing. *Hi* or *Hello* or *How are you* – what should he say and how? He had practised in front of the mirror this afternoon, stood tall and jaunty, practised his wave, aimed to perfect the exact angle at which his head tilted and his arm moved, to appear casual. He felt anything but casual now.

He took one more step into the street, aware, vulnerable, away from the tree and the cars, without any friends or props. Just him. She was close now, he could see her smile. She laughed at something, a tinkling laughter, as she swayed her arms.

The girls came within a few feet of him. Close enough to reach out. Close enough to feel that silken dupatta. A hot flash coursed through him.

'He… hey,' *Sandman* said, emotion and passion brimming, but coming out haltingly as he spoke.

The girls did not pause in their stride. Or look his way. Her sister frowned. They passed by without even acknowledging his presence.

He took a fevered step, his face red, aware of the guard watching him. Then he stopped still in his tracks and watched them enter the gate, beyond his reach.

THURSDAY, 11.00 A.M.

Rockville, Maryland

'Emmie. Come here for a sec,' Dr Terence Small spoke into the intercom.

Short and wiry, Dr Small was a Senior Bioinformatics Researcher at Acel Laboratories. Which meant that he spent his days sitting at his large-screen computer, playing with statistical graphs of data on new drugs. Today he was looking at the testing results for Colare.

'What's up, man?' The strapping Dr Emmett Paul walked into the diagnostics room.

'Look at this chart.' Dr Small pointed to his screen, parsed into sections showing different charts and pictures.

Emmett peered at the chart. 'Looks odd, no, that dip?'

Dr Small nodded. He reported to two bosses – in the research team and in the legal team, both of whom looked at minutiae of data trends. But before he could raise an alarm to either one of them, he needed peer review. Just to be sure. Because two bosses hardly meant two mentors. It just implied double interrogation.

'What do you think it is?' Emmett asked.

'Research results are off. The drug is not working?'

Emmett whistled.

The US patent on Colare had been approved and clinical testing had just started. The final drug, if at all, was at best a year away from being on the market. But not many research projects ever reached clinical trial stage. Without any publicity, the two scientific papers published by Acel researchers in biotechnology journal *Cell* and a North East medical research publication had brought attention on Colare. Marketing had already started tom-tomming their campaign, but Legal had kept the lid on it. With the global patent filing deadline coming up and whispers of positive results, attention had transformed into hype. Suddenly the market had taken notice. Acel stock had shot up 30 per cent.

Now was not the time for any data to go wrong on Colare.

'Better check your data, man,' Emmett grunted. 'You don't want to raise an alarm, if you don't need to.'

Dr Small nodded. The stakes were high. He knew that.

After Emmett left, Dr Small sat down at his computer again. He wished he could break the silence of the lab. But with restricted access to the internet, he could not play streaming music. Nor was he allowed to bring his mobile phone or iPod inside. Security was paramount, the protocol pretty strict. Whistling to himself, he flexed his shoulders and downloaded the latest in vivo data again. Charts were created weekly. To assure that tests were trending correctly.

Beyond Dr Small, on the other side of a half-wall of glass, was the Lab. A clean room. Sterile white workbenches held diagnostic machines and computers. Scientists donned special gear of the thinnest polypropylene and passed through a compressed air fan to enter it. It was necessary to ensure that not a speck of dust or human fragment contaminated the tissue cultures. Behind the Lab, another glass-paned white door led to the room where tagged mice – control, infected and treated specimens – were kept in individual cells for daily monitoring over a 38-day period for mortality, remission and recovery.

Emmett stood in the Lab, in his white scrubs, mask and cap. He gave Dr Small a thumbs-up. Then went back to his task. Working with steady hands, he took tissue fragments extracted from a neonatal Swiss Webster mouse, smeared it on a plate glass, stained it with cellular reagents, and put it under a Nikon Eclipse TE2000-U microscope for high-resolution confocal fluorescent imaging. The image on the computer screen connected to the device automatically fed hundreds of gigabytes of graphical data into a complex imaging software, which converted regenerated cellular clusters into red pixels, calculated red pixels as a fraction of total pixels, to ascertain cellular growth.

It was drug discovery in action.

Hundreds of such animals, monitored daily in labs in the US and in India, generated terabytes of data, stored in specially protected servers in Acel's offshore centre in Mumbai. Through a VPN, Dr Small accessed this data, then parsed and analysed it, to detect the trends and aggregate results.

Soon clinical trial data would be added to the lot.

It really took an entire team to bring a drug to the shelves.

Dr Small frowned at the screen, as he manipulated the data once again. The data for last month was still off the trendline. *Strange.* He was sure it had plotted flat last week.

He hit the refresh button again.

THURSDAY, 8.00 P.M.

Ghatkopar, Mumbai

Suv drove his red Enfield into the compound of a large housing complex, with Raghu riding pillion behind him.

'What do you see in Jiggs?' he grumbled, parking the bike.

Raghu shrugged.

Suv scowled.

Raghu was his best friend. They had been inseparable since kindergarten, planning every mischief they could get away with. He could not fathom Raghu's recent buddiness with Jiggs.

Raghu had become quieter this past year, glued to the computer, learning programming, writing code. Then, out of the blue, right after their class ten exams, Raghu had revealed his secret passion for hacking. It was cool. Different. Suv had totally lapped it up, and in the absence of stringent study schedules in the aftermath of their board exams, had absorbed much of what Raghu spoke of. He had hounded Raghu to learn basic internet tricks like breaking into friends' email accounts and mobile phones. Hardly stellar stuff. Raghu, on the other hand, delighted in writing fresh code or devising new arcane methods of breaking into a poorly protected website. The pleasure was in the process, not the end result.

Suv had felt their bonding was the strongest. Then Jiggs had come in with his fancy gadgets and crazy subroutines.

They entered the marbled lift lobby and went up the lift to the tenth floor. The nameplate on the carved teak door said in ornate cursive brass: Bhavesh Mehta & Family.

Mr Mehta was widely known as the Kanda King of Konkan, being the largest wholesaler of onions in the western region. His multi-tentacled henchmen spread far and wide in the hinterland, collecting the onions from farmers, loading them up into lorries and tractors, hoarding them in large damp rodent-infested regional godowns, and duly released the stock into the criss-crossed veins of retailers in every *haat* and bazaar of the region. *Dhandha* was good. Cleverly timed stock management created a perception of scarcity just before peak wedding and festive seasons, and that was when he hiked the prices. Onion profits, like liquid gold, flowed into Bhaveshbhai's lockers, on the way lubricating the palms of the Bhais and Sahebs of the local politburos and mafia mufti.

Jiggs, as Jignesh preferred to be called, was Bhaveshbhai's younger son.

The boys were led through a pink living room. Pink marble spread on the floor, walls inlaid with gold-leafing. A large pink chandelier hung from the ceiling. Large stuffed sofas in pinkish-beige upholstery dominated the room. A kitty party was in progress. Large ladies shimmered in large diamond *kaanphools* and *naakphools* and colourful embroidered Gujarati saris.

'*Kemcho, beta*,' Jiggs's mother said, waving at them.

The boys headed to the bedroom.

Jiggs sat in front of his iMac, playing a game. His ample bottom drooped slightly on the sides of his large chair.

'Hey JMax,' Raghu greeted Jiggs by his online name. The name he had first known on *brownphyre.com* almost a year ago.

'RDX, sit, sit.'

Intrigued by some posts from JMax about patches for crack software, Raghu, or rather his alter ego RDX80, had initiated a chat. It had evolved into frequent online swaps, trading JMax's self-coded hacking apps for RDX80's tips on evading detectors.

They had finally met in person, bored with the captive pressure of pre-board study break and discovered much in common. Both were class ten students with a passion for gaming. And a secret – an underground identity and expertise in hacking.

'Video games?' Suv was amused that Jiggs was doing something so commonplace.

Jiggs gave a curt nod. He did not like Suv either. Just the mutual distrust of two people vying for a common friend!

Raghu scowled. Suv could be such a nut! Only looking at the superficial from his carefully cultivated world of branded polo shirts, foreign holidays, Golds Gym routines, and posh accents. It was a marvel he had remained friends with Raghu, though their financial circumstances had diverged over the years.

'It's Royal Rumble. An unreleased game. From the WWE site.'

'Really? Wow!' Suv was impressed.This was cool, indeed. Accessing an unreleased game from a global site.

The room became quiet as the boys huddled close to watch the contraband game. On screen, a large man in red thongs smacked his equally large opponent in black thongs. Arms and fists slammed, blood spurted from reddened noses, black marks tattooed across bare bulky bodies. Jiggs moved his stubby fingers with unusual speed on the Wi-Fi keypad, making the red-thonged man pound his rival to the exaggerated thuds and chip-chopped fractal music.

Raghu remembered why he had come. 'Jiggs, you posted about an exploit for penetrating video site management systems?'

'It works, bro.'

'Is it a remote file inclusion bug?'

'No RFL. Simple SQL injection.'

'I've tried a downloaded version.'

'Pah. Those never work. Mine uses time-based enumeration.'

'Where's it from?'

'I wrote it myself.' Pride shone in Jiggs's voice.

'What the heck?' Raghu exclaimed, alert and curious.

'What the *hack*, you mean?' Suv grinned at his own silly joke.

'Just some code,' Raghu said, not willing to elaborate.

He had shared many of his secrets with Suv, but some things he drew a line at. Suv was, as Raghu jokingly called him, a *quacker*, just a basic cracker, not scripting his own code, but tinkering with existing tools and tricks.

Suv narrowed his eyes, and let the matter go. Jiggs and

Raghu spoke in tongues. Some gibberish of Boolean algebra and nested subroutines and Linux open source platforms. Things that he cared not to understand. As long as there were apps to use, with graphical user interface, that he appreciated.

'Can I get a copy of the exploit?' Raghu asked. 'Can't believe it's that simple.'

Jiggs typed rapidly opening windows and files and quickly copied something onto a pendrive. He handed it to Raghu.

There could be anything in that pendrive, Suv thought.

THURSDAY, 9.00 P.M.

Bandra, Mumbai

Madhu sat in the middle of her books, looking like a pristine lily in the pads. She scribbled in small neat notations. A mix of Greek and numbers to the layperson, advanced mathematics to the wonks. Her hair, freshly washed, hung about her like a long silken veil, rippling under the overhead fan.

The warm evening breeze wafted in through the open window, bringing in the distinct fishy and swampy smell of Mumbai. Madhu wrinkled her nose. The barest buzz of traffic whizzed along the Sea Link and the Western Highway. Inside, she could hear the sound of Ankita tapping on her computer.

'What are you doing?'

Ankita seemed oblivious to her surroundings, with her headphones on, dancing in her chair to the beat.

Madhu crumpled a sheet and threw the paperball at Anki.

'What?' Ankita pulled one earphone off.

'What are you doing with such concentration?'

'Nothing.' Ankita put her earphone back on.

Nothing? That in Ankita-speak meant something she did not want others to see. Something mischievous.

Madhu stepped onto the braided dhurrie.

The wall above Anki's desk had a large kitschy collage of comic book characters. Manga and Anime creations; lush bodied heroines in peek-a-boo costumes; dark etchings of rough-edged DC comic superheroes; the eternal love triangle of Archie, Betty and Veronica. Painstakingly cut out and pasted.

Madhu peeked over Anki's shoulder and gasped.

The screen was split into many small windows. A chat site, various RSS feeds, a Bollywood music-streaming site, and blogs on cartoon animation. But the largest window was open to

Madhu's Facebook account, checking out her photos that her old schoolmate had sent.

Ankita giggled as she clicked on an old photograph of Madhu in unflattering tight plaits tied with ribbons and slouchy blue uniform.

'Anki,' Madhu snapped. 'What are you doing in my account?' She tugged the earplugs out of Ankita's ears.

Startled, Ankita looked up to see Madhu aggravated, a pillow in one hand, ready to be flung.

'What? Just looking. No harm done.' Her eyes held not a trace of guilt. 'But your friends. Really!' she said in mock horror. 'Such dowdy clothes! Like they are sixty and not sixteen...'

Madhu threw the plump pillow at Anki's head.

Anki grinned cheekily.

Madhu put her hands on her hips and launched into a mini tirade. 'Do you understand there are online rules? That it's illegal to get into someone else's account? What about my privacy?'

Ankita scrunched her nose and stuck her tongue out.

'How did you even get into my account?'

Ankita shrugged again. 'Just cracked it.'

'Cracked? You mean, Anki, you saw me type it?'

'No guesses. Just this crack software I've got.'

'Crack software?'

'It's really cool, it has this invisible key logging tool to track your password keystrokes, just standard stuff you know.'

'You downloaded a hacking software?' Madhu all but screamed, aghast that Anki was not a wee bit guilty.

'It's hardly hacking. Wrong terminology, honey.'

'Terminology?' Madhu yelled. 'Raghu and Suv put you up to this, didn't they? Why do they always bother me?' She huffed a hot breath.

'Why do you keep saying that? Why would they do that? They could do it themselves if they wanted to.' Anki flushed.

'Then how?'

'Okay, if you insist, I did borrow it from Suv.'

'I knew it.'

'It's not hacking, but. It's just trying out a new technology, just for fun. No harm intended. All I have seen are some pictures.' Anki stood up, stormy belligerence upon her face.

'That's how morally derelict people start! How do you even pick up these things?'

'Because I'm the Goddess of Geek…' Ankita preened.

'You?' Madhu giggled. 'You can't even figure out Newton's Third Law, stupid...'

The bedroom door opened, creaking on its hinges.

'Girls!' Mrs Sharma chided.

Ankita quickly minimized the screen, while Madhu looked on, amused.

Mrs Sharma surveyed the room. Comic books, papers, magazines and the laptop crowded Ankita's desk, in direct contrast to the neatly stacked books and study timetable on Madhu's desk. The large bed had two dissimilar zones too – one side piled with clothes and fluffy teddy bears; the other side neat, except for the books spread on it.

'Look at Madhu's things, Anki, look how careful she is, how organized she is. Learn from her.'

Mrs Sharma looked disapproving.

She rallied on. 'At least read some real stuff. Why, at your age, you're stuck with comics, I don't know.'

Ankita made a face.

'Don't make faces, madam,' her mother thundered. 'Stop wasting your time, or else I will ask your dad to give away the computer. Do you know why your father works so hard?'

That was a cue for Ragini Masi's favourite monologue. That Mr Sharma was a workaholic, clocking long hours and longer travels, and that he was steadily climbing up the corporate ladder was a moot point. Once started, Ragini Masi was like a runaway train, impossible to stop.

'Okay, okay, Mummy,' Anki grumbled softly, hugged her mother and pushed her towards the door.

'I will check in a few minutes,' Mrs Sharma called out.

Both girls were studying on the bed when Mrs Sharma checked in later, Madhu solving some maths problem, Ankita hunched by her side, trying to understand. Mrs Sharma smiled softly and went away.

'This is too much,' Ankita snapped. 'Not only do I have to go through this *I'm-serious-about-my-future* routine, but also have to do all these extra tutorials and worksheets. When I'd rather be doing something else.'

'What do you want to do?'

'I don't know. But something else, for sure. Not this course. Not this college.'

'Really?'

'Yes. Graphic Design. Psychology. Mass Communications. Cartoon animation. Who knows? Except with you here, Papa got onto this engineering bandwagon as well.'

'Why don't you just tell Mausa? He will understand.'

'Just by myself I could have neutralized Papa, but with you around, no.'

'Sorry,' Madhu appeared contrite.

How come I never think of my life like this, she puzzled. *Do I have no will of my own?* She had accepted goals set by parents. Was it because Korba was so tiny, so limited, that she had known nothing of other options?

A cool breeze blew in through the open window, bringing with it the sounds of compressor hums and the buzzing of crickets. She suppressed a yawn and stretched out. It was too late for homework. She decided to go to sleep.

Unbidden images sneaked into her mind, silent as night birds. *Raghu.* How he sat in class, how he sang at the fest, how he teased her.

'Arrggh!' she groaned, clutching onto her pillow, burying her face into its softness. But sleep eluded her.

The wall clock struck eleven. The house was quiet. Anki was reading a romance paperback. Madhu sat in front of her hand-me-down computer, to email her mother. Her nightly ritual. She missed home. Missed her ten-year-old twin brothers, the bane of her existence when she was at home. Yet now, in Mausi's house, thousand-odd miles separating them, life seemed almost incomplete without their vile presence.

From a small Kendriya Vidyalaya in her remote township, Madhu had topped the tenth standard national board exams for Chhattisgarh state and indeed the entire central India zone with a national ranking of third position. Her father had traded his dreams of sending his daughter to the local college and started imagining her in an IIT. But Korba was too small with no coaching schools.

So they had shipped her off to Mumbai. To stay with her Mausi and attend college with her cousin. And her uncle, Ankita's dad, perhaps dreaming a similar dream for his daughter, had welcomed Madhu, hoping she would be a good influence on her cousin.

Madhu could trace the family resemblance between her photo and Anki. The oval face remained common. But that's where it all ended. Anki was wiry and effervescent, a head shorter. Their personalities couldn't be further apart. Anki was like a pixie or a butterfly. Madhu thought of herself as colourless, almost boring.

Shaking her thoughts, Madhu sat at her desk and pressed a button to fire up the old computer from its sleep mode.

The screen lit up, frozen. Madhu pressed various keys, willing it to start.

Suddenly the screen went dark, then became alive, as slow as viscous fluid, morphing into an array of digits and Ascii characters, spewing badly tabulated nonsensical data.

'Oh no,' Madhu groaned as she desperately pressed more keys in an attempt to stop this slow slideshow of unformatted text.

THURSDAY, 9 P.M.

Chembur, Mumbai

Raghu opened the inner zippered compartment of his backpack, and took out Jiggs's pendrive.

With the mildest excitement, he leaned forward and penetrated the computer of the curly-haired geek, the sole other person sitting in the room, on terminal 24. Then using the host terminal as a base, he opened the website for Desi Rhythm.

Desi Rhythm's hottest new starlet, Anya, was releasing a new music video titled *Anya Aaaaahhh*. Its ten-second promos on MTV revealed a sultry-looking Anya, her eyes laden with kohl, two feet of black lace and not much else, grooving and gyrating in a breathy croon. His entire class in junior college, the boys, had been salivating at this promo clip ever since he had shown it to them.

He had tried to download it a few times. And failed. When Jiggs had mentioned a patch, he had felt maybe a solution could be found.

It was that pendrive that Raghu inserted into the computer. It had a clever little algorithm, which rode upon the query form on the Desi Rhythm site. As Raghu entered his inputs and the host website started processing the query, the algorithm mutated and injected itself into the website, tunnelling its way to the protected area which stored the video.

Raghu pursed his lips as the download began. It was amazing how most sites despite all the heavy duty firewalls they put in, left some loose opening. A cross-site script or an injection flaw, which a malicious code could detect and break into.

He waited for the download to complete, then logged off. He looked sideways at the lost student on the faraway terminal, who hadn't even realized that his computer had been compromised.

Tilting his computer screen away from the door, Raghu shot another furtive glance around him. He put his computer on mute and hit the play button on the downloaded file.

Anya emerged from a veil of mist, her glistening body shimmering on the screen. The cool air-conditioned room suddenly got too warm for Raghu; his breath nearly stopped, his eyes flared and his heated breath froze inside his body.

They didn't make girls like this in *real life*. Images of his classmates flitted in his mind's eye: studious girls. Worried about grades and not clothes. Ankita was the spunkiest of them all, even-featured, lively, but not gorgeous. Plus, he had known Anki since kindergarten. Madhu. She was tall and fair. Could be pretty. If she undid that hideous plait and junked her dowdy *choga*-type kurtas. As Anya fizzled out of the screen, leaving stunned pixels in her wake, Raghu exhaled a sharp little breath of hot air and copied the file onto a disk for Maganbhai. He deleted the file off his computer and carefully deleted every trace of his trail from the terminals and the server.

He went back to his customized browser page. Various feeds were coming in. His own personal flipboard. A campaign against violence on women in Northern Africa by *Avaaz*. Euro Top list of songs from a music site. A feed from Dark Net News. A button for an anonymous chat site he frequented.

He logged onto *brownphyre*. The screen became dark, molten swirls of black shot with brown. White links within the page in fine print. He checked out the posts. Quests that had been announced. Patches that had been developed. Something caught his attention. Money for some data transfer. It was a quest too. Like an online war game, a capture-the-flag-type game, where many competed in a live attempt and one succeeded. Neat.

Interesting, Raghu thought, as he clicked on to read further.

FRIDAY, 11.00 P.M.

Mansingh Road, New Delhi

High bass electric guitar riffs rippled through the darkened room. Leggy models sashayed down the ramp in exotic ripped and shredded and heavily embroidered dresses that plunged deep, displaying cleavages and toned backs. Feather and diamante-encrusted headpieces accentuated the Gothic eye makeup. Unsmiling faces glanced imperiously at the audience, the who's who of Delhi, watching the iconic Ethnic-Gothic collection of designer Anangmitra Dutta in a charity fashion show at Taj Mahal hotel on Mansingh Road.

'Oh, I want that dress!'

Dr Tracey Ward looked at the impossible creation, a floating, flared, multi-hued kaftan dress, riddled with mirrors, sequins and crystals that winked in the pulsating light. *Whoever wanted a dress like that?*

Tracey shifted her gaze from the stage to her companion for the evening, her hostess and wife of Vir's school friend Harry Singh – the skinny Pammi of bouffant hair, bountiful jewellery, and tufted pink Dior bag – who was squealing in delight at the dress.

'I'm sure you do,' Tracey muttered in a wry undertone.

Sitting on front row plush chairs inside the beautifully arcaded Longchamp ballroom, amid expensive women eyeing expensive clothes and sipping the best of Ivy Brut, the dusty footpath reality of India seemed unreal.

Was this Vir's India?

Such a far cry from her commonplace life in Bethesda, Maryland, where she lived in a mid-century maisonette, and commuted down Rockville Pike to her office at NIH, the National Institute of Health, the renowned research facility. She was a Research Fellow in the paediatric onco-immunological department. Routine defined her life. In the predawn, she jogged along the Bethesda Trolley trail. It was the best time of her day, cares of yesterday diluted by sleep, watching dawn gild the sky, the shadowy leaves turn emerald, and morning dew droplets below newly opened sepals. In the winter, it remained pearlescent, skinny bare branches piercing the greyish shroud. At that moment, she could believe easily in new beginnings, in resurgent hope.

The days were another matter. She divided her time between the clinic, the lab and classes. But even away from the clinic, instead of finding refuge in data collection or lectures, the patients stayed in her mind, their brave but faltering smiles tugging at her. Only the harshest cases came to the NIH. Neuroblastoma, cancer of the peripheral nervous system, was a deadly killer of the young. Against its vile dendritic spread, she fought with experimental immunotherapy. She was running a clinical trial, using biopharmaceutical antibodies to target the cancerous cells and cytokines to trigger the immune system. There were positive signs. Yet, in that long-drawn battle of therapy against malignant carcinoma, the latter won more often, snuffing out another young life.

This was the life she had shared with Vir.

They had so much in common – their love for medicine and its wonders, their compassion for the sick.

Dr Udai Vir Dhingra. The wrong kind of doctor, if you will. An expert in bioinformatics and molecular modelling, rather than symptoms and treatments. Then he had forgotten all bioengineering and dived deep into trends of share prices, sales forecasts and return on investment on life-saving research.

A common friend had introduced the tall, strong-jawed Indian to her. He had cracked through her serious demeanour, making her laugh in a way she hadn't since grade school. His dark eyes twinkled with a vivacity that seemed so alien to the rest of her life. It had been spontaneous combustion. They had fallen into bed that night, crept into a relationship in a month. It had taken two years for him to propose. They had set a date for later this year. Then, this!

Vir had taken up an unexpected offer to head the growing India business of Acel, and had flown eastwards, begging her to join him.

After six months of this long-distance relationship, things had slid downhill. She had come to India two days ago. As much to understand the country as to understand the man she thought she knew.

To say it was overwhelming was the least of it. Street children with swollen tummies followed her. Her car passed through such utter decrepitude, it was unimaginable.

'*You will be immune to it in time,*' Vir's Mumbai friends had said casually.

Would she?

She had visited a couple of medical facilities on the second day, seen newer set-ups and older corridors steeped in disinfectant smells, talked to society cancer surgeons, no doubt good at their art, but instrument-happy enough to talk of capacity utilization and surgery statistics and asking rates that defied US rates. No different, then, from the insurance-driven US healthcare market, which itself needed fixing.

There was no sophisticated cancer research she could do.

But then what use was advanced medical research amid all the dusty devilment and abundance of diseases that was India. Primary healthcare was what it needed. Hell, hygiene was what it needed! But could she do that? Could she give up super-specialized medical research to do primary medicine for Vir's sake?

Tracey wound her fine blonde hair around one long unvarnished finger. And were she to remain, who could she even talk to? All Vir had introduced her to since her arrival were sophisticated men with wide world views and baby dolls with combined cerebral matter smaller than the pituitary gland of a peahen!

FRIDAY 10.00 A.M.

Rockville, Maryland

Andrew Rudd strode down the third-floor corridor along the internal perimeter impatiently.

Acel's headquarters in Rockville, Maryland, was built like a wide horseshoe around an open grassy area. Just a few kilometres off Rockville Pike, the area around the building was sparsely wooded, creating a sylvan feel. The spring morning heightened by early blossoming trees. A row of pear trees in cream finery stood like floss-flecked sentinels guarding the rolling greens. The gravelled walking trail along its inner curve had a couple of scientists crunching along slowly, eyes glazed into the distance, mentally working out some breakthrough formulation. A modernistic fountain in the middle replicated double-helical strands in brushed titanium steel and spewed a diffused spray of water eight months a year.

Andy, Head of Research at Acel, saw none of this. He turned a sharp corner and through a pair of swinging doors entered the onco-immunological research wing.

Andy pressed the four-digit code on a security panel next to the door and held his right eye at a security camera for a retina scan. The glass door silently slid to one side.

'Andy.' Dr Small waved nervously.

'What's up?' Andy strode over to the workstation. 'You mentioned some problems with the Colare data?'

'Something is odd. See this chart, with data from the US labs.'

He pointed to a straight line. This indicated repeatability. Proof that the cure worked.

Dr Small typed at a rapid pace. The screen changed. 'Look at this chart again, with the last three months, results from India.'

It was barely perceptible. But when Dr Small zoomed in, it was clear. The dip in the line. The results were awry.

'This is puzzling,' said Dr Small. 'I thought both labs were on track. Now I don't know what to make of it.'

Andy sat back in the chair and started swivelling. He looked grim. The chair made an irritating squishy sound, which he did not hear. 'Morons!' he barked.

'Perhaps the data got corrupted,' suggested Dr Small. But one look at Andy's face told Terence that Andy was buying none of this.

'Have you checked the backups?'

'I have requested backup data. It may take overnight.'

The data centre, an offshore entity created in a wave of cost cutting about a year ago, was now located in Mumbai. There were people monitoring it round the clock. But of course, the manager who could access and analyse the data would arrive next morning.

Andy crinkled his eyes. 'It's probably just carelessness. We don't know if it's the data or if their calibrations were wrong or the samples got contaminated or something else.'

Setting up an offshore data unit had been bad enough. He had resisted it. But sending top-notch drug discovery research on an Indian jaunt was sacrilegious. In fact, he had opposed the idea. Only to be overruled by the Founder Chairman of Acel.

Dr Adam Janlowski, a charismatic biochemist-turned-business mogul, whose initial discovery of a bio-insulin drug in the eighties, had spawned a global medical drugs empire. Acel had operations in Rockville, Santa Barbara, Budapest, Sao Paulo and Mumbai, where formulations manufactured in Rockville were assembled. But research had been a closely guarded process in the headquarters.

Until recently.

Until Dr Udai Vir Dhingra, a young smooth-talking bio-engineering doctor-turned-business executive, armed with a posh degree, had convinced Adam of global footprint and the benefits of having an R&D centre in Asia. Coursing along a newfangled trajectory, Andy's concerns had been ignored.

The India centre had been established. Dr Amin Ali, a senior researcher from the US team, had moved back to head the Colare project in India, the first molecule to be tested in dual locations. Vir, of course, had moved to India to head the entire India operation.

Every reservation that Andy had voiced came burbling back to him now. What with news of process disruptions and fudged data submitted by Indian generics manufacturers to the Food and Drug Administration in the USA, he could imagine the worst happening in Acel's captive unit in India.

'Have you told Peter?'

'He is sick. Can't reach him on his phone either.'

'Sick?'

'I have left him a voicemail and an email. He hasn't responded yet.' Terry shrugged. 'His assistant said he called in with conjunctivitis.'

'Let's call Vir in India.'

'Now?' Dr Small looked at his watch. It was nearing midnight in India.

'Yes, now.'

FRIDAY, 12.00 A.M.

Mansingh Road, New Delhi

'Your blonde is lovely, *yaar*.' The jovial Harpreet Singh Joneja, better known as Harry, chuckled and sipped his Glenfiddich.

'Must be the secret of your fitness, *patthe*! The rest of us are going soft with nagging wives and puking kids in wet nappies.' Nikhill Ahuja laughed. 'But you are still getting it, *haan*! Sex burns more calories. Says new research.'

'*Wow.* Which intern prepared this research report, I wonder.' Harry laughed.

Vir pursed his lips, disliking this banter. He was meeting his boarding school buddies after years.

Harry ran a construction business. Their residential complexes and malls and hotels dotted the changing cityscapes of Delhi and Mumbai. It had been a small contracting business in their college days. Mildly profitable, unknown. It had metamorphosed since then to cater to the growing acreage dreams of modern India. Nikhill had been on Wall Street, before starting the Delhi office of a US private equity fund.

The room was full of businessmen and dealmakers, animated on the umpteenth peg of neat Scotch, trading an endless string of 'how to engineer economic recovery' and 'the new *sarkar*' stories.

'Really, you Delhi-Punju types,' Vir said. 'No subtlety.'

'We *settle*. You *sat lo*.' Harry winked.

'Good one.' Nikhill high-fived Harry.

Vir rolled his eyes. 'You bastards will twist anything.'

He worked hard to stay fit. Boarding school habits had remained with him – waking up early and going on walks in the hills. Just the deodars had been replaced by pine and spruce in the US. He would jog in the early dawn or play tennis, and on weekends hiked up ferny trails in the Shenandoah ranges or cycled along the Potomac past the weekend barbeque groups to the quieter terrain upstream. He was still trying find that balance in Mumbai. But no point explaining that to these animals. It was easier to change the topic.

Vir forked a *makhmali kebab* and leaned back. 'Jealous, guys?'

He grinned. 'But tell me, Niks, what's with your name? All these extra letters? Going soft in your brain too?'

Nikhill rolled his eyes. 'Mothers!' He explained how his mother, in a recent spell of numerological fanaticism, had insisted on the extra letter to ward off the continuing perils of the global financial crisis from her son's life.

'And what do your clients think of it?' Vir was curious.

'They consult their own astro charts before placing their multi-crore bets, *saale*!'

'You've become totally Yankeefied, Vir. It's all okay in India.'

'How's your fund doing, though? It's been rocky for many.'

'I'm golden, dude,' Nikhill picked up his vodka martini with a swagger. 'We raised money before the crisis. I never deployed it.'

'*Right*.' Vir shook his head thoughtfully. There was merit in inaction at times.

'Saw you in a magazine, some licensing contract. Big story?'

'No biggie.'

Out-licensing agreements were bread and butter, a way to stay in the game with older products. He suppressed a half-smile – the real *splash* would come later, when news of Colare erupted.

Talk turned to classmates from their Shimla days – the jocks gone bald and the nerds metamorphosed into business jocks; those heading family businesses and those washed ashore to places as distant as Tokyo, Zurich and Santa Barbara, and the wives who were ex-models and ex-pageant queens and current reigning fashionistas.

'What happened to your dad's business?

'Sold off.'

'No pressure to come back to it, then!'

'There never was.'

Their small water bottling plant on the Sutlej had been sold to a company with a fancier logo and shaded plastic sleeves on bottles. All for the better. Civilization impinged upon rivers, the exploding population trotting upstream to form ragged hutments on once-pristine banks, soiling the once-sparkling clean waters. Could you promise purity now?

The apple orchards remained, the mainstay of his father's existence, with rows upon rows of sweet Himachali apples that were sold in *haats* and bazaars of Punjab and Delhi. The remaining apples were stewed in vats to make cider and apple wine. Vir's BlackBerry clattered on the mahogany coffee table. 'US,' he said, looking at the caller ID. 'I need to take this one, guys.'

It was past midnight, morning in America.

Why was someone calling him this late?

Vir moved towards the club lobby, wondering what new cross-border issue was behind this call. He had been up every alternate night these past six months, on scheduled phone meetings with the US teams. This was an unscheduled call.

'We have a problem, Vir.' Dr Terence Small's gruff voice echoed. Vir could hear agitation in his voice.

There was a crackle of static in the line, as Terence said he was switching on the speakerphone.

Andy Rudd's sharp voice boomed across the airwaves. 'Vir. We can't have India bloody screw up at this stage!'

SATURDAY, 1.00 A.M.

Telegraph Lane, New Delhi

'One more peg?' Harry waved a bottle. They had just returned to their fortress-like bungalow on a tree-colonnaded road just minutes away from the bustle of Janpath.

His wife suppressed a yawn. 'Oye Harryji, I'm sure these lovebirds want to spend time alone.'

Lovebirds? Tracey thought wearily. It implied a giggling frivolity.

Harry gave a nudge and a wink, and went up the staircase.

Vir stood beneath the Swarovski waterfall chandelier amid burnished gold sofas, lost in his thoughts. His mind abuzz with Andy's words. *Accusations*. His blood pumped hard.

'Let's get some fresh air for a bit,' he said.

He opened the French door and walked onto a wide verandah filled with fronds and ferns. A redolent bed of Asiatic lilies filled the air. Vir was quiet as he stepped onto the lawn, looking up, trying to locate a few dim stars in the hazy night sky.

'What exactly did Andy say?' Tracey frowned, trying to decode the tension in Vir's shoulders.

Vir gave a short dry laugh. *What exactly did Andy say?* Well, in essence not much. But from his choice of words, a sea of antagonism and waves of distrust had risen. He could not fathom what data had gone wrong and to what extent and how. 'The results from the Colare project. Something is wrong. The India data does not match the US data.'

'That doesn't sound good.'

'It's not. We have six weeks to go to PCT.'

PCT, or the Patent Cooperation Treaty, had to be filed within a year of filing the US patent. It gave the filing company intellectual property rights over a new discovery in all the countries which were signatories to this international patent law treaty. Many countries were still not signatories to the PCT. Especially emerging markets and their billion-strong patients. But still. It was an important hurdle to cross. Till then, any pretender could sneak in, claim the discovery as his or hers. Once the global patent application was filed, the discovery was protected, the capital invested safe from the pernicious wiles of international wannabes ready to muscle in with similar products. Once filed, the discoverer could go public, disclose the information to the market.

'Are the implications huge for India?'

'India is a signatory to the PCT. But the situation remains in flux, with the government ambivalent about its policy. Claiming exceptions. Calling some medicines essential needs.'

'Seems like wild lawlessness.'

'Everything is protected. Except for life-saving drugs.' Vir hesitated, Diti's words coming back to mock him. He did not feel like giving long explanations. The patent regime had been tightened recently. The government had intervened, ditching process patenting to allow multinationals to retain their patent protections. He breathed out, but the unease remained.

'It's the first that I've even heard of a problem. There was nothing unusual in last week's review. It's probably being blown out of proportion and Andy blames the India team of negligence,' he said, almost to himself. 'Blame' did not describe the vitriol in Andy's words, the cutting sharpness, the 'you-versus-me' arrogance.

Tracey arched her brow. She was not a fan of Andy either. She had met him once at a corporate event and he had struck her as narrow-minded, something in his manner hinting of disapproval at a white girl going out with a brown boy.

'What did he say, though?'

'He was downright provocative. It's always like that.'

'What do you mean *always*?'

'It's tough to explain.' Vir ran his fingers through his hair. It was hard enough perceiving it, this intangible divide of colour and country, but to explain it to Tracey, an American, was madness.

He had been one of the team till six months back. The driving force propelling new ideas and action. Or so it seemed. Now suddenly he was the outsider, the sloppy caretaker of the messy developing world, a market promising enough to not ignore, yet not promising enough to command respect.

'It's not just Andy. Some others too. They talk like I don't understand the bigger picture, the global perspective, the winning game, you know?'

'Uh huh.' Tracey nodded. Not quite understanding. But his impassioned voice spoke volumes. Whatever had happened had clearly incensed him.

Not that they had spoken about it in their patchy talks. She had been wrapped up in her own misery, in how his move to India was affecting her life, that she had never asked him. She had assumed it was all fine.

She looked at him now, tall, arms folded, those dimples she loved hidden. She raised her hand and stroked his face.

'It must be so hard.'

Was that hope in her voice? If it were hard, he could return to the US. Life could go back to normal.

'India is not hard, Tracey. India is exciting. It's happening. It's opportunistic. It's this constant calibration, this remapping of local realities into US perceptions, this constant explaining of why-to and how-to, which can be maddening. The trick is to learn to ignore it. As long as we are creating fresh history locally...' he said, chuckling despite himself.

'I have to miss Solan though. I'll have to fly back to Mumbai tomorrow.'

'I was looking forward to meeting your parents.'

'Why don't you go?'

'Alone?'

Vir gave a rueful shrug. 'I will be at work anyway. The trip has already been arranged. The place is beautiful. Why not just go?'

Tracey studied his face. She had met Vir's parents before. They were nice. His dad a distinguished Oxonian, his mother elegant old money. They had given crisp congratulations on the phone after the engagement. But she had come to India to meet Vir.

Does he not get it? She frowned.

She looked at the secluded garden. Glossy palmyra palms and rubber trees surrounded an oval pool. A large almond tree rose majestically, its broad leaves strewn upon the grass. Night jasmine spread its fragrance. An overhang of flowers created a perfumed bower near the pool. It was beautiful. Romantic. Meeting after ages, they should've been wrapped onto each other. *Yet they were standing here talking about work.*

Tracey gave a crooked grin. 'Do you really want me to go?' she asked and traced a finger on his cheek. A shiver rustled through her, a little current of awareness. Months of separation had crystallized into a need that pooled deep inside her.

'No,' Vir mumbled into her hair.

Tracey nodded into his shoulder, not sure what was written on her face – relief or desire. But did he really mean it?

She kicked off her shoes and stood barefoot, dew cooling her toes. She planted a fevered kiss upon his ear and wrapping her arms around him, drew him close. She arched into him, aching for his touch, filled with a maelstrom of emotion, like she needed to make up right now for the six months of living apart.

A dog barked somewhere. Was the guard on a night stroll?

Vir created an inch between them, the fresh air calming down his erratic breath.

'We have an early flight tomorrow.' He stepped away.

Anger coursed through Tracey. Could he not focus on her for a bit? She jerked away.

'Tracey, wait. I'm sorry.' Vir followed her, still half-distracted.

'Forget it,' she said, without looking back.

SATURDAY, 8.00 A.M.

Jet Lite flight, Delhi–Mumbai

Vir craned his neck to peer out through the plane window. A rift in the sea of fluffy clouds offered a glimpse of the shadowy arid terrain of the Deccan. He was headed back to Mumbai, sitting in a cramped middle seat. Tracey slept in the window seat.

He could have been in a car instead, speeding towards Solan. He could picture the final stretch amid the scraggly foothill deodars as the road turned up. Spring had its special beauty in Solan. Freshly melted snow in the high Dhauladhar ranges made the river rush briskly. Leaves had a fresh green hue, the first wild flowers of the season burst out in masses of pink and yellow and blue.

Gleneagle. Once a Victorian folly, built by a British officer for his delicate English bride, had been bought by Vir's grandfather. Painted lemon and white, the house was a confection of arches and thin fluted columns that ran the length of the frontage. From the sloping green lawn studded with calla lilies, the shimmering river looked bluer, the air so sharp and clean it pierced with its clarity.

Instead he breathed in the stale recycled aircraft air, the combined smells of masala aloo, buttery croissants, warm citrus, sweaty feet and musty cushions.

He stretched in his seat, exhausted from a sleepless night, but his mind was hyperactive, filled with thoughts of Colare.

He switched on his tablet and opened an image. Small crimson ovals lay scattered across a fibrous backdrop, their shading and striations adding depth, making them almost pop out. Thinnest green strands inter-crossed in the back, a million fibres webbing about, meeting at nodes, branching again, forming a woven basket around each oval. Variegated blue dusted the green strands in places.

It could be abstract art. Instead it was an image of a cancer cell viewed through a microscope, thousand times magnified. Produced by special antigens and fluorescent markers, it showed cells, their nuclei etched in red, the cellular skeleton in green, while the blues, the barely-there flecks of cobalt, the merest dots enmeshed in green, were cancerous growth.

He kept flipping between different images taken from mouse MUM102379, before and after a month of Colare medication, willing his naked eye to spot the differences. The blue flecking. Was it motile? Was it more aligned after the treatment?

Vir opened the report sent by Terry, a series of charts showing the average dimensions and density of tumour growth taken from multiple samples from rats and guinea pigs over the past three months. It was the isolated data from Acel India. The dip. The drug seemingly ineffective. It made no sense.

Vir had called Ali last night, right after Andy's call. Ali was equally surprised by Terry's report.

Vir had been awake all night. A thought had occurred to him: could it be *data error?* Yes, it had to be that.

Data corruption.

He had messaged Ali in the wee hours. *Check backup data.*

Vir rotated his neck to relieve a crick that refused to go.

The plane was descending, making a wide arc over the silvery grey Arabian, flying down over roads and dense habitation. The plane touched down with a thud and sped up.

SATURDAY, 11.00 A.M.

Bandra, Mumbai

'Why must you always dress like Amrita Rao in *Vivaah*?' Ankita threw a fit at Madhu. *Act like that too,* she thought.

Mrs Sharma sighed. Anki would not let Madhu rest in peace till she tried on the pair of skinny jeans. 'You don't have to buy it, beta, if you don't feel comfortable. Go on try it.'

'Mom,' Ankita scowled. 'What is the point of trying out and not buying?'

Ankita was tired of the churidar-and-choti look of her cousin. Sniggers followed them in college.

'Why don't you go buy those bedsheets, Ma?'

Mrs Sharma picked up her flouncy brown bag and shuffled away.

'Don't force Madhu, Anki.' She pinned her daughter with narrowed eyes. Anki pushed Madhu towards the trial room, a bunch of clothes in her hand. 'I want to see you in each of these.'

Madhu looked at herself in the three-fold mirror. The jeans fit well, the pink tee shirt snugly shaped her waist and made her feel oddly underclothed. Madhu made a face in the mirror. She just saw a small-town girl in the mirror.

'Mads, come out.' Ankita rattled the thin door.

'Coming, coming.'

'Wow.' Ankita whistled, making Madhu twirl. 'Don't you clean up well!'

Madhu pulled down the stretchy jersey of her top.

Ankita slapped Madhu's wrist. 'Look at your boobs, wow! Total Katrina-like! Oof!' She tugged at Madhu's braid, opened her waist-length hair. 'Better. You should layer it. Four inches short.'

'Never.'

'Okay, okay, don't get in a snit. Try the other things now.'

For the next half-hour, Madhu amused her cousin by trying out a variety of outfits.

'So?' Mrs Sharma demanded upon returning with her just-bought bedsheets.

'I'll take this set.' Madhu pointed at the light blue jeggings and the short-fitted teal kurti with khari printed butis in dark bronze and the barest hint of tiny bronze gota potlis trimming the edge. The dark print enhanced her dark-lashed eyes and the style felt closest to the churidar-salwars she was used to.

'That's the most *dehaati* of the lot,' Anki said.

'Let the girl take what she likes, Anki,' Mrs Sharma said, pursing her lips. Anki herself was dressed in three-quarter dhoti pants and shirred-fitted lemon ganji on top of a pale orange sleeveless tee shirt, a look her father would disapprove of if he saw her now.

'One outfit doesn't count as a makeover,' Anki said.

'Maybe she does not want a makeover,' Mrs Sharma said, shaking her head.

Madhu thought of her old computer. It had gone bonkers last night, throwing out strange numbers, it had remained frozen since morning.

'I will just take one set, Mausi,' she said, looking earnest. 'If we need to spend to fix my computer, I don't want to spend on clothes.'

Mrs Sharma felt a little tug. *If only her own daughter were so thoughtful.*

SATURDAY 12.00 NOON

Bandra, Mumbai

Not a flower or a speck of green was in sight. Mid-afternoon sun beat down upon the broken road, and rickety autos and two-wheelers with broken silencers whizzed past, dredging up loose dirt and foisting it upon everything around. The heat was searing. Faded multicoloured paper buntings hung upon a mud-caked house – remnants of a wedding. A loudspeaker blared somewhere and a group of kids in brownish vests and faded shorts burst into an impromptu dance.

A tired-looking bus drove under the Western Expressway and entered the small stretch of slums. It stopped in front of a butcher's shop. Flies buzzed around the carcasses of goats hung from a nail. Raghu stepped off the bus. A red cap shaded his eyes. He pinched his nostrils, overcome by the stench of raw meat, and entered the small space next to the butcher. Not quite an alley. More like the empty space between huts. He quickly moved to the third house, if it could be called that. He flicked a plastic sheet doubling as a door-cum-curtain and went inside. The tin-roofed space housed five ageing PCs linked on a wired LAN. Thick wires trailed along the floor.

Maganbhai's hidden cyber den. The streetfront cyber cafés were shutting, but from this hidden spot, Maganbhai did brisk business. Chawl boys studying in vernacular schools flocked at odd times, pretending to practise Microsoft Word while surfing online at ten rupees per hour.

There were no customers now. A dark, kohl-smeared baby lay in a steel cot, wrapped in a stitched old cotton sari. It was sucking its tiny fist. Maganbhai slept on the floor, a dark hairy forearm flung over his face.

A string of tiny bells tinkled as the plastic curtain flapped.

The baby woke up with a wail and the man sat up, his eyes bloodshot from sleep and his face puffy from the heat.

'*Arre tum*,' Maganbhai said, stretching, revealing hairy armpits. He calmed the baby with a few pats. '*Kaam hua*?' He scratched his greyish baniyan, looking expectant.

'Of course. Done.'

Raghu took out a DVD from his bag, once again overcome by the stench coming from the alleys. He wished he had waited until the evening to meet Maganbhai at his Linking Road stall. The endless crowds and smoke-spewing buses would have been more bearable than this. He couldn't wait to collect his fees now and head off to a music shop to buy that bass guitar he had been eyeing for weeks. Irritation flared in him for a second. He was smarter than his friends. Yet, he had to scrounge for cash.

'*Bhai wah*, very good,' Maganbhai chuckled, as he sat on his haunches. 'Give me.'

Raghu looked on with distaste, noting Maganbhai's hairy plumpness and grimy nails. *Whatever would Amma say if she knew?* But, but, whispered his inner voice, reminding him it was just a two-minute video clip. What did it really matter? It wasn't like looting a bank or for that matter weaving a web of scams. How easy would it be for him to access some stupid data centre records and sell them. He wasn't doing that, was he? Maganbhai slid the unlabelled disc into a computer.

Raghu waited for him to see the first few seconds of Anya suggestively writhing on screen to display her bounteous bosom.

'Good, good,' Maganbhai said with a twisted little smile.

He had many ways to source such videos. Bribing young courier boys delivering digitally mastered secret discs from the studios to the producers. Or keeping an army of small-time street-smart computer geeks who penetrated poorly protected studio sites to download videos. The shack and his DVD stall on Linking Road served as a front, really. There were clients who paid to get the unauthorized versions of movies or songs, feeding into a larger shadow business spread across the country.

'I am glad I found you, Raghu. Useful *ho*.' Maganbhai grinned.

Raghu shrugged.

'I had understood you the instant you had come to my stall. I knew this boy is smart. Very very smart. I also knew you were short of money.' Maganbhai winked.

Raghu grimaced. He felt awkward.

'I knew you wanted to fit in with your cash-rich friends.'

'Really?' Was he that transparent, Raghu wondered. All of Amma's training on simplicity reared inside him. But Maganbhai had literally swooped in, taking his number on some pretext, calling him up to seek help on small computer problems initially, then offering a paltry sum for a hard hack.

'You had been so torn that first time,' Maganbhai reminisced. 'Good schools create too much conscience. My street boys act faster and negotiate harder.'

Still, Raghu had succumbed, and continued doing a couple of other odd jobs for Maganbhai every other month.

Maganbhai fished out some crumpled thousand-rupee notes from his pant pocket, so folded and thinned with age that Raghu was sceptical if any shop would accept them.

'*Theek hai, jaali nahin hain*. They are not fake,' Maganbhai said.

Raghu carefully placed the notes in his wallet, and rather grumpily stumbled out into full sunshine. Taking a shallow breath to avoid inhaling too much of the gutter and raw mutton smells, he took out his sleek Maxx Mobile phone.

He breathed out any guilt he had felt earlier. He hadn't stolen money or killed someone. It was just a download, damnit.

He just had one more stop. The second-hand music shop. To buy the guitar he had asked the shopkeeper to set aside.

He sent an IM to Suv:

I'm on my way.

SATURDAY 12.00 NOON

Andheri, Mumbai

Vir pushed his sunglasses up his nose and leaned against the seat of the cool cab, hoping for a much-needed snooze. But a myriad problems weighed on his mind. Not just Colare. Another issue had brewed overnight. While lawyers had been squabbling over the *whereto* and *herewith* in the out-licensing agreement, the grasping local party had decided to hike up the agreed price. But more than anything else, it was Tracey. On her way to his apartment now. Vir did not know why he had pulled back last night. His mind had been clouded. There were tough questions to answer, indeed. But did she care that the very people he thought would bat for him had taken to vilifying him? So focused was she on her need to define life the way she wanted, barely masking the wish that he return to the States immediately. He had felt hollow, like she did not understand his predicament. To sweep her into a cinch that instant had been unimaginable.

Diti's face danced before his eyes. Diti, who had refused to carry on a long-distance relationship with him eight years ago. Diti, who looked vibrant and vivacious as ever now. He pursed his lips,trying to keep her out of his thoughts.

Life was coming full circle. The same dilemma cropping up again. *So much to resolve,* unease filled him. This Colare drama could not have happened at a worse time.

He rubbed his eyes as the taxi stopped at a black gate while a uniformed guard cursorily inspected the vehicle and let them inside.

Two steel-and-glass buildings flanked a central fountain. One neem tree, circles of aloe vera and tulsi planted underneath created a mini arboretum.

Vir went up to the sixth floor which housed the research

lab. The guard rose sharply, in an abrupt unfolding of limbs and *salaamed.*

Vir moved through the swinging steel double door. If he had been expecting any urgency given last night's phone calls, there was none. Sleepy silence reigned.

'Where is everyone?' he muttered impatiently, striding down a fluorescent-lit corridor. A glass inset in the wall provided a sneak peek at the all-imported, mini-me version of the US lab.

He walked to the HEPA filter zone and went through another set of steel double doors. Suiting up in thin filament gear, he entered an air scrubbing area. The pneumatic high vacuum system hissed into action. Intense puffs of cool ultra-clean air whooshed down, swished about him, then with another hiss, the pressure valves shut down and an automatic air-lock door slid open.

It had been important to create a clean-room environment in India. To keep away the dust and the humidity.

Vir strode into the quiet lab, grumbling agitatedly. 'People have no sense of urgency here.' Here he had cancelled his weekend trip, flown back from Delhi on the earliest flight. Only to find no one was even on the case!

Vir entered the control room. 'Ali!' he exclaimed, glad to see someone.

Ali turned. 'Hey doc.' Amin Ali had been working on Colare in Maryland with Peter Lee and the rest of the team. When Acel opened its R&D lab in Mumbai, Ali had gladly packed up and moved eastwards to manage the India end of the Colare project.

'Where is everyone?'

'In the diagnostics room. GS is checking the backup.'

'Any luck?'

'Not yet.' Ali shook his head in disbelief. He could not understand either what had suddenly gone wrong. Sifting through data, though, was like trying to find one crystal in a tub full of shimmering sand.

'What do you think caused it?'

'I can't understand. We track the readings on a daily basis.

I would have known...'

'Something has happened. We need to find out how and why. And fix it.' A forbidding look came upon Vir's face. 'You don't need me to tell you, Ali, but your job, heck, our jobs, may be on the line.'

SATURDAY, 1.00 P.M.

Andheri, Mumbai

The small R&D team of Acel India huddled in the diagnostics room, in an uneven circle of chairs. Ramesh Raut and V. Radhika, the young scientists. Shrishti Kathuriah, the lab technician who had taken to wearing excessive jewellery after being reprimanded for shimmering make up that threatened to increase the particulate per cubic metre count of the lab air.

'Thanks for coming on a Saturday...' Vir started.

The door opened and Dhananjay Tole, the biochemist, walked inside. 'Sorry, sorry,' he mumbled inaudibly, looking not in the least contrite. 'I had to go for a puja, sir.' He raised his right arm, a thick wad of red string visible between his lab coat and gloves.

'*Had* to go?' Ali said, barely able to conceal his exasperation.

'My own bua's puja, Dr Ali. Had to go, no?'

'Let's start again,' Vir began. 'I have disturbing news. Something could be going wrong with Colare results. It's happening here in India. How serious this is, I don't need to tell you. You know the global patent deadline is in six weeks.'

'I'm perplexed. How come we never noticed it?' Ali's brow furrowed in deep horizontal wrinkles. He had bet his career to move to India to drive R&D for global products. For nearly a decade, he had lived under the shadow of his own name. Meaning *noble*, his name had acquired other connotations in America of the noughties. So when the opportunity presented itself, he and his wife Latifah had only been too glad to relocate to India. But what if Colare failed?

'We must do root-cause analysis,' Radhika piped in seriously.

'Duh. Obviously,' Ramesh said wryly.

Vir exhaled deeply, having no patience for team theatrics. 'Let's list down the possibilities, and then investigate.'

The team went on a roll of ideas. The imaging of the machine could be faulty. The equipment calibration could be off. The machine code could have developed a flaw or rule error.

'Call the equipment suppliers today,' Vir said.

'The specimens may be infected,' Radhika said, adding another dimension to the complexity. 'Or perhaps some systemic contamination through the measuring process.'

'Oh no,' Shrishti said, her bangles jangling in emphatic denial. 'I am very careful. Process error is not possible.' Her saucer-round eyes glared at the others. 'Maybe recording error, when *you* do MRI?'

God! Veer hunkered down. This was complex beyond belief. The elements that could be faulty were endless. To have a bickering team on top of that! It was too much.

'Okay, okay,' he began frostily. 'We need to divide up the work. Shrishti, please review the process steps again; reflect if you are doing anything different. Dhananjay, check the animals, monitor their BP, ECG and all. Do it every two hours. Ramesh, you chase up the vendors, sit with them, recalibrate, make sure no equipment is malfunctioning. Radhika, look through the secondary databases, check all formulae, see if anything looks changed.'

'Let's move it. Chop-chop!' he said in a rush, clapping his hands together, anxious that the team begin the investigation at once.

The team filed out.

Ali sat there, fiddling with a pen, clicking it open and shut, the little tics tattooing a beat in the empty room.

'But what *is* this formula Terry's measuring now?' He sounded peeved.

After all, the per cent reduction in melanoma size multiplied by the square root of platelet count as a fraction of the cube of the micrograms of medicine administered, or some such idiotically complex calculation monitored over time, had the US guys in a tizzy. Third-degree trend analysis seemed more a mathematical uncertainty to him, than something real to worry about.

'He's been tracking it every few weeks for the past three months. I am sure he will call again tonight with more analysis.'

'Could be the data itself.'

The data, in this case the various indicators of the spread or decline of cancerous growth or the size of metastases, was measured in multiple ways. Magnetic resonance imaging and multi-spectral imaging of the diseased animals was done on a daily basis. Generating enormous imaging files for each animal. Every five days, tissue tinged with biomarker enzymes, extracted from each of the animal subjects, was studied under massive Siemens machines. Complex measurements of protein inhibitors and lipids and blood cell counts and the like were made. Workstations connected to these mammoth machines recorded the data using healthcare research software. The resulting imaging files and raw measurement data was transferred to peripheral data storage servers over 2 gigabytes per second fibre channels. Dual Xeon Linux workstations ran post-processing programs. Raw data was also copied to the file server using the file transfer protocol or ftp. Nightly backup happened, from Acel labs in Mumbai and Maryland, onto a 100 terabyte RAID array located in the global data centre in Goregaon.

'Perhaps,' Vir said wearily. *Any one element of that complex data map could be faulty.*

There was a knock on the door. Shrishti peeped in. 'Have you considered sabotage?' she asked softly. 'What about the cleaning and maintenance staff?'

Vir and Ali stared at her incredulously.

SATURDAY, 2.00 P.M.

Goregaon, Mumbai

Vir's car sped along the Western Expressway once again. Off the highway, the narrow arterial road was canopied by dusty mango trees and banyans. A mandir peeped out from amid the trees, red triangular flags fluttering above its small dome. The greenery gave way to a modern gated block of buildings.

The Acel International Data Centre in Goregaon was a secure facility inside building 4. A security guard in blue uniform and brass epaulettes noted down details of the car and the driver in a thick fraying notebook and gave a cursory look, before opening the gate.

'Waste of time, this security,' Vir muttered. What terrorist worth his detonators would drive into a building, batteries and wires in full display upon the seats or in the boot?

Rads, the unfortunately named Lakshminarayanan Radhakrishnan, stood at the steps of building 4. He was short, with neatly combed hair. A thin belt held up his baggy pants, highlighing the curvature of his potbelly. As Vir stepped out of his car, Rads pulled up his pants a bit, and slid down the steps in warm greeting.

'Hello, hello,' Rads mumbled.

'Hello Rads,' Vir said, placing his sunglasses on his head and gave a crisp handshake.

Rads pulled up his pants again and asked Vir to follow him.

Inside, the building looked like a massive warehouse with a warren of corridors, each zone with individually coded magnetic striped keys and secure pin codes.

Rads led Vir through an endless brown-carpeted corridor to the Acel secure zone. The data centre. The root cause of so many screaming matches on the decision to offshore.

Vir took in the room. The area had clearly not been designed with aesthetics in mind. Low grey dividers separated rows of cubicles. Young people in distressed denims and graffiti tee shirts manned large workstations. The data centre never shut down, there was always someone on duty, even on weekends and public holidays. The support staff rotated in three shifts. The main coders and technology wonks worked the day shift, but really were in and out even at the oddest of times, liking nothing better than being glued to their computers.

Beyond the seating area, separated by a glass wall, were racks of equipment. Floor-to-ceiling wired cages housed thick servers and routers in standard black and steel. An impressive array of lights flickered green and yellow, indicating networks in use and data under transmission. Thick black cables of electrical wiring snaked about the room, banded together with duct tape at intervals.

The heat emanating from the equipment could single-handedly notch up the case for global warming. The air conditioners were on full blast to counter the heat-emitting devices.

'Come this way.' Rads led the way to a small glass cubicle with a large desk and a sofa. The view was pure concrete. 'Coffee?'

Vir's eyes felt heavy, pent-up with sleep. 'Make mine black.'

'My team is working on the case, Vir,' Rads said.

Vir smirked. *My team* sounded like an assortment of qualified responsible adults. But perhaps this gaggle of youngsters in their distressed jeans and ganjis, earphones plugged to MP3 players, mouths moving in constant gum-chewing motion, were more attuned to the innards of networks and servers and open source codes than an army of serious adults.

He leaned back in the sofa. 'What are they doing?'

'Do you know how the data is stored, Vir?' Rads said.

Vir nodded his head in negation with the usual uncertainty of a business head on technology matters. He knew it was all on secure servers, but not much more of the technical details.

'A single MRI scan can create gigabytes of data. Factor in the scores of scans and tags for each specimen on a daily basis, you are looking at several terabytes of storage. The individual machines and the computers connected to them act like bottom-holed receptacles. They pool the data in, and funnel it out to the server.' He paused for breath. 'The server is then backed up on a daily basis.'

'How do you get the data from the US research centre?'

'We are on a VPN, a dedicated cable connection, like our private freight corridor for data, between the US and India.'

'And it's secure?'

'And some!' Rads gave a lopsided smile, and extolled the virtues of arcane network security protocols. 'We have a three-tier safety net. Like three rings of fire. Double firewalls protect our networks from attacks from the external domain. Each server is individually protected again, sheathed in layers of firewalls. Like fruit around seeds.'

Rads slapped his thigh, seemingly pleased. 'The best protection is at the file level. Each file is individually watermarked. It gets coded with an automatic secure encryption based on which an authorized user is uploading it. Then if someone checks it out, it gets watermarked again, coding the document with another encrypted signature.'

'In essence, it leaves a trace.'

'The back-end is a fortress, believe me.'

'So what happened?'

'Maybe machine error? Maybe operator error?'

Vir shook his head. That was what headquarters wanted to believe too – that it was arising from on-ground breach of process. Yes, the research team in India was young. But he wasn't sure this was the root cause. Ali was too experienced and too careful to have let handling errors perpetuate.

'So can we compare the data on the file server with the backup server data, just to ensure there is no discrepancy? No data corruption?'

Rads scowled at the thought that *his* data could be corrupted. 'That's what my team is doing. They are writing an algorithm which will automatically sift through the servers, compare like files and do a line-by-line comparison of the data.'

Vir winced. It sounded complicated. 'Can't we check manually?'

'Manually?' Rads's voice thinned in disbelief. Nothing could be more sacrilegious than manual data checking, when logical sieving could attain the same result with more elegance.

'Where's your team at?' Vir exhaled.

As Rads fished out his mobile phone, a skinny office boy walked in carrying a tray with coffee mugs and cookies and set it on the glass table with much flourish. Rads gave him a half-nod and called Peevs to come over.

Peevs, or Pranav Verma, entered through the glass door. His feather-cut hair had been artfully arranged in gelled spikes. He looked confidently at Vir and said, 'We are just testing the data verification code, sir.'

'Who's we?'

'The programmers, sir.' Peevs pointed beyond the glass window at the tech squad. Thin bespectacled lads in assorted denims, tee shirts imprinted with the usual geek graffiti like *I am Root* and *E=mc*^{2} and various calculus equations.

'OK. And after that?'

'Then we will run it on the servers to compare the data on the file server and the back server. If there are any discrepancies, the program will spit it out.'

'How?' Vir leaned forward in his chair, as much curious as eager to test the young programmer.

'Easy.' Peevs smiled. He knew Vir was the big boss and he was keen to impress. This was an easy question.

'It's basic cyclic redundancy test, sir. It uses basic polynomial algebra. Of course, we use cryptographic hash function, to do routine automatic checksums on the server data and store this in hash tables to make sure there is no accidental data corruption.'

Vir kept a straight face at the matter-of-fact answer, even though it seemed techno mumbo-jumbo to him.

'I don't think it will be a data issue, sir. Anyway, the test will verify all this soon.'

Tension burbled back. 'How long?'

'Two–three hours, tops.'

Vir nodded in dismissal. Peevs returned to his workstation. Two–three long hours, Vir mused. No point waiting here. Yet with global IP filing due in six weeks, financial stakes were high and tempers higher.

SATURDAY, 4.00 P.M.

Andheri, Mumbai

Vir surveyed the thin man in the blue uniform with brass epaulettes sitting across the table, finding his bushy moustache at odds with his skinny voice. Ali had called the supervisor of the security team for questioning.

'Our personnel are all trained and security cleared, sir,' the man explained.

'How?' asked Ali.

'Police verification, permanent address check, three references of people they know.'

'Show me the file of everyone who has access to the building.'

'The entire building? Not the Acel area?'

'Do your staff have master keys for all zones?'

'Only for emergency, sir.'

Vir and Ali exchanged a quick glance. Could the security guys have stolen inside to sabotage the experiments or the data? It was a strange thought that Shrishti had planted. But they had to explore the possibility.

'Where is it kept?'

'In a locked drawer at the main desk. Only the supervisor has access. That's me during the daytime and another person at night.'

'Let's see the file,' Vir said.

'I have it, sir. But you are facing computer troubles?' He looked from Ali to Vir for confirmation.

'My boys only know basic reading writing. Like signing in entry registers. How can they destroy your information, sir?'

The man has a point, Vir mused. Even if some of the securiy guards were graduates, they would likely have got a degree from some unregistered college. It was unlikely they'd know how to mess up the sophisticated machines or the complex data.

Ali and Vir went through the file of handwritten forms

with details of the ten men and women who manned the main entrance and floor lobbies of the two buildings.

'They have all been with us since the building opened, sir. Four years now,' the supervisor said. 'I have personally trained them.'

Vir flicked the pages, studying the profiles. All had signed their names, so were clearly literate. Most had SSC diplomas, from Solapur and Malegaon and other outskirts of Mumbai. A few showed that they had started a commerce degree but never completed.

'I don't know.' Vir looked up uncertainly.

'Yeah,' Ali said, equally at a loss. 'Send me a photocopy of this entire file,' he added in a strict voice, and let the man go.

'It can't be any of these jokers.' Ali shook his head.

Vir looked at his watch, aware of Tracey waiting for him. She had called him on waking from a nap; a hurried call when he had asked her to grab lunch. Since then, there had been a half-dozen messages.

He had not responded to any after the first one. She had come to India to meet him, yes. But what could he do now? He *had* to fix this first. His thoughts scattered for one brief moment on Diti, on her refusing to be swept with his goals. All those years ago. His luck with women was the worst, he thought ruefully.

'The maintenance supervisor is waiting,' Ali said. 'Probably not much use. But let's go through with it.'

The maintenance supervisor looked his part in green-trimmed blue overalls, with a thick belt upon which hung an assortment of keys, torches and tools.

Vir had lower expectations from this interview. After all, would the cleaners even be literate?

They flicked through a thin roster, seeing names and photographs.

'We have best staff, sir. Best soaps. Best training,' the man said. 'We do police verification.'

Vir raised an eyebrow. 'Always?'

'*Vell*,' the man said, shifting testily in his seat. 'Almost always. Emergencies happen. Someone sick. Someone absent. So sometimes...' He spread both hands wide, leaving the sentence hanging in the air.

'What happens when someone does not turn up?'

'We don't get notice, sir. Sometimes they call the one day before and take long leave. Can't even fire them – they will quit to take a leave if they want to. Sometimes no show,' the man offered.

'Are they unionized?'

The man gave a shudder. 'No.'

'So what happens when janitors don't show up?'

'We have extra janitors on call. Temps. People wanting to join but not hired yet.'

Vir nodded. In a population of a billion, there was much to be said for daily wages that came with regularity, especially when the alternative was occasional work in fields or quarries or up rickety scaffoldings.

'There is much demand then?' he said, making insipid conversation. There was not much to follow up here.

'Of course, sir. Clients want reliable service. We ISO certified,' he said proudly. 'Many people want to do this work. Except in harvest season.'

'How long have they been working in the building?'

'Six months,' the supervisor said, passing a printout of what seemed like the attendance record of the past month.

Most of the people had 'present' against their names. Against one name, Santosh Kumar Jadhav, there was a row marked '*absent*'.

'You had a temp person replace this guy?'

'He went. Family emergency. Sent his brother-in-law, sir, I remember. Nice lad. No experience. But we took him on.'

'And the brother-in-law's papers?'

'Jitendra Kumar Jadhav, it's not in file? I will check in office, sir.'

'OK send them to Ali here. Send them tonight.' Vir sighed, shutting the roster and closing the interview.

An inexperienced temp cleaner was unlikely to have caused any damage, even unwittingly.

SATURDAY, 5.00 P.M.

Goregaon, Mumbai

Rads took off his thick glasses and blinked. The blast from the air conditioner tickled his eyelashes. It was already evening. His wife would be spitting mad by now, looking after the kids alone on the weekend. The whole point of working for an American company was to claim his weekends. Yet there had been a major technology outsourcing project weeks into his joining. His weekends had gone for a toss. Just as life had stabilized, this problem had emerged.

He wondered if he should go home. *It's probably nothing.*

His intercom rang.

'Hey boss, check this out!'

'What's up, guys?'

'Something's very wrong, Rads.'

Peevs coughed. He scrolled down his screen, flicking back and forth between two congested data sheets.

Rads looked bewildered.

'Look, look.' Peevs pointed towards some tables in the two sheets. 'This is the data grab from the server yesterday, and this is the data I retrieved today. There's a mismatch.'

'How can it be?' Rads leaned forward, squinted his eyes at the screen.

'Dunno,' Peevs muttered, perplexity writ large upon his face.

They had designed a failsafe system, or so he had thought and prided himself in. Complete accuracy. Utter control. To imagine any system and server errors seemed incomprehensible to him.

'Is it a virus?' Rads asked, heart sinking as he looked at his watch. Had to be a virus! Could the latest protective gear ever match against the wits of a cracktivist on a mission?

'Don't know yet, but hope not.' Peevs looked distressed.

Rads nodded. He was in trouble either way – have his head chewed off by his wife or have the office declare he was not on the job. He chose the lesser evil.

'Do the data grab again, run the redundancy test again with the new grab. Get someone to do a complete system scan simultaneously. Check the server logfiles. Try all possible checks, before we raise a virus alert.'

He blinked behind his thick glasses and cleared his throat. 'Call me after the checks. If it's a virus, we'll need to alert everyone.' He called his driver.

'You're leaving?' Peevs said, his voice sounding incredulous. How could Rads go home at such a critical moment.

Rads knew he could not help by hovering. He couldn't start fiddling with server diagnostics. His ace programmers were totally adept at handling the work.

'Shouldn't we tell Vir now, boss?'

Rads looked at him.

'If it's a virus, he would want to know. This could be major!'

Rads pursed his lips. 'Nothing is confirmed. Vir will be compelled to tell headquarters. We don't want to cause US to hyperventilate needlessly. But we have to make sure it's not a virus either. Do the checks first.'

'Call me the minute you discover anything,' he called out as he left, feeling certain they would not need to call.

One scan proved *nothing*.

The test could have gotten corrupted.

SATURDAY, 6.00 P.M.

Bandra, Mumbai

'Well done, Madhu.'

KCS Sir pushed his thick tortoiseshell bifocals on his flat nose, nodding approvingly. At thirty-one, he was the oldest teacher in the coaching institute, and an IITian to boot.

The whiteboard was covered with the working of an advanced physics problem. A complex string of Greek and numerical letters in red and blue markers.

Madhu, dressed in her new teal block-printed kurta and pale blue jeggings, gave a wobbly smile, and walked back to her seat. She hated standing in front of the class. She hoped no one would notice the shivers that ran through her.

'Okay, boys and girls. Let's move to Lagrange's Theorem,' the teacher said.

Madhu hastily sat down in her seat, opened her Resnick & Halliday, and willed her cold shaking hands to calm down.

She turned to Anki. To see a notebook filled with cartoon doodles. Not a complex delta or sigma letter in sight. Quite elaborate designs, in fact, grey-shaded to define the action silhouettes and the facial expressions.

'Anki!' Madhu whispered. 'What are you doing?'

Ankita put her tongue out at Madhu.

Papers ruffled. The class sat, heads bent, taking notes while the instructor explained intricacies of advanced mathematics.

Madhu felt a tingle down her spine. Someone was eyeing her. She looked up.

Raghu was looking at her, easy confidence in his square shoulders. Suv nudged Raghu and they both laughed silently.

She felt herself go cold again. She had seen that look in college. Classmates laughing at her expense. She looked away, heart beating wildly, and peered at the half-written page.

Much as she had come to dislike Suv and Raghu, there was no denying their confidence. So different from the boys she had known in Korba. Suv dressed like a banker in the making, in formal shirts and chinos, hair gelled, riding an Enfield into college. Raghu, in contrast, was tall and lean; his tee shirt usually topped with a checked shirt left unbuttoned, his curly hair unruly. His voice was deep and dense, and when he sang at the college fest, strumming his guitar, looking the audience in the eye as he belted out blues and rock songs that Madhu had never heard of, a collective sigh rippled among the girls.

Their assurance, a jauntiness that came out of living in a megapolis, made her uncomfortable, feel inadequate somehow. They were popular. If they were insufferable, it was simply to her. Was it like Anki had said – Raghu was simply piqued that someone smarter than him had entered his domain?

Madhu had hoped to quietly fit into her new life in Mumbai, dreaming that impossible dream of quiet over achievers, of making new friends and being the academic star of the new environment.

She shone, no doubt. Teachers loved her. But what about the students? Sniggers followed her. Raghu and Suv had started it; but the others had gone ahead passing jokes about her on WhatsApp, repeating them within her hearing in the quad and canteen and corridors.

She suddenly caught Suv's eyes. He winked. *In front of the whole class. In front of the teacher.*

She looked away. Instantaneously, her phone rang out, a loud sudden trill. It rode over the instructor's voice as he explained the corollaries of Lagrange's Theorem. Madhu scrambled to get it out of her bag and silence the unwelcome sound. It broke the stillness of the room. Students shuffled, distracted.

'Phone calls in class!' KCS Sir shouted. 'Wasting people's time; wasting parents' money. If you are here to be on the phone, better not come. Boyfriends calling during class time!'

She felt all her hard work and brilliance shadowed. Girls

and boys smirked, and quickly hid their grins, glad it was someone else and not them.

Madhu stuffed the phone inside her backpack and shoved the bag under her chair, not wanting to peek at the called ID yet.

SATURDAY, 7.00 P.M.

Bandra, Mumbai

Ankita stood on the crowded footpath of Hill Road, fingering plump beads in azure and aquamarine and amethyst at a roadside stall. Some had dusty silver medallions strung upon them, some were interspersed with filigreed rudraksha or enamelled tin globules. Evening revellers huddled outside Elco's, bumping into each other, queuing up for panipuri and chaat. The smell of hot aloo tikkis frying and sizzling rose as thin flutes of smoke overriding the animal and petrochemical smells floated around.

'Let's go, Anki,' Madhu said.

The press of pedestrians, the noxious hot fumes of stalled vehicles, the constant orchestra of vehicle horns in abrupt tweets and syncopated protractions, the heat rising from the supersized tawa and frying pans of Elco, all made her want to escape.

'Coming,' Ankita mumbled, distracted.

This was her favourite pasttime. Dawdling at shops, enjoying the sheer tactile pleasure of touching beads or fabric, or heatedly haggling over a new pirated game only to let it go. Making up for the mindless boredom of two hours of pre-engineering jargon.

'Why must we waste time after every class?'

'But this is the best part of each class.'

'Right.' Madhu snorted.

Anki floated in the clouds. Like a cotton flower upon the whimsy of the barest breeze. Anki's gossamer dreams hovered over the latest waft of fashion or film. Social networking and cartoon figures.

'Who had called you in class, anyways?' Ankita picked a necklace of red beads and folded gold tissue accordions, slipped it on, fluffed her hair and peered in the small mirror held aloft by the grubby stall-keeper.

Madhu fished out her phone from her bag. The call was from some unknown number. But there were two unread messages.

A sent message. From her mobile to Unknown:

I can't help it, I keep thinking of you.

A hot flush rose up Madhu's face, the deafening roar of mortification drowning out all roadside sounds.

The second message was a response. From Unknown to her:

Hot for me? Love that look...

'What? What happened?' Ankita grabbed Madhu's phone and giggled. 'Too funny.'

Madhu scowled.

There was nothing funny. As to how a message like that went out from her phone to some unknown number was beyond her!

A motorcycle roared, a flash of red veering away from cars to brush close to the girls, and sped past them, weaving into the gridlock of cars. Madhu jumped a half-step back, bumping into the hard metal frame of the stall.

'Watch it,' the stall-keeper shouted, as the stall rocked.

'Let's go.' Madhu dragged Anki half a block, to the narrow lane where their autorickshaw waited to take them home.

In the rick, Madhu checked her phone again. Raghu or Suv. It had to be one or the other. Or both.

'How...' she mused, holding on to the side rod of the rick, covering her mouth lightly with her dupatta, as the city and the traffic spluttered past.

'What?' Ankita asked over the sputter of the rick.

'How could they send this strange message...'

'Who's "they"?'

'Raghu and Suv. Who else?'

'Too quick to condemn, aren't we?'

'Who else could it be!'

'Show me the message.'

Ankita took the small-screen Nokia, held it aloft to read

the message, and barked another loud laugh, much to Madhu's chagrin.

She typed a few keys. 'Your Bluetooth was on. You've been bluejacked, babe! *You* are the one who wants to be an engineer; *I* should not have to tell you to keep Bluetooth off in small public spaces.'

'Bluejacked?'

'Hacking into a mobile phone via Bluetooth, don't you know?' Ankita continued. 'It's pretty easy, I think. I personally don't know how to do it, but you know – instructions can be downloaded from the net. Easy.'

'I didn't even know my Bluetooth was on.'

'Yeah. Everyone forgets. They play music from their mobile onto a Bluetooth speaker, or use hands-free headsets, then forget to switch it off, and it's pregnable, especially in closed rooms.'

'I know phones can be hacked,' Madhu said, exasperated. 'But how could they specifically target my phone?'

'They got lucky.' Ankita shrugged her shoulders.

'You need Quick Heal. Do you know who lives in your phone...?'

'But how could they send a message out from my phone? That means breaking in, no?'

'Hah! You have a two-letter password! How hard can that be to guess... even I could *break in*, as you say.'

'But, but...' Madhu mumbled. 'Can they remotely send a message from my phone?'

'Well...' Ankita sounded disconcerted, as the rick turned a corner and street lights lit up her face, showing her unease. 'We'll be home in a tick.'

Madhu narrowed her eyes. Anki had been about to say something else. She knew that look, that catch in Anki's voice – it meant something was afoot.

'So, you were telling me, how could Raghu and Suv possibly send a message from my phone remotely?'

'I would just be guessing, you know.'

'Go on, tell me.' Hardness crept into Madhu's voice now.

'Day before in the canteen, you left your phone on the table when you went to buy a chocolate. It beeped. Suv picked it up, said your battery was low. His laptop was open, so he said he would charge it from his laptop.'

'I never saw this.'

'He took it off the charger before you returned. I never thought about it. But why would he charge your phone for a few minutes? That can't help much if your battery is low.'

'Why?' Seeing Anki hesitate, she added, 'Go on, take a guess.'

'He could have mirrored your phone.'

'Mirrored?'

'You know, copying your phone's content to his hard drive, or installing a malware to control your phone remotely. It would just take a couple of minutes.'

The rick geared into action. Accelerator whirring, the driver navigated between parked cars, thundering down the quieter road. Madhu stared away, not responding.

'I would have stopped him had I known,' Anki said, as the rick stopped and followed Madhu contritely. 'Believe me.'

Madhu swept into the lift lobby, eyes averted.

SATURDAY, 6.00 P.M.

Bandra, Mumbai

The aurous expanse of the sky was broken only by a couple of palms, silhouetted against the gilded backdrop, swaying gently in the wind. During the daytime, the sea looked green. The warm depths of the Arabian churned in the heat, bringing nutrient-rich phytoplankton to the surface. On this late Spring evening, the sea was a shimmering ripple, the waves diamond-crested gold.

Located upon a jutting rocky promontory in Bandra, the clubhouse seemed a lifetime away from the traffic snarls of Pali Hill.

Vir sat on the seafacing terrace, his mind still crowded with work woes.

'How can people live blithely when homeless kids crowd the streets.' Tracey looked into her cool drink.

Vir exhaled.

Tracey was really affected by the sight of poverty. Was the poverty in Namibia different, he wondered. How did Diti deal with Bantu-speaking ill and poor on the streets of Windhoek? He cleared his mind, and compulsively reached for his BlackBerry, though he had checked it minutes ago.

'Any updates?' Tracey said, annoyed that Vir was on his mobile every two minutes, even after having spent the whole day at work.

'Nope.'

Anxiety would not loosen its grip on him. Was it all for nought?

If data had gone corrupt at the server level, there would be mayhem. Acel saved backups of server data often. But was it hourly or daily? He did not even know. There was bound to be some loss between such periodic saves. Someone was bound to question why he did not know the details. If, on the other hand, there was no data corruption, but data had been captured wrongly due to operator errors or machine errors or calibration errors, it would bring down the credibility of the Indian research organization. That it had happened was bad. That it had been noticed by a statistician in the US after two months was worse. Either way, there would be repercussions.

'Vir?' Tracey prodded.

'What?' he said.

'Why can't you listen? Only your troubles are important?'

'I'm listening.'

'What is the future of "us"?' Tracey had an odd expression, part expectant, part nervous, eyes bright with unshed tears.

Vir exhaled and inhaled slowly, filling his insides with the warm air in one deep gulp. He focused on Tracey.

'I can't be a nobody. If I agree to move to Mumbai, that is.'

'I've spoken to more doctors in the city, Trace. Meet them. There are newer hospitals, and contract research firms.'

'I thought they ran call centres and managed medical records, billing and the like.'

'A lot more than outsourcing, babe. Some big ones are doing pre-clinical trials. Some are doing clinical research. Could be interesting.' He tried a disarming smile, unsure of what else to say or do.

Tracey frowned. Vaguely, she recalled some ethical concerns regarding clinical trials in India. *Could I work with issues like that?*

'There are some reputed organizations,' he said, reading her mind. 'There is a contract research registry. Why don't you check it up?'

His phone thrummed. Vir pressed the answer button hurriedly.

Ali was on the line. 'Vir, there may be a problem. Records of that temp cleaner came. He has a degree in computer hardware and networking from some technical degree college in Gorakhpur!'

'What?'

'There's more,' Ali said. 'He hasn't come to work for the last two days.'

SATURDAY, 8.00 A.M.

Rockville, Maryland

Dr Peter Lee dragged his feet into the Acel building, hugging his white coat for warmth. It was Saturday morning and the building was quiet. Only the technicians rostered for the weekend were in the lab, monitoring the animals, taking readings.

Peter liked the office on weekends. The quietness appealed to him, the silence sharpened his senses. Plus, a couple days of being away, and the walls of his barely-furnished home had started crowding in. He had wandered from one empty room to another, feeling lost, away from the only world he cared about – his research.

Peter lived and breathed work. His life was testament to the fact. He had never married. His closet was mostly empty. His kitchen stocked with ready-to-heat meals and instant noodles. He lived mostly on takeaways. He had been with Acel for decades, having started fresh out of grad school, assisting Dr Ron Thomson on *Zeta Block*, also known as NF2-613, one of the iconic molecules discovered at the turn of the millennium.

Many cancers were characterized by the over-expression of proteins on cellular surfaces, which caused tumour cells to multiply fast. *Zeta* specifically targeted a protein that caused ovarian stromal tumour and turned it off, thereby stopping the multiplication of rogue cells. It had started a wave of protein inhibitor drug research and Dr Thomson had become a legend, being widely quoted in the *New England Journal of Medicine* and making frequent public appearances on CNN talking about this wonder drug that had saved thousands of women from advanced stages of serous cystadenocarcinoma, a malignant form of tall ciliated fluid-filled cells which appeared on ovarian surfaces and invaded surrounding tissue.

Peter, since then, had been involved in a series of molecular discoveries that had been quickly patented on early promise, but fizzled out in pre-clinical trials.

He had conceptually dreamed of Colare after a conversation with Dr Adam Janlowski, as a unique mix of two techniques that Acel had been independently researching on for a decade – immunotherapy vaccines and stem cell drugs. Then Peter had made it happen, spending hours in the lab, painstakingly grafting cells, an overlay that seemed seamless in theory, but nearly impossible to achieve in active biological reality. He had succeeded eventually, and the molecule had proved effective in inhibiting the growth of human tumour lines. Since then, Peter had lived and breathed with Colare.

And then, Adam had done the unthinkable. Sent one half of it spinning to India. *Split* the project. *Split* its ownership. *Split* Peter's soul. Now the overbearing Andy, hand in glove with marketing, seemed to be ignoring his contribution.

Peter opened his office door with a heavy heart.

The global patent filing deadline was just weeks away. There was so much to do and so little time.

SATURDAY, 9.00 A.M.

Chevy Chase, Maryland

Adam Janlowski adjusted his cap, took position and focused his attention on one single thing – the tenth hole on the fairway of the Columbia Country Club, across a sandy pit and beyond a little man-made pond. The first grass of Spring spread around him, green, soft, freshly mowed. Adam adjusted his stance, bent upon the club, stood poised for one long instant, then sliced his arms up in the air and down, in a graceful arc, hitting the white ball.

'Good shot,' said Lara Andrews, his Chief Legal Counsel. She was dressed in casual chinos and a warm jumper, a change from her usual crisp suits.

'Hmm.' Adam nodded, pleased with himself. At seventy, not much perturbed him, other than his game.

Lara took her position, swung her club and sent her ball flying, matching Adam's score.

'Good shot,' Adam returned the compliment.

'What about your other long shot?' Lara asked gingerly.

'Long shot?' Adam frowned.

'India.'

'It will sort out, Lara,' Adam said impatiently, not caring for this unexpected line of questioning.

'Yeah?' Lara raised her brows. 'Have you read the latest on the Indian patent regime? Its unstable, if anything. To send Colare to India at this stage...'

Adam raised one finger. 'That decision is in the past, Lara.'

He is losing his grip on the business, she thought. 'But making amends is in the present. Especially when you can see things starting to slide down at our India office.'

'Slide down? Not the words I would have used yet.' Adam

dug his club in the ground, and stood holding it for support. 'What would you rather have me do?'

'Cut your losses.'

'And what? Shut the centre down? After all that investment?'

Lara looked frosty. 'At least let Colare proceed without India.'

Adam stared thoughtfully into the distance.

'Sort local operations out in the meantime?'

Adam looked Lara in the eye. 'It's too soon for surgery. We don't know yet why this data has gone wrong. We need to take few days to sort it out.'

Lara eyed Adam, doubt clouding her mind. He seemed to be losing his decisiveness. Was that expected of a chairman?

SATURDAY, 7.00 P.M.

Bandra, Mumbai

'Wasn't that a neat trick I played on Madhu?' Suv laughed.

'Infantile.'

'Still. You have to admit she was startled. And furious.'

'Then some!' A perky grin lit up Raghu's eyes. He had an evening off from his Sys Sec duty today and had told his mother that he would be gone for a sleepover. Wanting nothing more than some hours with his new guitar. 'Let's try out a new song.'

They downloaded guitar music instructional videos from YouTube. Raghu picked up his new wine-red mahogany bass guitar and plugged it. He tried to play the chords of the new song, following the step-by-step fingering instructions, Suv giving beat on the table.

Noises came in from the outside. Caterers setting up for a party on the terrace. Suv's mother popped her head in to tell them she was stepping out for a bit. 'Study hard, boys,' she said, closing the door.

'On Saturday evening? Yeah, right!' Suv spoke to the shut door.

'Entrance exams don't worry you, clearly.' Raghu winked.

'Naah. Dad wants me to do tuitions just to improve my SAT scores. It's easier to apply overseas.'

'If you can pay for it.'

Suv shrugged. 'People go on scholarships too. Super brainy types, anyway.'

Raghu considered this for a moment, listening to Suv talk about standardized tests and such, a path different from the one extolled by his mother.

Suv rifled his box of games, and they settled for *Diablo III*. Eerie riffs of music filled the room. Rings of purple-green lighting rippled across the darkened screen, while a fierce witch doctor battled an undead monster in the centre of that vortex. Suv's body moved in sync with the motion of the fearsome masked witch doctor, as he combatted the shape-shifting monster. Raghu sat next to Suv, hawkishly glued to the screen, awaiting his turn.

There was a brief knock at the door, which the boys barely heard over the rippling music of the game.

Suv's father came in. 'Studying, boys?,' he teased.

Suv turned, glazed. 'Oh Dad.' He paused the game. The witch doctor froze on the screen, both arms raised in attack.

'Just taking a break, Dad.'

'Your mom's just pulling in,' Suv's father said, closing the door.

Suv exited the game.

'Dude, I downloaded these two cool books on hackers.'

Raghu raised an amused eyebrow. Suv was funny. Dropping names like Kevin Mitnick, the original cyber bad boy-turned-ethical consultant, and Jeff Moss, aka The Dark Tangent, the Black Hat founder. He had guzzled up a lot of trivia about white hats and grey hats and black hats. Shared the latest news about snoopers and counter-snoopers, from China's Byzantine Candor to the reports on Snowden.

Just a few years back, the spate of denial-of-service attacks and hacks were attributed to teens, trying to prove their crackerjack mettle. Now, everyone from shadow online Mafiosi to government outfits had joined the fray.

The rules had changed. New-generation chips relied on distributed computing, breaking down complex calculations into small steps and doing each calculation on a different processor at the same time. With so many machines connected to the internet, hackers used the same concept of distributed computing to launch widespread attacks. Like d-DOS, a distributed denial-of-service attack.

'I am trying to create a phishing email.'

'Cooler than reading about how to "jailbreak" apps,' Raghu said witheringly.

'I wonder if I can get into the Income Tax site?' Suv wondered. 'See who is hiding what.'

'Too complicated.'

'That's the fun. Imagine convoluted formulae and factors of calculating taxes, the number of evaders and the entire parallel economy. How easy to wreak havoc by changing one formula?'

'On half-baked knowledge, you'll never mask your trail.'

'I can claim I was exposing systems flaws.'

'Come off it, Suv! Such actions will only get you into trouble.'

This conversation bored Raghu. He hadn't the least interest in breaking into government sites or launch a denial-of-service attack. To tell the truth, India had become one of the top five global destinations for hackers to cause mayhem. Even the sleepy Indian government had woken up to the threat of hundreds of pings that tried to illegally enter their secure data sites, and started talking of online security.

Suv got annoyed. 'And when you do it, it's cool?'

'What I do, dummy, is advanced Boolean logic to decode security gaps. I would never follow mundane wiki-how commands!'

Raghu did not hack to belong to some imaginary online tribe or get his kicks by unauthorized entry in easy-to-pick sites. Over the last two years, he had learned programming and scripting languages like Perl, decoded locks in Firefox and anti-virus softwares, checked out web libraries for information on software and malware, and pored over detailed treatises on the physical configurations of routers and servers, the intricacies of machine language and programmable logic. He had shared code with other programmers, pitching in to create small logical loops that fed into the larger digital building blocks of applications. Like sewing a few stitches to make the communal quilt.

What I do for Maganbhai, for a bit of pocket money, is harmless, he told himself. Some things you did not tell even your best buddy.

The smell of roasting chicken tikka skewers and tuberose fragrance from a diffuser wafted in as the door opened. Suv's mother tottered in a fuschia silk dress.

'Come have dinner, beta,' she said.

'We have to leave, Ma. For a birthday party,' Suv fibbed. Last thing he wanted to do on a Saturday evening was to hang out at home with his parents' friends!

SATURDAY, 8.00 P.M.

Bandra, Mumbai

The sound of chatter enveloped the girls as soon as they emerged from their compound. People overflowed the ramshackle eatery, wolfing down greasy keema patties and soggy peanut-encrusted brownies off thick china plates.

Madhu surveyed the room. There wasn't one empty table. 'This is so busy,' she complained. 'Let's go home.'

'Don't be silly. You can't eat at home on a Saturday night. Someone will get up soon.'

As they reached the counter, Anki rattled off their order.

Laden with plates and cups, they edged towards the corner, waiting for a gaggle of teenagers to finish their high fives and goodbye hugs.

Anki looked around. 'You get to see the world pass by. Look, I think that uncle and aunty are having a fight.'

Madhu smiled and bit into her greasy keema pav, thinking that it was always Anki who forked out pocket money.

'I shall offer tuition lessons to kids. Earn some pocket money. Then I can treat you as well.'

'Don't be silly!'

'I'd like to have my own money too.'

'Hah! Set up a palmistry stall at our college fest. The boys can line up to get their hands held by you, while you read their palms.'

'Don't be silly.'

Anki was interrupted by a loud thwack on her back.

'Hello, hello.' Suv and Raghu made a pleading hand gesture. 'There are no tables. Can we join you?'

Suv flipped a chair around and sat astride, before Anki could say yes.

Madhu stiffened. 'It's *may we*, not *can we*!'

'Whatever...' Suv muttered, flushing a bit.

Madhu looked away, her mouth a straight line.

Raghu sat down, a bit uncomfortable. Silence fell upon the table. The girls sipped their cappuccinos and Suv fiddled with his smartphone, then got up. 'I'll get food, RDX.'

'What's with the name?' Anki looked curious.

'Not much,' Raghu said as soon as Suv was out of earshot. 'Look, I want to apologize for what happened.'

Anki goggled. *An apology?*

Madhu continued to glower.

'That was a mean trick,' Raghu said.

Suv returned, carrying lemonades. 'What are you saying, dude?'

'I was just apologizing to Madhu for the poor trick you played.'

'Aww, how sweet! But wasn't it a neat trick?'

Anki sniggered. She was always game for pranks. She had been in school with Suv and Raghu since kindergarten. Anki had been a tomboy growing up, till she had a partial transition in her early teens, had her first crush on Suv, which she had soon outgrown. Unrequited love was not for her. Her breeziness precluded such intense depths of suffering.

'That's it!' Madhu stood up, arms on her hips, eyes liquid. 'I've had enough. I don't want to listen to this rubbish. You've had much fun at my expense. All these past weeks! Don't think I don't know who is passing around these jokes. Do you think I can't hear the sniggers when you walk behind me in college? No doubt you will have a few more laughs about my computer.'

She rattled off, faster and more furious with each syllable, face reddening, voice thick with emotion. 'I thought my computer was conking off. Now I'm sure you have done something to it! Crooked and evil! That's what you are.'

She stomped off.

Shock froze the others. Ankita looked up, catching with surprise the sudden bereft look in Raghu's eyes.

SATURDAY, 10.00 A.M.

Rockville, Maryland

'I need you to solve a problem,' Jake Livingston, the Head of Security at Acel, said looking at his young team member.

'Happy to,' Scott said. It was perhaps the longest sentence Scott had uttered in months. Usually he preferred silence, letting his partner Dean do the talking. But Dean was on leave.

Jake's division looked not at just the technology security, but the overall policing of the company. He had crack experts designing online security. Part of it had been rendered toothless after the data centre had been outsourced to India. Physical security was also monitored by his team. Staff could not take their mobiles or tablets into the labs. Carrying USB sticks or rewritable CDs inside the protected zones was forbidden. Online connectivity was nil inside the labs, and heavily monitored in the offices. Trash bins were collected and sent to a central shredding facility before being piled onto a dump site. Even the cleaning staff went through a series of psychometric tests before they were employed for the chores of vacuuming the carpets or wiping the formica surfaces.

Dean and Scott, a tag team, operated alone. Like a specialist bomb squad. They sat atop all the IT infrastrucre of the firm, to conduct vulnerability pen tests against each new piece of spyware and malware sent into the world by a malicious hacker. They tested shellcode and app protocols, wrote complex javascript patches, remained on perma-alert and ready to invade any employee's password-protected domain, to protect every bit of front-end and back-end code and data.

That they were ready to intrude into systems and servers outside the company at his behest was something that Jake kept to himself. It was good to have his white hat systems architects, security analysts and battalions of coders and offshore specialists. But today he was especially glad for his secret arsenal.

'I am worried about India. I worry more when I hear "We're on track".'

Scott nodded. It could be a fudging stance, he knew. Drop-the-bomb-later tactic.

'I am worried something deeper is going on.'

Scott nodded again.

'So I want you to run some penetration tests at our end. See how much we've been compromised.'

'It may take two or three days to check every part of our systems.'

Jake eyed his twenty-two-year-old cracker. He had been working with Acel since he had emerged out of nowhere, declaring he had found some vulnerabilities in Acel's website. He had been in high school then. A zit-faced gangly lad. He had temped through his engineering degree in computers and networking, and joined them full time. He barely looked his age even now. It always worried Jake. Running background security checks and doing personnel profiling was a must. But the bottom line was always the same. You had to trust these kids. And yet, you never knew. If they turned rogue, the company would be the last to know.

'Sure, don't want you to dumpster dive. Lets start from the systems that Colare data touches,' Jake said. 'And our external website,' he added as an afterthought.

'You'll give me permission now?'

'Yes,' Jake said, took in a deep breath, and sent an approval email from his mobile.

As the firm's in-house security expert, Scott had access only to certain systems and the external firewalls. But unfettered access to data servers, mail servers, domain network servers was another matter.

'You be watchful now,' he said, leaving. 'I'll call you later.'

Scott nodded again and sat down, a Dr Pepper in his hand, and fired his workstation. It wasn't as much as a commune with God, as feeling akin to God, when he sat in that pen-test mode.

SATURDAY, 9.00 P.M.

Colaba, Mumbai

Vir sipped a sharp-tasting champagne of young vintage, bottled locally in Nashik under the shadow of the temple of the *somras*-drinking Trayambakeshwar.

He was at Galerie Saloniere Star, at an art talk hosted by a friend's wife, escorting Tracey to meet people, trying to act normal.

Christine, the wiry anchor for the evening, a photojournalist with *Time* magazine's India desk, introduced the artist Anushri Sen.

'Silver gelatin printing, uncommon since the emergence of digital techniques, was the primary photo documenting process for decades.' She described how the artist used silver halide paper and morphed new sensibility and edgy shots with old world techniques, washing prints by hand and toning them with a coating of selenium for a luminous effect.

Vir did not know much about art, but he appreciated it. One of the lessons he had learned from Diti. To look beyond structure. He scanned the black-and-white photos. Touching images of old people in Art Deco and Victorian bungalows of Mumbai. Last sentinels of an era gone by. The room was a sea of chiffons, and diamonds, people stopping on their way to some other party du jour.

As Christine spoke about the history of silver gelatin printing, Vir's mind wandered off to the phone call earlier that evening.

Another biting exchange with the US team. Adam had been disappointed. Peter silent but standoffish. Andy volcanic. This trouble about Colare data had created fault lines at work, leaving Vir in the middle of a rubble. Unsure of where to run or who to ask for help. Sharp accusations had flown. *Lack of supervision. Inept team. The background pounding of tables.* A hot flash of anger coursed through him.

He took another sip of his champagne. When did worry solve anything? Yet he felt guilty being here, when he should have been back in Goregaon along with his team.

≈

'Give it time, you will come to love India,' an effervescent Tara Malhotra said, bright as the solitaires in her ears.

They were sitting in Ziya, sharing the degustation menu of a Michelin two-starred chef, downing white tomato soup served in tiny shot glasses, with a dollop of Bloody Mary jelly. A sophisticated charcoal-and-gold backdrop merged modern interior lines with a traditional gold leaf-overlaid trellis.

Raj laughed at his wife. 'You hated it when we first came.'

Vir felt a sliver of envy at this easy camaraderie. Life and its loci of stability still evaded him. He looked away at the sodium shimmer of Marine Drive.

'It was hard initially.' Tara shrugged.

'But you're Indian. How hard could it be? You understand the context. These maddening multiple realities.'

'Perhaps,' Tara said, spooning an avocado mousse.

Tracey fell silent. Vir toyed with his glass of Scotch, not looking at Tracey. It look a leap of faith to accept the chaos, the cacophony. Would she be able to handle it? But more than that, he could feel his own emotional estrangement. Did he really want to worry about her adjustment with India, when there were so many real challenges to be faced?

Raj broke the silence, turned the talk to something about an expected exit in his portfolio. 'That's where the returns are. Mid-caps.'

'Not start-ups?'

They spoke of the fuzzy investment scene, the interest in biotech and medical devices, in rural applications. Vir feigned an enthusiasm he did not feel. How positive had he felt just last week! He had always viewed himself as a planner. Imagined himself part of the tribe that built cathedrals, rather than slapped bricks together. Not just this Colare data debacle which could have far-reaching effects on Acel and his own future, but also the slippery downward slope of his personal life. *I need a long run to clear my mind!* he thought.

Vir's phone rang and he almost jumped.

Rads was on the line. 'Vir, we have a problem. The server had an open port.'

SATURDAY, 9.30 P.M.

Bandra, Mumbai

Madhu lay curled on her side, the thinnest wrap covering her. The weak light from the table lamp cast its penumbral glow, making the room a dim cocoon.

A storm welled up inside her. Home seemed far away. Another reality. Through the rosy lens of memory, it became sweeter, friendlier. Forgotten was the Ladies Wing gossip her mother abhorred. Forgotten was the nosiness of a closed township, where everyone knew what everyone else did, where common diktat decided what everyone wore or ate or spoke or how they behaved. Instead, it became a magical domain whose customs she understood, whose simplicity she liked.

Downstairs, the evening revelry continued, its sounds carried upwards like a bass drone upon the still air.

The door opened softly. Madhu hid her face in the pillow.

'Madhu, why are you alone? Where is Anki?' Mausaji's voice startled her, and she scrambled to sit up.

Mr Sharma stood, one hand upon the doorjamb, tired, having just flown in from Delhi.

'I just came back, Mausaji. Raghu and Suv are with her.'

'This girl,' Mr Sharma muttered, walking away, annoyed.

'I will call her,' Mrs Sharma called out from behind him. She shot a glance at Madhu. 'You okay, beta? Were you crying?'

Madhu shook her head. 'Just missing home.'

Ragini Mausi leaned forward, clasped Madhu's face to her stomach. Madhu's arms went around her bulk, soaking in the tenderness, the soft caress upon her hair.

'Have you called home today? Or Skyped?'

'I will try.' Madhu offered a crumbling smile, feeling calmer than before. 'My computer was not working earlier.'

'Really? Check, or we will get someone from Mausaji's office to fix it. Let me go call Anki now.'

Madhu switched on her old computer, hoping it was okay. Miraculously it *worked*.

She opened her inbox. There was a flood of emails, responses to a rogue message from her account saying that she had lost all money and was in desperate need of some cash. A spam? A random happenchance? Or one more incident in a series of episodes crafted to trouble her?

She started replying to each email, telling them it was a scam.

'Telling tales to my parents?' Ankita's whine disrupted her.

Madhu turned around.

Ankita stood grumpily, cheeks puffed out. *Madhu was such a goody-two-shoes! Even normal behaviour seemed deviant in comparison.* 'What are you doing anyway? Studying again?' she said crossly.

Madhu simply folded her arms and stared back.

'What now?'

'Someone spammed my email account.'

Ankita shrugged. 'So?'

'You won't ask me who?'

'Oh, the princess persecution complex has kicked in?'

'I can guess,' Madhu said.

'Hah.'

'Can't be chance. Mobile bluejacking, email spamming.'

Anki snorted.

'It has to be your *dear* Raghu and Suv.'

'You are insane.'

'Who else?' Then struck by a surpising thought, she said in a startled tone. 'You? Its not your idea of a joke, is it? Like you got into my account yesterday...'

'Don't be silly. Of course, I did not do it. Show me.'

Madhu showed the emails.

'It's a spam alright. Probably spear phishing from some link you clicked on. There's even a bank account number to send money to.'

It was an old trick. A scamster would set up a fake bank

account in sub-Saharan Africa, break into someone's email account, and send out fake emails to the person's contact list. Gullible friends would transfer small amounts, placing it at the disposal of the scamster.

Anki made a face. 'Really! Who falls for dumb old tricks now? These fraudsters continue to live in hope.'

'I was reading somewhere,' Anki said, 'one online gang from Europe had set up a series of fake accounts, recruited journalists across California to write in support of charitable trusts and invited the public to send aid dollars to these accounts. At the same time, these fronts siphoned money from e-commerce sites, selling fake goods. Before anyone suspected, millions of fake transactions on countless sites had dot-dotted real money away, leaving the authorities scrambling.'

'You read such stuff?'

'Sometimes.' Anki lifted her shoulders up.

'But how complicated!' Madhu forgot her worries.

'Isn't it? The goons are always so inventive,' Anki said sagely. 'That when three-fourths of all email traffic in the world is spam.'

'Isn't spam illegal?'

'In many countries. Yet, it generates billions of bytes of useless data, causing millions of dollars in loss.'

'Not that any scamster has come forward till now, claiming to be the *master* global job creator!' Anki explained. 'But thanks to a few crazy people, it must be a trillion dollar industry.'

'How do you know all this?' Madhu frowned.

'Just like that.' Anki shrugged, and stepped in front of the mirror, evaluating her reflection. Too thin.

'Aren't there laws against such things?'

'Since when have laws prevented people from breaking them?'

'Like Raghu and Suv.'

'Tch, I give up!' Anki said and went to the bathroom.

SATURDAY, 11.00 P.M.

Goregaon, Mumbai

Vir was on the Western Highway again after dropping Tracey home. The suburbs sped past, lit in the uneven neon of intermittent street lights. At its chaotic best the traffic veered in and out of lanes, tiny scooters overloaded with entire families zipped between cars.

Vir was lost in thoughtt. What had seemed logical, this much-feted move, touted by the desi business dailies as yet another example of a talented executive jumping ship from foreign shores to desi coasts, suddenly verged on the farcical. Rather than receive plaudits for market making, he would receive public flak for data leaks. *An open port!*

The cyberworld's equivalent of the lawless shore. Unfettered by civic rules, allowing pirates to dock and jostle at will. To think of millions invested in firewalls and layered spywares, not to mention Rads and his team, was all useless if the servers had an open port.

The worst thoughts came to him. He knew how important it was to close all unused ports. A port was the channel or gateway through which applications on one device could communicate and interact with applications or software on another device. When a user accessed a website, a port in the user's computer talked to the port in that website. Ports acted like haughty visa officers at a company's online borders, allowing only those data packets to enter a server that had proper identification, while booting out the rest.

Hackers used port scanning software to locate an open port.

An open port, like a broken lock on a door, was an open invitation to hovering cyber bandits.

Should I tell Andy right away or wait?

Vir exhaled sharply, wishing for answers he did not have.

≈

'I'm glad you are here.' Rads mopped his sweaty brow.

Peevs stepped forward. His hair was in complete disarray, possibly from pulling at it for the past hour.

'So, we redid cyclic redundancy tests to mirror and map out the large data banks.' Rads explained that it was a very complicated form of spot-the-difference.

'Then we actually detected differences between data on the server from the data on the backup server.'

Vir could barely contain his annoyance.

'Yes, it made no sense. We thought it was a virus.'

'Oh yeah?' Disbelief tinged Vir's tone.

Virus. The deadly scourge of the online world, these electronic worms could rip through systems and processes. Every new epidemic, from Stuxnet to Bleeding Heart, attacked new vulnerabilities in machines controllers or computers, stymieing users and geeks for weeks until they unravelled it.

But virus was also a copout. The perfect excuse when issues escalated beyond understanding or control.

'So Rads asked us to check again, do all kinds of tests.'

Vir leaned back, hands in his pockets, and shuffled from foot to foot in nervous irritation. Clearly the team had had time to mull over this, do their tests, and get their story aligned. While, he had swum and watched the sunset and drunk champagne, unaware!

'That's when we discovered the open port.' Peevs had discovered it, quite by accident.

'How was it left open? Was this sabotage?'

'We don't know,' Rads said, tetchily.

It was hard to admit. But in a world of a million possibilities, it was hard to actually pinpoint the truth. Such was the world of cyber crimes. You could never be sure.

'It could be a mistake,' Peevs said.

'Could someone be using this to access our systems, our data?' Vir asked.

Peevs and Rads exchanged a troubled glance.

'We have a hunch,' Peevs said.

Vir's eyebrows rose in question.

'That our data may have been altered.'

It was a bomb which fizzled out without detonation.

Vir remained quiet, unable to even comprehend what Peevs was implying. 'What does that mean?'

'Look, this is just conjecture. But the data grabs over two days did not add up. Now we find an open port. So it's possible that something, some virus, may have entered our systems and infected the data.'

'Oh God!' Vir raked his frantic fingers through his hair.

Data in drug research was sacrosanct. That was what determined progress, proved drug efficacy, allowed the authorities to see effects and after-effects to hand out licences and patents. Data was what enabled the creation of new billion-dollar markets. For data to go out of hand, at a time when the global patent application was due to be submitted in weeks, was simply awful.

'Is it just the data from India, or global data too?'

'Maybe more.'

'All Colare data?'

'I don't know. Maybe beyond.'

'You mean global data from other projects?'

After all, the entire global data centre had been offshored to India a year back. It was the nerve centre of all their corporate knowledge.

Acel had been a late convert. Internal debate had racked the company. Management had been riven. Those opposing the principle of job and information transfer across borders crowed against it. Those with inherent faith in global delivery rooted for low-cost options. Vir had been one of the supporters of the global data centre.

Convincing the insular research team, wary even of its own shadow and protective enough to ban iPods and phones in the research area, had taken longer. Hot arguments had raged. Adam and Andy had refused to see eye to eye. Eventually a compromise had been reached. To start a captive research unit in India, one that could be closely monitored, following a path that would eventually help costs from spiralling up.

For this to happen, then, was a severe blow. To say the least. His personal credibility was in shreds.

Vir strode around Rads' small office, towering above the others, compressing the already compact space. 'Who do you think is entering our systems? Can't you trace it?'

'We will try. But if it's a sophisticated user, he will muddy his electronic trail.'

'He'll *Tor* it,' Peevs said.

'What?'

'It enables online anonymity.'

The Onion Network, called Tor for short, enabled a set of volunteer servers across the world and allowed its users to travserse the internet networks without trace. Entering websites, posting comments and online messages, all the while concealing the identity of the user from the most sophisticated of surveillance technologies. Like layers of an onion, data was encrypted multiple times and then sent across Tor relays in utter secrecy.

As Peevs spoke about this, Vir exhaled. 'I will have to tell Adam and Andy.'

'Should we run another test before you do that?' Rads asked.

Vir shook his head. 'That time is past. We have known of this for a day now. I am amazed Andy has not hounded me with phone calls yet.'

Weekend had started in the US. People were likely with friends and family, hitting the latest jazz bars, throwing ball in the park with their kids, or doing their weekend chores. But come Sunday, pressures of the week would start and calls would come reeling in.

'We have to rule out a virus attack.'

'Is that what you are trying to do now?' Vir's eyes bored into Peevs, then swivelled to pin Rads.

'We are running virus scans and looking at all data sectors in the data server and the back-up server, comparing byte by byte.'

'The backup server!' Vir felt relieved. Surely, it was a matter of restoring backups. It could turn alright.

'I am afraid the backup servers may be affected too.'

Vir did not respond. But his heart sank yet again.

'Have you closed this port then?' he asked.

Peevs shifted uncomfortably in his chair, and exchanged a panicky glance with Rads.

Rads pulled up his pants. 'Vir, I hope you will keep this to yourself for a day or two.'

Peevs leaned forward. 'The thing is, we want to lay a honey trap.'

SATURDAY, 4.00 P.M.

Rockville, Maryland

Spring wore a shroud. The watery sunshine of the day before had disappeared. Clouds curdled the sky in blotches of grey, promising snow, threatening to throw the city in hoary disarray.

Beating the snow predictions by the weatherman, the Acel management team had flicked up the collars of their winter coats and zipped up their featherlite parkas, sped on empty weekend roads to the headquarters, cursing the buffoons across the world whose ineptitude required this unusual weekend meeting.

An emergency conclave to discuss the repercussions of the news from India. Of protected data compromised weeks before the global IP filing.

Tyra Gladstone, assistant to the Chairman, bustled about the large boardroom without her usual burst of energy. She had promised to take her seven-year-old son to a special screening of the *Transformers* at the local mall. As a single mother, these promises meant a lot to her. But Adam had called her in. Hardly a request she could say no to, when her boss – and the single largest shareholder of the company she worked for – wanted work done.

Adam Janlowski, the Chairman, walked in, his brisk confident gait slowed down with age.

'Thanks for coming in, Tyra,' Adam rubbed his ginger beard.

'Trouble, Mr Adam?'

'Maybe. In India.'

As his assistant, Tyra was privy to most decisions.

Andy walked in, exuding brooding energy, and took his seat in the boardroom after a brief nod to Tyra. The rest of the team arrived within minutes. Lara and another member of her team, Peter Lee in dark glasses that contrasted against his sallow skin.

'This is unacceptable.' Andy thumped the table.

He had never hidden his dispproval of the research facility in India. At least, he had squashed Adam's thought of handing out work to some third world outsourcing outfit. Units that promised everything from informatics and molecular chemistry to safe testing upon animals and humans. With fewer laws strangulating the research process, such testing could go faster, but would the data be equally credible before international juries?

'It seems hocus to me,' Andy thundered. 'What are our facilities there? Have we outfitted them with old machines bought at dumping rates?' A large vein along his right temple throbbed prominently.

'You know we built it to mirror our US lab,' Adam said curtly.

'What levels of training and know-how do the staff have?'

'It is headed by someone from Peter's team.' Adam had gone to India for the opening of the lab, and had come back thinking that the new set-up was in good hands.

'Look at all the stories of process violations coming in.'

Jake Livingstone interjected. 'We should review the security levels in India again.'

He had been to India twice. To set up the data centre network and then to set up the research lab. He had sent routine manuals to the local team, but to what degree were the rules followed, he did not know. 'I want to confirm that security protocol is actually followed.'

'Research should never have been sent out to India,' Andy said, fuming, his deep-set eyes flashing darkly.

'Sad situation. It shouldn't have happened,' Peter Lee slurred in his strong accent.

No one looked at Peter.

'Utter disregard for brand image,' Andy spat out.

Adam listened to them for a few minutes, letting them vent. He looked kindly and spent. Thin veins criss-crossed his papery face and wrinkled hands. He looked approachable, but his voice was authoritative. He still commanded the sole grip upon Acel. A successor would have to be appointed sometime soon, groomed and cosseted. In fact, the board was stuck on the issue of planning his succession, but they just hadn't found the ideal candidate yet.

Adam felt a bit sad to hear Andy talk about the brand. None knew more about creating the brand than him. He had lived and breathed it for four decades, but always from the perspective of creating something new, experimenting, being inspired to help those in sickness and in need, bettering the products created. Never from the ossified view of brand preservation.

'These are all valid concerns, gentlemen and ladies,' he said. 'We should do a due review on processes being followed in India. But first, I want to understand the legal ramifications.'

Adam looked at Lara.

Lara Andrews, in a red power suit, even for an emergency weekend meeting, looked straight at Adam. 'I cannot comment if there will be material consequences yet, without understanding the extent of this data problem.' Her voice sounded deadpan. 'The international patent filing deadline is next month. Five weeks away to be precise. In fact, Martha here has been working on the details of the application submission.'

Martha, a younger and softer version of Lara, in a mauve twinset, gave a vague smile. 'The Paris Convention allows us to file the global patent application within twelve months of filing the US patent and retain the US priority date. The deadline is next month. We will submit the application one week before the deadline.'

'Why wait so long?' Andy asked impatiently. He could never see eye to eye with Legal upon their due processes. He viewed them as pond scum, immaterial to the biological activity below the water.

'We have filed the provisional applications in different countries. But you know we always wait to improve our products between filings.' Martha spoke slowly and clearly. She knew of Andy's reputation as a hot-headed fanatic.

It was complicated, actually. Companies waited for a few months after filing the patent in their home country to further the research and see if the results changed, so that they could tilt the patent application accordingly. If the description changed too much, the priority date of the original application might not hold. So it was crucial to start with as broad a description of the new product and its production process as possible. Circular patenting allowed companies to lock in every variation, every angle, in effect picket-fencing a competitor from the territory. Local attorney partners had to be deployed in these markets, further adding to the time, complexity and cost of the entire process.

There really was no universal global patent either. Rather, companies had to file a series of patents in different regions of the world they wished to operate in. Adding to the complexity was the fact that several countries, especially in the emerging world, allowed process patents. Patent protection was not available against copycat products, made with just a slight variation in the manufacturing process. It defied the spirit of intellectual property rights. But the risk remained.

Lobbyists and international trade institutions were working hard at changing these legal frameworks. Indian laws had recently changed. An old act granting process patent had been repealed and global pharma and biotech firms operating in the region had breathed a sigh of relief. But there was always the threat of compulsory licensing for life-saving medicines. Like Acel's products.

'Where are the competitors at?' Andy asked.

The usual global patent searches were done regularly, to see if competition was warming up. No one had filed a patent on a similar product yet. But two other companies were working on a similar idea of grafting a gene onto a stem cell. One in Saarbrücken, Germany, and one in Guangzhou, China.

'Both the German and the Chinese firms have got patents in their home countries.'

'Ignore China,' said Andy. 'Hardly the hotbed of innovation.'

'You can't be sure,' Lara said. 'But we've been watching Karl Gütenbach, the chief scientist in the Saarbrücken firm.'

Unbeknownst to Karl, his prior publications and new blogposts were being studied carefully to elicit any clues.

'That's fine. But why can't you expedite the filing?' Andy asked.

'It is a lot of paperwork.' Acel had decided to file in seven countries as a start. Each of these dossiers needed to be complete in accordance with local laws and terminologies, with reference to local precedents.

'Four weeks is too long. Put more teams on the job.'

'We've already done that. Even so, it would take two weeks. We don't have deep bench strength. We are going to outsource some work.'

'That word again!' Andy roared. It seemed the scourge of twenty-first-century existence, which took work away from Western workers, whether for lack of qualified bench strength, as Lara mentioned, or for better profitability, as Adam had done before.

Lara raised an eyebrow, clearly not amused by Andy's theatrics. 'We have a team of freelance experts in California and Boston that we typically use when we need help.'

'Any chance the Germans can file something in the next two weeks?' Adam asked.

'I doubt it.' Lara's snoops sent her briefings on a routine basis. No burst of activity had emerged in Saarbrücken.

'Can we just use the US data to file globally?'

'Will just the US data be enough?' Peter asked hesitantly.

'The large volume of data is more for our own sake, to show more safe and repeatable results. FDA is more interested in these details than a global patent officer,' Lara elaborated. 'So, yes, we could use the US data only.'

Peter nodded thoughtfully.

As the team filed out, Adam stood at the picture window that framed a perfect pre-storm sight. Tall evergreens and deciduous trees rocking in the rising squall against a silver sky.

It was a bad situation, at best, bringing out hidden agendas and rivalries to the fore. Vir had been on Adam's radar as someone who was willing to take risks. But had he gone too far?

Work never stressed Adam. He had seen worse upheavals in his forty years at Acel, from the bacterial contamination scares of the seventies to the automation failures in the eighties to the prohibitive costs of the nineties.

There had to be a way forward.

SUNDAY, 6.00 A.M.

Bandra, Mumbai

Vir pounded the empty promenade of Carter Road, one Nike-encased foot lightly touching the ground, knee flexing and the other foot reflexively leaping through the air.

Waves swished against the stones lining the foreshore, their lapping the only sound at this hour.

He turned inwards, going slightly uphill, puffing upon roads that suddenly seemed broad when bereft of people and makeshift stalls. Every now and then, tucked within the mossy fronds of jasmine creepers and bougainvillea, he spied old Victorian bungalows, their fluted columns and arched windows now decrepit, narrowly hanging on to their existence in the face of modernity.

In a street corner, men in checkered sarongs sat shuffling piles of newspapers, inserting leaflets and handing them to tattered boys. A lorry was unloading crates of milk packets. Up ahead, the heavy bulk of the Bandra–Kurla flyover snaked towards the Bandra–Worli Sea Link.

Vir ran towards the Reclamation area, where an oblique glow was lightening the dark envelope of the night. He watched the orange essence seep across in a thin line, diffuse up and down in graded shades of vermilion to gold, tingeing the sky, tinkling upon the water, rendering it ablaze. Light splintered across every surface, the jagged rays making the entire panorama glitter like gold.

Just the wonderment of a beautiful sunrise – a rare sight in Mumbai – made Vir look at possibilities. Today was another day. After a quick breakfast, leaving Tracey asleep, Vir drove out to join Ali for a meeting with a private detective.

Jasoos Detective Agency was a narrow street-fronted shop off a crowded stretch of S.V. Road. Flanked by a toy shop and the crammed display window of a shoe shop, it neatly disappeared.

Vir and Ali sat on black office chairs, contemplating the portly round-faced man with a thin moustache, who had just handed them a card that said:

Sunny Singh, Proprietor
Jasoos Detective Agency Private Limited.
Missing Persons. Cheating Spouses. Lying Employees.
Trusted since 1996.

Vir felt unsure.

They had googled detective agencies in Mumbai, called the few listed in the western suburbs and arrived at the one place willing to open on a Sunday morning. To find a tiny shop crammed with cheap posters of snoops and private eyes from Hollywood flicks, and a dusty steel filing cupboard filled with box folders. There was a decrepit-looking computer on the steel desk, zipped inside a thick plastic cover.

How inept can he be? Vir thought, as he forwarded a printout of the hiring application form of Jitendra Kumar Jadhav.

'This is a temp worker we had. Cleaning staff. He has been missing for two days.'

Sunny Singh raised one eyebrow. There had to be more information than what the man was giving out. No one tracked missing cleaning staff. Must be a swindle job! Missing money. *No matter. He would ferret it out.*

SUNDAY, 8.00 P.M.

Bandra, Mumbai

Tracey sat on the terrace of Vir's apartment, staring blankly at the dark horizon beyond the moonlit sea. Vir had still not returned home, after stopping by briefly for lunch.

A beautiful night breeze rushed in, rustling the potted palms. Occasional peals of laughter wafted up from the swimming pool of the building next door. In the living room, a business channel was blaring. Not that Tracey was listening to the news. But television was company.

She fumbled to strike a match, the phosphorus flaring in the shadows. She lit a votive and placed it in a mirror-encrusted bowl. The door to the apartment opened and Vir walked in, looking exhausted, his shirt rumpled, evening stubble on his jaw. He gave her a smile from the distance.

Tracey walked inside stiffly, refusing to smile back.

'Hey. Bad day,' Vir said, apologetically. After reviewing security procedures with Ali, he had written a status report for Andy and Jake, then driven to the data centre.

'Why don't you freshen up, sit outside for a bit,' Tracey said, moving towards him. He looked handsome, even dishevelled and stressed, the faint lines just adding allure. But she did not want to thaw so easily.

'I still have a report to write,' Vir rotated his neck, trying to loosen the stiff nerves.

'Your cook made some snacks. Relax for some time.'

'Sounds good. I'm famished.' He smiled and sank into the sofa.

Tracey looked outside, wistfully. The flickering candle had created a hushed bower of light. She recalled the beautiful Cape Cod cottage in Vermont they had rented for a skiing trip last year. After an exhilarating day at the slopes, they had cuddled by an open log fire, when Vir had proposed unexpectedly. She moved her hand. Her two-carat engagement ring flashed. Yearning filled her. For that perfect moment, that intensity they had felt for each other that evening, that complete exclusion of outside reality.

'I'll pour some wine.' She turned to face him.

Vir sat slumped on the sofa, staring at some ad on the television screen.

Feeling irritated, she went to the kitchen and carried platters of food, wine and flutes to the terrace. *Keep it light*, she said to herself. *Not wedding plans*, she told herself mentally. *Not India versus America*. Topics that dominated her mind. Topics that could not be resolved tonight. Exhaling deeply, she went to call him.

He lay sprawled, watching the same ad again. Some earnest-looking girl inviting people to watch the 'Jaago India Hour with Diti Rajan', sponsored by a major tea brand.

'Vir.'

He kept staring at the screen, lost to her.

'Vir,' Tracey called out louder.

He looked up flustered, took in Tracey, standing arms on hips, looking hostile.

'I'm sorry, darling,' he said and stood up, his face softening. 'I feel guilty. You're here. And here I am, stuck in this bloody mess.'

She stepped away curtly. 'You can try to let go, perhaps?'

SUNDAY, 9.00 P.M.

Bandra, Mumbai

Sandman walked fast, head down. He was skinny. His dark skin glistened in the much-sieved brightness from the low-wattage lamps inside the chawl homes and tin-roofed squat dwellings that lined the lane. His curly hair fell messily around his face. He swept a furtive look about him, swung his slipping backpack up on his shoulder, and continued walking.

The tall lit spire of a church dominated the main road behind him. The hush broken by the sounds of cable television serials and dance shows coming from the chawls and hutments. A few men sat outside a corner paan shop, playing cards. A naked young child played on the street, while a figure wrapped in a muddied shroud, possibly a parent, lay next to him. He stopped in front of an almost invisible alcove between two shop fronts. A small board was hung above the mezzanine space. It read Caress Massage Parlour. He fumbled in his pocket, took out his phone to verify the address he had noted down. This was it.

He glanced back at the men. They still looked busy in their card game. He took one shallow breath and disappeared into the dimness, almost running up a narrow staircase to reach an unlit landing. He pressed a buzzer next to the rickety door, still huffing, and waited to be let inside. His heart beat a strange tattoo, a mixture of anticipation and anxiety.

The room inside was red, from the red cellophane-covered bulbs that lit the room. The boy inhaled deeply. The room smelled sickly sweet. Like burnt jaggery. Shahnewaz, the owner of Caress Massage Parlour, stood at the door, looking flinty-eyed. His mouth was a permanently red-stained thin line beneath a straight henna-dyed moustache. The boy hardly looked like a paying customer. In fact, barely legal age.

Shahnewaz put his hands on his hips and barked, 'What is it?'

'I have a delivery,' the boy mumbled blankly. 'For Mir.' That was the name he had been told to give.

Shahnewaz gave him a measuring look, led the boy inside and locked the door behind him.

'*Dekhoon toh sahi.*' He was curious to see what was to swap hands for which he had to give a fat brown paper-covered bundle.

The boy fished out a small plastic packet from his backpack. He opened it, laid out four small square objects in colour-blocked grey and chrome.

Shahnewaz stood, brow raised, not comprehending the thin bricks. The size of the bundle indicated it contained notes of *thousands*. For these silly little things? 'What is this?'

'Storage devices,' said the boy.

Shahnewaz narrowed his eyes.

'Computer stuff,' the boy added.

Shahnewaz nodded. He knew about computers, even if he himself had never used one. Each box had a name: *Seagate*. Some information worth lots to someone. The money had reached him through a complicated network. A boy in Bhiwandi, who lived near a trucking station, was a regular at arranging shipments for Shahnewaz. Cash, usually in crisp numbered bundles, travelled thousands of miles in those trucks, taped inside bonnets, underneath greasy pipes or sewn inside hard matted coir seats. Sometimes, girls came too, hidden behind stacks of regular shipment. Passing through several state excise checkpoints and city *naka* toll booths.

This particular bundle had come on a truck from Guwahati, inside the salwar lining of a thin girl. The girl was Bengali from a tiny border village outside Dimapur. Not for him the doe-eyed sylphs from Manipur. The visitors of his parlour liked girls with bigger boobs. 'You have the cash?' the boy asked.

Shahnewaz was jolted from his reverie, and gave him a red-toothed smile. He walked over to the small sunmica-covered desk, fished out a key from a chain on his neck and opened a drawer. He took out a brown paper-wrapped bundle, held it in his palm, tossing it up a few times, as if feeling its weight and looked at the boy wonderingly. He lobbed it across, at the boy, who stumbled but caught it.

'Count it,' Shahnewaz said.

The boy nodded. His heart was racing, his fingers cold. Never had he been paid so much for his skills. But, that was how it was in the wide interconnected online world. If you had skills, and you let it be known, you could make money. Real money in the real world. Why care for real-world employers, who verified degrees and assessed English-speaking skills?

He tore open a side, licked his thumb with his tongue, flicked the thousand-rupee notes, and counted. Two hundred.

He looked up. Shahnewaz was watching him, a wicked red crescent of a smile on his face, a plotting look in his beady eyes.

'Here.' He moved forward easily, fishing out a cigarette.

The boy stood frozen.

'*Kya*, never had a cigarette?' Shahnewaz winked. 'Try. It's free. I made good commission from whatever this is.'

Shahnewaz had indeed made a small packet himself. Now he would give these computer bits to his intermediary. Perhaps they would travel north again, to Guwahati, then to Dimapur. After that the trail got fuzzy. But Shahnewaz hardly cared where it went. It was clearly not a weapon. Neither gold. Nor white powder.

'Here, try it.' He lit the cigarette with a lighter and slipped it into the boy's hands.

He took a puff. Smoke filled his mouth, his nose, his stomach, burning his insides, scratching his nerve endings. He coughed. Looked at Shahnewaz dazedly, the smoke getting into his head, his brain.

Shahnewaz's lips curled into a half smile. 'Want to try a girl?' he asked, looking at the spindly curly-haired boy, clearly at unease just talking to him. 'Just five notes from your bundle,' he added in a soft encouraging voice.

MONDAY, 1.00 A.M.

Goregaon, Mumbai

'We just traced an intrusion from Croatia.'

Rads had called Vir with this dramatic announcement just after nine. The intrusion had lasted mere seconds, then stopped.

But Vir had rushed back to the Goregaon office, leaving a fuming Tracey behind. He sat occupying the small office, blearily staring at his laptop, writing out another report for Andy and Adam.

Which meant that Rads had to hang around as well.

An internet call flashed on Rads's screen. Jake's grainy face appeared on the screen. 'Rads. How's it going, man?'

'Going on,' Rads mumbled. One more reason why Rads was chained to his desk. With so many persistent callers wanting updates, be it night or day, it would be impossible to explain remote monitoring. He said patiently, for what he thought was the fiftieth time, 'We are comparing the data not just for the Colare project, but also for all of our projects.'

'Have you transferred Colare data to an offline drive?'

'It's under way.'

'Hi Jake,' Vir jumped in. 'Can't we switch off the server?'

Jake wavered. 'Even if we do shut down the servers tonight, tomorrow we'd need the network back up again.'

Someone would complain if they brought down all the servers indefinitely, while they probed this current problem. Customers still understood if a site was down. But Acel's own researchers would kick up a fuss if he shut off the data tap. 'Let's hold on. Take that decision later.'

After Jake ended the call, Vir let out a shaky breath. 'Jake did not ask about the open port.'

'It's an open secret. If his analysts dig any, they'll find it,' Rads responded glumly.

Vir knew he was courting danger by not telling Jake. Not just to the firm. But to himself as well. If heads had to roll, the first would be his. 'Let's track this intruder first. Then we'll tell Jake. I have a hunch he may not be in Croatia.'

Rads decided to take a walk. Clear his head a bit. The team was camping in the office, fed on yet another round of pizzas and Coke. With enough sugary supplies to last the night.

Peevs sat at his desk, taking a break, listening to Black Eyed Peas on his earphones, eating a large slice of a brownie. A scan ran in the background, but the screen was open to a game. One of the perks of working in back-end tech support. He loved his work, loved debugging the viral logic of malicious codes, and mostly self-monitored himself. But when scans ran in the background, he felt no flicker of guilt in playing a game. Who policed the police anyway?

Peevs was an undisputed master of *Shogun 2*, adept at making strategic moves and thinking three steps ahead of his adversaries. The battle siege ended in flames of destruction and victory. The tall bulging Yoshitomo retired to his tent to the ministrations of Masami, his screen Geisha Avatar. Just as the nubile Masami pulled the red ribbons to undo her bun, letting her sleek long raven hair fall upon her shoulders and looked up from the screen with wide-lashed eyes, moving her hands to undo the obi of her mauve silk kimono embroidered with white chrysanthemums, Peevs felt a hand upon his shoulder.

'What, what?' he muttered exasperatedly. A million battle points and many scars had to be gained to earn the pleasure of a Geisha.

'Hot move, eh?' Vir grinned at him.

'Oh Vir,' Peevs said, sounding flustered. 'Just a short break. But scans are running in the background.'

'Don't stop on my count.' Vir went back inside.

With a sigh, Peevs stole one quick look at Masami slipping out of her kimono to reveal a blushing pink under-kimono and with a heavy heart, exited the game.

One of the young programmers came up to Peevs. 'This is not making sense.'

'What happened?'

'My head is swimming! I have mapped the two data sets a million times. I swear my eyes are dancing now. Maybe, I missed this before. Or miscalculated.' Doubt wavered in his expressive eyes.

'What are you saying?'

'Yesterday there was a ten per cent mismatch between the two data banks. It doesn't make sense. But it's twenty per cent mismatch now.'

'What?'

Additional ten per cent mismatch in a day? Had the intruder released a virus? Was it now spreading from sector to sector, erasing correct data, overwriting the databank with gibberish? How else could data mismatch increase so rapidly?

'We must hook off the backup server, then back it up once more into a new offline server. Store the Colare data separately. We should have done it earlier.'

'It's a virus then? Is there a signature?'

'Don't know. I need to dig some more. It might be due to that intrusion from Croatia through the open port!'

Peevs looked at Vir sitting on the other side of the glass cubicle. He started to get up, to inform him. Suddenly another young techie rose from his seat, waving frantically. Peevs ran over. Vir rushed from the inner chamber.

'Boss,' the youngster whispered in awe. 'We have another intrusion. But the IP address is from Kyrgyzstan.'

SUNDAY, 5.00 P.M.

Gaithersburg, Maryland

Mystic Mir stood in his barren sideyard, took a puff of his hand-rolled cigarette with trembling fingers and watched smoke freeze into a swirl against the darkening sky. His fingertips were browned from nicotine stains.

A strong tarry odour surrounded him these days, as he snuck out again and again to the designated smoking area at the office

'You stink, man,' a colleague had said yesterday.

Emotions were not something he usually expressed. Or, even felt. Except lately, control was wilting. And he found himself fishing out and cataloguing hurts from the recesses of his memory. Plans gone awry. Friendships never developed. Brief moments of attraction unexpressed or unrequited. Expectations not met. Remembered with all the precision of scientific enquiry.

Yet, once remembered, clinical dispassion deserted him. Along came anger. Anxiety. Then, he crushed them away. He needed a methodical approach. Making his plans. Alone. Quiet. Wanting recompense.

Inhaling deeply, he felt his internal tremor subside a little as the smoke filled his lungs. He dropped the stub on the withered grass and crushed it.

Inside, his house was fairly basic. Just as it had been for years since his father had set it up with cheap furniture and cheaper decorations. The only thing that seemed to grow was his wall of books, mostly technical tomes, and the cornucopia of gadgets in his home study.

That's where he went, to his large desk by the slatted window, mind tick-tocking, running scenarios, visualizing actions and plans. He fired his large-screen computer, logged in and as always, ran a scan for open servers. After two hops from his own service provider to random open servers located in Paris and Bangladesh, he connected to the dump server in Romania. One that he had paid for from his newly accumulated stash of bitcoins.

Bitcoins, started as crypto-currency amid digital enthusiasts, a veiled exchange on an open source platform, had proved to be handy. His payments had come easily, without the taxman asking questions. Yet.

Its anonymous developer with the alias of *Satoshi Nakamoto* could not have imagined bitcoins would catch on like wildfire among cyber enthusiasts, who solved complex problems to mine the currency. With the bitcoin exchanges awash with hustlers and black marketers, regulators had started to hover. *Mystic Mir* knew he could not trust in technology completely. The more he learned about the mutli-tentacled spread of online transactions, the more he understood how easily it could be tampered with and misused.

So he had converted the bulk of his crypto-coins into silver then converted it back to bitcoins on another exchange, not worrying about the conversion losses. He had spoofed an identity, created a spurious bank account in Hanoi, connected it to the new bitcoin exchange, converted digital money into real money and transferred it to a nested account in a regional bank in Haiphong.

Silently, he scrolled through the directories on the Romanian dump server, each with its own pin code. He smiled. Even rogues wanted their privacy. He clicked on the account that he had created and typed in his password to access his rented space. Terabytes of space. His personal virtual hideaway.

An auto-dating subroutine tagged each stream of data transfer. Something he had coded. Not that coding was his special forte. But he had gone through a hacking phase in college. He had simply brushed up old tricks and learned some new ones. It was logic in the end. Whether he applied it to one domain or another.

He checked the data on the server. A new batch of files had

been uploaded. The files from the day before had been checked out, copied off the dump server.

Good job, he thought mentally of his new recruit. Someone he had found through a mini-quest. Someone he had instructed through emails that were never sent. Seemed like a young guy. You could never tell for sure. Just something in the language in the few emails they had exchanged.

Mystic Mir felt excitement course through him.

The plan is on.

MONDAY, 11.00 A.M.

Bandra, Mumbai

'*Arre*, still asleep?'

Sandman felt himself being hauled out of deep sleep. Feeling sluggish, he opened one eye and shut it again. Brightness crept in from the sides of the plastic curtain. Like a burning ring of fire eclipsing the door.

'Get up, get up.' His mother pulled the thin sheet off him.

Sandman curled up, wanting a few more minutes of sleep, to let the movie reel of last night play in his mind. Getting paid, and then getting laid. He stifled a giggle, wondering if he should share it with his friends.

His mother burst into a cough that had been persisting for a few days. He sighed and slowly sat up.

'That cough is still there.' He eyed her sleepily. She looked haggard in her old sari, her well-oiled hair in a neat bun at her nape.

'I work with water all day.' She rubbed her throat. 'How will it go quickly?'

'Are you taking your medicines?'

'Of course, I am.' She sat on the edge of the bed. 'But the doctor has asked you to meet her this evening.'

'Why?' *Sandman* asked, thinking perhaps the doctor might want to prescribe more medicines. For once, he felt calm when thinking of money. For years, he had felt the hopelessness of his circumstances, held back by his government school education and lack of good spoken English. For years, he had honed his one skill, discovered by chance while working in the corner mobile and computer repair shop, earning meagre rupees. Today was different. He could spend.

'Maybe new medicines,' he told his mother. 'Don't worry. I will also buy you a new sari today. I got some extra money.'

'That little money from the corner shop turns your head, beta,' his mother said. 'Get that certificate. It will make your life.'

So she thinks. *Sandman* grinned. He had had nowhere to go but enrol in a low-cost vocational training course which taught him less than what he already knew. Would that certificate then transform his life?

He got up. 'I'm learning lessons from life.'

'You will regret it later.'

'Never.' He smiled, full of optimism. His skills were going to make his life. He knew it.

MONDAY, 12.00 NOON

Andheri, Mumbai

'Just one more shot. Turn to the left. Good.'

Vir felt a stab of annoyance at the photographer. He wanted nothing else but to shut the door to his office. But the interview and the shoot had been scheduled weeks in advance.

He quickly posed as told, appearing nonchalant. As the shoot wrapped up, Vir quickly called Rads for an update. *Nothing further.*

Vir felt restlessness return. And exhaustion. He had sent Rads home in the wee hours, and snoozed on the sofa in the data centre after mindlessly trolling YouTube for teasers of Diti's show. Ignoring the stream of messages from Tracey, he had reached the office early morning. She would be asleep now, and he had regular business to manage. Clients to meet. Emails to send. *How futile it seemed when such uncertainty hung over Colare!*

Ali walked in with a sheep-faced Shrishti.

'What happened?'

'Why don't you share it, Shrishti?' Ali encouraged.

Shrishti held her head high. 'You know the data we collect from daily samples of tissue culture of control and infected mice. I used to make a note of some key variables.'

Scientific enquiry demanded a clear tabulation of clinical and pathological variables in animals with different virulence and spread of tumours, to chart the effect of different doses of a medicine. Or in late-stage research, as in Colare, auto-recording the response across specimens over time.

Vir frowned. Given strict security protocols, employees were forbidden from maintaining any notes or documentation. What process rules had been omitted now?

'Well, not all data, Vir, you can understand. The files are so huge,' Shrishti said, speaking fast. 'Just some daily readings. I meant no harm.'

'And?' Vir stared at her.

'So I checked the data that Ali sir has got from the US against the readings for last week that I had recorded in my notebook. The numbers are different. There is a mismatch.'

'Rads and his staff detected as much over the weekend.'

'We can verify the data with my notebook. Prove to the US that we did not do any process errors,' Shrishti stated plaintively.

Vir's heart sank. Yes, partial hand-recorded data could be proof. But dare he share it at this stage? When there were clear global instructions on information storage and retrieval? Wasn't it indicative of broad-scale ineptitude in the country! *How could I have been so oblivious? How could Ali?*

'The less we say about it the better.'

'Another thing...' Ali began.

There was more? Vir looked from Shrishti to Ali.

'The thing is, Vir.' Shrishti wrung her hands now. 'This notebook was in my bag.'

'You mean it had been leaving this building with you everyday?'

'Yes, but...' Shrishti plodded on. 'It was a new notebook. The other three notebooks with data from the past three months were in my drawer.'

'Were?' Vir stared at her incredulously.

'They are missing, Sir. I can't find them.'

MONDAY, 6.00 P.M.

Bandra, Mumbai

'What?' *Sandman* stared at the doctor, an odd vacant look in his eyes, his mind refusing to comprehend what she was saying.

'I know this is hard. I wanted to tell you face to face.' The doctor looked into his eyes steadily.

He stared back, his slack jaw and spaced-out teeth giving him a slightly-demented air. 'How could it be?' he croaked.

'Idiopathic,' she offered, not taking her eyes off him. There was no explanation she could give. Except share the report, in black-and-white print, showing the protein marker off the normal limit, the biopsy result marked *Positive*.

Sandman looked down at the report, willing the letters to reform and change.

'Look at me,' the doctor said.

He kept looking down. He would never be happy again. Ever. He knew that. Trouble was pressing upon him, crushing all joy, singeing reality, crumbling him like burnt cinder.

'You have to be strong.'

Strong? He could not lift his eyelids, a terrible lethargy drowned him. Hope, that fleeting, almost tangible thing he had caught just this morning, had fluttered away on flimsy wings. How could he be strong when he knew what was to come? He remembered his father. What was to come, but that same very end, of limbs warped in relentless pain, the cough whooping into a wet wheeze, the pallor of skin as it lost elasticity, crumpling on itself like paper. There had been two of them then. Taking turns, crying on the other's shoulder. How would he manage now, alone?

'There are some injections,' the doctor offered, ineffectually patting his hands with her cold fingers.

He kept staring at his hands.

'Look up,' she said again.

'You will have to tell her. If you want, I can explain it to her.'

He sagged further, trying to control an involuntary shiver. How could they tell her? She would break before her time. Once she knew what lay within her, what was eating her alive from within, how many days or weeks before she succumbed to the inevitable despair?

'You can't,' he croaked, refusing to look up. 'Just give her the injections. Just give them. I have the money. I have it. Just give her the injections. But please don't tell her.'

MONDAY, 7.00 P.M.

Mira Road, Mumbai

Sunny Singh tied a handkerchief over his nose, as he walked from the Mira Road train station to the narrow lanes behind Anand Hospital and Indra Hospital.

The train had been crammed with daily workers. He had battled sweat and grime to cling to a pole at the door, one leg inside and the other precariously hanging over the tracks as the train sped past stations and suburbs. Anything for a whiff of fresh air. He had been glad to hop off.

But the bustle continued outside the station. Vadapav sellers did brisk business. A group of girls in shiny garish salwars hung around, chatting, eating vadapavs. A slimy-looking boy sidled past, brushing deliberately against one of the girls. Immediately the entire gang assaulted him with their shiny fake-leather purses.

Sunny Singh smiled and moved on.

'Which way to Anand Hospital?' he asked a paanwallah.

He had traced the address of the chawl where Jitendra Kumar Jadhav shared a room with four men. He had waited till evening to make sure one of the residents would be home.

After several twists and turns, asking another paanwallah on the way, he arrived at a ramshackle building. As expected, it was dark, unpainted, with thick bars across small square windows and a steep unlit staircase that went up.

Sighing, Sunny Singh took out a slim torch from his pocket and ascended the staircase. Huffing, he arrived on the fourth floor landing and moved along the narrow corridor to room number 413.

The door was partially open. The room was barely large enough to house one man, leave alone five! Someone was sleeping on the floor. He knocked on the green-painted door.

The man woke up. 'Who is it?' he asked sullenly.

'Where is Jitendra?' Sunny Singh asked.

The man rubbed his eyes. 'He hasn't come home in two days.'

'Where could he be?'

'How do I know? Maybe he ran away home.'

'He has not gone to his village.' Sunny Singh had traced Jitendra's cousin and through him the number of his uncle. No one had heard from him, or seen him. 'So, any ideas? Otherwise, *bhai*, the local inspector is my friend.'

'So go to him,' the man spat.

'Or I could go to the ACP too,' Sunny Singh said camly.

'Why are you troubling me, *babu*? If I knew anything I would have told you.'

This wasn't leading anywhere. Sunny Singh tried another tactic. 'Where could he have gone? Any friends?'

'Try New Friends Bar behind the station.'

Sunny Singh stood in front of New Friends Bar, a quiet-looking establishment with a guard manning the entry. The inside was neon blue and dark. A handful of men sat at the tables, small glasses in front of them. Perhaps Monday night attracted fewer clients. But what struck him as odd were the curtained cubicles in the back. There was a rustle inside one of them. Someone was in there.

What was this place?

Curious, he started moving towards the cubicle. Suddenly a brawny hand held him in place.

'Kya, bhai? Where?'

'What's going on?' Sunny Singh asked the beady-eyed man, whose thick arm held him back.

'Why?'

Sunny Singh considered his options. He had heard of bars pimping girls. But he would have expected some squatty rooms in the back, not cubicles off the main room! But surely a place like this could never survive without the protection of some local goons. Maybe even the local authorities. He decided to take his chances.

He swished out a 500-rupee note. 'Can I go now?'

The man sniggered. '3000 for a room in the back. 1000 for a cubicle.'

Sunny Singh took out another note, then entered the cubicle. A thin, sickly-looking boy sat inside on a little stool.

'Are you clean?' The boy looked sick. Really sick.

'I have HIV,' the boy said. His thin cotton ganji molded his rickety frame. His shorts displayed spindly legs below. His Adam's apple bobbed as he spoke, his eyes protruding.

What sort of a joint was this? Sunny Singh wiped his brow. 'Have you seen a doctor? Are you being treated?'

The boy threw his head back and laughed, a loud cynical laugh, the motion highlighting his bony shoulderblades. 'My hands are still good. So is my mouth.' He made a suggestive gesture, revealing yellow teeth. 'So, what is it? Don't waste my time otherwise.'

Sunny Singh took a deep breath, his mind full of questions. Like how many people worked here? Boys only or girls too? Where did they live? Why did they continue in the trade after getting sick? He had heard of places like this. *Silent bars*. Desperate girls. Desperate boys. Low-heeled clients.

Maybe Jitendra did come here, perhaps because this is what he could afford. The boy was hardly his concern. He fished out a photograph taken from Jitendra's employment file. 'Ever seen him?'

The boy looked at him. 'Information? Are you a policewallah?'

'Would I give you money if I were?'

'Two thousand rupees, then,' the boy bargained.

'Thousand,' said Sunny Singh.

The boy shook his head. 'Fifteen hundred. Or go.'

Sunny Singh fished out three crisp notes and held them in front of the boy. 'Tell me.'

'He used to come every week. Lonely.'

'Where has he gone?'

The boy shrugged.

'OK did he come to you, or the other boys? Other girls?'

'Boy only.' The boy grinned, taking pleasure in Sunny Singh's discomfiture. 'Sometimes to me, sometimes others.'

'When was the last time he was here?'

'Yesterday,' the boy said. 'There is more,' he added slyly. 'Give me five hundred more and I will tell you.'

Sunny Singh let out a low curse and held his eye as he fished out one more note. He would have to claim it back as expenses, anyway. 'No more. Now tell.'

'He was here when this Chinky came looking for him.'

'Chinky?'

'Maybe Nepali. The man just pulled and dragged him away. He had a knife, it looked like a knife.'

Chinky? Nepali? That was hardly much to go on. The city was full of immigrants from the north-eastern states. It could be anyone.

A dead end. Sunny Singh cursed his luck and went out.

MONDAY, 8.00 P.M.

Andheri, Mumbai

'Let's seal this with a drink,' the safari-suited Mr Kanakia said.

Vir glanced at his watch. It had been a long afternoon, pitching Acel's products to the owner of Kanakia Healthcare, which ran a set of hospitals across Gujrat. Now that the negotiations were done and the deal agreed upon, the man understandably wanted to party.

'I have come down from Amdavad for two days. I cannot eat room service.'

'We could use a drink,' Vir said. 'Its been a tough week.'

'Good, good. Lets have a Scotch or two,' Mr Kanakia said, beaming. Away from the prohibition regime of his hometown, he was eager to swig a peg.

Sleep deprived as he was, Vir longed for nothing more than his bed. Except home had become more like a war zone. The woman he had wanted to marry had been possessed by a forbidding creature, and Vir wasn't sure if he had any patience left to woo her into a better mood. There had been one frosty message from her, then silence. Mr Kanakia was hardly a scintillating dinner partner. But a night about town was better than heading home. He agreed to meet at the hotel later.

He quickly sent a text message to Tracey.

Work dinner with client. Just signed a new deal. Don't wait up, will be late.

An hour later, scrubbed and showered in the office bathroom, dressed in a trendy purple shirt and khakis, Vir stepped inside the glittery suburban hotel. Some minor movie stars tottered about on high heels, unheeded by the other patrons. Crossing the pianist tinkling in the lobby, he went to the restaurant.

'When in Amdavad...' Mr Kanakia was regaling Prashant and Arnab over double pegs of smoky whisky. 'Come, Vir, settle down,' he said, patting an empty chair, then went on to complete a story about his favourite city and its amazingly efficient bureaucratic machinery, the Gujju *babus* aligning business permissions with financing, which had his audience all agog.

Their food arrived – platters of creamy vegetable gratin and saffron-scented vegetable paella and fried greens topped with lemony mayonnaise. It was one of best Tapas restaurants in town, but in deference to Mr Kanakia they had ordered Jain options.

Over dinner Mr Kanakia's one-sided monologue continued, leaving Vir's mind to wander back to Colare and the tech team. *No messages. That was good. Or was he being an ostrich?* He looked at his watch. He should head to Goregaon.

'Someone waiting for you, Vir?'

'His girlfriend is in town,' Prashant said, winking conspiratorially. Not often did he get a chance to rib his boss. But after a few pegs, it was fair game.

'Girlfriend?' Mr Kanakia quizzed. 'You haven't been snapped up and married yet?'

'Et tu,' said Prashant, laughing. 'There are bets going on in the office on his state of singlehood.'

Really? Vir frowned.

'My apologies if I have kept you away from a romantic evening.'

'You haven't,' Vir responded, nonplussed. Like it would have been anywhere close to amorous had he been home. 'Excuse me for a second though,' he said, getting up.

'Yup, you go call her.' Mr Kanakia's voice followed him.

Vir exited the restaurant abstractedly and rounded the corner, when he collided into someone with a cry of 'watch out'.

Vir steadied himself. 'Diti? What are you doing here?'

'You must stop bumping into me in the oddest places,' she joked.

'You must stop being in the oddest places.'

'Oh yeah?' She gave him a wry look, stabbing the errant thought that he looked delicious and fit, the very poster child for executive dressing down.

'Yeah, but so good to *bump* into you. I didn't realize you were going to be back so soon.'

'Yup. Back.' She shifted her long length accentuating her figure-skimming top over flared palazzo pants.

'So good to see you again.' The words shot out before he even thought them. 'You look lovely.'

'Flatterer,' she teased. 'Like it's been ages, right?'

'Maybe. Maybe not. I've been seeing you in your ad on television daily.'

She gave him an odd look. 'Well, I must get back before my friends ditch me.'

'Meet me by the pool in five?' He clasped her wrist, a handcuff buzzing jolts of electricity back to him.

She gave him a quelling look. 'We're going for a pub crawl.'

He wanted to knock away her assuredness. It was maddening. 'Join them late,' he urged. 'Please.'

Diti stood in the shadows, on the far end of the pool, facing the Arabian, in an awning created by dwarf palms and redolent frangipani. Water tinkled nearby from a fountain, drowning out the sounds of the sea.

'It's beautiful here, isn't it,' she said, sensing his presence.

'Beautiful,' he intoned, not that the outdoors were on his mind. 'When the city doesn't crowd in.' How was he to blank out that he had been crazily in love with her once, a level of maddening intensity he had never felt since.

'Why are you partying on a Monday night?' she said. The diffused light from the hotel lit up her beautiful face.

'Work dinner.'

'Hmm. You saw my ad, did you?'

'I have it saved on my phone.' He patted his pocket. He felt foolish admitting it. Bit light-headed.

She gave a flirty smile. 'Wanna come and see the shooting of the opening episode?' She mentioned a prominent politician who was going to be the first guest, sharing his outlook on the current mire holding back the Indian economy.

'It's not live, then?'

'No. Makes it less sensational. But the flexibility of editing wins over stalwart guests.'

'Their PR watchdogs, you mean?'

'Them too. And advertisers. It's a package deal.'

'Would love to. Be there, I mean.'

She nodded.

Silence reigned, amplifying the slow drip of the fountain.

He watched her bundle her long hair and scoop it to one side, baring a slim shoulder, revealing a delicate ear. Why was he so attuned to this woman like some moonstruck teenager, aware of the slow rise of her breath, the way her eyes had widened just a little? He steadied himself.

'I saw you are on Twitter now.'

'Someone is observant. The studio needs me to.'

'You're making up for years of anonymity in one go,' he teased, 'thousands of online admirers in a week.'

'A girl needs some,' she said, smiling, a provocative flash that seared through him. 'Admirers, I mean.'

'You lacked them, you thought?'

He stepped forward, into her space. Half step more, and they would touch. She looked inviting. He was dying to reach his hand out, close the gap. He needed to keep his cool. It was deserting him when he needed it the most.

Blood rushed up to his ears, reality forgotten in the searing intensity of need – for possession and pain, for subjection and worship, for erasing the past and writing the present.

He reached out, clasping her with pent-up emotion, the present forgotten, the lost love and befuddlement of the past, all in a messy writhe. His hands spanned her waist, snaked up, knotting her hair, wrenching it, his lips in a crush of power against hers. How had she let him down then? Carved him out of her life? And how dare she flirt now? He moved in closer, taut against her, his nerves in a thrum. Everything forgotten. Just this moment, him and her, like they had been in Delhi all those years ago. She broke for air, tracing a finger on his cheek. 'I should go now, my friends would be wondering.'

'Yeah.' He stood there, feeling foolish. What was he doing? He shook his head and breathed in the cool night breeze, the balmy air of the sea.

MONDAY, 9.00 P.M.

Antop Hill, Mumbai

'The usual again?' Yunus Ansari said, grinning. His roadside stall did brisk business each evening, selling mutton rolls, kormas, and sheer khurma mostly to local regulars. Paul Zhang was a regular.

'It's the best,' Paul said, smiling. His teeth stained black from chewing tobacco. His black-framed glasses gave him a teacherly air, barely masking the aura of danger around him.

He tore into a rumali roti and scooped up some mutton korma. Three decades of living in Mumbai, and he relished nothing more than the spicy meats of his adopted home. Not that there was anything official about it. Other than an unmarked tombstone less than a kilometre away, where his father was buried.

'One more roti, Paul?' Yunus called out.

'No more,' Paul said, scooping up the last of the mutton from his plate.

His phone vibrated, but he put it on silent without looking. He enjoyed this interlude, this peaceful time between his day job at a men's salon and his other tasks at night. He sat savouring the lingering taste in mouth, then shuffled to wash his hands.

He fished out his phone. It was a fancy model, belying his day earnings. There were no messages, just his alarm.

Time to go.

Paul lit a cigarette and drew in a deep drag. 'Khuda hafiz, Yunus mian,' he called out.

He moved away into the night with stealth and agility, born of his early years. Initiated by his father, he had spent his childhood in the hills and swamps of Manipur, following village poachers, silently moving through the forests. Tiger hunts. Not the loud drumming, fire-torch flourishing kind of a hunt. No, theirs was a silent kill. Alert, full of nervous energy released in one snap of a precise bullet. Once the tiger had been killed, his father would pay off the villagers and work swiftly through the tiger's body, dismembering the claws and the penis, skinning the fur, taking out the organs. Each part served a different purpose, had a medicinal use. Worth thousands of dollars.

Tiger and other animal parts then found their way to the border. They were swapped for mini assortments of pistols and rifles with Burmese insurgents and sachets of opium powder, and made their onward journey to the hustle and bustle of the Ta Chi Lek market along the Mekong, and from there wending their way up the river into Yunnan.

Managed by the network of Blue Lanterns working for the 14K.

It was a way of life. Harsh, elemental. But it paid well.

After a brush with a tigress in the Kasom hills had left him injured and less nimble, his father had to choose another way of life. Sam Zhang had escaped Yunnan as a child and gone back only once. To get married. He knew he could never fit back in there again. He took a one-way train trip to Mumbai without a ticket. He was already in his late forties.

Paul, who had never been to school, picked up a job in a salon as a sweeper and worked his way up to become a master stylist, and taught himself to read and write on the side.

But members of his father's Triad had found him. Led by a master infiltrator, borders became porous, and Paul found himself making the long trip across land and up the Chindwin river, to the rugged hills and plunging gorges of Yunnan. He had no childhood memories. But the beauty of the region exhilarated him. He had taken his oaths in a beautiful room lined with medallions and swords in a hidden back lane in Chongqing.

Now he had a flourishing side profession. He sought danger of another sort. One that involved drugs, human trafficking and breaking in. Linked into a shadowy network of middlemen from Mumbai to Manipur and beyond.

He fished out his mobile again and scrolled through his

messages. He paused on the one he was looking for. It had instructions.

An address. The patent office near Antop Hill.

A name. A certain Mr Dhumade working in the building.

A file. For some patent application of a drug.

Paul moved briskly now. His was not to question, but to follow instructions.

TUESDAY, 1.00 A.M.

Goregaon, Mumbai

The rack of servers and routers blinked and hummed. The scans went on interminably. The honey trap remained set, the port still open. But there had been no new intrusions since last night.

Peevs was tired of waiting.

He had barely slept in days, catching winks glued to his chair and finally unrolling a sleeping bag under his desk at 2 a.m. His hair stood on its ends now, greasy, spiky.

'Go home, Peevs,' Vir said, coming up behind him. 'You stink.'

Peevs glanced at Vir, looking tired but well groomed, his stubble adding a certain jauntiness. 'I was thinking of checking the file logs. Check who all have been accessing the Colare server these past few days.'

'Wouldn't that be crazy? Researchers logging in and out.'

'There might be a pattern.'

'Check on it, then.' Vir went over the cubicle. He had co-opted it as his night office. He had to be here, he felt compelled. With the team. Or maybe he was just avoiding Tracey. Not that they'd spend much time together, defeating the purpose of her trip. Conversation had fumbled and bitterness had crept in now. He had started feeling claustrophobic. Like a thick blanket had been flipped on him, blanking out all joy.

Vir settled on the sofa. He had spent years studying bioengineering and then business. Infotech was a deep dive now. He read instruction manuals to understand the details of Acel's multi-tiered security firewalls and encryptions. He called jittery youngsters from the floor to understand the coding and the protocols. He still felt he was swimming in the depths.

Outside, Peevs munched on a stale pizza. His fingers typed rapidly, opening various systems screens, typing instructions and watching the spew of data. He checked the system log file to see which IP addresses had logged in over the past two days and tallied it against another dataset of dynamic IP addresses allocated to various authorized users.

At three in the morning, Vir left, his body aching, unwilling to spend another night on the sofa. 'Call me as soon as you find anything.'

Peevs nodded absently, lost in his tallies. There were multiple log ins from the usual suspects. Ali, Jake, Andy, Terry. Most of all Peter. The man lived and breathed Colare. Then there were twenty-two accesses to the system by IP addresses assigned to someone called Dr Lauren Sandler.

Who was she? Peevs had never heard of her. In just a couple of days, he had come to know the entire cast of characters involved in Colare research, including technicians and lab assistants. Dr Lauren Sandler's name had not cropped up.

'Hey, check this out,' he called out to a teammate. 'Is she a new researcher?'

They tracked her logs in the Colare database. All odd times, including the weekend. Each night someone had hacked in.

'That's a pattern,' the team member observed. She was clearly working late nights. Or, what was the off-peak time in the US, after the day's work ended.

Peevs logged in as admin and accessed the System Access Control List. Access was given after a strict approval process. A physical form had to be signed, scanned and submitted for each person. People had access to different parts of the system. Lab assistants and technicians could upload data and retrieve only what they uploaded. Some executives had access to only the data summaries and reports. Only the lead researchers could access all the data. There was a list of clinical researchers signed up for Colare. They could upload their data in Acel-provided formats, and retrieve only what they uploaded. Peevs found Dr Lauren Sandler on the list.

'Damn,' he muttered. There had to be a mistake. 'She had full access to all the data.'

'How is that even possible? This is so strictly controlled.'

'Who authorized Sandler's account?'

Peevs typed in another request, and the machine spat out the digital authorization for the opening of the Sandler account. There was a typed cross on the form for 'Full Access'. Duly signed by Peter Lee, as was the norm.

For once Peevs was glad these permission settings were granted in the US. But the actual execution of the work order, he knew with rising dread, happened in India.

TUESDAY, 10.00 A.M.

Andheri, Mumbai

Vir stared blearily at the quarterly sales forecasts. He had barely slept in two nights.

He forced himself to consider the numbers now. They looked aggressive, more hope than reality. Non-communicable diseases were on the rise in India. A combination of poor eating habits, sedentary lifestyles and too much stress. It offered huge market potential for drug manufacturers. But Vir knew where Acel's arsenal of superdrugs suffered. It was their pricing, driven in part by the formulations that were imported. They just had one local licensed manufacturer. The new licensing agreement was crucial for market share. But for supply of ingredients, he needed a manufacturing set-up in India. He had been trying to convince his bosses. *Would they ever agree now?*

Ramesh snuck his head inside. 'May I come in?' He introduced an engineer from the equipment manufacturer.

'Bad news?' Vir jumped the conversation, unsure if he could handle one more piece of bad news at this point.

'Not really. We checked the electron microscope calibrations. It was off by a 0.1 per cent deviation.'

'I've just recalibrated it,' the engineer added.

Vir exhaled. One-tenth of a percentage deviation would have drawn some ire under normal circumstances. In the current situation, it was almost good news. One variable eliminated. At least it was not machine error.

Ramesh left, and Vir closed his eyes momentarily, wishing he could put his head down on his desk and nap. Except sleep would not come, but recollection of the events of last night, with it the embarrassment of Diti pulling away and the deep drag of guilt. He had not reached out, neither had she.

His phone rang. Tracey. Sighing, he took the call.

'You're ignoring me. When will you be home?' she said.

'I'll call you by six...' Vir said. He had left early morning, not wishing to face her. Then again, he did not know how the day would proceed. It was not just the unfortunate timing of her trip. He felt reluctant to be with her. The smart, cool, cheerful woman he had met had become a whiner. One far removed from his concerns.

'Can you send the car? I'll connect with Tara.'

'Of course.'

Vir was in a sales meeting in a boardroom lined with photos of striations and dots that could have been galaxies but were actually cells and nerves, thousand times magnified.

'We need stretch goals,' Prashant argued.

'Make it realistic,' Vir said. Under-promise and over-deliver was his motto.

'There is huge untapped potential in the North and West markets. We can't pussyfoot. We need hard targets.'

They were deep in conversation when Delna walked in.

'Rads is calling. He says it's urgent.'

Vir picked up the phone with utter distaste. It was always the bearer of bad news of late.

'We found something disturbing, Vir,' Rads said.

He explained how Peevs had detected a certain Dr Lauren Sandler had been accessing the system data multiple times over the past few days, that too on full access. This secure encrypted VPN connection allotted to her, invisible secret tunnel between her account and the Colare server, allowed unlimited access to protected data inside the proverbial *four walls* of Acel. Sans any glitches, hitches, controls or surveillance.

'Did the team know this when I was there last night?'

'I think they detected it soon after you left. Peevs had a suspicion. He confirmed the details before telling us.'

'Damn it!' Vir swore softly. *Whatever was going on?* Intruders in his systems. Chinese walls inside. Information coming to him twelve-hour post facto.

'We have installed a capture software to monitor network traffic coming into the Colare server, to sniff all incoming TCP/IP packets. You won't believe what they found, Vir.'

'What?'

'We know this Dr Sandler has been accessing Colare data. Specifically some of the files in sectors adjacent to where Terry has reported data error.'

'So, she's our person!' He mused in a soft voice. 'Do you know if she is actually sabotaging the data?'

'Not yet.'

'Have you told Jake?'

'I wanted to speak to you before that. Peevs wrote a javascript – a patch of sorts, to sit on the TCP/IP port and monitor Dr Sandler's VPN login to the Acel system. It tracked every time her login was used, triggered a relay and recorded her movements.'

'And?'

'The IP address was from Kyrgyzstan.'

'And?!' Vir felt he was on autopilot, parroting the same words. Nothing made sense any more.

'There's more. The link dropped or was severed, we don't know. The boys waited, then there was another ping. The next login from her account came from an IP address in Romania.'

Outside, the sunlight was blinding bright. Inside, it felt like the womb of a catacomb, dark, constricted and hard to escape from.

'Don't you see the pattern, Vir? We saw an intrusion from Kyrgyzstan. Then we find the lovely doc is logging in from the same country. Then we see her logging in from another country.'

Rads was high-pitched, as he rambled on. 'Vir, either she is a master saboteur trying to muddy her electronic trail, or someone is spoofing her ID to get access to our data!'

TUESDAY, 8.00 P.M.

Goregaon, Mumbai

'This really can't be happening.' Ali paced the cavernous room. The tests and tricks of the IT team seemed incomprehensible to him. And he did not like one bit the few things he understood.

The room was warm due to an overload of equipment and computers that had been running on continuous scans over the past few days. Every few minutes, some machine spat out a string of stats.

'Something is terribly wrong,' Peevs said. 'The mismatch is fluctuating!'

The mismatch between the datasets on the servers had moved from ten per cent last week, to twenty yesterday and eighteen now. Had a router turned rogue? Become an open transmitter, leaking protected information to the world?

'How can we watch this happen?' Ali asked, anguished.

'The core data is safe, Ali. We copied it to an offline server. Fifty-six hours it took! All the petabytes of video imaging.'

They had gone old-fashioned, lining up portable servers to do tedious backups, and keep them offline. Safe from the intruder. New data was being similarly stowed away every few hours.

'What if data got corrupted during those fifty-six hours?'

Peevs did not have an answer.

'You've found a pattern though?' Vir was eager for scraps of welcome news.

'Partially,' Peevs said. 'The log files show she logged in Friday and Saturday nights, but not on Sunday. Then again on Monday. We are tracking her closely now.'

Ali swore. 'Could it be a virus?' Virus seemed like a lesser evil than a sociopath. Then again a virus could easily plague other parts of their knowledge banks.

'We haven't detected any signature pattern yet. The scans don't spit out traces of any known virus.'

'Don't we keep updating our security?' Vir demanded.

They did. Every layer of the protective system, and then some. Yet there were hacks and online jocks who made a living beating it all. The hottest new start ups in the Valley, naturally, were no longer those creating social networking sites or geo-tagged apps. Rather they were the obscure little firms creating new anti-virus programs and protective security systems. That's where the money was being poured.

'But why is Dr Sandler logging in so many times?' Vir was puzzled. A virus was self-replicating. If she was planting a virus, she wouldn't need to be in their system so often.

'Perhaps the lovely Dr Sandler, or whoever it is, is infecting the sectors. Bit by bit. Byte by byte.'

Peevs continued, 'We don't know yet if it's happening live. It might be pre-programmed in one of the machines, any small link. These current intrusions could be a red herring. A distraction.'

'That seems like a conspiracy theory.'

'Not really. It could even be in one of your diagnostics machines. Maybe one of the suppliers is trying to sabotage your results.'

Vir felt a flash of annoyance. This was all over the place. Then dread descended. He had to be the bearer of bad news again. His credibility, already low, would be mud now! What of the lives and families that relied on him to manage his act better. His entire team. He felt the start of a headache coming on, but he had to be present and take charge.

He interrupted the tech-talk. 'So we don't know. We are only guessing that Dr Sandler is infecting our systems.'

Then a thought struck him. He said, 'Have you guys monitored if she is also copying data out?'

TUESDAY, 12.30 A.M.

Bandra, Mumbai

Vir found Tracey asleep on the sofa when he walked in. She was still in her day clothes, her skin translucent in the dimmed lights. They had not really spoken since Sunday lunch.

She stirred and opened her eyes. No warmth in them. No love. Chill and anger lashed out at Vir.

'What's the time?' Tracey sat up. Her hair was mussed. Her clothes were crumpled. Slumber still lingered in her posture, but her face was already rigid.

'Near midnight.'

She had been trying to reach him since evening. Sixteen missed calls. Five text messages. He had only seen them now. On the way back home. He had never felt this helpless – in work or in life. At midnight, the team had literally shoved him out, saying they would call if something happened.

'I'm sorry, Tracey,' he started, feeling dull. He did not know what to even *call* that emotion. Guilt, in large parts. Affection, in small parts. But above all, it was weariness, anxiety and distance.

'*Sorry?* I don't care,' Tracey snapped back. 'I don't even know why you asked me to come over to India.'

Yes, he had wanted her to come to India. It seemed an eternity ago.

'It's not all about you, you, you! Your career decision is consuming you. But life is happening around me. You want me to ignore everything, and sit and hold hands?'

'You can at least respond. Explain. Send one stupid text message!' Tracey flung back, fury writ on her face.

'In the middle of a crisis?'

'Its common courtesy.'

'*Courtesy*? That's what you expect from me? Courtesy?

Niceties? In this big drama, this major catastrophe? While my credibility is on the line?'

Tracey stood there, sullen.

'And what about niceties for me?' Vir said with disdain. His voice low, but slicing. 'What if I wished someone understood *my* troubles? Stood by me? Soothed my worries away?'

'Hah. Did you try me, even?' Tracey said. 'Did you tell me what's happening? Share your feelings? Keep me involved?'

'You want me to talk about *feelings* at this time?'

'I. Want. Squat,' Tracey shouted back. 'You can stew in there. In your troubles. In your non-feelings. In your whatevers.' Her voice rose with every sentence. 'I don't care!'

'I can see you don't.'

Anger settled inside Vir's solar plexus. A damp anger. One that did not rise or explode. Rather it sat there. Simmering, spreading, seething. He turned on his heel and walked into the bedroom, slamming the door behind him.

TUESDAY, 12.30 A.M.

Mira Road, Mumbai

Senior Constable Anant Ghoble cursed his luck as he ambled along the narrow lanes near the Mira Road station. Normally he did not mind the night shift. It meant, he could evade his wife by sleeping during the day, scream at his son over homework in the evenings and then doze again in the police station at night.

But, of late, these strange sudden monitoring duties cropped up, based on tip-offs, to walk the streets, enforce the moral code. *As if he was Emperor Haroon al Rashid or Jahanpanah Akbar!*

There was no one here, except what looked like harried workers getting off late night shifts from work in shops or restaurants. A few could be coming from one of those dance bars in the neighbourhood. It was hard to tell.

He twirled his baton, whistled for his junior, Constable Vrushal Doiphode, to bring the standard-issue light motorcycle. Doiphode, who had been waiting while Ghoble inspected the entry points near the station for late night revellers, drove up. Ghoble climbed up to ride pillion, tapping his baton. 'Let's go, let's go.'

It had been an incident-free evening, and now he was looking forward to his post-midnight snooze at the police station.

Doiphode zigzagged through the silent bylanes. He turned a corner, startling a group of strays clawing at a dumpster. The dogs turned towards the vehicle, barking madly, yapping and nipping, throwing Doiphode off balance. The motorcycle careened and slid. They glided on the rough concrete and slammed into the dumpster, the motorcycle on the ground just a metre away.

Cursing, Ghoble felt his hefty limbs for any damage, and with many groans and shouts at Doiphode, he hoisted himself up.

The dogs were back now, yapping at him, some scratching away at a bundle of rubbish. Foaming mad at the beasts, Ghoble twirled his baton and started beating them up, till his stick fell upon the garbage bag, poking something solid and fleshy.

'*What the...*' He cursed some more and asked Doiphode to help him inspect the bag.

Doiphode stopped breathing as he tore open the stinking bag, beating away the dogs who wanted to hover and crowd in.

There was a man inside. A body. Bloated. Face puffed up and red. Limbs unnaturally splayed as Ghoble kicked the body with his foot to see if the man was drugged or comatose.

'He is dead, Sir,' Doiphode whispered. He had just joined the service. This was his first dead body.

Ghoble cursed again. Sleep tonight was done for. *There would be paperwork to do now!*

WEDNESDAY, 10.00 A.M.

Andheri, Mumbai

Vir was on his smartphone, deciding what witty thing to post @ditirajan or whether just to retweet something #ditirajan. He had pressed the 'Follow' button yesterday. The flimsiest connect.

This morning, she had 'followed' him back.

Not that he had posted anything half exciting yet.

He scrolled up through her tweets – all about current affairs and economic development, but with a tinge of sardonic humour that had her followers multiplying.

Vir rubbed his nose. Could he write on an open platform, for the world to see?

He typed a personal message.

'@ditirajan Magnetic lines ~ your followers queueing up'

Within a minute, there was a response.

'You're following me. Again ☺. Coming for my recording tomorrow night?'

'Yes.'

He wrote back immediately, smiling, then gripped by the question whether he should have waited before responding and shown some restraint, exhibited general busyness.

'Vir, check this out.' Delna walked in without knocking.

She spread out the front page of the pulp broadsheet *Half Time*, known for its sensational local stories. There in bold typeface, accompanied by a grainy picture was a caption.

Cleaner of Global Drug Company Acel Found Stabbed to Death.

There were quotes from Senior Constable Ghoble and a commiserative sentence from Mahto Ram, a roommate of the dead man. It ended with a speculation. The man was identified as Jitendra Kumar Jadhav, accused of stealing from the very company that employed him.

'Damn,' Vir said, and pounded the paper, hitting his knuckles hard. His heart sank, skipping several beats.

As if on cue, his landline rang. It was the detective, Sunny Singh.

'This story. *Ji aisa hai*, I was trying to track this Jitendra,' he panted into the phone. 'It seems some Nepali or Assami is involved.'

It was surely unrelated to Acel, Vir mused. *Or was it. What if it was linked to Shrishti's missing notebooks?*

'I was just in the police station, sirji,' Sunny Singh said. 'Some reporter was there. Crime beat. Wanted your official comment.'

Vir felt gravity desert him. His heart plummeted, expelling all breath. His fingers tingled, his head buzzed. *Whether linked or not, paparazzi could never be good news in this situation.*

He let out a spate of expletives. There were enough troubles on so many fronts. He was already having conversations with Andy twice every day. Even the Chairman, Adam Janlowski, had been calling up every day. Everyone was on high alert. Nerves were frayed. Patience was low.

Things on the personal front were a nightmare. Tracey had flown to Delhi in a huff, to drive to Solan to spend three days with his parents. Out of his hair. Hopefully the green hills would calm her down. He was texting Diti like a fool. His inner voice had nothing but contempt.

He had been desperately hoping his travails would end in a few days. *Now this?*

WEDNESDAY, 7.00 P.M.

Goregaon, Mumbai

Vir and his team huddled in Rads's cabin, aware of their precarious position. The entire India operation was a castle of cards, ready to tumble at the merest nudge. Their heads were on the line. Perhaps, legal wrangles with their employer would follow later.

'Let us take stock of the situation,' Vir began. 'Let me summarize. The scanning machines are working fine. Shrishti's notebooks have been stolen. Temp cleaner Jitendra has been found dead.'

'It may not be connected,' Ali offered weakly.

'Connected or not, I don't care. Not to mention the clear violation of security procedures. But both incidents are not good.'

He knew there would be an intensive internal enquiry. In a company like Acel, process was paramount. There were clear guidelines on who could be allowed inside the research labs and when. As in the US facilities, tech gadgets and connected computers were not allowed inside the labs. No handwritten notes were supposed to be kept, every observation was online. Clearly many protocols had been transgressed here.

Vir sighed. 'Next, we know that we had an open port on the main data server housing Colare results and Dr Lauren Sandler, a certified clinician in Virginia, is accessing protected data.'

Rads took off his thick glasses and wiped his eyes. 'We know she has full access to Colare data. But she never logs in directly – its likely a multi-hop. IP addresses from all over the world.'

'And remind us about the timing pattern of intrusions.'

'Only at night, Vir. After the US shift ends.'

'So, not a virus then?'

Rads shrugged his shoulders. 'We've secured old data, haven't we?'

'But something more is happening,' Vir interjected. 'Bad sectors were increasing. Suddenly the mismatch decreased, meaning fewer bad sectors! Tell me, could this be analysis error?'

'I don't think so.'

Vir spoke sharply. 'Like I said, check if she is taking out any files. Dig deeper.' He had read something to the effect on some site.

'FTP is a fusty old technology. Too slow. No one will use it,' Peevs said.

'Rule it out then,' Vir said. Hacking happened to others, in news or movies. But in real life, to his company, on his watch?

Rads shifted nervously. 'It can't be pinned on us, Vir. What can we do if Dr Sandler has been given full access? Her forms have the approval signature.'

Someone should have double checked, Vir thought. *Someone should have raised a query. Why was a third-party clinician being given full access?*

'It won't matter now. We've told them about Dr Sandler. Not about the note-taking and disappearance of the notebooks.'

Vir looked around. Rads looked sheepish. Ali lost, his Adam's apple bobbing from trepidation.Vir knew it was a huge responsibility – the first ever overseas research centre for Acel. Set up against much doubt from many.

This at a time when local pharma companies and medical research labs were mushrooming in India, setting up huge gated facilities, with the latest technological sophistication learned from the West and mixed with the Indian notions of *jugaad* and cost efficiency. Indian patents were being filed, low-cost molecules being created, affordable alternatives being sought and frontier markets being reached. Patients across tracts of India and Africa and Asia, untreated until now, suddenly had options. But global headlines still screamed generics and patent laws protection, blanking out on a whole new changing landscape.

He had been one of the advocates of this changing landscape.

Convincing colleagues along the Beltway. Touting potential and promise. For this to happen now, to him, seemed utterly ironical. His career, was it all a joke now? Gone with the lost notebooks.

'Okay, so we haven't told them then,' Vir said, answering his own question. He sat there, utterly cornered. *Fuck!* He swore silently.

Hacking, if this is what it was about, would be breaking news. It would go viral in no time, reaching millions across India and US and elsewhere, affecting stock performance, market sentiment, regulator concern, and God only knew what else. Maybe even Colare's chances of getting the global patent approved! With data compromised, who would believe in them? And, in the midst of all this, as the commander watching over this debacle, Vir would be doomed. And his entire team. He *had to* contain this. He had to minimize losses. For the company. For the team. For himself.

WEDNESDAY, 9.15 A.M.

Rockville, Maryland

It was wet and windy. The unseasonal cold from the North had reached the capital region, carrying icy mositure from the Lakes, condensing upon the mid-Atlantic terrain as sleet and black ice, hanging upon the still air as grey fog. Schools had declared an emergency closure, sending unprepared working parents in a tizzy. Roads were slick, an odd but to-be-expected car slide on the Beltway had created a multi-car pile-up and radio traffic news reporters continually gave brisk commentaries.

Battling an unending commute, Jake reached the Acel parking lot and drove into his usual slot. He had been on the road for two hours, and even now many slots were empty. People were either still mired in traffic queues, or had decided to work from home. That wasn't an option for Jake. Not today.

Switching off the ignition of his sturdy Volvo, he zipped his parka and dashed across the parking lot. Once inside, he was glad for the warmth of central heating and the friendly smile of the receptionist. He made his way to the room where his duo of grey hats sat. Rads had sent an email about some Dr Sandler accessing Colare data. Dean, back from his mini break, had sent a strange message about open ports, which the Indian team had kept mum about.

'What's the news?' he barked on entering the dark room.

'We've been compromised, Jake,' Dean said, looking weary after an all-nighter. His black turtleneck jumper intensified the blackness of his eyes, odd against his thin blond hair.

Umpteen cans of Red Bull and Diet Coke littered the table. Scott lay asleep on the floor, hair mussed, dark circles under his eyes.

'Scott's been up all night. He just rolled down an hour back.'

'Tell me,' Jake said.

Dean, barely in his mid-twenties, but an expert at intrusion and protection, corroborated what Rads had emailed. It seemed a wild tale. Some Dr Sandler running in and out of Colare data willy-nilly.

'How did she get full permission?' Jake burst out angrily.

'That's the rub. I checked the trail of permissions, saw her original application embedded in it. The document categorizes Dr Sandler as a clinician, gives her PI tag.'

PI being Principal Investigator, the title assigned to clinicians who signed up to test a drug, giving them limited access to upload and view and edit their own data.

'Who created it?'

'Dr Peter Lee.'

'That's as per process.' Dr Peter Lee, as the Chief Scientist on Colare had the final say on who got access to what data. 'But the key question is how did Dr Sandler get full permission? To enter all sectors of Colare data.'

'A systems error?'

'Wouldn't that be the easiest copout.' Jake pursed his lips. 'Could she have tampered with permissions?'

'Hard to say,' said Dean, an uncertain look in his eyes.

It was a tacit understanding between Jake and him, that it was fine to make online forays and do a clean sweep of any computer he wanted to access, as long as he did not unleash some malware on his way and covered his tracks as he exited. But he hadn't managed to sweep Dr Sandler's machine yet. 'She is offline. I have to check her computer, see her systems files and logs.'

'Where is Dr Sandler located?'

'Right here, in Maryland.'

'Well, let's go meet the good doctor. If she's our person, we need to check her out now.'

'Shouldn't we just suspend her account? Stop her access to our systems?'

That would be the swiftest way to staunch the matter. But Jake shook his head, unwilling to take on the bullying of Andy unless he needed to. He was no expert on clinical research, but knew enough to know that doctors were accepted for clinical trials after rounds of interviews, and trials were carefully modulated to ensure perfect randomization. He could not go about messing with it on his own. 'We will need to inform Andy and Adam beforehand. I'd rather check out the doctor. Build the case first.'

'While she wreaks havoc in the meantime?'

It was a tough call. 'Well, that's a chance we have to take,' Jake responded to the aghast look on Dean's face.

'We should also get on-ground support in India'

Jake narrowed his eyes. 'I've been thinking too. The India team seems out of depth. Plus all the things they don't tell us. Like that open port they haven't owned up to yet.'

Dean shook his head. The Indian team had done well as amateurs. More than he could have expected, with honey traps and all. But they were trained data operations guys, not cyber crime analysts. There was much at stake here. An expert could certainly come in handy. He explained as much to Jake.

'How would we find someone? And by the time we go through sourcing and signing a contract, it will be too late.'

'There's this guy we met at Def Con,' Dean said. 'Good clean guy, studied at Stanford, helped various companies in the Valley track intruders while he was still doing his Comp Sci major. He runs his own cyber sting op in Mumbai.'

'Get him, then,' Jake said.

The business of Dr Sandler's permission form bothered Jake. As did the India team. With so much at stake, if they hid information like the open port, could they be trusted? Heck, could Vir be trusted?

He turned to Dean. 'Do you think someone in the India team is helping Dr Sandler?'

WEDNESDAY, 3.00 P.M.

Rockville, Maryland

A salt truck was ahead of Jake's car, slowly inching along sprinkling salt to melt the thick snow. The sky gave an ominous obsidian glow, the sun hidden behind the low snow-laden clouds that had been dropping heavy flakes since morning.

He drove impatiently, anxious to reach the Shady Adventist Hospital, Dean following behind him.

Dr Sandler was at the reception when they entered. Her evening appointments had been cancelled, a few patients had called in early. She was now waiting to go for a ward round before heading home herself.

'Dr Sandler?' Jake wiped his wet shoes on the doormat and offered his hand for a crisp shake.

Dr Sandler nodded and led them into her office.

Wondering how to proceed, and whether to ask her directly about the intrusions, Jake introduced himself as Acel's Head of Security.

'So, you are a PI on Colare. How is it going so far?'

If Lauren Sandler was confused as to why these two men had insisted on meeting her on a cold, wet, windy afternoon with a routine question, she kept her cool.

'It takes a while in trials for results to be observed.'

'Nothing unusual then?'

'Is anything the matter? Surely you did not come to see me on a lousy day like this to ask if the trial had started off?'

'Well, yes, there is an urgent matter. We think there is a problem in your computer linking to our systems.'

'Systems? What do you mean?'

'Meaning, may we just check your computer once, ma'am?' Dean said politely. 'Just to make sure it's all in order.'

Jake eyed her closely. They were trying to wing it, without

a clear plan on how to establish Dr Sandler's culpability. Now, meeting her, he could sense her irritated vibes. But was there more to it? Was it the cold hostility or the nervousness of a hacker?

Lauren Sandler frowned. High quality data gathering and reporting was crucial, she knew. She was a trained clinician, well aware of dataforms and medical codes. What to measure and how to record entries and keep data trails, even if she did not know much beyond that, about how that data was merged, extracted and locked in the overall trial being managed by Acel. She certainly did not have time to waste with yet another data wonk, wanting to check her computer for some updated file or the other.

'One of your medical reps just came down a few days ago, and installed your latest software and tested it. Why do you need to check my computer again?'

Jake and Dean exchanged a surprised glance with each other. An Acel rep coming down to a PI's office to install a software? How unusual. What was that about?

WEDNESDAY, 7.47 P.M.

Rockville, Maryland

Dean sat alone in his cold apartment, a sole vigilante wrapped in a blanket, patrolling the online periphery of Acel's networked servers, sniffing at the honeypot that the Indian team had created. He was waiting for the good doctor to log in.

A much better way to be working on a day when the snowstorm raged outside. Dean had understood that Jake needed some evidence before making the case against Dr Sandler.

The rep angle had been unexpected. Was she fibbing? Creating a red herring to distract attention from herself? Or, was there really some employee on a kamikaze mission? He would get to know soon. He had asked the HR team to put together the dossier of all mid-Atlantic reps. They would send it tomorrow on priority.

Dean rubbed his palms, and drew the blanket closer. It was so cold, even with the heating on, he was literally freezing despite being dressed in multiple layers.

There was a ping. Data flowing through the network. Dean felt his pulse quicken. He quickly checked the systems log. It showed Dr Sandler had logged in. An authorized access, as far as the system alerts went. She was legit. She had right of access. No alarms would be triggered. With a thudding heart, Dean rode the internal pipe, tunnelling through. He was in pursuit. Hot-footed and silent. She wouldn't know he was watching. Unless she was on the lookout. But people usually overestimated their cleverness. They knew how to find the vulnerabilities in others' systems, but forgot their own.

He would catch her today.

Dr Sandler's unique machine ID, the MAC code, had been

recorded in her authorization file. All he needed to do was connect his machine to hers, access her computer and see what she was up to. If she remained online for a while, he could even mirror her computer and do the clean sweep he hadn't been able to do so far. Dean knew Jake was sitting at the end of his mobile, waiting for an alert at any time of the night.

Dean typed in the ARP command to find all the devices connected to Acel's network. He stared at the screen counting the seconds, impatient for the system to spit out the details of the IP addresses and corresponding physical addresses of the connected machines. He felt his excitement rise, loving this armchair cyber chase, this counter-surveillance.

He leaned forward. The log table popped up. Lots of people logged in, despite it being late in the evening on a wild day. He scanned through the list, tracking the alphanumeric code that was Dr Sandler's listed machine address. Then he went down the list again, slowly, his finger on the screen, line by line.

She was not online!

How could it be? Had she simply logged in from another machine? But was she clever enough to bypass the machine-specific authorizations and log in from some web browser. It seemed inconceivable.

He needed time to investigate. He was glad Jake had had the foresight to not rush to Andy. But whatever was happening was a risk. The least he could do was bring the server down! People would just blame it on the storm.

THURSDAY, 4.13 A.M.

Goregaon, Mumbai

'We got him. The bastard! By Jove, we got him,' Peevs said, grinning owlishly at his team. A wave of exultation ran across the room.

They had a lead.

'Bandra! My God, can you believe it?' Peevs said.

They looked worse for wear, encamped in the office overnight, eyes glazed, breaths fogged, jaws grainy. But excitement shone through them now.

'It could be a false trail,' someone said.

'Why do you believe this IP address, when you did not believe the ones in Romania or Kyrgyzstan?' Vir said, sounding stern and sceptical, after being called at that odd hour.

Peevs stared at the speakerphone, struck silent.

'We can't be sure this is the correct one. But we can at least try to check this one out.'

It had been a long night, not knowing if it would yield any results. A quick pow wow had yielded no fresh ideas. They had already set up security measures to capture the IP address of the computer from where the attack originated. But IP addresses in Croatia and Kyrgyzstan shed no light upon the identity of the attacker.

'Is this a random attack and specifically targeted?' Peevs had wondered out aloud.

Who it was and what the motive was, was hard to deduce.

But they were on the lookout this time, on both the TCP/IP and FTP ports. These protocols allowed the computer to connect to the external world and transfer data. Either could be the pipe through which the Colare data was being accessed.

Peevs wrote an application to create an additional layer

upon the database architecture, to deflect and detract the intruder, and capture illegitimate activity at the open port.

A honeypot! He created a high interaction feature, a comb of virtual links to slow traffic by seconds, providing just enough time for counter-snooping. Like a motion detector at the periphery of a yard, this counter-surveillance spyware could buzz and alert the team if anyone as much as put a toe upon the edges of the system and servers.

Standard versions of such traps existed in the company's servers, to capture spamsters and bulk mailers aiming to abuse vulnerable links in open mail relays. Such traps would intercept the spam emails but not deliver them, and blacklist the bulk emailer. But Peevs's system was a specific one, zeroing in on the Colare server.

At dawn, the online stream monitors started beeping, alerting Peevs there was an incoming request at the open port. He nudged his dozing team members. They sat up, alert, backs sore, limbs stiff, hearts pounding.

A series of activities kicked into process. A sniffer was activated to check the incoming data packets. An autorule interface was established with an IP table to identify the origin of this request. Another sniffer sat upon the FTP gateway.

The intruder was sending a request to Acel's server. But just as quickly as the request had begun, it terminated. Before they had a chance to decode the request details!

But an IP address had been revealed.

Located in Mumbai.

THURSDAY, 7.00 A.M.

Bandra, Mumbai

'How do we know who owns this IP address?' Vir asked.

'We don't know. We've hit a stone wall,' Rads replied.

The weary Acel data centre team had driven to Bandra, eager for fresh air and real food. They sat in a tiny café near Hill Road, strategizing over egg bhurji, muffins and coffee. The day was already bright, with the damp promise of summer.

The ten-digit IP address had been tracked back to iTring, an internet service provider based in the western suburbs. But to get to the machine and its owner, they needed to go through iTring. Their server, which allocated dynamic IP addresses to all machines using its server to connect to the internet, would keep track of which machine had been assigned that IP at 4.13 a.m. that morning. It was just a matter of a simple search on the company's database to get the information. From there, ascertaining the name and address of who the machine was registered to was an easy path.

Technology was a small world and Rads knew Suresh Damani, the technology head at iTring, from some conference. He had called Suresh as early as he could in the morning. Suresh had sympathized, but refused to help. An intrusion originating from iTring's service network reflected badly upon him. He had no wish to divulge any details.

'If we get an FIR, he will be forced to reveal details,' Peevs said, fuming at being stymied. Usually the First Information Report had to be filed with the police before a telecom company could share data.

'I don't know,' Vir said.

An FIR meant revealing that Acel was under cyber attack. Even if they did not have to worry about the ramifications of such a revelation upon the Colare project, there could be adverse effect on Acel's stock or its perception in the market.

Anyway, it was not his decision alone. He would need board clearance.

Vir recalled his conversation with Andy last evening. Grenade explosions would've been softer than the verbal barrage fired at him. Rads had been called in. Jake had been patched in. Vir had been defensive, Rads deferential. Rads had explained what his team had observed, and how they had observed it.

Jake had voiced his surprise that the security clearance for Dr Sandler had been set to 'Full Access'. Dr Peter Lee had already been asked. His digital signature was on the electronic form, but he could not recall giving Dr Sandler full permission.

'It is highly irregular, a mistake perhaps,' Jake had said, and had asked Rads to investigate if system error or human error had led to this.

'Does the Mumbai police even recognize cybercrime as violable offence?'

'It does now,' Peevs said. For long, cybercrime was not recognized as an offence. The recently modified Section 66 of the Indian Penal Code offered a modicum of protection, allowing the cybercrime division of the police to investigate threats or search against suspicion of activities related to data theft, online swindling or stalking. But how many beat cops understood this was another matter.

'We have no options. We can't file an FIR,' Vir said. He wasn't ready to ask for permission from Andy.

'What then?'

Vir sat back and rubbed his throbbing forehead, a thousand aimless thoughts flitting in his mind. He exhaled, quietened his mind and a pattern began to emerge. *What would Harry do in a situation like this? Why not reach out to someone who knew people at iTring.* India, he was beginning to recognize, worked on contacts. Never from the bottom up, meritocracy and due process be damned. The thing was to reach right at the top. Only way to make things happen!

Vir called Harry. 'I have a favour to ask, *patthe*.'

'But of course, Vir,' Harry said smoothly.

It turned out that Harry's father's golfing buddy knew a builder friend in Mumbai who was negotiating long-term contracts with iTring to become the sole internet service provider in his series of housing complexes across the eastern suburbs. Nothing persuades more than money, Vir was discovering. Thus introduced, the owner of iTring could only but agree to help Vir.

It took a few hours for the gears of connectivity to click in and turn, but greased through referrals, the cogs had meshed, generating action. A sullen Suresh had to accede to Acel's request.

By 9 a.m., the team was sitting in iTring's office. They had a name and an address.

Mr Sharma. Santhal Building, Bandra.

THURSDAY, 10.00 A.M.

Bandra, Mumbai

Mornings were always chaotic in the Sharma household. Mrs Sharma bustled about, supervising breakfast and tiffin. Hoping that Lalti, the daily maid, would turn up today, recovered from whatever ailment plagued her last week.

Mr Sharma, tired from a late night flight from Vietnam, could not take it easy. A series of meetings awaited him at the office and files needed to be cleared. Despite global aspirations, his company was a strange amalgam of old and new. Younger staff asked for requests and approvals on email. But older staff and senior executives preferred thick paper files, and the ritual of a bellboy bringing in a sweet cup of tea.

Mr Sharma sipped his morning tea, prepared just the way he liked it – strong and boiled with tulsi leaves. He opened the newspaper, scanned the headlines, then surreptitiously read his daily horoscope. *Unexpected matters will claim your attention.* He harrumphed softly.

'College excursion fees are due,' Mrs Sharma reminded, dishing out poha on his plate.

'When is some expense not due?'

'You have a teenage daughter. Expenses will be there.'

'College fees, yes. But shopping bills?'

'She could be worse, Sharmaji.'

'Madhu has simpler tastes.'

'She is new here. But poor thing...' she said dramatically.

'What happened?'

'Anki's old computer that we gave her has been crashing all week, she says.' Mrs Sharma made a face. She did not understand much about computers, let alone whatever a *computer crash* meant.

'Okay, I will send Tarun from the office to look at it,' Mr Sharma replied as he left.

≈

'That's Sharma Saheb,' the car washing lad said pointing out a man outside Santhal building. Vir's driver duly slipped him a fifty-rupee note, and gave a thumbs-up sign to his boss.

Vir and Peevs sat in a car from across the building. The middle-aged man getting into a white Honda Civic hardly looked like a hacker. But could you tell?

'Does he have children?' Vir asked absently, unable to decide whether to accost Mr Sharma or not.

'Two girls. Ankita didi, Madhu didi,' the cleaner responded, eager to help, wondering if he could wangle another fifty.

Girl hackers? Could be. But to think that two young girls could stymie Acel's security systems seemed hard to digest.

It wasn't that long before two young girls emerged from the gate, carrying backpacks, looking fresh and utterly guileless. A petite short-haired one in a yellow top and three-fourth jeans. A taller long-haired one in a red-and-white churidar kameez.

These were the potential perpetrators? The ones who had hacked and slipped out hundreds of millions worth of data? Perhaps they were crackers who got lucky. Vir felt perplexed.

'What the...' Peevs muttered.

Vir stepped out of his sedan. 'Ankita? Madhu?'

The girls turned, startled. 'We need to talk to you,' Vir said in his sternest voice. 'About hacking.'

'What?' Ankita frowned. 'Is this some joke?'

'We'll be late for class,' Madhu whispered.

'Look Sir. You are confusing us with someone else,' Ankita said, taking in the posh man standing in front of her. 'We will miss our bus.'

'We have proof,' Peevs added, hands slipping nonchalantly into his pockets.

'What proof?' Ankita snapped, coming in front of Madhu, a stubborn glint in her eyes.

Vir took a deep breath. 'My company's site was hacked. We have tracked it to your connection. Your father's name actually!' Vir glowered at the girl, hoping to intimidate her into confession.

'You are making no sense,' Ankita said.

'Unless you think you father hacks into company websites in his spare time,' Peevs added, in a droll tone.

'Whatever it is you've tracked,' Ankita began. 'It's obviously a mistake.'

'It is no mistake. We captured the IP address of the machine from where the last intrusion into our server happened. iTring is your internet service provider, isn't it? They have confirmed that IP address was given out to your machine at the time of the intrusion.'

Doubt clouded Ankita's eyes.

Peevs continued dramatically, quite enjoying his double-cop routine. 'If you have a wireless router, someone could've used your connection to hack into our system.'

Ankita stilled. Madhu blanched.

Vir exchanged a quick glance with Peevs. Something had clicked. The girls knew something, maybe suspected someone. They were surely onto something now.

Madhu became flustered. 'My computer has been acting strange.'

'We need to see your machine then.'

There was more to it than the girls were letting on, Vir suspected.

'You can tell your mother that we are here to fix your computer.'

'You hardly look like a computer repair guy,' Ankita snapped, taking in Peevs' green jeans and navy-striped rugby tee shirt with some sort of crest on it. Hardly designer stuff, but definitely too cool for a computer repair guy!

'You don't want us to involve the police now, do you? Or talk to your father?'

Vir put the pressure on, though he knew very well he had no intention of going to the police. He did not even know if there was enough of a case to suggest a warrant and inspection of premises, if he went the police route.

Wordlessly Ankita shook her head. She would have to lead these two past her mother.

THURSDAY, 11.00 AM

Bandra, Mumbai

'Such quick service,' Mrs Sharma cooed approvingly, pegging Vir as the supervisor sort.

Vir dissembled. 'Just wanted to make sure we fix this today.'

'Aren't you girls getting late for college?' Mrs Sharma asked.

'It's just an English period, Ma,' Ankita said. 'We want to be around in case we need to give some passwords.'

'Show the work done to me before you go,' Mrs Sharma added authoritatively, going out of the door.

Peevs crouched down to check the router cables, then ran a scan at the command prompt. 'Who set up this router?'

'I helped Dad,' Ankita said, proud of her tech competence.

Peevs smirked.

'What?' Ankita said tetchily. Really, this guy had the nerve!

'The router setting is insecure. Easy for anyone to ride on,' he shrugged. 'Common mistake.'

'It's easy enough to buy a router off the shelf. A *Made in Taiwan* one, with warranty, or a *Made in China* one, without warranty. Unwrap the box, read the instruction manual, attach the cables. Presto! You're ready to go. But if you don't set up network security, you don't know who can crawl in and ride your connection.'

'Really?'

'Your Wi-Fi has no lock.' He pointed to the available Wi-Fi networks. Some protected, some unsecured. *Sharma* was broadcasting itself to whoever wanted to see as an open network. 'It's a risk.'

'Describe how this computer has been acting up,' Vir asked Madhu.

Madhu haltingly spoke about the frozen screens and screens scrolling numbers.

'You never suspected hacking?'

'Uh,' Madhu stuttered. Could Raghu or Suv have used her computer to hack into Acel? Surely, it wasn't Ankita? After all, she had been downloading hacking softwares.

'But what has the hacker done? Embezzled money? Leaked customer data?' Anki butted in. Whatever had happened was huge.

'That we can't tell you.'

'We just thought the old computer was dying off.'

Vir could see from the girls' expression that *hacking* had been discussed between them before. Did they do it? Did they suspect someone?

Peevs fiddled with the old desktop again, typing up DOS commands at rapid speed, checking settings and firewalls. 'Vir, check this out.'

The girls crowded in to take a look.

'There is a Trojan on this machine. It keeps the transmission protocol port open, allowing remote access, letting the sender tunnel through this machine!'

Trojan malware easily spread through mails and links. It could be used to connect the host and the victim computers, gain absolute remote control of the victim machine, or be an online voyeur. It could be used to destroy the hardware or software of the infected computer or to conduct nefarious activities on third-party systems. 'Trojan? How?'

'May be through a phishing widget on a site, or a rogue email.'

The unsuspecting person would click on a seemingly harmless link. While the surface activity happened, usually accessing a website or filling an online sign-up form, the host computer would covertly run a malicious executable program in the background. The installed server code would then bind itself to a particular port and furtively wait for open connections. When the attacked computer connected to the internet, the Trojan client installed on the attacker's system could get the IP address of the server machine, usually by posting the IP address to a random site which the attacker could access. Using this, the attacker would create a backdoor link between the two machines.

'Have you clicked on an unusual email recently? Files gone missing?'

Madhu was uncertain. She was missing one English essay, but suspected it was because she had not saved it properly.

Anki narrowed her eyes. 'Could it be that e-card site you clicked on?'

'It did start acting up after that.' Madhu looked doubtful. Could a site as cute and ordinary as an e-card site hide malicious code?

'It could,' Peevs said. 'A hacker will usually package a phishing email with something attractive. Something the victim will click on.'

'What next?' Vir asked. They seemed nowhere closer to finding the real culprit.

'I will install a software, to trace where this incoming signal is originating from. Of course, it could be anywhere. Croatia. Kyrgyzstan.'

Madhu and Ankita exchanged surprised glances.

'It could be totally random,' Peevs said. 'But usually, if a hacker is installing a Trojan to control a machine, it is someone within their ambit, someone they may even know. Or know of. I think this will lead somewhere.'

Madhu shot a worried glance at Anki. This conversation was skittering on the edge of unreality. Raghu's face, his confident swagger, flashed in her mind. Was Anki thinking the same?

'Make sure you don't tell anyone,' Vir said, and shot a censuring look at the girls, fully certain they would approach who they suspected.

It would be as easy as that.

THURSDAY, 3.00 P.M.

Santa Cruz, Mumbai

Vir dabbed his forehead with a white handkerchief, feeling the warmth recede as the TV camera lights panned away to focus on another speaker.

He was on stage for a pharma and biotech industry conference, in a silk-panelled hotel ballroom aglitter under crystal chandeliers. Beyond the stage, executives in suits and saris sat fiddling with toffee wrappers and drank labelled water, perhaps longing for the cocktail service to begin.

On stage Mr Satarsondke, a grey-haired, thick-jowled industry veteran and popular speaker of choice, droned on about recent mergers and acquisitions in the industry. 'This is where the action is. Demand for healthcare is going to rise in emerging markets.'

Vir snuck a sidelong peek at his watch. He couldn't wait to call Peevs for an update. Sunny Singh, the detective, had assigned a field operative to follow the girls. An innocuous-looking *maushi*, dressed like a cleaning lady.

Meanwhile, Satarsondke carried on. 'Affordable healthcare is the mantra. Generics drove growth in the past and biosimilars will emerge now.'

'Like many cheap hot dates instead of a steady expensive girlfriend. More action, eh?' The moderator, more known for his deep baritone than profound understanding of sectoral dynamics, took charge. The crowd tittered. He turned to the next speaker. 'What do you think of indigenous innovation?'

'There is not enough venture investment in Indian labs,' a young firebrand CEO of a biotech start-up thundered. She made the case for small nimble players gunning for innovative products with niche expertise.

'Big players are only worried about *quarter se quarter*

tak pressures. We start-ups are the ones who innovate.' She scanned the audience to see if any provender of hot venture capital money was taking notice of her.

The wide lens TV camera rolled on, under the broad sweep of floodlights. *Who would spend an evening watching this on TV*, Vir wondered. Especially when a dozen *saas-bahu* serials and teenybopper dance shows vied for viewer attention.

He thought about the media buzz that could have been generated by talking of Acel's research work in India. Not that he could have mentioned Colare. Even in normal circumstances secrecy was paramount. But, as matters now stood, he could only hope that Colare would eventually reach the stage of public disclosure.

He felt like a fraud. Pretending nothing was the matter.

When his turn came, he drolly began, 'I shall be succinct. Cocktail service is infinitely more attractive,' and proceeded to talk in general terms about the need for low-cost medicines for the masses.

As the session ended and a press of card-swappers descended upon the stage in manic frenzy, Vir quickly extricated himself from the scene and called Sunny Singh.

'Any news?'

'Not yet, *ji*. The girls are in class. *Maushi* is hanging around.'

'The girls have not spotted her?'

'You've seen *Maushi*?'

Vir had only seen a photograph in a folder.

'Well, you saw the photo, *ji*. She blends in. Kids think she is staff. The staff think she is a guardian. And professors don't think of such things. It's fine.'

'Tell me the minute you see anything.'

'Of course. Peevs bhai is also here. We will call you.'

Vir hung up, not quite satisfied, but knowing that there wasn't much else he could do at that moment. He checked his messages.

There was one from his dad: *Tracey has reached. You should have come.*

Vir wrote back: *Work stuff, Dad. Will make it up to you guys and make a special trip.*

Another message pinged on his phone.

Quick reminder. Recording today. 7pm. National Studio. See you then.

Can't wait.

Vir responded immediately. Then fretted over his words. Maybe he should have written 'Looking forward' or 'See you'. Something simple. Meaningless. Less eager. He probably should spend the evening at work, anyway.

Then again, what harm could a few hours do?

THURSDAY 5 P.M.

Goa, India

It looked like an innocuous conference in a five-star hotel. Bright fluorescence streaming in the semi-frigid banquet room. Some flowers, a strange dendritic etching on a wall mirror.

But instead of afternoon stupor, the attendees, mostly young men and a few young women, all earnest faced, sat at the edges of their seats avidly listening to the speaker. The screen behind him stated: 'Introduction to Symlinking: By Karthik Viknesvaran'.

It was a gathering of enthusiasts at Null Con conference.

'I will assume you've experienced nix environments before,' said Karthik, better known as *HazMat* in his digital persona. He was clean-shaven and tall, with a curly mop of hair.

'You begin with a shell. If you don't have access to images in a site, you can gain access by symlinking'.

He toggled to switch to the dark prompt screen, and typed commands in neon green text. He clicked his laser pointer. The screen changed to an instruction. An array of jumbled words, separated by hyphens and slashes. 'Now, let's check the file called "sym-test.txt" in the 01 directory.'

HazMat was legend online, a Superman of Spyware. A certified black hat hacker, rumor had it that he had directly apprenticed with The Dark Tangent, aka Jeff Moss, the founder of Black Hat and Def Con. Then there was his pedigree, a dual degree in Computer Science and International Law from Stanford, that too on full scholarship. He was courted by spyware makers in the Valley and cyber crime authorities on four continents, but chose to run his consultancy from Mumbai employing a small, highly select team of ethical hackers.

The conference agenda lying on the table listed sessions titled 'Honeypots/Honeynets', 'UTM Evasion Techniques', 'Software

Fuzzing' and 'SCADA Networks Security'. But nearly half the room had paid their two thousand rupees solely on the hope of catching *HazMat*'s eye for an apprenticeship.

The session went on for two hours. The audience filled their notepads with arcane codes of computer commands.

As his session ended, Karthik was swarmed by a bevy of youngsters, aiming to impress or even just shake his hand.

His phone rang. 'I need to take this.' He extricated himself from the painful monologue of a girl.

'Hello,' he said, walking down the corridor, simultaneously typing a message on his tab.

'Hey, *HazMat*,' the voice said, with a distinct mid-Atlantic drawl. 'This is *DCaf*. We met last year, at the Riviera, at Def Con?'

'Hey man, yes.' Karthik smiled, remembering the enthusiastic American whom he had defeated in the semi round of a *Capture the Flag* contest.

In the carnival that Def Con gatherings really were in Vegas, with hackers and crackers, Feds and criminals, posing to be ethical of course, speaking, listening, socializing, gaming, competing in hackathons, bonds were forged fast, business connections established and maintained thereafter on underground networks. So, *HazMat* and *DCaf* had met in person through a contest, but had remained in infrequent contact over the year.

'So what's up?' Karthik said, plugging in his headset, and dialling on his other phone to call his driver. He was flying back to Mumbai tonight itself.

'I have a situation at work, dude,' said *DCaf*. 'I need your help. In our Mumbai office.'

THURSDAY, 6.00 P.M.

Bandra, Mumbai

'Hey, what's with the secrecy?' Suv winked conspiratorially.

They were on the rooftop of Santhal Building, against a dramatic sky etched with deep gashes of amber. Beyond the building, the Arabian Sea stretched.

'Why do you make a joke out of everything?'

'And why do you take everything so seriously?'

'Stop bickering, guys,' Ankita snapped.

'Okay, spill. What's so urgent?'

The boys had skipped college to knock on corporate doors, seeking sponsorships for the college festival. The girls had sent a string of messages to both. Telling them to bunk coaching class and meet them here.

'You ignore me always, sweetheart. And the day I am not there, you can't wait to meet me urgently,' Suv teased.

Raghu stood sullenly. Anki shifted from one foot to the other.

Madhu scowled. Her pink dupatta trailed upon the unfinished floor. She wasn't smiling, but when did she ever smile? Even in a snit, even in that infernal dupatta-salwar combo, she looked fresh.

'So is this where you confess your undying devotion for me?' Suv chuckled.

'Are you mad?' Madhu spluttered.

'Be serious, Suv,' Ankita said.

Madhu looked away. Here she thought she was helping the boys by warning them. So they could clean up their act before they got into real trouble. Before those Acel folks rounded up the police or CBI or something. And Suv chose to joke!

'What is it?' Raghu said.

'I know what you guys have been up to,' Madhu started baldly.

'What have we been up to?'

'Hacking.'

'Have you gone mad?' Suv said laughing. Sure, he liked goofing around on the internet. But this was absurd.

'Are you denying it?'

'Denying what?'

'That you have bluejacked my phone, that you cracked my computer passcode and snooped into my computer and accessed unauthorized websites?

'So you accept it, then?' Madhu said like an ace litigator. 'I knew it.'

'Knew what, dammit?' Suv was annoyed.

'That you have used my computer to gain access to Acel data. You had better confess it, you know, and stop this mucking around before you get into real trouble. Why, you may already be in trouble.'

'Did you launch a denial-of-service attack?' Raghu frowned at Suv.

'What?' The girls spoke in unison. They had been lancing in the dark. They hadn't for a sec thought they would hear about a plan for launching a denial-of-service attack.

'Hey, hey, back off, guys,' Suv said, raising his hands in the air, sounding perplexed. 'I have done nothing of the sort.'

'But there is proof, Suv.'

'Proof of *what*?' Raghu interjected.

'Someone installed a Trojan on Madhu's old computer and used the connection to hack into the Acel company site. The trace led back to Madhu's computer. We don't know exactly what happened. But it's something serious.'

Raghu's heart skipped a beat, he tried to keep his face impassive. He had snooped into Madhu's computer. But hadn't he cleaned up his trail?

'They've threatened to call the police. They suspect us,' Ankita said.

'They rather suspect we suspect someone,' Madhu said in a quelling tone.

Suv stared at Raghu now. Raghu stared back stonily.

Suv mused, 'You are such a pro. It would be easy peasy for you.'

'You're a hacker?' Madhu was shocked.

Anki raised her hand to cover her mouth.

'Not me, buddy,' Raghu said.

Suv whistled, eyes narrowed. 'It was the hacking tool you borrowed from Jiggs? Wasn't it?'

THURSDAY, 7.00 P.M.

Andheri, Mumbai

Vir was in the recording room at National Studio. A small group of people sat in the audience. Diti looked fabulous in a red sari and perfectly groomed hair. The powdered and primped Minister of State looked suave in his black bandhgala.

Vir gave her a little thumbs-up sign. His heart lurched when she smiled at him.He felt a little proud. His Diti, the confident outspoken brat he had known, was on her way to becoming a national celebrity. The ads had been running for days now, gathering pre-launch buzz. The industry was waiting to see the show ratings.

A technician walked up for one last mic check. The lights flickered. Music started, the screen behind the speakers lit up to show the snazzy opening sequence of *Jaago India Hour with Diti Rajan.*

'Welcome,' Diti started in her gravelly voice, flashing her beautiful smile at the camera.

As she opened a conversation on the need for affordable healthcare, the price of medication sold in India by global firms, and the ethics of regulations around it, Vir stilled. *What is she doing?* It felt like a personal conversation had been started, a subliminal message, aimed just at him. Like every probing question she had asked him in private had been opened up on national television. A reckoning perhaps. To confront the very issues he had skilfully avoided. He felt a warm flush rise in his cheeks as he listened to Diti and the minister debate policy and principles.

Vir's phone buzzed against his thigh. He had half a mind to ignore it. But with so much going on, he could not. He fished out the phone from his pocket. *Fuck.* It was Andy. Not a call he could ignore.

He swore again, and with minimal noise slipped out of his seat. The producer glared at him for disturbing the recording. Vir mumbled a silent sorry to the producer and made his way out of the recording room. He hoped that Diti did not notice his sneaky exit.

'Vir, this is Andy and Jake on the line.' Andy sounded sharp.

Another unplanned call. There were too many these days. None to bring good news or spread cheer.

'We hear that the perps are some teenage hackers in India, and you are playing along letting them free?' Andy said, sounding caustic.

'Dr Sandler...' Vir began, but was effectively cut off by Andy. 'Who is the security expert from our end, Vir?'

'Rads and his team have been working on this around the clock, Andy. The boys are excellent. They traced the incoming IP. True, there are some teens involved. But we think they can lead us to the real culprit.'

'It's no joke,' Jake chimed in. 'Rads and his boys are just regular IT guys. Not cyber surveillance experts.'

Andy cut in. 'This is gross ineptitude. How could you let amateurs handle such an important matter...'

'I was thinking of getting a local agency, a cyber crime expert...' Vir said, as calmly as he could, though he felt like a stunned blow had been delivered in his solar plexus.

'May I remind you that we need utmost secrecy?' Andy's nasal twang interrupted Vir, before he had a chance to complete his sentence.

Jake took over. 'My team is on it. We need an external expert on the ground, I'm told. Discreetly, of course.'

'Of course,' Vir agreed smoothly, glad he had spoken to Peevs just this afternoon and sussed out a friend of his, a security expert with a team of ace ethical hackers.

'We would have interviewed vendors ourselves...' Andy started.

'However, given the urgency, we cannot.' Jake's sharp voice came on the line. 'My team has identified an expert based in Mumbai. He will be working directly for my team, Vir, let me tell you. But I will tell him to call you right away – he will need support from your team.'

'What about Dr Sandler?' Vir asked.

'What about her?' Andy said.

'I know that Peter said he had not given her the full permission. But have you met her? She could be the perp.'

'My team is on it, Vir,' Jake answered, unwilling to share more.

'We have a hundred million invested, and a billion at stake, Vir,' Andy said. 'Don't forget that.'

Vir remained silent. It was undeniably complicated. More so, these personality clashes framing the whole episode. *They blame me*, he thought bitterly.

THURSDAY, 7.00 P.M.

Bandra, Mumbai

Peevs was parked outside Mr Sharma's residence, eating a soggy sandwich. He had followed the hired *Maushi,* unwilling to trust her.

Maushi came down. She had been squatting patiently in the landing above the Sharmas' door, having fobbed off the guard by saying she was going for an interview. She had seen the girls go to the rooftop, followed by two boys.

Peevs sat in the darkness, drumming the steering wheel, staring at the gate. Finally he saw two boys coming out.

'These two,' whispered *Maushi.*

'Come with me, bastards!'

Raghu felt a strong hand upon the nape of his neck, as he was summarily grabbed and shoved into a waiting Toyota.

'What are you doing?' Raghu said.

'What the...' Suv said, kicking. 'Someone will call the police.'

Maushi pinioned the boys in her vice-like grip, one hand on each. Peevs closed the door on the boys and drove off to the Acel office in Andheri, calling Vir on the way.

Vir knew he was in the doghouse with Diti for stepping out of the recording. He drove the few jam-packed blocks from National Studio to his own office. Telling himself he would go back by the time the recording ended. It was way past that time now. Diti would have left the studio by now. The bunch of hydrangeas and calla lilies, an unusual find in Mumbai, had probably wilted in his car.

He sat impatiently on the edge of the table, arms folded, watching Peevs conduct his interrogation.

Raghu looked at the boardroom. Very American, very posh. He did not know much about Acel, but clearly it was a big company. There were some framed photos on the walls. Were they molecules? Chemical company, perhaps?

'Why have you been illegally entering into Acel's systems? Are you trying to sabotage something?' Peevs stared at Raghu, clearly taking him to be the sharper one. 'Or trying to prove your skills?'

'I don't know what you are blabbing about,' Raghu said tetchily. Nothing more would happen. These guys looked too sophisticated, too soft, to be real goons. Just disgruntled employees, trying to figure out who had got into their systems.

'You look like a reasonable man,' he said, looking at Vir. 'You are barking up the wrong tree. While your real hacker walks free.'

Peevs responded, 'Do you want me to go to your parents? Maybe your college authorities? Your career will be finished.'

'What's the proof we have done something? But if you want, I can help you find your culprit.'

'This is priceless,' Peevs said, bursting out in a dry laugh. 'We are a team of professionals and you, Mister Teenage Hacker, can *help* us?'

'Don't call me that. And I have never been near your site. Ever.'

'But you've been into other sites?

Raghu ignored the question.

'How much do you know?' Peevs was curious. He rattled off a series of questions about sniffers and Trojans, transmission protocols and network protocols, Perl and java coding, freewares and open source platforms.

Damn, Peevs thought with rising gloom and admiration. The kid knew the stuff! He was good. He reminded Peevs of his own youth, when he had played around untethered. Yet, somehow he had never strayed too far, always returned to the ambit of safety, of rules. The world had been a simpler place then. Lesser tools to play havoc with. Kids today stood on the shoulders of giants. Each year newer, darker and more dangerous tools emerged. The chatrooms of his youth had gone further underground. Had become cult. Harder to access, even as access itself became easier. The world had split in two – one of light, the social networking, the gaming apps, the music downloads; and the other of darkness, on the fringes, devious, distorted and experimental.

How far had this kid gone? How bad? Peevs shot a glance at Vir. Vir looked inscrutable. Diti was forgotten. His larger worries were forgotten. He did not quite know what to make of the boy. He was clearly skilled and clearly devious. Yet with a hint of sincerity about him.

Vir grilled the two boys about their lives, parents and friends. Suv was the weak link here, likely to be afraid of his up-and-about parents. Though Raghu could be equally scared of his earnest-sounding mother.

'I'd rather you come clean than me having to complain to your parents. Or your teachers.'

'Look, you've got the wrong guys,' Raghu said again.

Vir shook his head. There wasn't much progress to be made, quizzing these two. But he could not detain them either. He took Peevs aside for a quick confab.

'He's clever, that one. Could be fooling us,' Peevs said.

'Can you put electronic surveillance on him?'

'Impossible. We could track the account he tells us about, but we won't know all the accounts and IDs that he has.'

It was not ideal. It felt like unfinished business. If Raghu wasn't their suspect, they were back to square one. But there wasn't much else they could do at the moment. For now, he had to let the boys go.

'I can really help you,' Raghu said again.

'My best people are on this. You stay away,' Vir said. 'One bad move from you two, one more attack and I shall personally crush you twits.'

THURSDAY, 8.00 A.M.

Rockville, Maryland

Dr Peter Lee sat in his small office, barely noticing the frigid outside. He pushed his glasses onto the bridge of his nose and stared at his computer screen, comparing the latest analytics reports sent by Dr Terence Small. Papers lay scattered on his desk.

Work consumed Peter. He had started at Acel as an outsider. An Asian genius, ahead of his time. But always in the shadow of the legendary Dr Ron Johnson, whose commanding white-haired presence and patrician East Coast voice generated instant confidence in a way that Peter's first-generation accent and slim sallow presence did not.

He still felt like an outsider. Someone knocking on the doors of the establishment. Waiting to be let in.

He had been counting on Colare to break out of the shadows, to declare his brilliance. But with all the turmoil, would it come to pass? And, even if the approvals came, the glory would be split between the US teams and the Indian teams and the lawyers, Andy at its forefront. Would it still get him accepted into the intellectual elites of drug discoverers?

He had devoted his life to research. He had had no hobbies, no other activities, not even a family to distract him from his purpose. To create the next best cure for metastatic pancreatic cancer. *What now?* He found no consolation in anything any more.

He absently googled a travel site. Perhaps he needed a break. Let Acel solve its problems.

An alarm beeped in his computer. He went back to his reports, making neat notes in the margins. But his head was swimming a bit. Maybe he was going to get the flu.

'Peter?' A knock sounded on his door.

Peter looked up, confused to see Adam, Andy, Jake and Martha crowding inside. He was unsure of what they wanted, but was nonetheless overwhelmed by their combined presence. He cleared his throat and muttering a garbled hello, tried to offer his seat to someone. Martha perhaps? What did manners dictate? Peter was never ever sure of such proprieties.

Martha waved her hand, dismissing the offer. 'Sit, Peter. This won't take long. We need to expedite our global patent filing.'

Peter blinked expressionlessly. 'Why would you rush it?'

'We have detected systemic intrusion into Colare's database.' Jake looked grave. 'The intruder could be using the ID of one of our principal investigators to get into our system.'

Peter goggled.

'A Dr Sandler.'

Peter blinked.

'She looks bona fide. Her permission form even has your signature.'

'But I give permissions to every clinician.'

'We know, except somehow she had full permission to all data. And we think it was not an error. It was deliberate.'

'Why do you think so?'

'Someone hacked into Dr Sandler's machine, installed a Trojan. We just found what it's doing. It is posting her dynamic password on an open site. The hacker bypassed her machine-specific code and is using that to enter Colare data from an internet browser.'

'How do you know this?' Peter asked.

'My team is on the job, Dr Lee. We will catch this hacker.'

'But you see why it's urgent we file the application urgently.'

Andy paced the room, like the pitbull his colleagues likened him to. 'What are our competitors for Colare doing?'

Martha explained. 'We've been tracking both of them. In Säarsbrucken and in Guangzhou. Both have shown a spate of recent activity. There's an increase in research papers being submitted by both teams, there's also an increase in the frequency of press releases.'

It was always like that. Ideas remain latent. Till they have sudden currency. Clear to many all at once, creating a race.

'Dr Small is waiting for you in the diagnostics lab,' Martha added. 'My team needs additional reports. Now. Will you join him?'

Peter gave an involuntary twitch. The room felt chilly. 'Ye..e...ess...' he stammered.

THURSDAY, 8.00 P.M.

Bandra, Mumbai

Sandman leaned against the corrugated tin wall, and fingered his refurbished Dell laptop, his dream possession. Bought with his own money. Earned from his own skills.

But today he could not bring himself to smile. Happiness had left his life forever.

His mother was asleep on the bed next to him, visibly thinner within days. He had told her to go watch television in a neighbour's house. *Naach Dekh* was on, and his mother, once a movie buff, used to love seeing her matinee idols' dance moves recreated on the little screen. But today, despite his cajoling, she had not found the strength to go. The first injection had been given, consuming a hefty portion of the money he had earned. The next injection was due in three weeks. To be repeated in a cycle regularly after that. Distress mounted, and desperation that refused to go.

In an auto-loop, images of his father invaded his thoughts. If the malaise was genetic, where did it leave him, after inheriting the rogue gene twice over? It wasn't a thought to dwell on. Did his mother even believe him? Did she not suspect what the doctors hid in plain sight, lying in that cancer ward in a government hospital surrounded by other patients? Sadness had crept into her eyes, a faraway look, like she had detached herself from reality, like she knew the unspoken secret they were both not ready to acknowledge.

He shivered. How would he survive after her? But even before that, how would he survive *with* her, tend to her, manage the costs? He racked his brains on who he could ask for help. There was some family in their village, but they could hardly be asked.

His phone vibrated.

'I am coming,' a friend said. '*Tera mast naya laptop hai.* We can play games.'

'*Nahin re, Sallubhai* will come online today. Live chat *hai.*' He fibbed. He did not feel like meeting his friends any more, sharing their everyday concerns of cigarettes, snacks and the week's movie release.

He fired his computer, scanned for open networks in the neighbourhood, and connected to the internet.

He clicked on *brownphyre*; he hadn't visited the site for a few days. There was a new blog on how to crack password-protected Wi-Fi networks. Ignoring it, he scanned through the list of challenges, the extbasic and stego missions. There was a new stego mission posted by *WeedRawker*, to decrypt a video file. He clicked onto the link for personal messages. There was one.

From *Mystic Mir. 'New login ID and password posted. Mystic@25. Old one invalid.'*

Cryptic, though the message was, *Sandman* knew where to go.

He had met *Mystic Mir* by chance. Who knew where he lived. Perhaps in America, *Sandman* guessed. But he could never have met *Mir* in real life. That he was sure of. No. *Mir* would have judged his face, his clothes, his English. Then paid no attention to him. The online space was a leveller. His willingness mattered. And, his skill.

Not that he had to test his skills here. It wasn't even real hacking. He had been given a login ID and password. *Mir* had sent detailed instructions. Where to go. What to copy. What script to run afterwards. Just the timing was key. Early hours in India.

He exited *brownphyre* quickly and opened Tumblr. He typed in the keywords till he found what he was supposed to find. A site titled *Mystic@25*. A beautiful compilation of ten thought-provoking photo blogposts. He scrolled through the essays offering mystical wisdom for youth. Soppy stuff that he did not like. What was he supposed to see? Then he found the answer staring him in the face. There was one name as the writer of each essay.

Charles Mason. Next to it an alphanumeric email address.

Sandman knew what he had to do tonight.

But for now, he needed to cook dinner. Impossible to expect his mother to get up. She lay there, half-awake and nauseous, tossing in pain that radiated from her stomach to her thighs. He looked at her raggedy hair which would soon start thinning. Helplessly, he shut his laptop and squatted on the floor staring at a meagre pile of potatoes and gourds, wondering how long he could manage with his limited cooking skills.

THURSDAY, 11.30 A.M.

Rockville, Maryland

Jake and his team were rehashing last night's breach. The IP address traced to the teen hackers was one thing. But more perplexing was the fact that they had logged in using Dr Sandler's account, that too from some unconfigured machine.

Dean had gone through the log files again.

Jake peered at a printed report, not quite seeing it. 'Did we not program the security such that a doctor could only log in from an authorized machine?'

'Clearly someone overrode that security code,' Dean responded, trying to piece the puzzle.

'This is a clever breach, for sure,' Jake said with a forbidding look on his face. 'But what worries me is how did it happen. How could the machine-specific logging rule be bypassed? This is no mean trick. We are up against an expert.'

'It could be those boys in India,' Dean said, used to the weekly reports of some teen punk or the other causing some major site to crash, or tunnelling into forbidden government sites.

'But are they alone? Or is Dr Sandler masterminding it?' The innocuous-looking doctor could be letting others access the data through her authorized ID and passcode.

'She seemed unaware,' Dean responded. He had met the doctor only once. But she did not strike him as tech savvy enough to pull it off. 'What would be her motive, anyway?'

'Sell our data to competition?'

It seemed unlikely to Dean. He had been gathering information on Dr Sandler since yesterday – her past, where she lived, where and what she shopped, where she went online, and even a list of her lovers. It was amazing how easy it was to piece together the puzzle online, if you put your mind to it.

There seemed to be no stray or suspicious conversations going on with a third party. But then, could one ever be sure these days? There could be aliases she used. There could accomplices.

'Should we shut down Dr Sandler's account?'

Jake shook his head. 'Too much explaining to do to Andy. Keep it open, see if she logs in again, let's see what we can gather. The data is backed up anyway.'

Jake rose up to leave. 'You need to check on her. And trail those Indian boys.'

THURSDAY, 11.00 P.M.

Juhu, Mumbai

Vir had sent several apologetic messages to Diti, and got no response. So he had landed up uninvited at the celebratory post-party hosted by the producer of *Jaago India Hour*.

The bungalow and its terrace garden were overflowing with creative types and film financiers, models and advertisers, minor celebrities and wannabe actors. Guests were meandering in and out, in typical Mumbai style. No one kept tabs on who was invited and who not. Vir blended in easily, found himself a drink and looked around the room.

Diti had changed from her power sari into a skimpy metallic dress that highlighted her toned legs and accentuated her shapely back.

'Hey, congrats,' he said, walking up to her.

'Thanks,' she said, giving him a cool smile, and proceeded to ignore him.

He saw Diti flitting between groups, sparkling, that celebrated gravelly voice rising above the din with her laughter. He made small talk with strangers, getting annoyed by the minute. She had a way of getting to him. He felt transported to the past. To his twenty-five-year-old self. To the little tiffs that had mattered so much. Caused him so much heartache. When she, younger than him by years but more confident, would network effusively and pretend to take no notice of him. Making him pay for any little mistake or a turn of conversation she did not like. Reduce him to a bundle of ire, stewing in his own misery.

That she had the power to do the same even now, and that he was even letting her do it, years later, was incredible.

I've had enough, he told himself. Full of indignation, he walked up to her. 'Shall we walk outside for a bit?'

'Okay,' she said, and extricated herself from the group of advertisers she wanted to avoid anyway.

The terrace was beautiful. A wide-boughed almond tree hugged it, creating a rustling arbour. A few lanterns hung from the branches.

'That was a thought-provoking topic,' Vir started.

'Then why are you apologizing so profusely, anyway?' she said icily.

'For walking away in the middle of your recording.'

'And why did you?'

'There was a crisis at work. I had to attend to it.'

'So, then, why apologize?'

He shrugged.

'Why are you here, Vir?' Diti turned, giving him the shoulder. 'Isn't your girlfriend in town? Fiancée, I mean.'

He knew Tracey would be back tomorrow. His dad had called to tell him the flight number. Tracey hadn't messaged throughout her time there. Neither had he. Things lay unresolved with Tracey.

Was it him this time, the one running away from commitment? From compromise? Like Diti had, all those years ago.

But what of this could he tell Diti?

'She's gone to Solan. Because of this same crisis at my work.' He knew it sounded odd. Incomplete. A weak response, if there ever was one.

'It's an ongoing one,' he added effetely.

'Then go work out your problems, Vir. Don't stand here and keep apologizing to me.'

She turned and walked back inside, her tattoo shiny black against her bare back.

Inside the party continued, the festive din like distant background noise. He stood there, alone, gloom descending like the silent night.

THURSDAY, 1.00 P.M.

Rockville, Maryland

'Owww.' Dean nearly slipped on a frozen patch of ice, his arms flapping in the air like a moth, till he grabbed onto the edge of a postbox and prevented himself from slipping on the slick pavement with a thud.

He exhaled and steadied himself. Yesterday's snow was piled in thick deposits on the kerb, solid and slippery in places. The day was dull and dismal. The weatherwoman had promised grey skies and stiff winds for one more day before it started clearing up. The wind chime hung near the door tinkled as he walked into Dr Sandler's office. The doc was standing at the reception desk with her PA. She looked up, surprised. 'You again? Wow, you guys are persistent, or what?'

'I wanted to see which rep visited you before.' Dean flashed his ID sheepishly.

Dr Sandler lifted an eyebrow. 'I don't have the whole afternoon.'

'Half a minute.'

Dean pulled out a dossier he had received from HR. It was an employment record of Acel medical reps in the mid-Atlantic region, complete with their photographs and biodata.

Dr Sandler scrolled down the document. 'None of these,' she said shaking her head.

'Are you sure he said he was an Acel rep?' His mind raced ahead. Could it be a rep from another region? Or someone else?

Dr Sandler frowned. 'He said he was a rep. What's happening?'

Dean weighed the odds. Explain to Dr Sandler and tip her off. Or not tell her, and not get a chance to inspect. 'Would you mind if I examined your computer? The thing is the data you have loaded up reads totally garbled on our end,' he said, making it up on the spot.

Dr Sandler bit her lip and peeked at her slim watch.

'It won't take long. The portal on your machine is likely corrupted.' Dean tried a conspiratorial frontline approach. She could hardly say no. Not unless she was trying to hide something.

Dr Sandler sighed. *Corrupted.* Such an unusual term. Was there more this man was not letting on? 'Make it quick,' she said, typing in the password of her desktop.

Dean connected his own machine, mirrored the desktop on his own computer via Bluetooth access and opened a utility to run an advanced scan. He drummed his fingers upon the table, in a quick two-step beat, while Dr Sandler hovered, peering over his shoulders, asking a stream of basic questions which Dean tried to tackle patiently.

He typed command scripts, read the query messages, checked the drives and directories and usual hiding spots. The machine seemed clean. He checked the firewall, a two-way protection, linked with the McAfee system. It was up to date.

Then he found it.

Hidden inside the outer shell of a *Grey's Anatomy* video game, a 42KB unaccounted file in a 435MB folder.

It was common for a freeware game to install a malware along with it. Hackers delighted in gaining secret access to unknown machines and users. This was a remote access Trojan, a real leech of a worm, hiding in the shadows and leaving the computer unprotected so that a roving evildoer could enter through a backdoor and use the computer for a malicious purpose. To what end, he could guess. It had to be connected to Colare. But was it the only end? The hacker could have easily accessed Dr Sandler's passwords and protected PIN codes. What else had he done? Was there a connect with the doctor?

Dean rechecked the computer directory, looking for any recent executables that had been created or accessed. There was one. Could it have been installed by the rep when he accessed the Acel site? No doubt he would find an open port if he checked further. Left open by the Trojan. Dean made a mental checklist of all the tests he needed to run when he got back to office. On top was a diagnostic for checking if any malware had been embedded in the Acel website.

'Found it!' he told Dr Sandler.

What he didn't know yet was who had installed this! And whether it meant Dr Sandler was completely in the clear.

FRIDAY, 1.00 A.M.

Goregaon, Mumbai

Vir settled down next to Peevs, legs propped on a desk, a tablet on his lap, reading up on firewalls and hacking. He had a lifetime of knowledge to catch up on.

They sat on their nightly vigil, to get any fresh clues from Dr Sandler's next night-time crawl.

The more Vir read, the more his helplessness grew. The expert hired by Jake would arrive tomorrow. Meanwhile, his reputation was toast. Andy had as much as screamed ineptitude on the phone, and even Adam, who always backed him up, had been chilly and disengaged. His challenges seemed monumental, and the certainty with which he had lived his life, seemed hollow. Where were the colleagues he could trust, and who trusted him back? Where was the system that was straight and rewarding? It wasn't about Colare's curative powers any more. No, it was a race. Plain and simple. Diti's earnest questions seemed to mock him. He stood demonized, accused of not just lack of control over his team, but vilified for knowingly letting potential hackers walk away.

He put a finger to the throbbing in his temple, which threatened to morph into a full-blown migraine. 'You need to crack that boy.'

He felt an urgency like never before, reading an article on password-cracking algorithms. The net was full of alarming hoaxes and spurious advice.

Peevs stared back. Did Vir actually ask him to hack into Raghu's account?

Vir professed self-defence. They were under siege. It was surely permissible. Not that the young punks could complain to anyone!

'It's not working,' Peevs grumbled, after playing with a

random password-cracking tool, trying various combinations to open Raghu's email account. 'Even if I get in, it would be one account. Who knows how many accounts or aliases he has? Or, access to hundreds of computers – in his house, in college, in a friend's house. How can we track that?'

'There might be clues in his email account. Try the obvious ones. Variations of his name. His birthdate. Check his social profile. Recently favourited movies and songs.' It was amazing how much information was available just through social media.

'I've tried those before. No luck,' Peevs called out.

'Try the girls' names,' Vir suggested on a sudden impulse.

Peevs raised an eyebrow, taking in the dark circles under Vir's eyes, the crinkles on his forehead. 'You're looking wasted, man. Coming up with funky ideas at this hour.'

It was past midnight now. They hadn't slept properly in weeks. Dean and Scott had offered to tag-team and keep a watch. But given how tense the situation was, Peevs felt it would be foolhardy to accept that offer.

'Give it a try. What do we have to lose.'

Peevs shrugged and started typing. It worked – with a combination of Madhu's name and the current year. 'Heartache makes you smart, hmm, boss?' he teased, knowing that Tracey had flown from Delhi to Goa.

He charged up. This was better than waiting. Maybe the account would indeed yield some clues.

Vir wheeled his chair behind Peevs. 'Let's dive in.'

They scrolled down Raghu's email account, reading the messages and drafts. All harmless exchanges – the usual dirty jokes, censored images and homework discussions. They moved to his GooglePlus account, noting his posts on social media and comments on video sites, his recent chats and hangouts. The picture was getting clearer.

'This boy is in the thick,' Vir said, looking at his posts on dark sites and the torrent downloads. 'But how do we prove he is our perp, in cahoots with Dr Sandler?'

THURSDAY, 8.00 P.M.

Rockville, Maryland

The wait was never fun, except when it was.

'Let's go.' Scott touched his keyboard. Dean drew his chair closer. They toggled between screens, checking out latest security softwares for mobile apps and social platforms.

'Look, this one uses a hypervisor to control computers virtually,' said Scott, reading a product review and searching about the founders and the funders. Three venture capitalists had bankrolled the promising idea, started for a change not by some teen-punk, but by a balding and bearded man in his mid-fifties.

Scott looked at another site. 'Just listen to this, dude. Homomorphic split key encryption on the cloud. Ciphertext as a gatekeeper to disperse data.' He looked at the intense-eyed handsome founder, who had rounded up an impressive board and oodles of risk money.

'We need to give this shit up, and write some code,' said Dean, enviously.

After all, cyber deviants were getting more devious. Finding newer loopholes to invade private territories, creating fresh havoc, driving up the need to create newer security systems to detect social spammers and identity spoofers, email phishers, ransomware developers and unlawful entrants into personal or enterprise data domains. It made sense then that the hottest new start-ups, flush with funds, were those dealing in network security.

'Let's float that airgap client for cloud security.'

'After we catch this perp,' Dean said, stifling a yawn. They had been stationed for hours on the watch. He put down the remote keyboard and flexed his shoulders to ease his back muscles.

He was perplexed. There had been a pattern to the intrusions. Wee hours India time. Now it was late, already touching morning halfway across the world.

'Where the hell is this perp?' he said aloud.

FRIDAY, 8.00 A.M.

Nansha District, Guangzhou, China

The manufacturing floor of Wusan Labs was in complete hubbub as the morning shift workers, wearing white overalls, sat in rows, operating desktop grinders, measuring ingredients and mixing formulations. One floor above, the two rooms occupied by the research wing were in relative quiet.

'Someone better have a good reason why we are waiting!'

Min Ha, the owner of Wusan, was livid. He wasn't used to waiting, and this plan, complicated as it was, tested the limits of his patience.

Wusan had come up the curve as a generics manufacturer for heart- and tumour-related medicines. But its start, by a gravel contractor-turned-medicine man, had been less than salubrious. Jin Ha, the po-faced owner, had once run it as a drug-counterfeiting operation, selling fake medicines to villagers in the northern provinces.

Then fate had intervened. As his political contacts and clout had increased, he had perforce added a veneer of genuine copies to his business of bogus pills.

The counterfeiting industry continued to grow globally, raking up billions of yuans in profit from selling fake anti-malarial drugs in Africa or selling fake Viagra in the States. But by the time, his son Min Ha took over the helm of the roaring gravel business, riding the curve of China's construction boom, the medicines arm of the business had acquired a respectable patina as a manufacturer of generics. Behind the façade, the fake business for everyday medicines continued, making inroads into far provinces.

Now Min Ha had set his sights higher.

'This is a clean way,' assured Tu Yi, one of the old guard.

He had started as a floor chemist and become the President of Wusan Labs.

Min Ha looked out of the window, across the street to the shiny new ten-floor glass-and-steel building of Sino Qi.

Sino Qi was his main concern.

Once a poor cousin, helped by his father, the company had changed itself in the past five years. His tall young cousin, fresh faced and fashionably dressed from his years of studying in America, had come back full of ideas. Min Ha had always been more interested in Wusan Gravel. It needed low investment and yielded steady profits. It was only when Sino Qi had upgraded itself, by tying up with China's university professors to develop new biotech drugs and raking in hundreds of millions of dollars in global private equity investment, getting cushier recognition from the Party, that Min Ha had woken.

It was not the money. Min Ha had more of it from Wusan Gravel. It was this sudden lionization that totally irked him.

He wanted a part of it.

And, to bring down his upstart cousin. Sino Qi was working on a wonder drug, and had gathered recent press in Chinese media as an example of the modern firm, focused on innovation. His cousin had been invited to join the national committee of healthcare.

Min Ha felt his gut burn at the thought.

'Our team is on a roll,' Tu Yi said calmly.

'Let's wait for the showdown, then,' Min Ha said with relish.

FRIDAY, 11.00 A.M.

Churchgate, Mumbai

Madhu spent her free period in the college library, hogging the sole open computer in a corner, tucked between two long rows of psychology texts. She did her best to turn the screen away from the corridor, and read surreptitiously in the pale overhead light, soaking up the details.

She had fibbed to Anki she needed to borrow a physics book, and left her in the canteen chatting with some old girlfriends. Anki hadn't complained. Madhu sat resolutely, reading and partially thinking how amazing it was that they had stuck out so long, being as dissimilar as they were. But it was high time she took charge of her own life, stopped being the soft victim.

As for Raghu and Suv, well, how could she continue to be hazed? When they were just moronic surfers strangling legalities.

A student walked up, stopping at the psychology rack. Madhu turned her computer away further, shielding it from a stray glance.

There was much to learn. But she wasn't a national topper for nothing. So if being strong and self-sufficient meant she needed to be on top of hands-on tech stuff, she would get there.

With steadfast intent, she focused on decoding the differences between PHP, Python and Perl, languages she would start learning.

Meanwhile, Raghu sat alone at his favourite dosa place off-college thinking of the way Madhu and Anki had reacted in horror. They had refused to even look at him in college. Even Suv had acted weird, cutting off conversation.

His misery faded into indignation. How could his friends brush him with tar without proof? It went on to prove how real their friendship was, a decade of growing up dismissed on the accusations of a mere stranger.

FRIDAY, 11.00 A.M.

Goregaon, Mumbai

There was an urgency in the Acel data centre unlike any other.

Three young men in nondescript pale shirts, dark pants and colour-rimmed glasses had their laptops plugged into the Acel LAN, scrolling screens of command prompts, sending queries to the database, comparing results.

Karthik aka *HazMat* moved around, hands dug deep in his bespoke tailored trouser pockets, peering at the retrieved responses, muttering suggestions.

Rads stood back, uncomfortable at his personal domain being invaded by these security consultants hired by Jake. Karthik had arrived early bringing the drama of questions, running diagnostics to compare results with what had been done. Peevs, meanwhile, jumped from foot to foot and fidgeted with his tee shirt, clearly disgruntled.

'Pull up this chart.' Karthik instructed his team member to maximize a chart, and called everyone to look.

'We've laid down all the unexplained intrusions and logins by Dr Sandler on a timechart. Look at the pattern.'

Peevs scowled. This was old news. Trust this guy to seek glory with minimal effort.

Karthik said, with a reassuring smile at Peevs, 'You were on the right track. I am amazed at the clever work done.' He spoke sincerely. They were amateurs, after all.

Peevs bridled, unsure whether Karthik was patronizing.

The door opened. A waft of Armani perfume accosted the team even before they saw Vir step inside, stubbled and tall. He had spent the night on the office sofa and gone home in the morning for a shower. 'Where are we at?'

'We've plotted intrusions against time,' Karthik said, showing Vir the timeline on the screen.

'But he broke the pattern last night. What happened?'

Karthik pursed his lips. 'My guess would be as good as yours.'

'What do you think this guy is doing?'

'He is tampering your data. We've studied the data mapping you did. We've repeated several tests. The mismatch between the datsset is sixty per cent now.'

Alarm flared in Vir's eyes.

'This guy is slowly corrupting your data.'

There was a subdued stillness. They had suspected as much. It just felt strange when an outsider said it baldly.

'Is he using a virus to contaminate the data? But why go slow? Why not in a single go?'

'Have you wondered if he may be copying data out?'

Vir stared back. He had asked the team the same question two days back. Now the forensic expert thought the same.

'Yes, copying. Using FTP to copy out large datasets, then tampering whatever he copied out.'

Vir let out a series of expletives. He should have called in an expert like Karthik earlier.

'I would classify this as Advanced Persistent Threat.'

'Isn't that term used for defence infiltrations?' Vir said, trying to take charge, even as courage was failing him inside.

'Usually, yes. When cybercriminals target important financial or military systems. But sometimes someone tries in a systematic way to steal a company's secrets.'

'Like patentable recipe for breakthrough medicine?'

'Most definitely.'

If someone was copying data out, it could be positively disastrous. For Colare. For Acel.

A thought struck Vir. 'Tell me I'm not the only one wondering why we are giving free access to our data to this guy. Why have we set transmission protocol to "open"? Have we gone nuts?'

'We've created a decoy, Vir,' Peevs said.

'Peevs had a great suggestion.' Karthik was probably the same age. But he had been brought in as the expert. His reputation at helping governments, police and companies preceded him. But he had also learned to be diplomatic.

'We have masked the data deliberately. So the intruder cannot see the real stuff.'

'What do you mean?'

'They deliberately changed some of the data on the live server. To fool the hacker.'

'What about the real-time data being collected? What about the data that's needed by Terry and Peter for the legal paperwork?'

'That's being redirected to a new proxy server.'

Things were happening at a rapid pace. Vir struggled to keep up. Just when he mastered some details, new things came up. 'Who knows about this?'

'The IT team. Jake. Dean and Scott. Adam, of course.'

'Colare researchers? Peter, Terry?' Vir knew that the legal team was working around the clock, drawing up the PCT papers. They needed updated data charts to submit with the application.

'We have set up the auto-redirections for some users at the system level, Vir. So, if they send queries as normal, data will be retrieved from the new proxy server automatically.'

Jittery heaviness filled Vir. There had to be a loophole somewhere. He just did not see it yet. He looked at Karthik.

'So what happens when the intruder comes in tonight?'

'We'll get the MAC address of the machine that's sending the request.'

'But we already tried to find the IP address.'

'Another idea, to get the machine address. The type of machine could tell us something about the identity of the intruder.'

Vir did not understand this piecing together of identity through scraps of information. Seemed hocus to him.

Karthik added, 'I have the staff of iTring and other internet service providers in Mumbai on standby. They will trace the MAC address of the machine as soon as we get a ping.'

'Without involving the police?'

'Yes, without an FIR.' Karthik's deep voice carried a surety belying his years.

'Wow, we had such a hard time getting information.'

'I've worked with most internet service providers. They understand it's important to share information with a security consultant.

'That's not the only thing.' He smiled wickedly. 'We have placed several hotspots near Madhu's house. Open Wi-Fi connections. We will add tracking spyware to her computer. Let this guy get comfortable, let him begin the downloads. Then we'll switch off Madhu's Wi-Fi and hope the guy logs back in through a spy hotspot.'

'You suspect Raghu then?' Vir quizzed.

Karthik shrugged. 'He seems your key lead. Could be someone else too.'

'Won't he find it suspicious to suddenly find these new open hotspots?'

'We have to take this chance.'

'Isn't that leaving it to chance? That he does log in again immediately?'

'We typically wait for five minutes, let him get into his session. If the *Sharma* router hangs up in the middle, he will be frustrated. He will log in again.'

'That sounds slow.'

'It's behavioural dynamics. We need to triangulate his location to catch the bastard.'

Triangulation. The intruder would need to dial in from three separate hotspots. That information would then be pieced to find his exact location. Would a hacker smart enough to spend days in their systems undetected fall for a cheap trick?

'It's a bait.'

'Let's catch him then,' Vir said, feeling lighter than he had in days.

FRIDAY, 3.00, P.M.

Churchgate, Mumbai

'Don't be silly,' Madhu snapped angrily. The slanted rays coming through the stairwell made her glow.

'Come on, Madhu. Believe me. I didn't hack into Acel. But I am better than those smart pretenders!'

Raghu had insisted they meet. They sat on a stone staircase off an unused corridor in the Arts building, where none of their Science classmates would venture.

'Tell me you're joking.'

'No computer-support types can beat my skills.'

'So you're a hacker, then?' Her disappointment was palpable. She jerked her hands crossly.

The crocheted silver edge of her dupatta flapped towards Raghu and he held its edge. There was something in his eyes. An intent watchfulness.

'Come on, Madhu. These guys can't just walk in and doubt me.'

She pulled away her dupatta irately.

'Even if I believe you didn't do it, those guys are pros. Didn't you hear them tell you to back off?'

'They suspect me, anyway.' What could he say to make her believe in him again? And, why did it suddenly matter? Expectancy hung in the air.

Madhu looked down at the patch of sunlight, as if studying the photons. *What is happening to me*? Her heart chugged like a runaway train. She was very aware of the boy sitting next to her. Where had the dislike flown? There was an invisible force running between them, making her want to look at him. It scared her.

It was the first time in her life, ever, that she had missed a bunch of classes. Yesterday, when she was trying to message him, she'd been worried sick that he had done something wrong. That the police and the courts would come after him. Today, again. She had skipped an important class. Given the miss to Anki. To be in the middle of this impossible conversation. Trying to stop him from hacking to trace whoever was getting into her computer.

She bit her lip, recalling what she had read in the morning.

'Madhu?'

She looked up at his thin face and bright eyes. 'I've been thinking,' she murmured feverishly. 'The fact that someone is using our Wi-Fi to hack means one thing. The person lives within a fifty-meter perimeter of our house.'

Raghu stared at her, mouths wide open. How the heck did *she* think of that?

FRIDAY, 8.00 A.M.

Rockville, Maryland

'This APT report is dismal,' Jake said.

Karthik had sent in a mini dossier overnight, laying down the various threats to Acel's proprietary information.

'It's deliberate then?' Martha asked.

They were in an exclusive confab with Adam to decide upon the next course of action. Minus Andy and his theatrics.

'It can be nothing else. First malware is installed in the machine of one of Colare's clinicians, allowing the hacker to use her login ID and password to enter our systems undetected. Then, there is the matter of the same doctor having full permission to flit unfettered through all data servers.'

'Just Colare data?'

'Maybe others, but we don't know yet.'

'What else?'

'Then, there is the data corruption. What was recorded originally and what's stored now is different.'

'This is dreadful,' said Adam. 'We've spent a hundred million already. Metastatic pancreatic cancer is one of the most prevalent forms of the disease. Our estimate of market size is two billion worldwide. More if we prove it's effective for adjuvant treatments.'

Jake whistled. There was a lot at stake here.

'How could we have missed all this?' Martha was puzzled.

'Look, for what it's worth, the hacker has been in our systems for a week. Ten days, tops. Do you know what's the average time for detecting corporate espionage and hacking?' Jake said, speaking in his best rational voice.

'What?'

'Four hundred and sixty-one days.'

'That's crazy.'

'Isn't it? We are doing fine in comparison. Not that it takes away the extent of the mess we are in.'

'Look, with all this at stake, we need to protect European markets at least,' Martha said.

'Agreed.'

'And, we need to cut our losses in India.'

'What are you proposing?' Adam asked. He had been facing scepticism and obstruction from his top team on the India expansion ever since the start. Other than Acel's CFO and its board, other top management had continued to be suspicious.

'It means that we remove India data from our application. We also remove India as a country we file in at this stage.'

'Why?'

'My legal advisory expert has been watching the whole patent debate closely.'

'You mean *Big Pharma* versus *the State*?' Adam kept abreast of international industry news.

'Yes, the very same. The Indian Patent Board is deliberating on this whole process patent loophole.'

'There are also progressive factions that support a stronger patent regime.'

'Possibly. The tech firms could stand to gain from stronger protection. But the government could equally appease the masses.'

Adam polished his bifocals. Without his glasses, his eyes looked watery and weak. There was a time when advanced research led to cures, and thus to return on research investment. Now, lobbying with international trade organizations and global governments was equally or more important than investing in top-notch innovation.

'Do what you must, then,' he said.

'Fine. One thing, though,' Martha said, and paused deliberately. 'With so much at stake, let us keep this plan to the people in this room. And contain news of the hacking as much as we can. We don't want panic across the firm.'

FRIDAY, 7.00 P.M.

Bandra, Mumbai

They had to work on a group project. That's what they had said at home. Instead, they sat inside the empty church. A gilded cross sat atop a carmine velvet cloth up front. Evening mass would start in an hour. Soon the church would begin filling up.

'It has to be someone in *Santhal*, or the building next door,' whispered Raghu. Once he had got over the admiration that Madhu had come up with the idea, he had been happy to probe that line of thought. Because it meant, even if she did not say it, that she believed in him. Because it also meant spending time with her.

'But who?' Madhu glanced as a priest in a white cassock came to dust the altar, worried that he may shoo them away if they spoke too loud.

'The Wi-Fi signal cannot go too far.'

'Can you think of any shady neighbours?'

Madhu shook her head. They lived in a government colony, housing senior executives from public companies.

Madhu thought of the random ramblings she had heard from her friends. 'Well, there is Ruksana aunty's daughter. She is dour and hates every girl in the building. Chopra uncle kills lizards for fun with an airgun. Sapna aunty is visited a lot by her neighbour, whenever her husband travels.'

'Creepy. But they don't seem tech savvy.'

'Well, there is Mehta uncle's son. He spends all his time inside on his computer. A bit demented I heard, he's failed BCom twice. Mehta aunty complains that he is always playing computer games.'

'Sounds like Jiggs,' Raghu said, then mouthed *someone*, as Madhu gave him a questioning look. 'Can you check him out?

Fake an excuse, say you have computer problems, something. You need his help. See how he blinks.'

Madhu sat in the pew, looking down, almost penitent, wondering how to approach Mehta uncle's son. She hadn't spoken to any of the neighbours, leave alone a reclusive boy.

'Let me see. I will ask Anki.'

People started entering the church in groups, for the Friday evening mass. A pianist tinkled a few notes on the piano, then retreated behind a red velvet curtain.

'It's late.' Madhu had asked Anki to cover for her, but soon Mausi would start asking questions. As to what her parents would say if they knew was best forgotten. Madhu exited the pew, followed by Raghu.

Outside the iron-clad wooden door, the rising moon shimmered and reflected off the latticed glass window. They walked silently down the steps, close to the wall, Madhu stiffeningly conscious of Raghu right behind her. A quivering squirrel scuttled out of nowhere, scurried across the steps, brushing its furry tail on Madhu's foot. She squealed and jumped, stumbling on the steps. Raghu's arm reached from behind, steadying her. She stood with her back against the wall, Raghu's hand still on her shoulder, pinning her, her hand clutching the cotton of his shirt.

Raghu stood electrified, the runaway thud of his heart beneath her palm. He could see the rise and fall of her breath, rapid and shallow, beneath the fabric of her dupatta. Perhaps from the shock of her near tumble. Perhaps from something else. She continued to look at him with dark kohl-rimmed eyes. A hundred butterflies rose within her, crowding out any sound, any reality. Nothing existed but the tremble of his hand as he lightly wove a loose strand of her hair around his finger and leaned forward.

She stood there, first petrified then reckless, arcing up, her lips soft upon the edge of his mouth, until she felt she would die of the sensations that gripped her.

FRIDAY, 8.00 P.M.

Bandra, Mumbai

Sandman was on a mission. He would collect another payment today, there were new data drives waiting to be packed and given. Then he had to complete the rest of the work. Get paid again. That was the only way out.

He needed to decongest, before he got to work.

With determination, he plugged his fourteen-inch laptop into a floating socket, created by ducktaping the live wire borrowed from the pole outside with the wire of a multipin plug. The plug powered a hanging light bulb and a side fan. And now his new laptop.

He had used a borrowed computer till a month back. A slapdash arrangement of a crumbling monitor and ancient CPU, loaned to him by an old lady, who thought herself charitable and pious by giving him a contraption too old to have even scrap value. Yet, it had served his purpose. Taught him skills. Enabled him to earn. Given him a chance to buy his own machine.

He fired up, scanned for networks. *Sharma* was open. But in the list of networks, many with a lock sign signifying password protection, were three new open ones: *ZyDon. Gulati. Tan.*

ZyDon. He liked the sound of it.

He clicked on *ZyDon* and logged onto Facebook. He had created his *Sandman* account some years ago, when the only access he had was pocket internet using Nimbuzz on his second-hand Nokia. That too had to be shared between friends, who took time to apportion the precious prepaid minutes to surf or network or download games. That phone had been a treasure, too, paid for by the work he did at Rahmanbhai's corner kiosk near Mohammed Rafi Chowk. That was his evening job. Assembling old mobiles, repairing broken handsets, troubleshooting, cleaning viruses, or jailbreaking stolen phones. That had been another time. Since then, he had learned to troubleshoot and repair computers in his spare time. From there, teaching himself how to enter and exit domains was but a step up.

He whistled tunelessly, checked updates and forwarded a photocard to his list.

He clicked on *brownphyre*, out of sheer habit, and posted a question about a new ferreting tool he had heard of. That was his trick, posing the best questions, waiting for someone to share the tools. He took what he could in the online world. In the real world, he could gather precious little.

'Beta,' his mother called.

With a pebble in his throat, *Sandman* quickly logged off, and went to the bed.

'Water, Ayi?'

She hadn't got out of bed the whole day, weakened by nausea and wracked with pain in her legs. Not eaten anything, not even the thin lentil soup he had tried to spoon into her mouth. The neighbouring aunties had tried to come in and help, all concerned. *What happened to her? Tell me if you need anything.* There was nothing he could tell them. 'Ayi?' He bent down to his semi-unconscious mother, put his cheek upon her feverish cheek.

'My legs,' she mumbled incoherent with pain. He sat on the edge of the bed, rubbing her legs, feeling a desperation that never seemed to leave him. Tears brimmed in his eyes, but he held them.

FRIDAY, 8.12 P.M.

Goregaon, Mumbai

'Hey. Check this out,' Karthik said.

Peevs looked expectantly from Karthik to the computer. It looked like a command screen.

```
Hello. Z33d10.
```

'Cool.'

It was an active hello message, an auto-response sent by a router labelled *ZyDon*, along with its six-digit identifier code. This was one of the monitored but open routers installed by Karthik's team at various distances around Madhu and Ankita's building.

Karthik fired up the diagnostics software which listened to and monitored traffic on connected Hot Standby routers. He typed:

```
Router# show standby
```

The software spit out its response.

```
Ethernet0/1 - Group 1

  State is Active
  5 state changes, last state change 00:17:27
  Virtual IP address is 10.21.0.10
  Active virtual MAC address is 0000.0c07.ac01
  Local virtual MAC address is 0000.0c07.ac01
  (default)
  Hello time 3 sec, hold time 10 sec
  Next hello sent in 2.276 secs
  Authentication MD5, key-string "z33d10",
  timeout 30 secs
  Preemption enabled
```

```
Active router is local
Standby router is unknown
Priority 110 (configured 110)
IP redundancy name is "hsrp-Et0/1-1" (default)
```

'Do we have him?' Peevs bent over Karthik's shoulder peering at the screen.

'Don't know yet.'

'Are other routers active? Can we triangulate his location?' He hot-footed on his spot, eager for action.

'There are no other hello messages yet.'

'Damn.'

Karthik typed furiously, opening screens to check the status of the other standby routers, toggled to another screen to see the activity on *ZyDon*. The router had been programmed to send the exact string of instructions going through it as a set of message posts to pre-programmed locations.

The intruder was accessing Facebook. The end of the string was what looked like English words.

'*Sandman*?'

'Maybe his name. Let's check it out.'

But Facebook offered no insights. Search showed a page called *Sandman*, but there was no publicly available information, other than the person was male and lived in Mumbai. The accompanying photograph was of a muscular young man, in spiked hair and rippling iron-pumped biceps. The cover photo was of Taj Mahal Palace hotel.

'That's obviously not him,' Peevs said. 'I have seen this picture before. In an insurance ad, I think.'

'Don't stress. It's likely a fake.' Karthik sent a friend request to *Sandman*. But would he respond? When, was the other question?

'Check his friends, in case someone has a public profile.'

'Doxing! Cool!' Peevs said.

He had only recently heard of doxing, the new technique used to track, trace and gather information on something or someone, by piecing together little bits of data to create the full picture.

'Let me do it on another computer,' Peevs offered.

It hovered on the border of legality, tracking all publicly available information from various online and offline sources to piece the puzzle. Social engineering was getting a bad rep, especially getting the scoop on someone through phishing or baiting or tailgating or one of the other shadowy techniques. But this, doxing, was harder to track. Thrilling even, Peevs thought.

But how to begin when there wasn't even a name or a picture?

He settled down at his workstation, trawling through the friends list of *Sandman*, to see if any of them had posted anything that was useful. Every now and then, he would get up and scribble something on a large whiteboard hung on the wall.

Soon the whiteboard was filled with a complex diagram of boxes and arrows, with *Sandman* in the middle and a series of names like *Irrfan, Pednekar, Ray Man, Mann Dola* and so on. Most of these pages were private as well, and Peevs painstakingly sorted through their friends lists to see if something could start unravelling.

Karthik continued to seek traffic updates from *ZyDon*.

'He could remain on Facebook for hours!' he exclaimed.

It was impossible to know what the target was actually doing on Facebook. He could be checking updates or posting photos. But then again, he could be playing Farmville or Scrabble or some other game, stuck there for hours, offering no information to the investigators.

'Should we switch off *ZyDon*? See if he logs in from another router? Then we could triangulate him.'

'Look, there's a new command.'

Sandman, or whoever he was, had logged off Facebook. The next traffic update showed him accesing a site called *brownphyre*.

'*Brownfyre*?' Peevs frowned.

'Let's check it.'

Karthik opened another window and googled '*brownphyre*'. A site opened, all dark brown, with leaping flames in overlapping shades of ochre, bronze and gold. It had blogs on hacking and RSS feeds from other sites. There was a members area, which allowed users to participate in virtual hackathons or try out the latest hacking challenge. There were public posts, largely tips and challenges posted by users with names such as *Viral, Plastic Nuke,* and *Malingomer*. There was a private chatroom, and what appeared to be a private person-to-person messaging zone.

'Bingo,' said Peevs. 'That's our proof. That's it. We have a hacker here.'

He was almost relieved that it was a hacker, and not some virus run loose, spreading past the multilayered protections, encryptions and locks that his team created and maintained.

'Yes, but who is our suspect? These aliases tell us nothing.'

Karthik rubbed his chin. 'If he is not registering on other bots, then he is too close to *ZyDon*. Tomorrow we should tweak the locations. Move the other bots in closer?'

'Can't we do something tonight? Now?'

'Tough. Auto-toggle works only if the bots are physically close.'

Just then *ZyDon* sent a goodbye command.

Karthik swore. Would the perp dial back in again tonight?

'Hey, I found one public account in *Sandman's* network,' Peevs called out.

Karthik stared at the open profile of Suhas Patil. The photo showed a skinny young man in white shirt and sunglasses, leaning against a red motorcycle.

'Could this be a real photo?' Karthik said. 'Scroll down his home page.'

Most of the posts were photocards, of nature or Bollywood actresses or Manga men, some with inspirational quotes and comments like '*purrfect*' and '*kya jawab hai*' and '*chhaa gaye boss*'.

Karthik sighed.

It would be a long night. Hoping and waiting for the hacker to log in again.

FRIDAY, 10.37 P.M.

Bandra, Mumbai

He had left his mother sleeping, muttered in her ear that he had to meet Rahmanbhai on some urgent work and left. In reality, he needed to collect his next wad of cash.

But as he turned the corner, thoughts of another spilled onto his consciousness. 'Would she be alone?' He pushed his backpack up his shoulder.

Dull excitement stirred inside him as he walked the streets. Obliterating the pain. He needed the mindlessness, the loss of focus, that would make him forget his life. He had met her just once. Been lucky just once. His heart had made an instant about turn. Dumping the long-haired one, the daughter of the rich. She was out of reach. But this one! He had been back there three more times, hoping to catch a glimpse. But she had not been free, Shahnewaz had said.

Would he see her tonight? 'I will offer double,' he told himself. He would give her the phone. A cheap one he had refurbished himself from spare parts in Rahmanbhai's shop. Worth a few hundred rupees. Prepaid card for another hundred. At least they could talk. She could be his secret. His one source of joy. But did she even know how to type? Would she be allowed to use one?

Inside the neon-red interior of Caress Massage Parlour, Shahnewaz looked at the spindly boy. On the television behind him, Kareena gyrated in a skimpy sari.

'One more?' He eyed the boy keenly.

'*Bas*. Few more.'

'*Kyon*? Done?' Shahnewaz did not like to see easy custom go. But such was the nature of his efforts.

The parlour was a front, the nub from where he spun his other business dealings. And these things, passing money and contraband items through his network of contacts, were easy pickings. Not much effort on his part. Assignments just came to him. Enough people wanted to use grey *hawala* channels. A cut for him, rest to the party. He was scrupulous. And honest. He had to be, or customers would never return. He had repeat customers, those who slunk about on the other side of the divide, amid the so-called respected citizenry, parading at fancy parties, getting photos clicked and waiting, watching, planting ideas and connections, making money move and goods transport without a trace, when needed. Secrecy was important. Nothing escaped Shahnewaz's lips. No identities revealed, no details gossiped about.

This assignment was a little off-key. Money had come to him through the North East, in lots, hand-carried by truckers, as bundles of notes stowed under seats or in the lining of spare tyres, slowly working their way across the country. Just wait, his contact had told him. Shahnewaz had hardly expected a scrawny boy to turn up!

'What's in these boxes?'

'I told you. Data.'

'What is data?'

The boy sighed. '*Uff. Kaise bataun*? Tough *hai.* You will not understand.'

Shahnewaz was curious. 'What happens with these boxes?'

Gold bars, he understood. Too much trouble, in his opinion. Diamonds, he liked, easy to carry, openly worn in rings or bracelets, or cleverly hidden. Once he had to take a man to a local dentist, to get tooth caps fitted with diamonds stuffed inside the resin-bonded porcelain crown caps.

But these black boxes were new.

The boy shrugged. He wasn't being paid for nothing. He knew he was stealing something. What exactly he did not care. 'I don't know,' he said.

Shahnewaz scratched his groin, mind active with scenarios.

The runner who carried the boxes away in a shabby cotton rucksack was another shrivelled lad, wiser than his years. Despite being pushed for information, he evaded questions with the laughing ease of a stripling. Haribhai Dalal, Shahnewaz's contact, had arrangements at the international airport, and a set of high-flying couriers, traders and businessmen, who hand-carried small packages, usually in innocuous ways.

Haribhai had let slip '*Guzu*', making Shahnewaz wonder if he had heard wrong? Did Haribhai say '*gujju*'? It made no sense.

'*Bhai,' Sandman* interrupted. He really wanted to meet the girl. His heart sank. How to ask this man, he wondered. '*Woh ladki.* I want to meet her again.'

'*Lat lagi,'* Shahnewaz said, giving him a wicked, paan-stained grin. 'Another girl today?'

'*Wohi ladki,'* the boy insisted. He *had* to know her name.

'Caught your fancy, that bitch?'

Sandman felt anger spurt from his skin. But he suppressed it. He hated it when Shahnewaz talked about the girl like this. He could hardly fight back. The girl. Focus on the girl. He did not even know her name. He was so scared last time. He had to know her name today. He needed the money, but he needed to meet the girl more.

'I'll give you ten of these notes,' he offered, waving the bundle Shahnewaz had just given him.

FRIDAY, 3.00 P.M.

Rockville, Maryland

The room was frigid. The day had fast deteriorated into another hoary afternoon. Most teams were zipping out early, taking advantage of the impending weekend. Except the Colare teams, those working on the documents for the rushed patent application job were preparing to camp out at work.

Dean and Scott were preparing to do the same.

The air-conditioning system never worked well when the office was empty, and this afternoon it blew icy currents down the ducts and into the room.

Dean shivered, drawing the sleeves of his thick jumper onto his fingers and hugging himself.

'There's a blizzard warning.'

Not that it could be seen from inside this windowless room, but he had just walked out to make a cup of tea for himself and seen the thick flakes tossed about by lashing winds. The parking lot was already buried under snow.

'We are trapped then,' Scott said.

He knew full well that he had more fun cooped up inside, than going home to do laundry and cook his own dinner. Though, twice removed from the action, they had to rely on *HazMat* for help. But these were the moments, of live surveillance, of active snooping, that made everything else he did come alive.

Dean winked, settling back in his chair. He drew a blanket about him. No one waited for him at home, either.

A corner of Dean's monitor screen crackled to life, showing a flashing telephone icon. Dean pressed a button, a window popped up showing a curly-haired man.

'Hey *HazMat*.'

'Hey *DCaf*.'

'All set, man?'

'Yes,' Karthik responded, his head pixelating for a second, then nodding on the screen.

He had shared the news that the hacker had logged in for a few minutes on the sniffing bot, *ZyDon*. That they had an online name was progress, the next step was mapping the digital avatars to the real-life person. Dean and Scott were as eager to nab the culprit.

'Ready to trace the MAC address when the intruder comes in?'

'Yup, the *Sharma* router will remotely shut down as soon as we detect traffic on it. Three open bots have been set up nearby. We just sent a techie to move in the location of the other bots closer to *ZyDon*.'

They had discussed the strategy on an earlier call.

'I've spent the day with your guys in India. They've been doing a good job for amateurs,' Karthik said.

Having lived overseas for a few years, he understood unsaid geopolitical kinks, knew full well that *DCaf* and his bosses perhaps trusted him more on this than they did their own offshore team. He was an entrepreneur, as much as he was a hacker and a gamer. Not for him a blindsided approach to his machine and all that was linked to it. He responded well to people, knew how to make them respond to him, trust him. That was key to his consulting assignments.

'Good,' said Dean. 'So now we wait.'

SATURDAY, 12.00 A.M.

Goregaon, Mumbai

Peevs longed for his bed and a full night's sleep, stretched out under a thin sheet in the whirr of his small window AC unit. Longed for it, with the desperate longing of a man who knows it was not to be. Every muscle in his back was knotted. 'I'll be back,' he said, and decided to take a walk.

Karthik and Vir had stepped out for coffee. The others were sitting idly, watching the port scans, playing a game of cards as they spent another night of vigil. Perhaps a hopeless vigil. While the perp slept in comfort and slipped back into anonymity. They had all been so sure they would catch him last night.

Peevs walked to the podium. Beyond the trees and tenements, the lights of the city spread out. A few scraggly stars glittered in the sky. With trembling fingers, he unearthed a packet of cigarettes and lit up. Inhaling deeply, he took in a drag and saw the end of his cigarette glow red in the night. Smoke filled his mouth and his lungs, and a momentary peace descended.

Even at night, the city had a gritty smell to it. Crushing the stub beneath his sneakers, he broke into a spot jog, alternating it with a few jump squats. It had been days since he had exercised, since he had done anything except sitting in front of a computer. He felt the tension drip away bit by bit, as he sweated it out. The night was long. He had the time.

Finally he stretched, bending backwards and forwards, his skin prickling as the sweat evaporated in the slight evening breeze.

His phone rang. 'Where are you? We're onto something.'

THURSDAY, 12.00 A.M.

Chembur, Mumbai

Raghu sat at the Systems Administrator's desk in the computer lab at TISS, leaning into the screen. A scan was running, a thin bar filling up bit by bit, showing the percentage completion. A routine weekly check to ensure the servers powering the bank of computers remained clean. Nights were the best time, really. The lab was at its emptiest, the traffic through the campus LAN at its lowest.

But his mind was far away, recalling the touch of Madhu in his arms. The madness of the moment. As if all the blood had pooled in the centre of his body, cobwebbing common sense.

His phone clattered on the table. It was a message from Maganbhai. *Disk is ready?*

He wanted to talk to Madhu, go meet her. But the kilometres might as well have been a continent separating them. No way to reach there by public transport. On his bicycle, it could take him an hour of huffing and puffing. He mentally calculated what it would cost to buy a motorbike.

With trembling hands, he sent an instant message:

Hi...

He could not have sent a sillier message. He cursed himself.

He should negotiate with Maganbhai and save up to buy that motorbike. But he needed to get the data first. The computer lab would shut down soon. He had an hour.

The scan was just halfway through. He opened another screen, remotely logged on to another terminal in the room. He quickly ran a port scanner file to find open computers in remote locations. A stream of IP addresses filtered into his screen. He put his finger randomly on the list and checked it against the permissible IP address range for countries.

The open port was in China.

He swooped in and entered. A zigzag path to retrieve the data that Maganbhai wanted.

SATURDAY, 1.00 A.M.

Goregaon, Mumbai

Karthik sipped his chai latte. The eatery was busy, the only one in the area that served late night munchers with coffee and cakes.

'Intellectual property theft is unusual, isn't it?' Vir asked. 'Banking frauds or consumer information leaks are more heard of.'

Hackers were sophisticated now. Phishing, defacing, stealing passwords. New security softwares arrived, public awareness increased, but malware outwitted them. With many cool gadgets to play with, people barely managed security.

'IP theft is more common than you think. And worth a lot more.'

'No kidding.' Vir was very aware of what was at stake at Acel. Not just their careers, but the billions in potential revenue.

'Consumers facing hacking gets attention. Stealing of financial information or passwords or medical information. Consumer fraud. Cash siphoned off from bank accounts. But data espionage is very real too.'

'Not just *Mr & Mrs 55* then?'

'It's a very real threat. It's probably an insider, you know.' Karthik spooned a piece of cake into his mouth.

'What makes you say that?' Vir said. He could not think of anyone in the firm who would do this.

'I've been doing this for years now. There are patterns.'

'What patterns?'

'Companies don't want to hear this. But seventy per cent of the time, in a planned intellectual property theft, an insider or someone connected with the company is involved.'

'But we have so many firewalls, such safe practices.'

'You don't want to hear the stories, dude,' Karthik joked. 'Of IT helpdesk guys who brought in viruses on pendrives.

When people started suspecting pendrives, then they started coding malware in fake web links.'

'I've heard of those.' The biggest scoop of the times involved protected information being carried away by a former NSA employee on thumbnail drives.

'What about the malware coded into the mouse? Or the bankster hackers sending upscale clients champagne and cake, to be received with signature and mobile numbers. The phones were then switched off for half an hour, giving the hackers a window to swipe money out of bank accounts without any SMS alerts.'

'That's inventive.'

'And bank accounts are not even insured, so no recompense. Do you know that in Mumbai, I can go to a place in Dharavi and get the details of your phone bill? All your call record data, regardless of your provider?'

'Say you're joking. Not the Chinese mafia, then?' Vir said feebly.

'Yeah, that's the headline news,' Kathik said.

He had been involved in cases with ministries and defence establishments. India had become one of the top countries in the world where cyber crime took place. Not just for origination. Rather, a place where others got into the country's systems and databases. Partly, the blame lay on the poor awareness about cyber crime. Many systems remained weakly protected. Much of the incoming chatter and snooping could be easily traced back to foreign shores, China in particular. Some real, others spoofing overseas infractions.

Not that these cases were much publicized. It wasn't just national security, but national pride at stake.

'But, realistically, in this case, the way the hacker is using Dr Sandler's information, it could only have come from an insider.'

'The missing rep.'

'It's the era of insider leaks, man. Every righteous enthusiast has the ability to blow the whistle.' Snowden had left a deep impression on the notion of corporate loyalty in the face of common good.

'But this is data for a life-saving drug,' Vir said sounding aghast. 'What's there to blow the whistle about?'

'The rep is disgruntled about something else. Does not wait to think about the implications,' Karthik said cynically.

Vir knew they were trying to track down the rep who had visited Dr Sandler. Acid rose up in his guts. He just wanted to wake up into a new world. One where work proceeded smoothly. One where success came unequivocally. One where girlfriends did not huff off to Goa on their own. There had been a cryptic message from Diti: *Brunch tomorrow?* Like yesterday hadn't happened. And to top it all, he'd accepted. That his life was a mess was an understatement.

'How did you get into this line, anyway?' Karthik looked too young.

'As a student, like everyone else.' Karthik shared how he had got hooked onto computers during high school when his father had been transferred to New York. Without many friends in those early months of transition, he had spent hours on his computer. Learning to code and jailbreak. After India, the American high school curriculum had been easy. Time had sat heavy on his hands. From there to minor hacking was a small step.

In college, on the West Coast, he had got into ethical hacking, helping the university administration at foiling a hacking attempt. He had caught the eye of the local police cell, and helped them in a case, getting attention as a young hacker on the right side of the law. Not that there was too much money in being on the right side. Still, it had felt like a calling. He had hung out at Def Con, participated in hackathons, and made friends in the community. After a degree in computer science, he had made ethical hacking his profession. His parents had relocated to India, and so had he, to start his own cyber security firm.

'Wow,' said Vir. A man who knew his mind and his path. 'So, mostly you uncover corporate thefts or terror plots?'

'It's not quite as exotic as being in the NSA,' said Karthik. 'Mostly we help companies against fraud. Stealing of consumer data. Embezzlement and swindles.'

'Conned consumers?'

'A lot of fraud happens with individuals. Cons via mobile banking or unprotected passwords. But individuals don't help pay the bills. Companies and local authorities do. Usually to nab people trying to spread anarchy through spoofed social media posts. Religious and regional unrest, you know.'

Vir looked confused.

'You don't know?' Karthik puckered his brow. 'It's probably kept under wraps from the media. But serves divisive politics. People so easily believe things. A photo, a compromising one – against a religious minority or regional interest – speaks a thousand words. Ordinary citizens don't quite think about authenticity. Like is it coming from a spoofed ID? Or is it a doctored clip? Has the picture been morphed? News spreads like wildfire. Riots break out.'

Vir's phone rang above the chatter in the room.

'Come immediately,' Peevs said.

SATURDAY, 2.00 A.M.

Goregaon, Mumbai

There was frantic excitement. Peevs and Vir hovered, watching the cyber security experts toggle screens to track the intrusion in real time.

Karthik had laid a series of traps, barely observable mini loops in the digital strands of the Acel network, thin pieces of code hidden at ports left deliberately open, ready to catch the digital footprints of the intruder. These traps were hidden in data servers and the corporate firewall, inside Dr Sandler's computer through a remote administration tool, and inside Madhu's computer installed physically earlier in the day.

A map-like app was open, lighting up in visual motion the intruder's path into Colare's data warehouse.

Someone checked the data feeds from the bots. *ZyDon*, *Gulati* and *Tan* were not in use. The *Sharma* router was inactive as well. How had the intruder connected?

'Run a trace on the intrusion,' Karthik said.

'Fat lot of good that'll do.'

'We can't triangulate.' Vir felt let down. 'He is not using our decoy routers.'

The team had reprogrammed the decoy routers to toggle on auto-loop. Had the hacker used any one of them, they could have got an exact location.

Karthik pointed towards the map-like app. 'The guy is in our system, through open port 443. We can see incoming and outgoing traffic through the port.'

'Is data being transferred out?' Vir felt a frisson of tension.

'I fear.' Even without forensics, that seemed a fair guess.

'You say it so casually!' Vir squirmed.

Karthik shrugged. 'This is clearly an informed intruder.'

'You keep saying that.'

'He is very sure-footed. This attack is not exploiting any of the security holes in your base browser, any vulnerabilities in your database package. He knows exactly where to tunnel to. Using known passwords, as we know.'

Vir observed the thrum of activity at this uncertain hour between midnight and dawn, amazed by the ruckus. Could it be the work of a lone hacker, sitting in some shack in Bandra?

'Who inside your firm could be doing this? Think,' Karthik suggested softly, his eyes still trained on one screen, his fingers typing away on the command prompt, checking on the trace.

Vir raked his fingers through his hair. *Who?* He felt sick.

'It is also possible that this person just masked his location as Bandra. He is elsewhere actually,' Karthik said.

Vir frowned at this new theory. Was this a wild goose chase? A guessing game? 'Didn't you just say two minutes back that it could be an insider?'

The trace sent to detect the address provided an IP address, and another little window mapped it to geo-codes.

'Wow, this is Guangzhou, China.'

'China?' exclaimed Rads and Peevs in unison.

'China!' Karthik rubbed a bony finger upon his upper lip. 'Didn't Jake say something about one of your key competitors trying to create a similar molecule is in China?'

'It could be, you know. It could be,' he mumbled softly, almost to himself. In his business, he had seen many instances of competition by stealth, of companies trying to acquire intellectual property through nefarious means, planting moles or scooping technology.

Vir stared at him with rising dread and comprehension. 'So we can't triangulate him because he is from China?'

'Is Dr Sandler's spoofer really sitting in? That I don't know. We just see the last hop of the incoming ping. If it's a multi-hop intrusion, the person could be sitting anywhere. In this room even.'

Vir looked pained. 'You are doubting us?' If Karthik could even utter this, what stopped Andy and Co. from totally believing it?

'Just stating the obvious. Don't get in a snit,' Karthik said. 'Check the systems logs once.'

There was another flurry of activity as his team checked the systems log files to verify the ID of the incoming connection.

There was no Dr Sandler.

There was only one active user. It was another name altogether. Charles Mason.

'Who the hell is Charles Mason?' Karthik asked incredulously. 'Is this a valid entry?'

'Check, guys, quick,' Vir urged.

Peevs typed at rapid speed, querying the database of users.

'Who is this? What is happening? Shut him out,' said Vir urgently. 'Shut him out.'

'Dr Charles Mason is a registered clinician on Colare clinical trials. Based in Baltimore.'

On cue, a face flashed on the computer. Dean, calling VOIP over the internet. Asking Karthik to shut down pronto. Till they could reassess, see what next and how best to lay a trap.

Karthik used a Wi-Fi clicker to switch the server off and terminate the session.

As ominously as a little bar had blipped on the screen, indicating data transfer out from the protected confines of Acel to some unknown location in the wide world, it stopped.

Just a flashing dash in green bisected the dark screen.

SATURDAY, 4.00 A.M.

Antop Hill, Mumbai

'Fuck,' Paul Zhang swore at his vibrating phone.

He had forgotten to put it on silent last night. Now the few hours of night sleep he had managed were history.

It was eerily quiet outside. His neighbours in Maratha chawl huddled in their rooms and in corridors. Even the street dogs were crouched behind bins and boxes. Perhaps the only time of the day the city was actually shrouded in silence.

'Does this bastard ever sleep?' He fumbled to find his reading glasses in the dark.

It could only be one person messaging him at this hour. But when you signed up with the 14K Triad, you signed away your right to live life on your terms. The group, a brotherhood really, kept a tight leash on its members spanning across Asia. Paul knew that.

The sender was who he had expected.

The subject, the irritating assignment that seemed to be taking up too much of his time. Paul preferred simplicity. The narrow track he had established over the years. Girls and drugs, making their way across the subcontinent, to the nerve centre of India. To *wadi* pimps and dons. He knew what to do. He knew how to operate. This fucking company spying business was different. Too many new tasks to be done, for no better pay.

The message was cryptic.

Clean up. Leave no loose ends.

Sighing, Paul got up to get ready.

Shahnewaz was the last link.

That was the place to start then.

SATURDAY, 11.00 A.M.

Park Hyatt, Goa

Tracey dived into the sun-speckled pool, a flash of red in the blue water. Pausing for breath, she treaded water, when she heard a deep American-twanged Hey there!

Turning back, she saw a crinkle-eyed man, too easy on the eye, his legs dangling in the pool. 'How about a race?'

It was bright and the large amoeba-shaped pool largely empty, except an Indian family lounging in the shallows with babies in floaters, swimming rings and water toys.

Tracey smiled. 'To the end and back.'

Without waiting, she dived and swam away, hearing 'Hey wait', then powerful slashes behind her, as he churned the water trying to catch up. She flipped at the end, losing by a mere fraction of a second despite her headstart.

'Andrew.' He extended a dripping hand.

'Tracey.'

They swam a few more lengths without a word, then towelled dry, put on dark shades and sat under a large white umbrella with drinks. 'I was in India on work, so came here for the weekend,' Andrew said. He was negotiating on a major infrastruture project for the World Bank. He lived in Washington, DC, a few stops away on the metro from where she lived.

'We were meant to meet, huh?' He regaled her with stories of his journeys through Odisha, and through places as exotic as Azerbaijan and Vietnam and Costa Rica.

'What brought you to India?'

'Work,' she said obliquely, casting a quick glance at his hands.

He caught her look and spread his hand, a thin tan line marking where a ring should have been. 'Recently divorced,' he said, ruefully. 'She did not like the fact that I had to travel.'

Tracey gave him an empathetic smile. Her sparkling engagement ring, safely locked in the hotel room, was too new to have left a tan line. 'There is someone?' Andrew noticed the slight gesture.

Tracey nodded, feeling bitterness tinged with sadness brim over. 'I don't know.' Wishing for an instant that she had liked someone like Andrew. How uncomplicated life could have been!

'I understand,' he said, not wanting to dig further. 'Shall we forget our shattered love lives for a bit and order another drink?'

Tracey nodded.

Later in her villa it came to her. *She had to return.* What was the point of staying on? The future seemed unimaginable. Passion had subsided. Laughter had disappeared. It was the misery of the end. Of a beautiful phase of life. Of love that was dying.

FRIDAY, 10.00 P.M.

Nanshang Province, China

Min Ha was throwing a fit. 'Why this drama,' he asked tetchily, 'when we have the best teams right here to infiltrate this company and get the data?'

Tu Yi looked at his boss with a steady eye. His contact had not told him, but he knew the plan had already met its first hitch. He had warned Min Ha against this foolhardy goal. Why seek the glory of originality when you have the wealth of a mercenary?

As the President of Wusan, Tu Yi had led the company on that same path of success. Wusan applied genuinely for generics licences. But when it wanted a particular recipe, such as a new cure for heart disease or chemotherapy still wrapped in patent protections, sealed shut to the world, a secret network would click into action. The easiest places to break into were the patent offices in Eastern Europe or Asia, and Tu Yi had assembled shadowy mercenaries, building linkages with the Triads, to get what he wanted. But that was after the full application had been submitted. Preliminary petitions, he had found out, contained sketchy technical information and weren't valuable for his purpose.

The adjoining set of rooms housed a recent initiative. A small team, sophisticated in the art of cyber penetration. Hired from a government IT lab. Pharma company sites had layers of protections, and occasionally his team had managed to get past. But they would routinely ping American government medical organizations, and look at the new ideas being tested at the National Institute of Health.

Since China became a signatory to World Trade Organization agreements, swearing to protect intellectual property rights, such things were becoming tougher. Tu Yi had engaged a British legal firm, whose Chinese partners had strong connections with the State Food and Drug Administration, and managed to hold his own.

'We had to go the insider route.' Tu Yi gave a half-smile. A flash of silver-capped teeth. He liked the idea of shifting allegiance, of bendable morals.

'We can trust him?'

'I think so.'

'All according to plan, then?'

Tu Yi debated whether to share the details with Min Ha. He would not understand the intricacies of the operation, just kick up a fuss.

'I have a Plan B.' Tu Yi always had a Plan B.

Min Ha nodded. He did not want to know the details. Just that they had a backup plan.

'Tell me again why we couldn't just air-lift the guy? Get the material directly.'

'Because even then we would need to copy out the data. There are petabytes of data, Min Ha. One person's intellect is of no use.'

'If you say so.'

Tu Yi pursed his lips. Getting all the data had not been his idea. Just getting the recipe was easier. They could cook it locally. Change a few minor things. Get on with it, make the money. Like they always did. But, no, Min Ha wanted to make a splash with this one.

Min Ha tested his patience. There was an arrogance about him that had not been there in the old man, Jin Ha. Not that Tu Yi could voice it. He had risen through the ranks, become powerful in his own right in Wusan. But the purse strings were always controlled by Min Ha. If Tu Yi had created contacts with the different ministries that had purview over Wusan Labs, it was on the back of the cash and connections of Wusan Gravel. Tu Yi knew his limitations. At fifty-three, if he was forced to take early retirement, there would be no recourse for him.

'I just want to beat Sino Qi,' Min Ha said childishly.

'I know. And that's what I have planned. My contact has

shown the way. The man in the middle is the obvious cog. A paid hack. We download the data from the dump server in Europe. The trail, when they find it, will lead to Sino Qi. We will derail the American company, and point a shadowy way to our neighbour.'

'Good,' Min Ha said.

Tu Yi looked away. *Plan B*. The glitch was not trivial. He might have sent a mercenary to get the data, but his own team was riding the chatter of his target. Min Ha knew that his adversaries suspected foul play. They were on their guard, trying to dig deeper.

Even if there were no more glitches, could he afford to let any loose strings remain?

SATURDAY, 11.00 A.M.

Bandra, Mumbai

'My kind of place,' Diti said, sipping her coffee.

She looked casual in denims and a floppy shirt. Approachable, Vir thought, unlike the statuesque goddess of two nights ago.

'So why are we here?' Vir folded his arms.

He had come, of course. Perhaps he just liked inflicting self-wounds. Just his luck then that every time a woman crossed his path, he couldn't make the cut. That he had to change life's course to fit with them. Never the other way around. First Diti. Then, when he had finally learned to trust again, Tracey.

'Not to eat these lovely nutella crêpes and drink coffee,' he said sardonically.

Diti looked away for a second, playing involuntarily with a demi spoon, fiddling with it, moving it on the table.

'I had to tell you.'

'What?'

'That you're distracting me.'

Vir stared at her, dumbfounded.

'There,' she said, and started playing with the spoon again. 'I said it. What I had come to say.'

'Okay.' Vir let out a measured response. What was he supposed to say? Diti considered him for a moment. Observing the way his jaw looked tight. Like stuck with cement.

'I need to know that the city is big enough for us.'

'What?' Vir said, goggling, looking confused.

'Look,' Diti said, leaning in, all earnest. 'I am back here. For good. For the moment. My show is on, the contract is done. I am here.'

'So?'

'That's the thing. So are you.'

'So am I *what?*'

'Here. In this city. For the moment. For some time.'

'This is priceless. Are you asking me to leave?' He shook his head.

'Of course not. That's your decision. Look, be calm.'

'I am calm.'

'Okay, so, we had unfinished business from the past. You left India...'

'And you left me.'

'Whatever,' she said turning red. 'Simply said, we have this unfinished business from the past. This connection. This unclosed loop. We need to close it somehow. Learn to breathe in the same city. Without guilt, without remonstration.'

She paused, her deep-set eyes looking darker. 'Without expectation.'

'As you say. But remember, you called me. I did not message you after Thursday,' Vir said, feeling the heat rise up his neck. Whatever was she going on about?

'I know,' she said, reaching out to place her hand on his. 'I'm sorry I'm coming out all wrong. Look, this is for me. I need the closure. I need to close the loop. In my mind.'

'So are we done then?' Vir asked, leaning back in his sofa seat.

'Look, you have a fiancée and all.'

'A fact that I never hid from you.'

'So basically you are beyond the pale. Untouchable.'

'Yet you are touching me.'

'What?' She jerked back, lifting her hands and placing them on her lap, below the table.

'Shall we, then?' Vir said, scrunching his napkin and placing it on the table.

She opened her mouth to say something, then simply spread her hands, looking baffled. 'I just needed to meet you. Say this. For whatever it is worth, I once loved you. Dearly. But I wasn't ready to even think long term. It's been years. Longer than whatever I could imagine at twenty-one. So, meeting you now. It's just odd. This remnant attraction, this it-might-have-been. A wisp of the past which must float away.'

Vir shook his head.
She could not dump him.
Not now, when they weren't going out.
So why did it feel like he was being dumped?

SATURDAY, 11.30 A.M.

Bandra, Mumbai

'What filth! Couldn't we go on a better excursion, Madhu?' Raghu jumped across a puddle of uncertain colour.

They were scouring the ramshackle spread of hutments behind Santhal Building, peeking through tattered curtains that flapped from openings in mud-brick and rippled tin constructions, drawing sullen stares from children and old men. A family of pigs lolled about, with dried mud on their backs.

Madhu avoided a fluttering hen pecking upon vegetable peelings. 'Since I could not think of any suspects from the buildings, the next option was this slum.'

'How likely is that?' Raghu grumbled.

They moved along the makeshift path, skirting rubbish and faeces.Televisions blared from inside some of the huts. Raghu lifted a random curtain acting as a door and peeked inside. A woman squatting at a makeshift oven screamed at him. He dropped the curtain.

A young boy crooked his finger. 'Why are you here? Are you police?'

'Does anyone have a computer here?'

'Why? Your computer stolen?' the boy asked in pidgin English.

Raghu nodded.

The boy shrugged, walking away.

'Wait,' Raghu called out, but the boy just walked on. There was no one else to ask. They left the slum.

'There may be one other person who could help...' Raghu began. If there was a hacker in this mohalla, Maganbhai would surely know. But could he take Madhu there? Let his worlds collide?

'Let's go then.'

'I can't take you there.'

'That's silly. Remember I am smarter than you, I can fend for myself.'

She walked fast past the buildings, lest a neighbour or a guard spot her. Raghu followed a few minutes later. On the motorcycle borrowed from Suv, Raghu whizzed off to the *galli* beneath the Kalanagar flyover.

'This way.' Raghu led her down the crooked alley.

The grimy space housed decrepit computers on narrow tables. A beady-eyed man in a checked green lungi lounged on a green plastic mat, watching a half-naked baby crawl among a few toys.

'*Arre, arre*, Raghu baba,' Maganbhai said, beaming with *paan*-stained teeth. 'You brought a girlfriend. Got my CD?'

Madhu stood impassive, wondering how on earth Raghu knew such a shady-looking character, and whether she should have paid heed to his hesitation in bringing her here.

Raghu avoided looking at Madhu. 'I needed some information, Maganbhai. Do you have any sources in the slum near Reclamation?'

Stillness descended. The baby continued to dribble and coo on the ground, but Maganbhai bolstered himself up to stand tall.

'Why? You getting into police business or what?'

'No, no, nothing like that.'

'I don't know anyone from there. It's too far. And if you are smart, you will stop asking questions. They lead to no good.'

Raghu nodded and led Madhu outside to the motorcycle.

'I won't ask now how you know him. But I have a hunch we should wait,' Madhu said. Part of her wanted to leave. What had come upon her? How horrified her family would be to learn she had visited a place like this.

Barely minutes later, Maganbhai whizzed past on an old Kinetic scooter. Keeping a safe distance behind a couple of cars, Raghu tailed him, weaving past footpath shops and slums, buses and pedestrians, turning a swift corner into a quieter tree-lined area in the shadow of a giant stone church. Maganbhai stopped in front of a row of shops. The building had a peeling signboard of *Caress Massage Parlour.*

'What's this place?' Madhu strained her eyes in the shimmering sunlight. 'Should we go up?'

'Don't be stupid,' Raghu snapped, loath to hang around in that area with a girl.

Raghu waited for a minute, then revved his motorbike and sped back along the tree-lined road, turning onto the main road to go home. Suddenly a jeep came up behind them, swerved, rammed into the motorcycle, losing control for an instant before speeding off. The motorcycle slid onto the ground, trapping the riders underneath its heated bulk.

Raghu's helmet flew off. His torso hit the ground, the harsh edge of the footpath cutting into the side of his chest.

'Damn,' he said, spitting out dust, dislodging a shaky breath.

He looked around at Madhu, buried beneath the motorbike, a gash near her temple. 'Fuck,' he swore silently, as he hauled himself up to give her a hand. How could he have been so stupid?

SATURDAY, 5.00 P.M.

Aksa Beach, Mumbai

The sun was angled above the horizon, turning the Arabian Sea into a rippling sheet of unending gold. The sea breeze gently rippled the palm trees. The sand was smooth and powdery. In the distance, local fishermen navigated their boats and the day's catch away from the naval ship that stood moored in the distant shallows. A postcard scene Diti did not notice.

Behind her, in the gated garden of a sumptuous bungalow, things were readying for a weekend party. Her friends were setting up the karaoke system and putting beer bottles in an ice-cooler.

Her heart was bleak. She walked to the edge of the shore absent-mindedly, steeped in her sadness. She had told Vir to stay away, but was that what she truly wanted? Love, once carelessly tossed, had returned to haunt her. No one had measured up to Vir over the years. It wasn't just that simmer of magnetism between them, but his patience to stand her ribbing, her lofty world views. Yet he had never sought her out, and stubbornly, neither had she.

Diti Rajan, clever as she could be, steady in the face of hardships, hopeful champion of the unfortunate around the world, put her head on her knees and wept.

For her botched love affair.

For her dithering heart.

For her unsettled life.

Utterly spent, she wiped her eyes and lifted herself up. She paced the sand, then stood facing the shimmering horizon.

Vir entered the torchiere-lit garden, the incense of *loban* warding off the evening insects. Beyond the palms, lay the sea. Tall candle pillars flickered artfully in glass jars.

The party was in full swing, a bartender briskly sending

around green and pink drinks decorated with cherries and paper umbrellas. A woman was crooning melodiously to a ghazal, the audience swaying in appreciation, humming in response.

The bottle of champagne in his hand felt futile.

He hadn't wanted to come. Yet he had to escape.

He took a glass of Scotch from a passing waiter, and absently sat on a folding garden chair. He should have gone to Goa instead, been contrite with Tracey. It was too late. He felt effete. Laid bare.

He stared into the darkness, the music barely a salve.

The last two weeks sat heavily on his mind. What had started with much fanfare just months ago, was heading nowhere. His career, even after the Colare drama ended, would take a while to ramp up again. Colleagues he had assumed to be friends were giving him grief, questioning his intent.

The dilemmas Diti had invoked – the needs of the masses and how far his trajectory was from anything imbued with empathy and meaning. Why did they meet again? *Of all the gin joints...* he wondered.

So Tracey's call had just staked his moorlessness. '*This will hang between us like an unsaid divide,*' she had said. It was over. In one surreal phone call. If his heart had been broken once with all the splintering pain and uncertainty of youth, this was worse. It was blankness, bleakness, an utter void. He gulped down his Scotch.

It had happened again. He had been dumped.

Then he saw her.

Diti. Sitting in a corner of the carpet, among a sea of women, and all he wanted to do was walk up and crush her.

He had to escape for his sense of self, for his sanity.

SATURDAY, 4.55 A.M.

Gaithersburg, Maryland

Mystic Mir sat at his desk, frantically looking through the ongoing conversation strings on *brownphyre.* All he could think of was that ominous message on Scrabble.

Plan B.

Two words that could be innocuous, an idle threat, but likely meant a great deal. People who dealt in hot money rarely threw around threats they did not mean. If Sandler was bust, how long before Mason got found out?

What had seemed an infallible plan, safe in its complexity, had knotted on itself. The path had been found. His contacts knew it too. How long before it led to him? There was no certainty who else would be on the watch now, from the state department to the airlines and the banks. Thank God he had transferred his money. But if the plan failed, was the money really his? How long before the mercenaries arrived, ready to slit his throat.

He had to inform *Manic 18*. Tell him to pause. But where was he? Was he simply hiding in the shadows, listening to the chatter, under another alias?

Mystic Mir logged onto his email account and left a draft message. Titled *Urgent.*

Outside his slatted window, the sky had turned cerise and aubergine. He drummed his fingers upon the table.

Plan B.

Something was about to click into action. Something he did not know. Something he could not control.

He needed to have his own Plan B.

SATURDAY, 8.00 P.M.

Bandra, Mumbai

'Abort. Don't do anything else until my next instructions.'

Sandman stared at the draft message in the inbox of the account he shared with *Mystic Mir*. It was dated today. There was another message dated yesterday, saying the same.

Something was up.

He had done as instructed. Step by step. Logged in as told. Copied the data. Run the scripts. Delivered the Seagate hard drives. Received payment for each lot. He had come to enjoy it. That sense of power. That feeling of absolute command.

But there was more.

It was complicated to know exactly what his intervention was doing. But whatever it was could twist the fortunes of this medical company. He had read briefly about Acel, its various fancy cures that only the rich could partake in. A company like the one which had conducted the bogus clinical trial his father had been a part of. The gut-wrenching pain tormenting his Baba in his last days, as he had contorted senselessly on a narrow iron hospital cot, swam before his eyes.

He needed to cobble together every rupee to pay for medicines for his mother. This work had personal significance. It was sustenance. It was a mission. It was life itself.

It was even vengeance. Could he just let a company like this get away? Abort? Not do anything else?

And what about the two 750GB hard drives that sat in his backpack right now? He hadn't been paid for those. If he froze now, then how long before he received any further payment.

What about the shy dark-eyed Mishti? The one spot of excitement in his dull life. He had blown a lot of cash to meet her, find out her name, sneak her that prepaid phone. Would he get to meet her if he was of no use to Shahnewaz?

He felt brittle. Molten inside and frozen outside, stretched and stressed from the sudden shifts.

He logged out and shut down his laptop, wrapped it in bubblewrap, stored it in a makeshift cupboard of planks and bricks.

'Sandesh, beta.' His mother dragged herself and set a plate of *subzi-roti* next to him. She looked bedraggled. Worn down by the disease, yet insistent that she scramble up the strength to cook for him. 'Let me walk you next door, Amma. Watch television for a bit. You will feel better.' Anything to distract her.

She shook her head, sat and leaned against the wall, eyes closed. 'No, just give me one *roti*. I feel like sleeping.'

Sandesh nodded helplessly.

Poor Amma. He felt bitter. So content with the hand-me-down scraps from Mrs Sharma. So happy just to watch her favourite show on television. Not concerned that the uppity women looked down upon her. Upon him. Not concerned that life had meted out a lot of ill luck to her. She took it all in her stride, guilelessly. Blaming neither fate nor the world. Whatever she faced was written for her. So she believed.

How could she?

He felt strangled by the unfairness of it all. *He would show them all.*

He went to the makeshift kitchen, brought food for his mother, sat her against a pillow and waited for her to finish. Then giving her the medicines, he flicked off one bulb, letting her doze off.

Silently, he sank to the floor and finished his dinner, chewing mechanically. How long till she became bedridden, unable to cook, or even go to the bathroom herself?

He washed the thin steel plates and cooking vessels, stacked them on the shelf. *Time to go.* Get the money from Shahnewaz before he got the instruction to stop.

SATURDAY, 2.00 P.M.

Rockville, Maryland

Dean sat in the cyber security meeting room and dialled out. The room was featureless, an inside space with a pretend view of a landscape. He flipped a pencil on the table, making it clatter, his mind racing through a million scenarios, while an automated voice on the speakerphone informed him that he was the only person on the line. It was getting to be routine, this working on weekends.

'Hello,' Jake's voice crackled into the room.

'Hi Jake. Just me on the line for now,' Dean said wearily.

'Fill me in while the others join in. So, you saw a second intrusion from a new ID?'

'Yes, a Dr Charles Mason, listed as a PI for us, working at the Howard University hospital.'

The line crackled, and a series of *hellos* filled the airwaves. Adam, Andy, Terry, Lara and Martha came on the conference bridge.

'Are we waiting for anyone else?' Lara's sharp voice was like blade through chiffon.

'I left a message for Peter. But he hasn't called back yet,' Dean said after a moment's gap.

'Let's continue,' Jake said. 'So is this Dr Charles Mason a bona fide clinician on Colare?'

'Seems so. Strangely, he too had full access to the data.'

'Like Dr Sandler.'

'Yes. We checked his permission forms. He had authorization.'

That means our intruder may not be Dr Sandler?'

'Probably not. Probably not Dr Mason either.'

'Those punk teens then?' Andy asked.

Dean hesitated. He had been on the phone with *HazMat*

who hadn't met those teens yet but had tracked their account. If there was a tenuous connect between them and the shadowy mastermind, it wasn't clear. So where did that leave them? With a clear breach, and no suspect. Not what his bosses wanted to hear.

'I'll ask *HazMat* to question the teens.' What else could he suggest. He was short of any fresh ideas. 'We'll go meet Dr Mason anyway. Maybe he will remember something useful.'

'Do that today?' Jake was eager for urgent action. 'Is the paperwork ready to be filed, Lara?'

'Just some more charts, some more background.'

'The important thing is,' Adam enunciated, clear as a foghorn over the spectrum, 'we must decide to file the patent application first thing Monday morning Geneva time. Lara?'

'Monday,' Lara affirmed. 'I don't know how, but we'll swing it.'

SUNDAY, 8.00 A.M.

Bandra, Mumbai

Vir opened his eyes lazily, luxuriating for a moment under the soft duvet. Then last night returned in one bitter moment. Tracey had said she would leave the ring when she came to pick up her luggage.

The end was always complicated.

His head was heavy, the Bollinger he had finished alone sluggishly coursing through his veins.

What did he really feel now? Heartbroken? Or, just empty?

Vir padded up to the kitchen, switched on the kettle and shuffled to the door to get the newspaper.

As the kettle hummed, Vir scanned the broadsheet.

'Shit,' he burst out loud. 'Shit, shit, shit!'

He stared at the newspaper. On the left hand of the front page was an article. Small but conveniently placed.

Daily Times, Mumbai & Goa Edition

Saturday, Mumbai

Data theft from Acel global data centre in India

Data stored at Acel's global data centre located in Mumbai may have been compromised. Inside information from the Goregaon campus, where the data centre is located, suggests that cyber forensics experts have been at the company's data centre. This news comes at a bad time for the Indian BPO industry, which has been struggling from the economic downturn and increased concerns from global clients around data security at offshore centres. Global banks and financial services providers have been especially concerned about data security and financial fraud. In the past two years, many of them have shifted from third-party service providers to captive units. But this news of data theft from a captive unit is of concern, given the US rhetoric around outsourcing jobs to emerging markets.

Inside sources! Bloody hell! Vir pounded his fist upon the table. Personal crisis slid from his mind.

SUNDAY, 9.00 A.M.

Bandra, Mumbai

Sandman squatted on the floor, sipping tea, the sounds of the morning filtering in through the flapping curtains. His mother lay asleep, after a restless night.

His laptop lay open. He had not cared to understand what he was pulling off. The quest had been enough for him. The thrill of getting inside a protected domain and sneaking data out. Then money became the motive. He knew the company was making cancer drugs. That much he had learned on Google. There had been a mention of a clinical trial. *Bastards.* He hated clinical trials – they offered hope for the rich while the poor, like his father, were turned away. Did he really want to know more, dig deeper?

Last night he had sent a frantic message to *Mystic Mir,* putting it in the Drafts box as instructed.

'We need to go on. The work remains incomplete.'

But it was almost complete. He had gone sector by sector, as told, downloading and transferring to the Romanian dump server. Only a little bit remained. Maybe two more days, two more payments. Then what? His expenses had ballooned, a large wad spent on just one injection. The doctor had said there were more injections to be given, and medicines to go along.

His phone rang – it was the repair shop where he worked. 'What has happened? You haven't come to work. The boys say you have bunked college for days.'

His voice nearly choked in response. 'Rehmanbhai, Amma is very unwell. I can't leave her.'

'You need some money, *bacche*?' Rehmanbhai promised to send some advance wages, a few thousand rupees to tide him over.

Sandman killed the connection and pulled out his stash

of cash from inside a burlap wrapping stored in an old tin box under the bed. He fingered its heft. Life was hell-bent on defeating him. *Why me?* The question heaved inside him. Then he checked his email. There was no response.

The curtains flapped and a neighbour peeked in, carrying a plate of food. He placed a finger on his lips indicating her to be quiet, and the lady nodded, looked at his sleeping mother and left. He bit into a vadapav, relishing the pungency of the chilli-coriander sauce.

He picked up his laptop and started surfing, checking on Acel, reading articles, Vir's interviews, randomly scouring through page after page, wherever the links led him. That's when he saw a mention of Colare, the same name that had been used in several of the filenames he had copied. He read on, devouring the words like hope itself. Colare, a wonder medicine for late-stage cancer. There was a trial going on in the US. Surely they must be starting a trial in India too?

Would *Mystic Mir* know these people? Yes, that might be the way. The only way. He had to get his mother onto a clinical trial. A real one. He could not argue for his father – he had been young, voiceless, his mother too simple to push through. He would find his voice now, for her, for her life.

He emailed *Mystic Mir*. Pleading would not help. The man was always curt. No, power had to be dealt with power, and he had some. He knew what he was doing meant money to people, not just to his faceless recruiter who was getting cold feet now. *Or else*. That's what he needed to communicate. The only way to be heard.

Should he leave it in Drafts? He needed faster response.

He hit the Send button.

Then on impulse, he looked for an email address for the local office of Acel, and sent them a request as well. To get onto a clinical trial. Just in case someone saw it and responded.

SUNDAY, 11.00 A.M.

Bandra, Mumbai

Vir looked sternly at the duo in front. 'How do you know Magan?'

'How do you know it was not an accident?' Raghu responded. He was wearing a full-sleeved tee shirt, but the white wrapping of bandage was visible near his wrist, covering a gash. There were bruises that he could hide from Amma. Madhu had a knocked-up look about her, with residual pain from a set of purple and blue welts on her body. There was a welt near her lip too. She had to lie to Mausi.

Vir sighed. Karthik had called him early morning, telling him about the accident. Or not an accident, perhaps.

They had to interrogate the teens, Karthik had said, and Vir had agreed. With all clues decimated, they were back to Raghu. He had to be the culprit.

They sat in a small coffee shop, one of the many that had mushroomed in the area, crowding its solo table.

'I can't be certain,' Karthik spoke up. 'But we can't rule out the fact. It looks too coincidental.'

He drank his black coffee, distastefully eyeing the confection of mini cupcakes in the glass counter. 'Let's go over it again.' He eyed Raghu, again wondering why Madhu had turned up, and whatever had happened to Suv. 'Why were you there? Why would the jeep try to bump you off?'

'Bump us off!' Raghu exclaimed. 'How colourful.'

'Tell me.'

Madhu cleared her throat. 'It was my idea. That the hacker would be living within fifty square meters of my house. We were investigating in the slum. In case, there were clues.'

'That's a smart observation.' Karthik noted the girl now.

'But you must leave it to us – we have better ways of tracking this perp.'

'How did you know we had an accident?' Madhu was curious. And suspicious.

Within minutes of the accident, Karthik had called Raghu's phone, organized for someone to take them to a dispensary for first aid. He had been miraculously prompt!

Karthik shot a glance at Vir.

'Look, I know you are keen to help. Play detectives. But you don't know what you are up against. Plus, cyber crimes are still committed by people from the real world. We have a team of security professionals who work with us.'

'Private eye, you mean?' Madhu suddenly decided to take charge of the conversation. She looked at Raghu irritatedly – he looked content to have his red velvet cake and cold coffee.

'My field guys are quite clued into every aspect of cyber crime.'

'Basically, you had us followed?' Madhu said baldly.

Raghu stared at her. Where had the shy Madhu disappeared?

Karthik shrugged. 'Standard ops.'

'Isn't that illegal?'

'No, it's not. Anyway, my guy thinks this vehicle was waiting at the corner and moved only after you sped past.'

'What a disaster.' Vir felt trapped in an alternate reality where nothing good could happen. His breath shrank in his chest. Someone was hacking into his systems. The cyber security expert was employing detectives to chase suspects. Media was drawing flak for a missing cleaner and hyping up data security. Now he sat facing teens who fancied themselves as punk hackers-turned-do-gooder snoops? Where was the safe world he had known? How had he come into this madcap reality of porous online borders? Of pretend cops and robbers, and feeling helpless.

'How does a kid from a good family know a creep like Magan?'

Raghu stonily ignored the question, very conscious of the girl next to him. How would she react if he told them the truth?

Karthik drummed his fingers on the table, waiting for the response that was not forthcoming.

His field operatives had already given him the intel on Maganbhai. He was a small-time thief, engaging in piracy, part of a whole grey market chain that plagued movie and video content makers, who spent large money on production and technology only to see their well-deserved profits siphoned off by black marketers like Magan.

'Were you buying things off him? Let me guess. Pirated things? Gadgets? Movies? Porn?'

'You haven't the least idea.'

'Tell us, then. Or were you selling to him?'

Noticing the slightest stiffening in Raghu, he smirked. 'You *were* selling to him. What? Porn?'

Madhu was hush, eyes darting from Raghu to the others. What the hell was Raghu involved in? Had she trusted him for nothing?

'None of your business,' Raghu snapped.

'Chill, Tiger,' Karthik said. 'Not my business what you do, but if you butt into my investigation it becomes my business.'

Raghu looked away, even more bummed that this conversation was taking place in front of Madhu. After their closeness, after that kiss, all he needed was this, for the girl to be disgusted and walk away. Damn!

'Look, the internet gives you a lot of freedoms. To be who you want to be. To act how you want to. But there *are* limits. There *are* rules. It's very easy to cross these lines online. To move from mischief to delinquency.'

Karthik looked sharply at Raghu, pinning him with a glare. 'What else have you tried?' He lectured on the demerits of testing the limits of the law, weak as they might be in India. He was reminded of his own high school days. The pull of the wild, before he had tamed himself.

Raghu mulled. What to say? What he had done seemed exciting, but hardly definitive. Mentioning the programming languages he knew, or the protocols he had played with, would hardly impress Karthik. Who wanted to impress Karthik, anyway?

'I've written patches for various intrusions, for mobiles and IVR and computer hotspots.'

'Hmm. Look, you may be talented. I don't know.'

Raghu bristled.

Karthik continued. 'Buddy, what you've done till now is hardly ground-breaking. I've seen many kids floundering in these shallows.'

Yeah right! Raghu remained silent, but his expression said it out loud.

'You have seen this before, haven't you, Karthik?' Vir interjected. 'What's that name my team calls you by?*HazMat*?'

Raghu looked stunned. '*You're HazMat*?'

He had heard enough mentions of the name online. The man was legend. Ace ethical hacker, expert in intrusion, detection and protection, consultant to corporations and governments, avid blogger followed by thousands of wannabes.

'Yes, I am.'

Raghu stared at him with newfound respect.

'Who's *HazMat*?' Madhu squeaked. She had been in charge one moment, the conversation had gone haywire the next. She did not even know what these guys were talking about.

'He's a genius. The best ethical hacker in the country,' Vir gave an admiring intro.

Karthik waved his hands, embarrassed by the praise. 'You had better come clean, Raghu. We've tracked you online, we know the type of sites you frequent. It's only a matter of time.'

Raghu felt like an animal mistakenly ensnared. With such effort, he had convinced Madhu to believe him. But what would make these two believe? 'Listen, it's not me.'

'Are there any leads?' Madhu deflected the conversation.

Karthik thought of the unsolved half lead. Was *Sandman* Raghu? He had no proof to detain the boy or even threaten him. He was not about to share details with these two cartoons! But that friend of *Sandman* – Suhas Patil. Maybe these kids knew. He showed them a photo on his smartphone.

'Seen him in the neighbourhood?'

'No, but Raghu, this thin one in the back. Isn't he the boy we saw yesterday in the slums?'

'It could be,' Raghu said, squinting at the small image.

SUNDAY, 2.00 P.M.

Bandra, Mumbai

Vir stood on the broken curb, eyeing the building across the lane. An unremarkable building, housing an unremarkable business. The sun exposed every fissure on its grime-coated walls, livening every newspaper-coated windowpane.

'Don't go by the name,' Karthik grunted, shielding his eyes against the hot brilliance of the afternoon. 'It's likely a den of iniquity.'

Vir had read enough tabloid stories of establishments masquerading as massage parlours while licentious prostitution went on behind the curtains.

'It's amazing that you got the kids tailed.'

Karthik shrugged. 'It's routine.' He employed full-service physical and digital security teams and plain-clothes detectives.

What was more amazing was that people assumed a cyber security firm would only rely on computer forensics. It never stopped at the digital trail. There was always a link to the real world. Security personnel, detectives, lawyers, police contacts, telephone companies, utility companies were all part of his extended network. The key to succeed, to solve cases, to take perps to court or recover money.

'Shall we go upstairs?' Despite his misgivings about a dungeons and dragons-type chase, Vir had insisted on coming along. He had tried hard to understand the logic of digital honeytraps and countersurveillance. But he had chafed at the sidelines, unable to actually help. Live recce he could do. How could he sit back, when his career was almost all but finished? With one news report out, how long before the media fished out the full story.

'What's the worse that could happen?' Vir said.

Karthik rolled his eyes behind his shades. A lot could happen. Especially with a rookie as a field operative.

They walked up the narrow winding staircase, its steps withered with use, but its cool darkness a welcome change from the heat outside. The door at the landing was left ajar.

Karthik pushed it open and stepped inside a dim room, the deep maroon blinds on the windows pulled down, creating a cool escape away from the heat and brightness outside. A fug of smoke hit their nostrils, sweet and sharp. Marijuana.

A man appeared from behind a curtain of rippling chintz. The corridor behind him led to the back rooms, which were full today. Sundays were peak business.

Shahnewaz crossed his arms, planted his feet wide and eyed them sharply. Their fancy clothes and smooth features screaming loud that they were not his usual clientele. Despite his best *chai-paani* to the beat cops, there was always a risk that some uppity officer would decide to take matters up. But they didn't look like the police, either.

'What is offered here? Massage? *Maalish*? *Champi*?' Karthik took in the small room with its cheap décor and low-wattage bulbs.

'Why?' Shahnewaz chewed upon a Chlormint. He was trying to give up *paan* and *khaini*, but the gum was a poor substitute.

'What's behind those curtains?'

It was easy to imagine a police siren and a raid that uncovered a human trafficking ring and scantily dressed men and women in haphazard escape.

'Busy day, Saheb,' Shahnewaz said. 'Come again.' He stepped forward, one burly hand pointing to the door.

'Why did Magan come here yesterday?'

Shahnewaz remained impassive. 'Never good omen to pry into others' affairs,' he said smoothly.

His stance became wider, broadening his burly chest. Aiming to intimidate.

'Are you threatening us?' Vir's blood boiled thick. Shahnewaz remained where he was, just his eyes darted, animosity in them.

'If you say so, Saheb.' His words were hoarse. No explicit threat in them, just a tacit menace, that rolled out like ripples.

Vir wanted to goad the man further, try to make him spill the beans on what was happening and his role in the Colare data theft.

'We may come back with a warrant,' Karthik said from behind.

'Now you are threatening me, Saheb?' Shahnewaz smiled, revealing yellow rotting teeth. 'People don't threaten me, normally.'

SUNDAY, 8.12 P.M.

Guangzhou, China

The Temple of Six Banyan Trees pierced the grey sky like a red-petalled flower, its tiered pagoda dripping droplets of rain typical to the season before the Qingming festival.

Tu Yi carefully wiped his shoes on the coir mat and entered the temple, and avoiding the touristy Laughing Buddha and the ancient relics, went straight to the main hall to the west where a large copper Sakyamuni was flanked by Amitabha and the Apothecary Buddha. Luckily the room was empty. Tu Yi bowed in front of the statue at the right, his personal adopted deity, fitting for a man working in the medicine business, and knelt to light a bunch of joss sticks. Traces of jasmine scented the room. Bowing to the Apothecary Buddha, Tu Yi inhaled deeply, absorbing a calmness that he hadn't felt in days.

He remained kneeling for minutes, seeking blessings he sorely needed, till a press of visitors disturbed his solitude.

Ruefully he got up, with one last look at the deity and its beatific eyes. It was a short walk to the People's Park, at its nicest in this season, where he would play a game of solitary chess in the afternoon after his usual Sunday dim sum lunch. His wife had passed away, taking with her all the charm and sparkle of life, that his estranged son and daughter-in-law chose not to fill. His cute young granddaughter was a stranger, the one who would inherit all the yuans he had amassed.

Tu Yi opened his umbrella and walked slowly, at peace with his solitary Sunday. A day when he liked to recharge, away from thoughts of business. His phone rang. He paused at a traffic light and took the call, hoping it wasn't Min Ha haunting his weekend.

It was some young man from the office, from the special team that manned the online chats of their contact, who wasn't as hidden as he imagined.

The young man hyperventilated in rapid Cantonese. There was a new message, a threat actually. Asking to get onto a clinical trial for the drug under question. Tu Yi let out an expletive. No one threatened his project, and got away. Standing at the south gate of the park, oblivious to the traffic honks behind him, he made a call to the mercenary and barked out his orders.

SUNDAY, 10.30 P.M.

Bandra, Mumbai

Paul waited on the dark landing. He was craving to light up. But he needed the element of surprise. Smoke would give it away.

He shuffled silently, checking the time on his mobile. The boy had been inside for fucking two hours now.

Paul had heard him from an inside room in Caress, where he had parked himself for the day much to the chagrin of Shahnewaz. Fucking waste of his day off. Shahnewaz did not know where the contact lived. He was just getting bloated collecting his cut for perching his fat ass on a chair and waiting for the boy to turn up with the goods.

The git, Paul cursed.

Ten hours later, he had caught a glimpse of the boy as he had entered a back room in the massage parlour. That was the one. His target. He had no photographs to go by. No identification marks. Just the knowledge that Shahnewaz would give him money in exchange for those computer bits he would transport back up his normal chain from Mumbai to Manipur and beyond.

Paul had decided to wait outside. He squatted now to rest his legs, hungering for a cigarette.

'Fuck it,' he whispered to himself and slunk down the staircase into the open street corner, and lit up. He took a few deep drags, feeling normalcy return.

There was movement at the staircase and Paul saw the boy come out, slinging his backpack, a sated look on his face.

Paul dropped his half-smoked cigarette on the floor, loath to let it go. But he had to hurry. He crushed the smoking stub with his boot, and followed the boy.

Paul felt his back. His father's *dao* was strapped to his back, tucked inside his shirt. A *dao* steeped in the blood of a hundred tigresses. He had sharpened it on a stone this morning before leaving home, the scraping noise taking him back to his years in the forests and the hunts. A dark alley was all he needed.

MONDAY, 10.00 A.M.

Bandra, Mumbai

Raghu and Madhu trudged along the rubbish-strewn broken earth in the slum behind Santhal Building. A man trailed behind, a plain-clothes officer from the cyber crime cell of Mumbai police.

With the news of data theft having already hit the local newspapers, the need for corporate coyness had disappeared. On Karthik's advice, Vir had lodged an official FIR at the Andheri police station last evening. Karthik had contacts in the cyber crime cell, so the complaint had been registered and listened to immediately.

'You're saying you saw your suspect on Facebook?' Inspector Faisal had asked incredulously, scrunching his dark face.

'Not the suspect, yet, Inspector. His friend.'

'Let's hope you are not taking us on a wild chase after nothing.' But he had registered the case, and agreed to take Raghu and Madhu to hunt for the suspect.

Raghu and Madhu nodded at the inspector. Karthik had called Raghu early morning, to tell them a car would pick them up from college to bring them back to Bandra for an hour.

'Go on,' Inspector Faisal told them. 'I shall wait here.'

Raghu and Madhu went deeper into the row of makeshift huts. Other than a man sleeping, wrapped in a faded flower-patterned sheet, his dark callused feet peeking out of it, there was no one about.

They approached a small hut with a curtain door and peered inside. A woman squatted on the dirt floor, slurping chai from a steel bowl. She called out grumpily, '*Kay*?'

'Suhas Patil *kuthe*?' Raghu asked in the local dialect.

'*Tu kaa aalas*?' she asked, already irritated by this intrusion.

She did not own a watch, but she knew instinctively that she needed to leave soon for her mid-morning duties. Most women who lived here worked in one of the buildings on the main road.

Raghu apologized briefly, mentioning that he needed to talk to Suhas for some school work.

'You don't look like you go to the same school as Suhas,' the woman said, eyeing them suspiciously, taking in Raghu's neatly pressed clothes and smooth features.

Raghu shrugged.

'Two houses down,' the woman said indifferently.

Raghu led the way, and two doors ahead, they found the boy whose photograph they had seen on Karthik's phone. The boy with the Facebook name of Suhas Patil.

'Suhas?'

'*Kya hai*?'

Madhu pressed the redial button to call Inspector Faisal.

'We want to know about your friend. *Sandman.*'

'Why?'

'We need to talk to him.'

Inspector Faisal walked in at that moment, hand on his holster. '*Chhokre*. Where is *Sandman*? Answer the question.'

'Why is the *thulla* here?' Suhas grumbled, looking away from the man in uniform and wordlessly led them three houses away.

They walked inside.

'*Arre*, Lalti!' Madhu exclaimed, seeing Mausi's cleaning woman on the bed, hair matted, clothes messy, eyes red, flanked by two other women. She had not come to work for weeks.

'What happened?' Inspector Faisal asked.

'What has happened?' screamed Lalti. 'Tell me, tell me.'

'Her son Sandesh has been missing since last night,' said one of the women. 'His phone is also switched off.'

Madhu stared at Lalti, covering the shock on her face with her hand. That boy, the one with the watery smile and put-on belligerence at having to ask for money, was *Sandman*?

Raghu frowned. Had *Sandman* managed to slip away?

SUNDAY, 10.00 P.M.

Bethesda, Maryland

Lauren Sandler snuggled in her bed, her paisley-printed down comforter pulled about her. She had been unable to sleep last night and sleep eluded her again.

The entire episode with Dean had left her shaken. They had suspected her, she deduced as much. It was there in Dean's voice, in his stance. He had been silent since then, not even responding to her proactive emails asking to see photos of more reps.

She hated the very thought of it. That her exemplary conduct through life could be maligned by some dirt hacker, sitting somewhere. She had to do something.

But what, Lauren thought absently.

She recalled that rep. It had been such a fleeting interaction. He had been nondescript. Medium height, medium build, sallow-faced, moustached. It hadn't struck her before. But there was one distinguishing feature. He was Asian. How many Asian reps could Acel have?

Mountain to Mohamet, she thought. She had to go after that rep. Clear her name.

She picked up her laptop from her bedside table, opened her browser, typed in Acel, and scanned through all images, till tired after several pages of scrolling down, she decided on another tactic.

Would he be on LinkedIn? Who wasn't these days. She logged in, found the usual rep who used to come to her office, and trolled through his contacts, and contacts of his contacts, searching for a face. And a name against that face. She tried different searches, scanned face after face. Where was he?

Maybe he wasn't a rep, the thought struck her. She remembered his hesitant manner, his slight accent. Would someone have really hired him for a sales role, to woo doctors?

No, there must be some other connection with Acel.

She typed Acel again, going through the news of the company, the usual corporate and financial news. She ran a search on Colare. Perhaps that would yield some answers. The first links were all connected with the US patent application, the US FDA application – legal words talking about the product that was going through its life cycle of discovery. There were technical papers as well, archives on medical sites, that briefly talked about the results, without really going into the details of how it worked. She kept scrolling down, and that's when she found it, buried at the bottom of the third page. A news article on Colare in *Health* magazine.

The missing rep. Minus a moustache. In a team photograph of the Colare research team.

She scanned the name below the photograph.

I have to call Dean now!

MONDAY, 11.00 A.M.

Bandra, Mumbai

'This is getting out of hand,' Vir said, forking his egg bhurji.

Karthik and he had met at a tiny joint in Bandra, to decide what to do next. Inspector Faisal had called last night. They had found *Sandman.* Except that he had been missing since Sunday night. They were back to square one.

'I'm stumped.' Karthik sipped his filter coffee. 'It has to be an insider, I'm convinced. But who? In India or in the US?'

Vir scowled. 'You still suspect my team and me?'

Karthik held his fingers in a V. 'Peace, man. I have to rule out options, no?'

'But you thought it could have been me?'

'It's common. Happens all the time.' He gave some examples.

As Karthik spoke, Vir's unease ballooned. How had he ever been deluded that he had any control? 'It could be someone in my team, you think?'

'More likely someone in the US.'

'Okay, let's assume it is an insider. But why would they do this? There is money to be gained from taking the medicine to market. Not in sabotaging it.'

'Let's try to decode how this set-up was devised. That may tell us why.'

'In the first place, the person could not have accessed the complete data from home. Or taken it out from the office. I am told the Acel building in the US is totally secure. Nothing goes in, nothing goes out without triggering a load of alarms. No dongles. No hard disks. No mobile gadgets, not that mobiles could store such data. Then there is the system security, all kinds of firewalls get breached, tripping signals if anyone hacks in.'

'Yes, but none of this proves that it's an insider.'

'What about the address in Guangzhou. You have a competitor there who is trying to create a similar product. Wouldn't it benefit them if Acel got behind in its patenting schedule, allowing their product to precede yours? Can you imagine how many hundreds of millions, or even billions, could be riding on such a thing?'

Vir looked at Karthik incredulously, suddenly light-headed.

'Unless it's your German competitor, masking as a Chinese operative,' Karthik said.

'Wow Sherlock, so when the IP address was Bandra, did you deduce that Ali, or maybe I, were stealing the data?'

Karthik shrugged. 'I can hazard a guess who we may be up against.'

'Who?'

'Peter.'

'Peter? Because he is Chinese,' Vir said with disgust. The very notion was astounding. 'Peter is the architect of Colare. It's mostly his work. He managed to do that first gene grafting. It made Colare possible. He knows it all. Why will he hack into his own data? Makes no sense.'

'I don't know the man. But clearly the two permissions were given by him.'

'Unless that was doctored too.'

'A set-up? Plausible. But unlikely.'

'Even if I believe this strange theory, how will you pinpoint Peter?'

'There is one catch here. The intruder had to install a Trojan on Dr Sandler's machine. In person. Presumably on the machine of Dr Mason as well. Dean was chasing medical reps, but I have now asked him to show Peter's photo to Dr Sandler.'

'So there is a way,' Vir was in shock. 'Let's call Dean now.'

SUNDAY, 11.30 P.M.

Bethesda, Maryland

Dr Sandler had finally managed to doze off, when her phone rang, startling her. It couldn't be her patients – she usually did not have emergencies.

She fumbled to switch on the bedside lamp, and picked up her phone. Dean. From Acel.

'What's the emergency?' She started, irritated, then the online search filled her mind. She needed to talk to him anyway.

'Good you called,' she said in a softer tone.

'It is an emergency,' Dean apologized. 'We have a trail. I just emailed you a photo for verification.'

'Look, I know who came to my office. I saw his photo in an article on Colare.'

'You did?' Dean mumbled. He had not alerted anyone in office, but given there was no other lead, he had listened to *HazMat* and not dismissed the wild notion. Instead, he had taken a photo of Peter from the internal directory and emailed it to Dr Sandler.

'Look, he wasn't a rep,' she was telling him now, and Dean knew in his gut without her confirmation that he was on the right track.

His mind raced ahead. He would need to call Jake, alert his contacts in the local Maryland crime cell. He should probably call Scott to drive up to Peter Lee's house in Gaithersburg. 'Do me a favour, Dr Sandler. See the pic I've sent and confirm,' he insisted.

She put him on hold, checked the image on her mobile phone and connected again. 'That's him,' she said, recognizing the sallow-faced man who had first come to her office late one evening, the one whose photograph she saw in the article on the web.

Except that the person was not a rep. Who could have imagined? He was the Chief Scientist of Colare, Dr Peter Lee.

MONDAY, 9.00 P.M.

Bandra, Mumbai

Vir breathed out taking in the emptiness of his room. Tracey had come during the day to collect her suitcases, saying she was too fragile to see him yet, so could he please step out?

He had.

He had spent the day in office, going over and over the fantastic idea that Peter was the culprit. Dean had already verified it. Except the rest was a bit opaque. Were the authorities after Peter? He had become incommunicado suddenly. They had huddled in a small team – Karthik, Ali, Peevs and him, hashing and rehashing all the ideas. There was work to be done, emails to be answered. But who could concentrate in the midst of such tumult? They offered arguments as to why Peter would do such a thing. But it was all conjecture.

Vir had returned home earlier than usual. He felt numb. So much had happened over one weekend. Tracey had left India to spend the rest of her holiday wandering by the Arno.

Life had changed in one decisive swoop. He sensed emptiness yawning ahead of him. He would have to tell his parents. They would be devastated.

He sank in the sofa chair in his terrace, gazing into the sea, a glass of whisky in his hand, his third peg in the last hour.

His phone rang, breaking the silence.

'Dude, the police have unexpected news,' Karthik said.

'What now?' Vir said with the slightest slur.

'That missing boy. Sandesh. *Sandman*. We retrieved his comp, so we know they are the same.'

'Good.'

'Yeah. But he's not gone missing, man. He's turned up dead.'

'Woah, woah, woah. Wait a sec!'

'Yeah. I know. In an alley near a butcher's shop under the Kalanagar flyover. Hacked by some sharp axe-type thing.'

Hacked? 'Literally?'

'Literally.'

'That's not the least of it, Vir. Prep up. It's not gonna be pleasant.

'What now...'

'Media knows about the FIR, and now this boy turns up all cut up. Acel will be in the news, Vir. Not the little snippet like this morning. This is going to get huge. Lie low.'

TUESDAY 1.00 A.M.

Bandra, Mumbai

Vir looked at his watch. Tracey would be boarding the flight right now. He had not picked up the unknown phone calls that had kept coming since Karthik's call.

Now shit had really hit the fan.

The first news feed said: *'Hacker hacked to death, Proprietary IP stolen from biotech firm Acel'*. It had hit the online newswire, copied by news bots across India and picked up by the crawler feeds globally.

Vir sat there in his pyjamas, reading each and every one of them. Over and over. Fixated upon the same news clip repeating itself from site to site.

There wasn't much he could have done. There was a grudging response from Andy, in an email trail sent by Adam a while back, explaining that the team had sent out alerts for Dr Peter Lee and thanking Vir for all his hard work over the past days.

Work that had cost him his sanity. Work that had lost him his love.

Vir took another mouthful of whisky. His mobile screen wavered. Would Tracey and he have survived were it not for this hacking incident? He wasn't sure somehow.

TUESDAY, 7.00 A.M.

Chembur, Mumbai

Raghu stared at his phone with a sleepy smile and a tinge of unease, reading the morning message from Madhu.

How desperately he waited for her messages. She had gone to the slum with him on Monday, but had refused to look at him. He kept praying for a little indication that he wouldn't be ignored forever.

This message meant nothing. It signified everything.

He stretched and yawned, his body still sore.

He thought about their meeting with *HazMat* last afternoon.

'Don't play with your future,' Karthik had said. They had sat in a casual dosa place close to the college precinct. Madhu had insisted on coming along, even though she wasn't speaking to him.

'Use your skills well,' Karthik had continued. 'Time once lost doesn't come back, and more importantly, credibility once shattered sets you on a path you may not wish to see yourself on.'

Without much preamble, Madhu had asked *HazMat*, 'Will you give me an internship? I could learn so much from you.'

Raghu had sat like a fool, aghast at Madhu's boldness.

Part of him wanting to second her request. Part of him knowing that any legit internship, even if it gave him access to the newest tools and tricks used by pros like *HazMat*, would never afford the little luxuries he so enjoyed. Was he ready to let all of that go?

HazMat had been equally surprised that Madhu would want to intern with him. She had pressed on, telling him about her academic achievements, stressing her national ranking, talking about the programming languages she had started to learn.

Her final remark had nailed the request. 'I don't want to be a victim. I have seen how easily people have gained access to my personal accounts, and I want to learn how to detect them or how to foil their attempts.'

Before he knew it, both of them had an internship.

TUESDAY, 11.00A.M.

Bandra, Mumbai

Vir woke up feeling drugged and parched at once. He fumbled his way to the fridge and drank a bottle of water. He bent down to put his head under the kitchen tap, letting the water run over him for a few minutes.

Then wiping his head with a kitchen towel, he went back to the bedroom to check his phone. Hundreds of missed calls. Hundreds of text messages. Some known numbers, many unknown. He scrolled, not reading any, till one name caught his eye. Diti.

You're famous again, Doc.

He paused, examining how he felt. Not his overnight infamy. That he would need to deal with. See how to tide over the issue. Surely, there would be some buried messages from someone in the US about how to best respond to negative publicity.

No, the question was how he felt about Diti messaging him after she'd sworn to cut off contact.

At this moment. When he was coping with a broken engagement. Not that she knew about it. Yet the heartbreak he should have been drowning in this morning was absent. Failure had bothered him last night. But now, despite the hangover, he felt lighter than he had in months.

Impetuously, he wrote back:

Famous and dumped. Quite like a celeb today.

Clutching his phone, he fired up his laptop and searched for his name online. Some twenty thousand links showed up. Articles, posts, ezines, twitter feeds. All the top items were about the current data leak. It had gone viral. Every newspaper seemed to have carried the story. There were video links from television media sites, carrying live footage from outside the Acel data centre.

Vir knew he had to get up, doll up in his best blue suit and red tie. Look and sound reassuring. Inspire confidence.

It wasn't his data centre anyway. Maybe headquarters had issued a press release? He should check.

But he wanted to do nothing except stare at his mobile. Would Diti respond?

He pumped his fist in the air when her response appeared.

Umm, dumped?

He typed back.

Fiancée gone. Engagement kaput.

There was an immediate response.

Oh no! Poor baby! You sound heartbroken.

Vir grinned now, feeling a thrill of excitement.

Dashed up. Maybe.

He drummed his fingers on his lips, thinking. What did he want *her* to say now?

A message arrived, quite unlike anything he had expected.

Hey, you need support?

Did he now?

Perhaps.

He typed back, flummoxed for a second. Should he express neediness? Should he display aloofness? Did it even matter what he said, and how she responded, when the rest of his carefully crafted world had crashed around him, and somewhere few kilometres away irate journalists were clamouring for a piece of him.

Diti's response came in, with a little ping, quaking him out of his reverie. She posed another question.

Should I come over?

Vir felt lightness wash over him. He took a deep breath, savouring the feeling.

There was a time for dithering, and a time to take charge. He posed a question in response, mentally chucking his plan of dressing for a corporate battle.

How soon?

He lay back in his bed, arms folded behind his head, sinking into the pillows, smiling at the ceiling.

TUESDAY, 4.13 P.M.

Guangzhou, China

'Boss, something is wrong,' a junior scientist, an expert in reverse engineering, said, walking into Tu Yi's closed-door meeting.

Tu Yi frowned.

'The opportunity lies in Africa,' he had been in the middle of saying, standing at the head of a long table, deciding rather than debating a new expansion strategy for Wusan Labs.

Wusan's supply fingers trailed across Southeast Asia. From the massive port in the Pearl river delta, containers carried low-cost generic medicines to populous countries in the region. The next obvious frontier was Africa. His sales directors huddled around the table, listening. Protocol was important, rank mattered most and when the President of Wusan spoke, he preferred that his team simply listen.

Tu Yi did not know if he was more furious at the interruption or at the fact that something had gone wrong again.

His tiny team of scientists had been studying the Colare data downloaded from the dump server in Romania. This whole exercise was beginning to irk him. He had not been enthusiastic about it from the start. So much easier to just re-engineer and produce a drug.

But, no! Min Ha wanted the data. Min Ha wanted to file for an original drug. Thumb down his cousin. Min Ha wanted glory. Tu Yi had no choice but to go along with what Min Ha wanted.

'Wait for me, gentlemen,' he said imperiously, then marched out stiffly behind the scientist.

From the corridor, he could see the thin brown Hua Di river sedately flowing to meet the massive Zhu Jiang river, and the sleepy buildings, their air of unkemptness masking the frantic commercial activity housed inside. This old part of town was being sold piecemeal to large developers, older buildings being demolished and replaced by glass-and-steel megaliths. Plans were being drawn up to revamp the area with parks and gardens around modern residential towers.

It was the end of an era.

He entered the research room and barked, 'What's wrong?'

Scientists clucked in rapid-fire Cantonese, resembling a flock of chicken running amok. He was annoyed.

'One person speak.'

'This data is all wrong.'

'What do you mean?'

'The trend lines are jumpy. They could not have filed on this data and got any approval. Nor is it matching with what Zhang Wang thinks the back data for this formula should look like.'

Zhang Wang was the expert. Their chief of innovation. Which in Wusan terminology meant that he pored over the latest medical journals from around the world, read the descriptions of new technologies, decoded the reports on formulations filed by these global companies with various drug approval agencies and deconstructed how to make a similar product locally.

How all these confidential reports even reached his table was something he chose not to ask. That was Tu Yi's domain.

Tu Yi stared down at Zhang Wang.

'Not good,' the man said, waving his arms wide.

'How can it be? Our person has been getting the data straight from their server.'

'First five downloads are consistent, everything from last week is lousy. They could not have dreamed of filing on this data.'

'So the Americans were trying to fool everyone?' Tu Yi said with revulsion.

'Possible. Or...'

'Or what?'

'We downloaded the wrong files.'

The gears clicked in Tu Yi's mind, imagining every devious possibility. Had the contact duped them? Given them the wrong data and run away with the advance money? He should have just engaged his own team to enter into Acel's systems directly.

He had to freeze the account right away.

He had given some ten thousand bitcoins in first advance. A newfangled trick he had been loath to learn, except the contact had insisted upon that method. That stack of crypto-currency amounted to almost ten million dollars. Small change for a product worth hundreds of millions. Tu Yi called his marketplace agent in Hong Kong, and spoke rapidly. The agent was reliable, someone he had found through a family connection after the source had insisted on being paid in bitcoins. The agent handled online transactions, tumbled up the crypto-money and sent it anonymously.

'It's gone,' the agent told him. 'Last week. I can't undo it, or freeze anything.'

'Gone where?' Tu Yi barked. It was all digital, for heaven's sake. Surely it could be reversed.

'I don't know,' said the agent. 'All I can trace is that it was used to buy silver. The metal. Not shares. After that, I don't know.'

Tu Yi cursed.

It had been Min Ha's idea.

But that wouldn't matter now. No, very possibly the plan gone awry would be pinned upon his head.

Tu Yi felt like a sheep at the stake, live bait for what lay ahead. Cold dread settled in his stomach. He had to clean up.

His contact would clean up the trail in India. But that was the tiniest detail of this plan.

The money. That's what counted. Acel would have to pay. No, Tu Yi could not let it go that easily. He had to recover the money. And some.

He made another call.

Time to set *Plan C* in motion.

TUESDAY, 6.00 P.M.

Bandra, Mumbai

The alert came in over SMS. Just a little scrip.

```
NYSE: ACL $79.1130.11 (-27.56%)
```

Vir was dabbing Gio Pour De Homme on himself liberally, whistling at his reflection in the mirror. He turned his face in different angles, looking at the little crows lines near his eyes. They had softened overnight. Vir could have missed the one SMS, except that the huge fall in the stock price had tripped all manners of online alerts. The one innocuous text message generated a flurry of communication, sending his phone into a spell of beeps.

'What now?' Vir picked up his phone, wanting to silence it.

He was taking his team out for dinner. A simple meal together after a week of vigil. It was the easing of the guilt and blame that had lifted everyone's spirits.

Not that there was anything to celebrate per se. Acel was still in a soup. Karthik had traced the traffic back to the Romanian server, which had been accessed by the domain name server of Sino Qi, the Chinese firm that had been working on a Colare-like drug. Lara was in a huddle with the regulator and the authorities, identifying the best way to press charges.

But the blame no longer lay with the India team, but with Peter, who had evaded detainment and boarded a non-stop flight from Dulles to Narita a full day before any alerts had been raised. From Narita, he seemed to have taken a train into the city and virtually disappeared. The US authorities had raised alerts with the Japanese cops, but no one could track him. His credit cards remained unused. His phone switched off.

'What the hell happened here!' Vir cursed loudly seeing the

alerts and fumbled through the rest of the messages. Acel stock had crashed, and with it his personal portfolio.

Acel's share price had fallen as soon as the markets had opened in New York. The investors were apparently spooked by the news of the stealing of intellectual property data, raising questions on the ability of Acel to actually file the global patent application. Acel's corporate communications team had been in overdrive, sending out press releases and circulars, calling up analysts individually. But the market was another beast with a mind of its own.

His phone rang. Ananth Rao, his colleague from the mergers and acquisitions team in Acel spoke agitatedly. 'Dude, you won't believe it!'

'I am seeing the messages now. Unbelievable.' But it was there. In black and white. In the news. In the alerts.

'Not the share price, Vir. That was an hour back. There is more. Someone's shorted our stock.'

'What?'

'I wanted to tell you. Before the media comes hounding again.'

Vir held his mobile against his neck and nearly ran into the bedroom to check his computer. There were no feeds on a stock short. No posts. No tweets.

'There's no news. What are you saying?'

'It will hit the wires in a big way. Any time now. But someone massively shorted our stock. Made a killing.'

'Peter?'

'Perhaps. He was the one who could have known in advance. Planned it all.'

'Wow! Some nerve.'

'And some vengeance.'

'I don't understand. Peter was Colare and Colare was his baby. How is all this even possible? So much of planning. Such an intricate attack. It is not like Peter.'

'There are theories being spun here, Vir. That he was depressed when Colare research was shared with India. He felt his thunder was being stolen.'

'He said that?' Peter was known to be tight-lipped, keeping thoughts and emotions close to his heart. No one ever knew what went on behind that impassive façade, or what happened in his life beyond work.

'Something to that effect. Barry from his team mentioned something.'

'Really?'

'He wanted to become the next Ron Thomson. The next messiah of cancer treatment. But even after the US data filing and the FDA approval for clinical testing, the masses and the media never quite hyped up Peter like that. Andy became the public face. Peter felt let down, I guess.'

'But to sell out to Sino Qi? To competition? How could he?'

'Just wait. It gets even more farcical,' Ananth said, laughing dryly. 'Sino Qi issued a press release this morning. That someone spoofed their DNS. Feigned the attack.'

'What? Is that even possible?'

'Possible. But no way to check now.'

'So we just believe them?'

'Likely not. I heard internal rumours. Lara has rounded up the Feds, who in turn have promised to pressurize every possible international trade organization.'

'What a crazy set-up!'

'Yeah, Embassy Row will be abuzz soon. Faxes are already flying, apparently. High-level delegations will be cooling their heels soon, with intergovernmental posturing.'

'All fodder for the viral faffers.' Vir sighed.

Chinese hackers were big global news any day. Some agencies estimated that three hundred billion dollars worth of intellectual property theft occurred each year. From infringements of patented or trademarked data. A large chunk of it was attributed to the Far East. Legal whizkids were already in a tizzy, pointing out the losses, raising a ruckus. This new incident was spark to tinder.

Add in significant IP espionage and stock shorting, there would be nothing less than a deluge of attention on the issue in the coming weeks.

'Yeah. While Peter is living it up somewhere in Tokyo, flashing his newfound millions. Having the last laugh.'

Ananth rang off.

Vir plonked down on his bed, stunned.

TUESDAY, 10.18 P.M.

Hanoi, Vietnam

The tiny eatery spilled onto the riverbank, diffusing the smell of meat being stir-fried in large woks and the steam of pho rising from large vats into the muggy night air.

The cook spoke in rapid-fire Vietnamese, supervising the rhythmic scratching of the metal stirrer against the iron wok. With his right hand, he lifted a batch of succulent chicken skewers coated in the tangiest of sauces and dished it out on a plate and with his left hand, sprinkled thin strands of scallion on the aromatic meat. He poured a ladle of steaming clear soup from a large vat into a deep bowl, and put both onto a tray.

'Here,' he shouted to his assistant. 'Table Four.'

The bow-legged boy waddled in slow steps, carrying the hot dishes carefully.

Table Four was placed at the edge of the unbanked riverwalk, on the very outskirts of town, its lone tealight in a tiny cracked votive reflecting upon the sludgy water of the Red River.

Peter Lee sat with his back to the groups of chattering families, staring at the water.

He nodded at the boy, and took a sip of the soup, inhaling the aroma. He had had nothing but pasty meat rolls and boiled vegetables for the past week. It was hot. Peter leaned back on his chair, savouring this freedom, this sitting under the stars in some unknown joint up a river where no one would expect him to be.

A few furlongs downstream bobbed the little fishing boat that had brought him ashore from the large oceangoing trawler, in whose mighty cargohold he had made the rocking journey from Tokyo to Manila and onward to Hanoi, as it stopped to load and unload cargo at ports along the South China Sea. A week of being cut off from news, Peter had had a lot of time to reflect bitterly upon his predicament. He had nowhere to go, no one to turn to. Like some fugitive, he had made his escape, bribing his way onto a Filipino ship whose captain had chosen to ignore his lack of papers on the promise of the last stack of greenbacks he had withdrawn before boarding that flight to Tokyo.

Not that he needed those dollars. He had a few million stashed in a small bank in Haiphong. In an account he had opened some months ago, under the name that had been used by his grandfather. The entire transaction carried out over a series of faxes, the most secure form of communication in the world today, when electronic trails could be so easily tracked. The bank had asked for an identity proof, and he had faxed them a copy of his grandfather's papers from China, carefully whiting out the dates and putting his birthdate in. The rest remained the same – he could pass off as his grandfather easily, and the bank manager had stamped the papers, not quite checking them under a magnifying glass.

Yet now that he was here, resentment ate through him.

The money sat like a smouldering hole in his life.

Peter had eagerly withdrawn some cash after disembarking and found a small internet café, longing to read the news. What had transpired after his hasty flight, if anything. *Plan B* had stared him in the face from a million newsfeeds. Acel data compromised. Question mark over the future of Colare. Its share price at unseen lows. Its stock shorted, causing the company to lose millions. The millions didn't just disappear into the interlinked cesspool of global markets. No, someone made that money. Who, Peter had a good idea.

His entire life's mission had been reduced to nothing. He who had lived for his work all his life, compromised everything personal for the sake of science, now stood disbarred from it for life.

There was no going back now. Never.

No, he was a marked man. Not just in the scientific community the world over, but by the United States government as well. If they got a whiff of his presence anywhere, they would try to extradite him. Like some common criminal. Just one country could welcome him for his prowess, respect his scientific skills. But could he trust them now?

Peter pushed the bowl away. He could not eat another morsel from it.

FRIDAY, 3.00 P.M.

Anna Salai, Chennai

Vaidy paced the wide corridor outside Annaswamy's office, feeling more frantic than he had in years.

He had been confident that the persuasive voice of global trade organizations would will its way. Now he stood to lose not just his fat variable performance fee, but the account altogether. Rumour had it that Annaswamy was making a judgment against the petition filed by his global client.

'Is he ready to see me yet?' Vaidy asked the peon once again, resisting the urge to dash inside. He knew Annaswamy was inside. Would maintaining protocol and acting without haste help his case?

Inside the cavernous chamber, Annaswamy sat in deep conversation with his assistant lawyers, putting the finishing touches to the ruling.

'The people stand first,' Annaswamy said, as he finished rereading the draft position statement. He polished his glasses with the edge of his cotton handkerchief and stuffed it back into his pocket. 'We need to ensure that care and medicine is available to the ordinary citizens at prices they can afford.'

The team nodded.

There would be a lot of noise they knew. Maybe an appeal to the Supreme Court. International trade organizations would heft their way in to raise a ruckus. Goverments would muscle in, driven to respond by their constituents, declare economic sanctions or global censure to try to get them to behave. Perhaps the whole thing could be repealed at some later date.

But for now they knew what they had to do. Be true to those whose rights to healthcare they defended.

Acknowledgements

This book was a long time in the making, in a surreal interweaving of life imitating art, and I must profusely thank Nandita Aggarwal for nurturing it over time and iterations. I must thank Thomas Abraham for believing in the concept and my editor Rohan Chhetri for his serious probing of the plot and sharpening of the prose.

This book would not have been possible without the help of several people. I am deeply indebted to:

Sumit Chowdhury for his patience, plot twists and introductions, and for teaching the nitty-gritty of cyber tech to a nuts-and-bolts type techie;

Satyajit Ranganathan, friend lost and found, for going through multiple drafts and constantly reminding me of the power of emotions in a story;

Bratati Ghosh Ranganathan for an important call I cherish;

Vijay Mukhi for insights on the current state of cyber security in India, and introductions;

Sahir Hidayatullah for tips on hacking and counter surveillance, technical validation of cyber tech written in my book, and introductions, and for bringing Karthik alive;

Professor Rohit Deshpande for the eye-opening HBS case discussion on the global anti-retro virals market, which gave me the vocabulary to express the underlying ethical dilemmas;

Rena Patel for those early discussions on global patent law and infringement;

National Institute for Health for spearheading the movement of public domain medical research papers, an invaluable source of information that gave me the material to 'imagine' Colare;

The team at Medicines Sans Frontiers for the heart in what

they do, and for being open-minded to see the serious issues they deal with being touched upon in fiction;

Nimmi Rangaswamy for sharing insights from her studies on internet usage in slums; *Sandman* would have been a mere sketch without her research;

Mona Sinha for the idea of text messaging inside gaming apps, and much needed laughs;

Bhaskar Pramanik, Microsoft; D Sivanandan, Former DGP Maharashtra; Rachel Lopez, Hindustan Times; Rajiv Vaishnav, Nasscom; Rohit Deshpande, Harvard Business School; Vijay Mukhi, cyber expert; Vijay Ramachandran, IDG Media; Vishal Dhupar, Nvidia and formerly Symantec; for taking the time from their busy schedules to speak with me, read my book, and offer their support.

Devdatt Kapadia; Kumar Dave; Raj Biyani, Microsoft; Uday Singh, Motion Pictures Association; the team at Mahindra SSG; Alok Vijayant, National Technical Research Organization; Jiten Jain, Indian Infosec Consortium; Bharath Subramanian, Anand and Anand; Shashi Dharan, Bharat Exhibitions; Rohit Srivatswa, Clubhack; Antriksh Shah and Aseem Jakhar, Nullcon; and many others for ideas or support at different stages of the book.

The boss from hell from decades ago, whose name I shamelessly borrowed;

Aastha Sayal and Chetan Verma for reading the book and giving valuable feedback;

Alaknanda Kumar and the team at Infini Systems for my website;

The beautiful, complex, fractalated, continually morphing digital world for being an inspiration, always moving ahead faster than I can imagine, and making the tricks and tools in this book old even by the time I have written it;

The cyber security and hacking experts I have met or read; yet, despite so many conversations and a shelf full of books by Mitnick, Russinovich and more, the details remain mysterious – I cannot even hack into my son's iPhone!

My colleagues at Harvard Business School, especially Anjali

Raina, for their unstinting support and warmth during a tough phase of life, and my team, especially Vijaya Nadkarni and Disha Mehra, for being there with me every step of the way;

My colleagues at Harlequin, the writers I work with and all our partners in book trade distribution and retail for helping me quickly learn more about the books business than I could have imagined;

My father, Dr Mohan Lal Verma, and my brother and sister-in-law, Chetan and Shalini, for the bonds that hold us together and the strength they give me; my in-laws, Shyamal and Deepa Chowdhury, and my sister-in-law, Soma Datta, for their compassion;

Sumit for being the anchor that lets me experiment with life, for his infinite energy and caring, for suffering sleepy midnight conversations on hacking that could not have waited till the morning and for backing every crazy idea like a research trip to experience Yunnan to scout character references.

My fabulously talented children Shoumik and Aishani, suddenly grown up enough to manage themselves, for allowing me to be frantic at work in the week and writing on the weekend, and for occasionally quirking their eyebrows with *'you're still writing the same book?'*. Phew, it's done!

9789350098554